All It Takes

A DCI Caroline Cramer Novel

Ali Steed

MONETA MEDIA

First published by Moneta Media Ltd in 2023

eBook ISBN: 9781739437206

Print ISBN: 9781739437213

Book Cover by Nick Castle

Interior design by Rebecca Millar

Dad, I did it! I finally did it!
I'm just so sorry you weren't here to see it in person.

‘The only thing necessary for the triumph of evil is for good men to do nothing.’

Unknown

Chapter 1

It always backed away when he moved towards it. It pulled away again, but not far. Not so strong without its helpers, was it? Not so clever now.

He looked dead into its frightened eyes as he moved the blade through the thick air. Ran it up and down its exposed flesh. It made him laugh. They always pleaded with him, begged him. But it was too late. Judgement passed, now came retribution.

It opened its mouth to speak, but words were drowned in tears. He moved around it, scoring the knifepoint over its ribs, around its shoulder blades, and under its uplifted arm until he was facing it again. He forced his face closer. Nothing for him to fear now.

'You must be punished,' he whispered into its ear. 'Say it. You must be punished.'

He could see fear in its eyes, more tears coming. They always did. Too late.

'Please, I—'

'Say it!'

'I must be... punished.'

'Again.' He waited for a reaction. There was none. 'I said, say it again.'

Suddenly, it was shaking, pulling on the blood-crusted cuffs above its head, desperate to get free. Struggling, gasping. Trying to back away. That made him angry. It shouldn't do that.

'Say it again! Again.'

'I must be punished.' Better.

'Again. Say it again.'

'I must be punished. I must be...'

He brought the knife out of the shadows, the blade bouncing splinters of light off its face. He smiled. It knew what happened next.

'Oh God. No. Please. No!' it screamed, crying like a baby.

The time was right.

He lunged towards it – 'I commend thy soul to the devil!' – and thrust the steel blade through taut skin, feeling warm blood flow down his hand. There was no room for error. He pushed harder, further. Yes, there it was, the exquisite feel of metal on bone as the blade scraped its rib. The wide eyes dimmed. It became heavy and limp. He'd done enough.

People didn't know the danger he had saved them from. They didn't understand, yet. People would thank him one day for the work he was doing. It was important work, and there was much to do.

Chapter 2

It's funny the things you notice when you feel uncomfortable. Today, it was the clock ticking in Dr Jill Traverne's office. Its ticking sounded so loudly in DI Caroline Cramer's head it was in danger of derailing her train of thought.

The metronomic nature of the seconds passing gave a rhythm to the session – the third in as many weeks – that in the past had been soothing, soporific even. A relaxing reminder of the beautiful antique grandfather clock that had been in her grandparents' house, the one she'd coveted as a little girl. Its deep, throaty 'tick tock' as the pendulum swung first left then right was mesmeric when she was a child. Jill's clock, though much smaller and higher pitched, evoked those memories now. She felt safe. But it still didn't relax her.

That grandfather clock had always reminded her of loss too. The clock had been the focus of her attention for the many hours as a child when she had stayed quietly on her own, coming to terms with what death meant to a family. Well, that was probably overstating it. She wasn't sure that was ever possible.

Cramer was looking out of the window while thinking of an answer to Jill's question. The summer sun was weaker today, entering the room in sunbeams that made the dust particles dance in the light. It was now July. Her former partner DS Adam Williams' funeral had been in May. It had seemed so unfair to her that the first signs of new life in a late British spring were appearing from the soil, just as they were putting her friend and partner into it.

'So?' Jill asked.

Cramer continued to stare out of the window. 'So, what?' she answered. It felt petulant, childish, good. Just like it had in those early sessions with Jill all those years ago at her parents' insistence. She'd hated every minute of it, but in the end, they had been right. She'd needed help. And she needed it now.

In the aftermath of her partner's death, those long-lost feelings had returned. She felt empty, guilty, angry. All emotions that were so very familiar to her, sensations that she'd thought she'd buried. Or had tried to.

Jill tried again. 'You're being evasive, Cal. Remember, I've seen this many times before. Don't try and kid me. It won't work.'

Cramer shifted in her seat. She dragged her gaze away from the window and momentarily looked at her shoes before travelling up to Jill. She tried to look her in the eyes, but she could only go as far as her mouth. That was close enough for now. She could both see and hear what she was saying that way.

'Better,' Jill said. 'So, you're still feeling guilt about Adam's death. Right?'

Cramer nodded slowly. She couldn't say the words that had caught in her throat. Of course she felt guilty, and so she should. It was her fault.

'It wasn't your fault, Cal,' Jill said. How did she do that? Cramer had always thought Jill had some kind of superpower for reading minds. But maybe it was easier than that. What she was thinking was no doubt written all over her face. She would never have made a poker player.

'How can you say that, Jill? How can you say it wasn't my fault? It was my call to put Adam in undercover in the first place—'

'He volunteered...'

'OK, yes, he *volunteered*, but at my suggestion,' Cramer said, giving Jill that much. 'I was in charge of the operation. I was the one who chased Robert Kane as he left the house and ran into the barn. Adam followed because I charged in first. He was protecting me, and I should have been protecting him. That's my job. And I didn't do it. Not well enough.'

Jill sighed, leaning back in her chair. 'I thought we'd got past the self-flagellation stage, Cal. Are you planning to carry this on for long?' She pursed her lips as she looked at her watch.

Cramer felt her face flush red. Did Jill really just say that to her? Her jaw fell open and then closed again without any words escaping. Jill was just staring at her, unflinching. Now Cramer was glaring back.

'That piss you off, Cal?' Jill said.

'Yes,' Cramer hissed through gritted teeth.

'Good. Now maybe we can get some different emotions flowing. Guilt, pity, anger, all so corrosive. You know better than that. It took long enough to let go of those before.'

Cramer broke eye contact with Jill and stared back out of the window again briefly. Jill was clever. She knew what buttons to press with her to shift the conversation. God knows she'd had enough practice.

Cramer looked back at her friend with a changed expression. The clock echoed in her head again. 'Surely we're nearly at the end of the session, aren't we?'

Jill smiled and shook her head. 'You're in luck – my next appointment cancelled, so there's no rush at all. You're not getting off that easily.'

Cramer smirked as she looked at the floor again. Yeah, that was too much to hope for.

'Now, can we stop fucking around and get on with what we're here for, Cal?'

Cramer knew Jill would never swear at any other clients, but they were closer than that. Jill, over the years, had become a firm friend as well as her doctor and confidant – Cramer had precious few of those. She steeled herself to go back to the night of the raid.

She took a deep breath in. 'You know the start. It was textbook: cleared the entry, controlled the room. The drugs were on the table, Kane was in cuffs. All was good. Until he slipped the cuffs thanks to a rookie mistake by a lid.' Jill would understand the force's nickname for uniformed officers through her role as a consultant forensic psychologist for Kent Police.

'Then when we got to the barn, it went haywire. Just haywire. Adam's radio was turned up, someone called through just at the wrong moment and Kane managed to stab him in the neck and the thigh. He knew what he was doing. Avoided all his body armour. He should be doing life for what happened here.' Her hands made fists almost impulsively.

When there was no response from Jill, Cramer looked up. Her face remained expressionless until she nodded after what seemed like minutes. But no words.

Tension rose in Cramer's stomach. 'Don't play me, Jill. I know what the silent treatment means – you're waiting for me to fill the gap. Not happening. I'm not going to do that.'

'You just did,' Jill retorted. She smiled at Cramer, but there was pathos in it. Love. And pathos.

Cramer smiled back this time, shaking her head. 'You fucker.'

Jill winked. It made Cramer feel like she was ten again. This was the same office she visited back then, but now the furniture, the paintings on the wall, and even Jill herself seemed so much smaller.

'You know what's happening here?' Jill asked.

Cramer sought refuge in the view out of the window again, but Jill wouldn't let her leave now, even for a moment.

'C'mon, look at me.'

Cramer did as she was told.

Jill continued. 'It's repeating the pattern. The self-blame, the thought that, somehow, you could have done things differently. You know, you had no more chance to do things differently this time than you did when you were ten. It's a different situation, but the outcome for you and the feelings you have are the same. You need to let go of this blame, this guilt.'

A tear escaped Cramer's eye, but she forced her expression to stay the same. Stoic. Like a golden-age film star crying on screen.

'I know, Jill. I know that. I just don't know how to. I'm not sure I can. Not again.'

'You have to, Cal, before it eats you alive. I've seen it before with you, and I don't want to see it again,' Jill said.

Woman Found Hanged in Westgate Gardens

By Jason Baird, crime reporter

A woman has been found hanged in the Westgate Gardens near Canterbury Catherdral in the city centre.

The body has not yet been identified, but police say they are keeping an 'open mind' about the cause of death until a post-mortem has been completed. It is not clear at this stage whether the woman committed suicide, and Detective Chief Inspector Jeff Bruce would not be drawn on the circumstances surrounding the death this morning.

'The body of a young woman was discovered at seven o'clock this morning in Westgate Gardens by a council worker. She was found hanging from the Plane tree and was pronounced dead at the scene,' he said. 'As yet, we have not managed to confirm her identity or the cause of death. We won't be making further comment until we have identified this young woman and informed her next of kin.'

DCI Bruce would also not be drawn on whether the woman could be Linda Burrows, a married mother of two who was reported missing six days ago by her husband.

This is the second body of a young woman to have been found in as many months after the body of teacher Angela Downs was found badly burned in fields near Blean just outside Canterbury last month. Her death is still subject to investigation, and a coroner's hearing into the cause of her death was opened and adjourned last week.

Chapter 3

Cramer rarely ventured up to the Chief Superintendent's office. Usually, she didn't need to. But since Adam's death three months ago, little was normal in the station. As she waited on the uncomfortable chairs in the corridor, she certainly didn't feel normal. She missed him, and that wasn't going to change, no matter how much time passed, or how many sessions she had with Jill.

Chief Superintendent Ron Davidson – or Davo for short – opened the door and beckoned her inside. It was a nod rather than an exchange of words, but she dutifully got up and entered as he closed the door gently behind her.

Davo moved around to his side of the desk, sitting down and making a steeple with his fingers, his elbows on the table. Cramer braced herself for what was coming next. Those habits only emerged when he was delivering bad news.

'DCI Bruce has decided to take early retirement, Callie. It means, for now, you won't have a head of department above you,' Davo said.

Her immediate boss, Detective Chief Inspector Jeff Bruce, had been on and off sick leave since the raid on Kane's house had gone south. He'd been diagnosed with stress-related illness, which had presented both mental and physical symptoms, and had been seeing the force psychologist to resolve the issues surrounding the raid and other problems he had been having. Cramer had seen the force psych too once in the past. He hadn't helped in the least.

Cramer would never begrudge mental struggles after her own experiences, but still, this latest move left her resenting Bruce, truth be told. He hadn't even been there in person at the raid – he was supposed to be supervising from a distance. But when it all went wrong, she'd been left carrying all the weight, at least that's how it felt. He was hiding from it, shielding himself by running away. That probably wasn't fair. But Adam dying wasn't fair either. So, suck it up, buttercup, thought Cramer.

Of course, she wouldn't say that to anyone but Jill. She hated opening up to strangers. But in the past, she'd also learned how badly holding everything in can affect you.

She suddenly realised Davo was still talking: 'So, until we find a new DCI, you will be the most senior in Major Crimes. Can you handle that?'

Davo never pulled his punches. It was a fair question given the loss of Adam, and the knock-on effect that had on the entire team. But Cramer didn't blink.

'Yes. I can handle it.'

Davo didn't look convinced. But he accepted her answer without question.

'OK. In that case, congratulations Acting DCI Caroline Cramer.' He shook her hand before letting it go and adding: 'We have work to do.'

He pulled a piece of paper across his desk and pushed it towards Cramer. She looked at him as she picked it up. It was a forensics report on a body that had been found burned in a field just outside Blean, near Canterbury. It was one of Bruce's cases, and although she hadn't been working on it, talk within the team suggested there was very little forensically they'd been able to get from the body because of the damage to it.

On top of the report was a photograph. ‘What’s this?’ Cramer asked.

‘A note, a Bible quote found near where the body was found. Farmer found it when he’d been working in the area two weeks after we’d released the scene.’

He reached into the drawer and pulled out the note within an evidence bag.

Cramer took it from him and moved it around until she could read what was inside:

> *'For all that do these things are an abomination unto the Lord: and because of these abominations the Lord thy God doth drive them out from before thee' – Deuteronomy 18:12*

She handed the note back. ‘Means nothing to me. You? No reason to think it was connected with the victim, if it was found weeks after the body.’

Davo shook his head. ‘No, but we need to keep an open mind. Because it matches this one, which was found yesterday.’

He took out another evidence bag from his desk and placed it again in front of Cramer. ‘See the similarity?’

She picked up that bag and did the same again, moving it to see what the note said inside the bag.

> *'Regard not them that have familiar spirits, neither seek after wizards to be defiled by them: I am the Lord your God' – Leviticus 19:31*

Same copperplate handwriting, ornate, which took time and patience. Looked like the same paper too. Her eyes widened as she placed it back on her boss's desk.

'Have forensics got anything from this?' Cramer asked.

Davo shook his head. 'Too early to know yet. But the second one was found at the same time as that body in Westgate Gardens, this time by one of the CSIs on scene.'

Cramer raised her eyebrows, and leaned forward to pick it up again. Within the force it was being widely anticipated that this was Linda Burrows, the woman who had been reported missing by her husband six days before, but no formal ID had been made yet. Initially it was thought to be a suicide, even though there was a puncture wound under the left ribs.

Davo nodded. 'Are we considering these two cases to be linked now?' Cramer asked.

'We can't directly link them, given the note near where Angela Downs was found came to light so much later. But we can't ignore this either.'

Cramer nodded.

'Simms is doing the post-mortem in the next two hours. This is going to be your first case as senior investigating officer, Callie. I want you there with DS Gulliver, so we don't have to wait for forensics to get round to typing up the report. Prioritise this, Callie. I hope this is just some strange coincidence, but if it's not we need to know what's going on ASAP. And why.'

Chapter 4

Many people don't like hospitals because they smell too clinical. But Cramer didn't agree with that. It was the nauseating combination of overcooked cabbage and faeces that got to her. And not necessarily in that order.

She'd driven with her DS Rob Gulliver to the William Harvey Hospital in Ashford from their station in Canterbury, and thanks to traffic on the A28, they had only just managed to arrive moments before the county's lead pathologist Dr John Simms was about to start the post-mortem.

It seemed strange not having Adam with her. The lack of chatter in the car was noticeable, but it was more than that. Gulliver was a good sergeant, but he lacked the charisma of Adam. Physically he didn't look dissimilar – he was tall like Adam, but had short, straight dusty blonde hair rather than Adam's near black curly locks, although he was athletic the same as Adam.

She thought maybe she was being unfair, she didn't know him as well yet after all and who really liked chatting to their boss? Especially on the way to see someone autopsied. But it felt different. Wrong.

As they waited outside the white double doors to be buzzed in, Rob gave a shudder.

'I hate these,' he said, his body taking its time to stop moving.

'No one likes them, Rob – it's not exactly fun being here,' Cramer answered, her own stomach feeling slightly knotted at the prospect of watching Simms examining the body.

Just then the doors buzzed and began to swing open. You couldn't see anything from the outside, apart from a desk behind which sat a member of staff in scrubs. She was tall, with long dark hair tied up in a neat bun on the top of her head, and no jewellery.

Both Cramer and Rob reached for their ID and showed their badges to the woman. 'Ah yes, DI Cramer and DS Gulliver, you're just in time. Dr Simms has only just gone into room two. If you could please use these' – she passed them both face masks to go over their mouth and nose, and shoe covers to go on their feet – 'then I'll show you through.'

Cramer and Rob dutifully donned their protective wear and followed the woman as she tapped the card hanging around her neck on a lanyard to unlock the door. The doors sounded like air brakes on a lorry as they opened, revealing three metallic mortuary tables within the room, two with closed body bags on. The last had the body of a naked woman lying on its cold steel, with Simms stood close to the woman's head, prepping his autopsy tools on a rolling metal trolly.

He turned as he heard the doors open. 'Ah, Callie, Rob, nice to see you.'

Cramer noticed Rob give another smaller shiver as they passed the body bags while crossing the vinyl floor. The coldness of the room itself didn't help, but she was sure that wasn't the only reason.

'Yes, you too, John. Busy day?' said Cramer, nodding her head towards the other bodies as they reached him.

'Well, yes. But at least my customers don't complain if they have to wait.' Simms smiled.

Cramer smiled back, but she was feeling as uncomfortable as Rob was.

No more small talk. Simms held up his scalpel. 'Shall we?'

Cramer nodded but Rob didn't move at all. He looked like he was focused on staying upright.

Simms started the recorder, which was clipped to his scrubs, and placed the microphone headset on so he had both hands free to work. He read the case number into the recorder and then moved towards the woman lying on the table.

Simms began: 'White female, Caucasian, five foot two, found hanging from the Plane tree in Westgate, Canterbury yesterday. Identified from a fingerprint match as Linda Burrows, married mother of two from Ashford, Kent, who had been reported missing six days ago...'

So, now they knew for sure, thought Cramer. Rob took his notebook out and wrote it down.

Simms continued: 'Normal complexion, looks as if she was healthy, normal weight for her height... Most body hair is missing. Shaved head, armpits, and pubic area. Cuts and abrasions to her scalp that have started to heal, along with a small amount of stubble regrowth. Unclear when these injuries were inflicted.'

He opened her mouth briefly. 'All teeth present, fillings in the back molars...' He was about to close her mouth again when he stopped. Looked deeper inside and grabbed his camera. He held her mouth open and took a photograph, the flash momentarily blinding Cramer.

'What have you found?' Cramer asked as she moved closer to see for herself.

Simms held his hand up to her in a gesture to wait, then put the camera down, got hold of his forceps and an evidence bag, and reached into her mouth. Cramer and Rob moved closer again, to see what he was doing. He very carefully removed a fifty-pence piece from the back of her throat, put it into the evidence bag, and added this information to the recording.

Cramer and Rob looked at each other with wide eyes.

'What the...?' Rob broke the silence first.

Simms nodded and started recording again. 'Fifty-pence piece found at the back of the throat. Highly unlikely it got there by accident. There is also an abrasion at the back of her tongue, with evidence of a brown residue surrounding it.' He took a swab, before putting the sample into an evidence bag to be tested.

Cramer got her notebook out and started writing her own notes while Simms closed the dead woman's mouth again and moved her jaw upwards by tilting her chin, exposing the ligature marks around her neck. They were a deep purple, and Simms reached again for the camera to document them. Another brief flash and then he put the camera down again on the trolley.

Then he made his way to the slit about an inch below her left breast. He washed the remainder of dried blood off her body around the wound, now all crime scene pictures had been taken, to get a better look. The red-stained water droplets made metallic clicks as they fell into the mortuary table beneath the body before draining away.

Cramer watched intently as Simms opened the cut with his fingers, tracking the path of whatever had caused it into the woman's body. She didn't bother to look at Rob – he would either be fine, or he wouldn't and there wasn't much she could do about that either way.

Simms moved back to his trolley and got a ruler to measure the size of the wound and carried on with his commentary: 'Opening under the left ribs, five centimetres wide. Would cause significant blood loss.'

He carried on down the body. There was other bruising, but it appeared superficial. The only other significant item on the outside of the body was a brown residue on the woman's wrists, which was barely visible through the wounds that accompanied it. Her wrists must have been bound, but with what?

Simms again took some samples using a cotton-bud swab to send to the lab. He took blood samples at the same time to check for any sign of alcohol or drugs in her system.

Now, he was ready to make the Y-incision that was the usual starting point for examining the body internally. The sight of skin being sliced is never a good one, but at least this time it was with a scalpel and care, rather than a knife and aggression.

'Clavicle, sternum both intact, deep wound underneath the left breast...' Simms documented everything he was doing and seeing into the microphone. He extended the incision, allowing him to explore the wound more easily from the inside. He bent down to examine the now exposed ribs more slowly, using his gloved finger as a guide, before looking up at Cramer.

'Take a look at this. There's damage to her ribs here where the blade went in.'

Cramer moved towards the body again, seeing the slightly leathery nature of the now dead skin first-hand as it had been peeled away, and was hit by the odour of death. She held her breath as she looked where Simms was pointing, and he pulled the overhead light closer to the body to make it easier to see. Yes, there was a nick in the bone where the blade had passed through.

'Could that have killed her?' Cramer asked.

'We'll need to check the heart before we can be sure,' Simms answered.

He moved around behind Cramer and grabbed the rib spreaders, which looked like some form of medieval torture tool with strong, metal clamps on a winding mechanism. Simms put them into the body and began ratcheting them open with a terrible noise until the heart was exposed. He used the scalpel to sever the aorta and some smaller veins and arteries, allowing him to pick the heart up and examined the front of it, where it was clear the tip of the knife had pierced after going through the ribs.

'Yes. This would have been enough to stop the heart. She would have died as a result. This was definitely pre-mortem as you can tell from the inflammation around the wound where the body has reacted to it. So, there would have been no way she could have hanged herself after she'd been stabbed. It seems, we have a murder on our hands,' said Simms.

Cramer and Rob looked at each other and nodded back to Simms. It wasn't a surprise, but the confirmation took things to another level.

'How quickly can we get the blood and other sample results, John?' Cramer was already thinking ahead.

'I'll ask them to be expedited, but I know they are pretty backed up at the moment. Leave it with me, I'll see what I can do.'

'Thanks. If there are any similarities between Linda Burrows' death and Angela Downs' death, can you let me know?' She was thinking about the two notes Davidson had shown her.

Simms hesitated. This worried Cramer: hesitation wasn't usually a Simms trait. He took his gloves off and moved towards the doors. 'Come with me,' he said to the police officers.

They followed through the doors and into the next room, where other bodies were being stored before they went to the funeral homes to be processed for burial or cremation.

Simms urged them to wait while he went into a room on the right. Through a window, Cramer could see him tapping information into a keyboard as he looked at the accompanying screen, which presumably showed where various bodies were stored. He rolled the wheel on top of the mouse, until he found what he was looking for.

He moved over to the doors and opened the one marked *11*. A faint smell of burning emerged. Simms rolled out a body that was in one of the now familiar white body bags. The metal tray screeched as it reached its full extent, as if it was complaining about being pulled that far.

Simms unzipped the bag, exposing the charred remains of Angela Downs. For Simms – given his full six-foot-eight height – the body was at the same level as his chest, but for both Cramer and Rob, it was closer to their faces, and their noses. Cramer wanted to gag at the smell but managed to stop herself. Simms wasn't finished yet, he continued to unzip the bag until what remained of the woman's left hand was visible. On her wedding finger was a silver band.

'Angela Downs wasn't married, John. Why would she have a ring on?' Cramer said, having read the case file briefly before she'd left the station.

'That's what I wondered. None of her relatives have asked for it, presumably because none of them knew it was there. We bag it, and test it, agreed?'

Cramer nodded hard. 'If we get lucky, maybe we'll get a print. Is that possible given the damage to her body from the fire?'

'All we can do is try,' said Simms.

Chapter 5

Stupid bitch. How dare it talk to him like that? Who does it think it is? It'll pay for that. It had no idea he was watching it. Watching and waiting.

The power it had was excessive. Too much for one of them. For a man, no. But for one of them. Definitely. Especially one like that.

It looked down on men like him. All men probably. Its words dripped with entitlement. With disdain. Charmless.

He was sitting in his car, reading the story it had written. What did it know? 'The Problem with Misogyny.' The headline screamed at him as he picked up the coffee he'd bought. He didn't really want it. But it was the best way to get close to it. To follow without being noticed.

Then it said that as they'd left the coffee shop. 'I don't need a man to hold the door open for me, thanks.' Fucking bitch. Then it had gone back in after making a phone call.

Didn't deserve him being a gentleman, sneering at him with that supercilious look. Like he was shit on its shoe. His grandfather was right. They had too much power. His own mother was the same. Had cowed his father into being a spineless sheep that followed everything dutifully to the letter. '*Can't rock the boat, can we?*', his father had said. Fuck that.

His grandfather had hated his mother. He hadn't understood at first. But that day, that day she bellowed at him in front of everyone, then he realised. He knew. He'd run to his grandfather to tell him. He was right. That he understood now and wanted to learn everything from him.

He took another sip of his coffee as he watched it leave Starbucks again. It got into a car at the kerb that had pulled up soon after. An Uber.

He put the paper down and got ready to start his engine, not too soon. But soon enough, to be sure he didn't lose them.

Its car swept away down the street, heading out into the countryside. He turned the key, his engine growling into life. It would be going home. Past 6 p.m. now. He knew where he needed to be. He smiled as he moved off, ready to track it again, back to its lair.

He parked up opposite its house as it went in, still unaware he was there. He blended in. No-one would suspect him. That was part of his skill. It was a waiting game now. He'd hacked its calendar, knew it would be heading out in an hour. He knew where, and he knew when. He had time to get himself ready.

He checked the cable ties were in his pocket. They were. He was ready.

Chapter 6

It was only around thirty minutes before it left again, heading back into Canterbury for a date, according to its diary. It was the perfect place, he would blend in easily. Then – *then* – it would be his.

He followed its car, careful not to drive too close – he didn't want to be picked up on CCTV. He watched as it went to the door and waited for ten minutes. Then, he set down the syringe and the cable ties in the space under the handbrake so he could reach them easily.

After silently opening his door, he stepped out, and closed it equally silently behind him, making sure he had the other bottle of liquid in his pocket. He walked with his hand on it, a comforting friend that would protect him. He walked slowly up towards the entrance, waiting patiently in line now.

From where he was, he could easily see his prey. It was getting frustrated. Far too important to wait in a line to get into the club, wasn't it? Precious little bitch. He held his head high. He'd followed, watched, waited, hunted for weeks now. Another half an hour was easy. He had the discipline to deal with whatever came.

Finally, it went into the club in a group of eight. It would never have noticed him – it was far too involved with itself. It moved through the crowd, looking for its date. Checked its watch. The date hadn't arrived. Good. It headed to the bar, and he followed.

'Double vodka and orange,' it said to the barman. It couldn't have ordered a better drink. From his point of view, anyway.

He just had to watch again and wait. But in less than twenty minutes, the waiting would be over.

Chapter 7

It had been nearly a week since Cramer and Rob had been at the hospital for the post-mortem, and they were still waiting for information from forensics.

Cramer's new status as acting DCI had been filtering around the station – she wasn't one to make big statements about something like that – yet to be fair, most of her team knew the same day it had happened, even before she returned with Rob from the hospital, such were the station jungle drums.

She thought back to how she'd buzzed herself into the office and her team had made a beeline for her. DC Leila Johnson, one of the newest members of her team had been one of the first to congratulate her. 'We always knew you were really the one in charge rather than Brucie anyway,' she'd said. It made Cramer smile inside at the time.

Yet it was only this morning, nearly a week later, that Davo had sent round a formal email to all staff announcing the change of status for Cramer. He'd never been that good at admin. *Or maybe he was deciding whether he'd made the right decision*, Cramer thought as she headed out of her office to the coffee machine where Leila was heading too. Cramer motioned for Leila to go first.

'Thanks. Hard to believe you've been DCI for nearly a week already, boss,' said Leila, clearly trying to make conversation.

'I'm still only Acting DCI, Leila...' Cramer corrected.

'For now,' said Leila with a smile. She was petite and certainly would have failed the five-foot-four height rule for women that had applied when Cramer joined the force. But her fine features and blonde hair had made her an instant hit in the male-dominated office in the last few months.

Cramer smiled back. 'Yes, well, we'll see what happens.'

Their conversation felt a little forced, which had been a feature of the office recently. Something that was mirrored at home with Cramer's husband Patrick, but for different reasons.

The office had been quieter these past few months since Adam had died. There was the usual joking and banter, but it seemed more muted than before. Like there was a heaviness in the air that none of them could come out from under just yet. As if his spectre was hanging in every workspace. Slowly, things were getting back to normal, but it was very, very slowly. And it was going to be hard for all of them to move on. Cramer knew that better than most, but she tried to put the feelings aside.

'How are you getting on?' Cramer asked.

Leila had already begun working through social media connections for both women to see if there was anything that matched. Friends in common, visiting the same places, and so on. Most murder victims knew their killer, so that was always the best place to start.

'Nothing yet, guv, but really, I'm only just getting started. There's a lot to go through. Both women were very active on social media, and it isn't always easy to spot patterns initially.'

Cramer nodded. They couldn't be sure there was any connection, but given the notes, and now the items found with both bodies, they couldn't rule it out yet either.

There had been no toxicology results from Linda Burrows yet. Only a few things had been confirmed so far – the brown residue on her wrists was iron oxide, better known as rust, as was the residue at the back of her tongue. It didn't make a lot of sense. And that the last place her phone was detected was near the Cognoscenti nightclub. They were still waiting for forensics to determine where Angela Downs' mobile was last placed from the network signal.

Cramer retreated back into her office with her coffee and sat down behind her desk. She moved the mouse on her desk to open the computer, and images of the Bible quotes materialised on the screen in front of her. What was the point of them? She needed to find out. A priest would be best to ask, and she knew just the right one.

Chapter 8

Father Joe O'Malley had been a staple in Cramer's life from when she was a young girl. Her mother had forced her to go to church from a young age, '*like a good Catholic girl*'. Yet it was his irreverence and wicked sense of humour – despite being a priest – that had made her keep in touch with him for so many years.

She could walk from her office to his church, which was conveniently just around the corner, and as it was a lovely day, she'd take some time to clear her head in the fresh air. St Thomas's Roman Catholic church was near Burgate in Canterbury, and stood opposite the grounds of the much better known and much grander Canterbury Cathedral. Its gothic exterior, adorned with angel statues either side of its steeple, hid a stark white interior, ornately carved, with modern pews that seemed a little at odds with its history.

As Cramer entered, her steps echoed in the still silence inside, making her reduce the impact of her stride until it was more of a whisper. She could see Father Joe busying himself at the altar, prepping for his evening service.

'Father Joe,' she called quietly, hoping he would hear her muted tones. He carried on with his duties. 'Father Joe...' Cramer called again, a little louder this time. He turned his head towards her, a large smile appearing on his heavily lined face as he realised who it was.

'Ah, Callie, how good to see you! What brings you here to see me today?'

He hadn't lost the delicate Irish lilt in his voice, which she had always found comforting and warm. It reminded her of home and her father.

'I need to ask you about something if that's OK? Can we have a chat?' she said.

He immediately held his right arm out to show her into the vestry and they walked together through the archway towards it. He smelt vaguely of incense, one of the key tools of his job, and when they moved into the smaller anteroom where his robes and other religious paraphernalia was held, the age of the room gave itself away in the ancient dustiness and scent of more sweet incense.

He motioned for her to sit in one of the chairs at the edge of the room.

'Now, what can I do for you?'

Cramer opened her bag and took out copies of the Bible quotes found at the crime scenes.

'These, Father Joe. I wanted to ask you what they might mean to you? To anyone?'

He put his hand into the pocket inside his cassock and pulled out his reading glasses as he took the photographs from her. Cramer remembered being scared of the cassocks when she was younger. The full-length line of small buttons that had run from the collar to the hem had seemed unnecessarily elaborate, and that, along with the stole, which changed colour according to the liturgical season, had fascinated Cramer. But that fascination had ended abruptly in her early teens.

Father Joe put his half-moon glasses on the end of his ample nose and peered at the papers in front of him. He read both two or three times before removing his glasses and looking directly at Cramer.

'Where are these from?'

'A case I'm working on, Father Joe. They were found at different locations. I've done a quick internet search, but that hasn't come up with much.'

He put his glasses back on to examine them again.

'They are from the King James' Bible, both referencing the occult. King James, I'm sure you know, had a bit of an obsession with it, the occult, I mean.'

She hadn't known that, but it wasn't surprising given the age he was living in.

He continued: 'Never used by us, you understand. It was the second version of the Bible used in the Anglican Church. Never ceases to amaze me that an entire religion was founded simply because one man wanted to get divorced. And with such bloodshed as a result.' He winked at Cramer. They'd discussed Henry VIII before, so this was no surprise.

'What are these quotes relevant to, though?' Cramer asked.

Father Joe rubbed his chin. 'Mostly, they refer to the heretics, to the non-believers, the pagans or druids. Those who would believe in other religions, not Christianity. He didn't have time for them, King James, and to be fair, neither did us Catholics, if we can be candid.'

'Are we talking devil worship, then?' Cramer asked.

Father Joe shook his head. 'No, not that, well, mostly not that. Just not Christianity. A belief in the gods of nature, of the earth, the seasons, the sun. That kind of thing. A sort of "Glastonbury" feel' – he did air quotes with his fingers – 'if you will.

'In the past, the Catholic church might have seen anything outside of Christianity as the work of the devil, but we've moved on quite a bit since then.' He winked again.

Cramer smiled and nodded. Her mother, she was sure, would have disagreed. After all, she hadn't even been allowed to listen to The Rolling Stones growing up – just the title of *Their Satanic Majesties Request* and 'Sympathy for the Devil' was enough to send her mother into a lather. So, Father Joe was making sense. But she still didn't feel much further forwards.

'Thanks, Father Joe, it's good to see you again,' she said, and she meant every word.

He looked slightly upset that she would be going so soon. 'You away already?'

Cramer nodded. 'Yes, sorry, Father, I've only stepped out to get some air and ask you about these, to be honest. I need to get back.'

Father Joe bowed his head briefly before looking back up at her again. She felt his disappointment.

'Well, let me know if I can be of any more help, child,' he said to her with real affection as he held her arm. 'Before you go, is everything OK with you?' he asked.

Cramer didn't answer, she just nodded. She didn't want to get into the Adam issue just now, but perhaps another time.

'You'll tell me when you're ready,' Father Joe said to her as she began to walk away.

It made her stop in her tracks. No, she wasn't OK, but she'd said nothing to him to make him think otherwise. How did he know?

She turned to him. 'One of my colleagues was killed recently Father, and I was with him when it happened,' she told him, surprising herself that she had let the words come out of her mouth. He had an almost supernatural ability to get people to tell him the truth.

'I'm very sorry, Callie, that's hard to deal with. Very hard. But that's not all, is it?'

Now, she felt shaken. She hadn't told anyone about what else she was dealing with, so he couldn't possibly know.

'Actually no,' her voice broke on the no. 'My husband has been having an affair with someone he works with. I only found out recently – I saw a message come through on his phone and confronted him. And I don't really know how I feel about it yet.'

'Patrick?' Father Joe asked. She nodded.

He gave her a hug, and there was real affection in the embrace. But she didn't have it in her to return it. She was grateful he didn't push her for more details.

'When you want to talk, you come and find me. I'll be here for you.'

She looked at his kind face, kissed him on the cheek, and left before her emotions had a chance to come to the surface.

Chapter 9

Cramer still felt shaken by Father Joe's powerful insight as she walked back to the station. She decided to go the long way around so she'd have a little time to go through the city centre before she got back to the office.

Canterbury was always full of students, tourists, and, to a lesser extent, locals who were going about their business, which meant weaving her way through crowds often surging the opposite way. A group of French school children being led by their teacher crossed her path, forcing her to stop in her tracks and wait for the chattering gaggle to pass.

To get some respite, she dodged into a doorway briefly. The window of the shopfront was adorned with crystals and tarot cards, an ornate display of black webs, and pentagrams in circles stuck on the glass. Dreamcatchers of various colours were hanging from the top of the window, with drums, feathers, bones, and a mishmash of items that could only be described as debris. She wondered how any of this could tempt someone into the shop but found herself wandering in just the same.

As she entered, the pungent smoke of jasmine incense sticks tickled her nostrils; it was sweet and sickly, yet enticing. All around the walls there were various items like Himalayan prayer flags, scarves, boho and gothic clothes hanging on rails, druid-like robes, books, more pentagrams, candles and more tarot cards.

It was so full that the shop almost seemed to groan as she made her way through, as if any more weight on the floorboards would cause everything to disappear into a cavernous hole.

A young girl with jet black hair, dark eyeliner, black lipstick, and nails to match looked Cramer up and down as she walked through the store. There was no question she looked out of place. She felt out of place.

'Can I help you?' the girl asked, more than likely out of politeness than through any real consideration that she was a genuine customer, Cramer thought.

'No, thanks. I'm just looking,' Cramer said. The girl continued to watch her as she moved objects on the shelves. The different coloured crystals were vibrant, almost hot. They didn't quite glow, but for those who believed in such things, Cramer could vaguely see what the attraction was.

She felt the girl's eyes boring into her back as she moved around the store and decided that if she was going to feel awkward, she might as well see if the encounter would prove useful.

'Actually,' Cramer said, 'you might be able to help. I want to find out more about alternative lifestyles, I mean...' She was struggling for the words. How could she discuss something if she didn't even have the vocabulary to articulate it? 'I mean, like, pagan, Druid, devil worship...' The words had left her mouth before she had a chance to catch them, even though Father Joe had said that wasn't what the Bible quotes referred to. Still, now they were out, Cramer left the words hanging in the air, hoping the girl would pick them up and somehow know what she needed even if Cramer didn't herself. The girl looked slightly shocked and simply stared at her.

'You're in the wrong place, lady, we don't have anything for you here,' the assistant said with real venom in her eyes.

'No, don't misunderstand me. I... I mean... Well...' Cramer fumbled around in her pocket for her warrant card, holding it out for the girl to see. She hadn't realised until that point how much her hands were shaking. Finally, the assistant put her out of her misery.

'I think you better talk to the owner. I just work here, you know?'

She disappeared out into the back of the shop, through a gloomy doorway covered with clacking beads, which was seeming more cavernous the longer Cramer spent in there. The girl hadn't been gone long before she came back and motioned for Cramer to come out back.

She hesitated. She couldn't say why. But she felt even less comfortable now than she had when first entering the store. *Just go*, she told herself and parted the hanging beads, following the sales assistant into the gloom.

Chapter 10

The room was very dark, lit only by three candles sitting on what looked like an altar at the far end. It wasn't a small room by any means, but there were so many things in there that it felt suffocating. The air was heavy with more incense, but it wasn't cloying like some, more delicate.

Cramer could just make out a woman at the back, kneeling down in front of the altar. The long, dark hair that hung down her back was all that Cramer could see. Shadows danced around the room as the candles flickered, and she picked out some of the shapes hanging on the walls. There was a pentagram to her right. In fact, there were two, one much larger than the other, and black like coal, while the smaller one below was a brass colour.

As Cramer's eyes adjusted to the low light, more shapes revealed themselves. There was a large crystal, almost a foot tall, which was a deep purple with so many angular faces on it that the candlelight leapt off it and moved languidly around the room, like a sea full of diamonds.

To her left, she saw a flat drum with a beater next to it, a beautiful deer head painted onto the skin. There were other, smaller drums near it too, some looking like those you see on the documentaries of African or Amazonian tribesmen playing.

There were other, much larger candles around the room too, although none of these were lit. But their melted bodies showed her that they had been well used in the past. Whereas on the wall to the left were some of the largest feathers she had ever seen. They stretched across a large part of the wall, and below them were animal bones, deer antlers, and deer and cattle skulls. This place was beginning to give Cramer the creeps.

'Alicia tells me you want to know about devil worship,' the woman spoke without even acknowledging her presence, still not turning around to talk to Cramer directly.

Cramer took a deep breath. 'Well, no...I mean, yes...or I mean, maybe I do, I'm not sure. But it's not for the reasons you might think.' She pulled her warrant card out of her pocket again. 'I'm Acting Detective Chief Inspector Caroline Cramer, Kent Police. I wanted to speak to you about the occult, about...Well, to be honest I'm not really sure I have the right words because I don't know anything about this...' Honesty was going to have to be the best policy.

The woman still had her back to Cramer, and gave a low, very deep bow to the altar she was facing before she got up from her knees and turned to Cramer for the first time. Her skin looked like ivory in the candlelight, and she had very fine features, a strong but delicate jawline and very dark eyes that in this light looked black. She held her hand out to Cramer in a greeting; the black robe she was wearing moved up her arm just enough for Cramer to be able to make out a series of marks running up the inside.

'Don't worry about those, I don't do that anymore,' the woman said, as if reading Cramer's mind. 'But I'm not ashamed of them either. They are a part of my journey of how I got to where I am. And I'm happy now.' She spoke slowly, deliberately. Cramer felt like she was giving every word the weight it needed to carry. She was fascinating.

'Now, devil worship...' The woman invited Cramer to sit on a low stool next to the one she had just taken. It was very close to the ground, and Cramer's legs came almost up to her chin. She watched the woman and then mirrored her cross-legged posture.

'Why devil worship?' It was a fair question to ask Cramer, after all, she didn't know her at all.

'Not for me, and I'm not sure that is the right phrase anyway' Cramer wanted to be clear about this upfront. 'I'm working on a case and there appear to be some occult connections. I don't know exactly what or how at the moment, but there is something here. Is the occult something you know about?'

The woman stiffened slightly. 'Yes and no. I have read around the subject but I don't practise anything of the sort, if that's what you were thinking?'

'Oh God, no, not in the least...' Cramer, to be honest, had no idea what this woman did.

'Many confuse devil worship with paganism, but they are totally, and very much at odds with each other. People who don't understand this world think they are the same. That couldn't be further from the truth.'

Her eyes were locked onto Cramer's, which made her feel uncomfortable. But there was a warmth from this woman that was palpable.

'Are there people who practise both locally?' Cramer asked.

'I'm not sure I want to answer that,' the woman said. Before adding: 'Yes, there are. But I don't know them, I just know *of* them. Some will come in here looking for tools for what they would call their "work", but I can tell them a mile off. I will always prevent them from being in here long, they are too negative, have a bad energy. And then I will cleanse the space afterwards so their energy doesn't have a chance to stay.'

'Cleanse it how?' Cramer was becoming intrigued.

'With sage. White sage smoke. It's called smudging. You know it?'

Cramer shook her head. Maybe that was the scent she could smell.

'Yes, it's what's in this room,' the woman said. She'd done it again! How did she know what Cramer was thinking? 'I cleanse the space before I commune with the spirits, which is what I was doing when you came into the shop.'

The woman's insight made Cramer feel uneasy. Yet her presence was also incredibly calming, a real dichotomy.

'Devil worship, are there any telltale signs for this? Any rituals?'

The woman got up from her seated position and moved towards the pentagram on the wall. 'You see this?' She gestured towards the top of the pentagram, where the point of the star was facing north.

'In devil worship, this will be facing south. The two points of the star that are at the bottom would be facing north, making the sign of a goat. They believe he appears as a goat.'

'He?' Cramer asked.

'The devil,' the woman said without any emotion.

Cramer nodded, taking her notebook out to write this down. She had no idea if it would be useful in the long run, but at this stage she wanted to explore all avenues.

'What else?' Cramer queried. 'Is there any kind of sacrifice involved? Could it be a human sacrifice?' She couldn't believe she had even asked the question.

'In all the years I have been aware of this world, I've never known that,' she said. 'But it's not impossible. Animals would be much more common,' she said with a practical finality. 'People are missed.'

Cramer averted her gaze and began to get up from her cross-legged position too, feeling a slight tingle as the blood began to move to her feet again. She was ready to leave.

'I'm sorry, I didn't ask your name?' Cramer said.

‘Isabella.’ She held her hand out to Cramer in what was both a greeting and a goodbye. As she held it, she stopped, her face suddenly very serious. ‘She isn’t dead. You know that?’

‘Sorry…?’ Cramer frowned. She hadn’t mentioned details of the case, and even so, it was a murder—

‘I don’t know what that means,’ Isabella continued, ‘but that’s what I’m being told to tell you. She isn’t dead. It’s not a recent thing, it’s from years ago. Does that mean anything to you?’

Cramer’s stomach dropped. ‘N-No. No, it doesn’t.’ She lied.

Isabella nodded, and Cramer knew the shop owner didn’t believe her for a second.

Chapter 11

Few things hurt as much as a deep love turned to hatred, and there's a fine line between the two. It was just one of many things keeping Cramer awake. She was still pondering the conversation she'd had with Isabella five days before – well, that and the usual thought going around in her head since she found out about Patrick's affair. Her initial anger and upset – for her there was a fine line between the two – had subsided, and she was now left with a seething malevolence towards him that just wasn't her style. She hated feeling like this, and she hated that he'd made her.

So, when her phone rang just after 2 a.m., she at least felt awake with a purpose. Still, the shrill ringtone slicing through the dark had made her jump, and the adrenaline kick was just subsiding by the time she reached the kitchen.

She was on-call anyway and had been advised a body had been found near the reservoir but hadn't been given any other details.

She wanted to take her husband's car, knowing it would piss him off to wake up and find one of his precious four-wheeled mistresses missing. Maybe he'd be in such a bad mood he wouldn't play with the two-legged one she'd found out about a month ago. Bastard.

She searched everywhere she could think of – pockets, coats, the drawer in the hallway table... but she couldn't lay her hands on his keys. Her normal work car had been pranged the previous week, and her Land Rover was having a new gearbox fitted, which left just one option.

She hesitated briefly. The keys for her third car were hanging in front of her, the Mercedes symbol glinting. She didn't want to use it, but had little choice. Besides, at this time of the morning, luxury trumped appearances. She grabbed the keys from the hook and headed out the back door.

The car door thwacked closed behind her, completing the luxury cocoon. She sat in the darkness. Maybe she should go back inside and find his Audi keys instead. But point-scoring wasn't the priority.

Cramer yawned as she headed down the last small, winding road to the reservoir, driving through a shadow tunnel of overhanging branches jet black against the night sky, her headlights illuminating the low-hanging boughs in sequence as she moved towards the scene.

She stifled a second yawn as she turned into the parking area, guided by the blues strobing into the night sky. The full moon glinted on the water, its light playing in the ripples created by a soft wind. The air was thicker tonight. The rain had stopped, leaving a lingering earthy scent, but the night was still warm, a muggy mix of heat and humidity. Summer was morphing into autumn.

A small gaggle of reporters were already congregating – was that the right collective noun? Maybe *a murder* of reporters was more accurate, she thought, like crows, picking over the bones of someone's misfortune.

Cameras were trained mostly on smartly dressed women bathed in artificial light, the amount of pancake on their faces to compensate for the glare created a smooth, blemish-free finish on TV, even in ultra-HD. But up close, after the lights had dried it out, it created deep, ploughed furrows on their skin. Unflattering, to say the least.

Cramer didn't know whether this was another victim in her primary investigation – she had three others ongoing alongside the Bible quotes case: one rape, one other murder, and one GBH. So, these reporters couldn't know either. But it didn't matter, a body had been found, and that was enough for the ever-ravenous twenty-four-hour news cycle to go into overdrive.

Her arrival prompted interest from the assembled hacks waiting for something to happen but they didn't follow. Her car swept past them towards the boathouse where a tentative HQ had been created. She slowed for the uniform walking towards her, torch in one hand, the other outstretched to stop her continuing. She thought about ignoring him, but he was just doing his job.

'Oi! Where d'ya think you're going? Only police allowed up there...'

She should have ignored him. Unwarranted rudeness really pissed her off.

Cramer fished her warrant card out of her pocket and held it out of the window. He examined it officiously with his torch and swallowed hard when he saw who she was.

'Sorry, ma'am, I didn't recognise the car. I thought you was someone from the yacht club.'

'Even so, is "oi" really the way you would address a member of the public? Much less a senior officer?'

'Err, no. Sorry, ma'am, of course not. It's just... well, sorry, ma'am.' He tried to redeem himself. 'Nice motor. I haven't seen a Mercedes S-Class for a while...' He'd said precisely the wrong thing. That was exactly why she hadn't wanted to use this car. It attracted too many comments.

She flipped her warrant wallet closed and stuffed it back in her pocket without taking her eyes off him. He immediately stepped out of the way, making an idiotic, grandiose gesture with his hand, inviting her to continue towards the boathouse.

Cramer kept an icy stare on him as she drove past. 'Twat,' she muttered as her eyes returned to the road and she headed towards the squad cars in a clearing above the boat ramp. She parked up alongside and got out of her car.

The small dinghies anchored in quite possibly the tiniest harbour she'd ever seen moved gently in the breeze, their karabiners singing to each other as the rigging swayed and they kissed the aluminium masts. *Ping-ching*.

She broke into a light sweat as she moved towards the scene about three hundred metres away, up a slight incline into a copse. Pearls of perspiration formed on either side of her spine and joined forces, building momentum as they rolled south into the waistband of her suit trousers as she hiked over the uneven ground.

The mud under her feet was slippery and cloying, her shoes no match for it. She tried keeping to grassed areas with more purchase, but she was navigating by her phone's torchlight, which gave her a pitifully small pool of illumination. It wasn't nearly enough for her to spot the slick-as-ice tree root. She gave an embarrassingly high-pitched yelp as she hit the ground, her jacket now wet, cold, and covered in mud – she hoped mud was all it was.

She looked around to see if anyone had seen her fall. All the torch lights seemed to be pointing in other directions, so she stood up gingerly and mud-skated the rest of the way to the police barrier tape marking the edge of the crime scene. Her hands were becoming stiff at the joints where the mud was drying thick and hard from her body heat, preventing her from moving her fingers properly. She was grateful it wasn't on her face. She touched her cheek to make sure, realising too late the mud at her fingertips was still wet. Dammit. Now it *was* on her face.

'What have you got on your face?' Dr John Simms asked as he headed towards the barrier tape to meet her. She tried to clean her cheek on the arm of her jacket but made it worse.

'One word, John, I swear...' She held his gaze briefly before holding out her hands to show him and broke into a grin two seconds later. She turned around to show him the side of her jacket, eliciting a belly laugh, as it was also now getting crispy from the drying mud.

'These bloody shoes – I should have worn my walking boots. These are like ice skates.' She was looking down at what was left of her heeled boots, wishing she'd spent more time dressing before leaving. Her faded Genesis T-shirt didn't go too well with her suit either but was the first thing she laid hands on at the top of the clean washing pile as she dressed in the dark. She thought it was plain black but realised the mistake once she'd reached the hue of the arc lights. She momentarily considered wearing it back to front, before remembering the Turning It On Again 2007 US tour venues were emblazoned on the back. Wearing it inside out wasn't too appealing either, as it would leave Phil Collins nuzzling into her cleavage rather than bobbling around on top of it, as he was now. No, she'd brazen it out.

Simms was holding a forensic suit for her to put on before she entered the crime scene, which, thankfully given her current circumstances, covered everything head to foot, with latex gloves to hide the state of her muddy hands. Saved. She accepted when Simms offered his hand to help her under the tape, noting he hadn't offered until she was inside the sterile forensics gear. Normally, she'd have politely declined.

The sporadic hiss of police radios broke the silence, along with the lapping of water at the edge of the reservoir and the rustle of nature's night-time. It always amazed her how much keener her senses were after dark. The smell of earth rising from the damp mud after the earlier rainstorm was potent, as if Mother Nature was showing off her favoured perfume. Or the mud scent could be more potent on her clothes now she was sweating inside her forensic suit.

Either way, the reservoir was far too beautiful a place to be sullied by death, she thought as she scanned her surroundings, the moonlight creating shadow trees that betrayed the landscape.

Simms and Cramer climbed up the bank in silence, heading towards the opening in the forensic tent that was shedding its light into the night sky, attracting a large population of moths and insects which had settled on the exterior.

Canterbury had a long and bloody history and while murders locally weren't unheard of, their provenance tended to be drugs, money, or booze – sometimes all three. But this was new. And disturbing. Someone seeking out women, tracking and targeting them before they were found dead days later. Cramer hadn't seen anything like this before.

She nodded hellos to the scene of crime officers as they were coming and going from the scene. She knew some of them well, thanks to recent events.

As she and Simms ducked inside the forensic tent, both were stunned into silence. The crime scene was on the far side of the lake, which helped keep reporters at a distance. That, at least, was a blessing. Although the details of the case, the items left at the scene and the apparent shaving of all body hair, had been kept back from the press, the fact two murders had happened within a matter of weeks already led to press speculation they could be related.

The girl at the heart of the heavily lit rectangle couldn't have been more than twenty-three. She was propped against a tree, hands by her side, head lolling forwards like she was in a deep sleep. Cramer noticed a fine stubble fuzz of early regrowth on the top of her head, mixed with healing cuts, suggesting they had happened some days before she'd died. Every bit of her body hair had been shaved, just like Linda Burrows.

The deep scarlet hole under her left ribcage was another signature injury. But if this was like their suspected first and second victims, that was merely a violent way to incapacitate her and may not have been her final torture. She would probably have suffered more before she finally died. The pattern was becoming chillingly familiar. Cramer was in no doubt that this was the latest young woman unlucky enough to come across the person they were all looking for.

'Do we have a note?' Cramer asked, still mesmerised by the girl in front of her. She looked up as Simms walked away without saying a word, folded himself under the crime scene tape, and opened the heavy metal case that had been carefully placed outside the perimeter to preserve evidence. Cramer moved outside the tent towards Simms as he produced a tagged evidence bag. He ducked back under the tape and passed it to her. Inside nestled the now familiar paper, expensive but not uncommon, and the copperplate handwriting that in any other circumstance could only be described as exquisite.

Through the plastic, she could make out the standard methodology for Bible notations but couldn't see which part of the King James Bible had been picked this time to illustrate the unknown point. She moved the paper around until it was clearer to see.

> *'A man also or woman that hath a familiar spirit, or that is a wizard, shall surely be put to death' – Leviticus: 20:27*

Cramer expected it would reference the occult. The previous notes had. There seemed to be a biblical fascination with paganism, even though the church had tried to crush it as an alternative religion for centuries, at times more viciously than others.

Cramer was unaware of the level of interest in paganism and the occult in Kent, but had looked into it more closely since her encounter with Isabella at the spiritual shop. She hadn't previously been aware that pagan religions always revered the goddess as much, or more so, than the God. But this was something a male-dominated Catholic Church couldn't allow.

She snapped back to reality as Simms pointed to the note: 'I don't imagine it'll yield more than the last two, but we can live in hope.'

Cramer handed the bag back to Simms, who diligently placed it back in his case before they moved back to the body. As she returned to the tent, Cramer noticed a glint of metal for the first time on the girl's left ankle, the only item on the otherwise completely naked corpse. An ankle chain was a sign of a prostitute, according to her staunch Catholic Irish mother. Catholicism – or more likely Cramer's grandmother – had put the idea in her mother's head and no amount of coercion would change her mind, even though it was a long-outdated view.

She pointed the chain out to Simms. 'Hers, do you think?'

Simms tilted his head to one side. 'I doubt it, if the wedding ring and the fifty pence piece are anything to go by. He likes to write, so why not his bloody name and address?'

'Come on, John, where is the fun in that?' Cramer countered with a wry smile.

Laughing is always so much more dignified than crying. And she had been doing plenty of that lately.

'Talking of which, no sign of any prints on either of those items Callie, both the ring and the coin were clean, so to speak.'

She nodded. The time taken with each victim suggested he was methodical in his approach. A fingerprint was too much to hope for.

She pushed the thought to the back of her mind and crouched down to look more closely at the terrifyingly young body. There were some deep scabs on the scalp, suggesting the shaving had been brutal, hurried, or resisted. Perhaps all three. The blood from the wound had dried in streaks down her well-toned stomach. This was a girl that had looked after herself. But there was no blood-pooling evident on the ground, which suggested they were looking somewhere else for the primary crime scene.

She realised Simms must have watched the track of her eyes, as he instantly put her thoughts into words.

'She wasn't stabbed here. There isn't enough blood.'

'So,' Cramer surmised, 'we are looking for a car, or van, I suppose, to transport her. Something easy to clean.'

'Probably a van. We've taken casts of tyre treads and they looked too big for a car, could be a four-by-four. We'll check them against the database.'

'Is that the cause of death?' Cramer pointed to the gaping wound.

'No way of knowing until the post-mortem. But this could be staging again.'

Angela Down's autopsy had shown she'd been alive when she was set alight. The smoke damage and burning inside her lungs proved it. You could only hope she had been unconscious due to a loss of blood, the kind of lie you tell a grieving relative to help them cope. It's hard to imagine any state of unconsciousness that would save you from the awareness and initial pain of fire as you breathe the searing heat into your lungs, Cramer thought. At least within a short time, the nerve endings in the body would be eradicated by the flames so there would be no more pain, as if anyone could consider that a kindness.

The ankle chain was another unspoken challenge for the police to find the relevance of the items being left with each victim.

Angela, a well-loved teacher, had been wearing a silver band on her wedding finger when found. But she wasn't married. The second, mother of two Linda Burrows, was found hanged with a fifty-pence piece in her mouth. Her husband's vocal push for answers resulted in many column inches for the local press and started to get some nationals interested. Much as Cramer hated it, it was hard to knock him. He wanted to know why it had happened. They all did.

As these thoughts chased each other through Cramer's mind, DC Leila Johnson made her way up the steep incline towards the scene. She bustled rather than walked, always in a hurry, on a mission. Cramer made a beeline for Leila when she saw her stop at the tape and flip open her notebook.

'I've spoken to the couple who found her, but nothing doing, guv. Apparently, there was some event here today at the sailing club, an open day. Cars would have been coming and going more than usual.'

'The techs said it looks like something bigger, maybe a four-by-four,' said Cramer.

Leila cocked her head to one side. 'Oh, great! There aren't going to be many of those at a sailing club.' Cramer's look quickly wiped the smile off Leila's face.

'Sarcasm doesn't suit your prospects, DC Johnson.'

Leila swallowed hard. 'Yeah, sorry, ma'am, just tired.' Cramer wasn't keen on the formal epithet, but it showed Leila knew she'd overstepped the mark.

'What were the couple doing on this side of the lake to find her at this time of night?' Cramer asked.

'They were sha— I mean sex, ma'am. But when they saw the body, they called us straight away.'

Cramer looked at Simms, who'd joined them at the cordon. 'How long would you say she's been here?'

'No sign of animal attacks, and you would expect rats to come thick and fast in this humidity, especially near the water. My guess would be not that long. But I'll take temperature readings when I'm ready to move her, which will give us an idea.'

'So, the chances are she wasn't here when everyone came for the open day – someone would have noticed her surely, she isn't exactly hidden away.' Cramer had started thinking out loud.

Simms shrugged. 'Unlikely,' he answered, 'but maybe no one noticed. She's on the far side of the reservoir, not in the direct line of sight from the boathouse.'

Cramer chewed absent-mindedly on the inside of her cheek, a habit she'd had since childhood. Her mother said at some point she'd wear away a hole, but so far, so good.

'Leila, get a list of everyone here for the day from the organisers. Speak to each of them and see if anyone saw anything suspicious – cars pulling up further down, someone behaving oddly, anything. I want to know about someone even taking a piss against a tree. He probably came up here to scout, and an open day would be the perfect cover.

'Also, get a list of all the members of the sailing club, and check out any visitor registers they have here for the last month.'

Leila's mouth fell open. 'That'll be hundreds of people. Apparently, today was really popular.'

'Well, the sooner you start, the sooner you'll finish. Get some of the lids to help you out, but you or Rob do any interviews if something relevant pops up.'

Cramer expected more backchat from Leila, but she just let out a weary I've-already-worked-a-fifteen-hour-shift sigh, then nodded.

As she left, Cramer pulled her phone out of her pocket and punched in a number. It was early, but she'd leave a voicemail.

'Hello?'

'Jill, what are you doing up?' Cramer said, surprised. 'I was going to leave you a message...'

'Don't ask,' said Jill wearily. 'What can I do for you at this hour?'

'We need your help again... We have a serial killer on our hands.'

Chapter 12

As a kid, Dominique Monroe never dreamt she'd be doing this for a living when she grew up. Little girls want to be ballerinas, film stars, or singers – at times, she had wanted to be all three – but none of them aspired to sell their bodies on the side of the road.

She looked suspiciously around her at the assembled crowds, lined up in an orderly fashion, the way that only British crowds do, failing to properly chastise anyone queue jumping. That was the trouble with the British, Dominique thought. They had no capacity to do more than raise an eyebrow at injustice.

Turning her head, she could see all the way down the road, past the few shops that hadn't gone bust on the street, most of them estate agents fuelled by the last property boom. There was very little traffic tonight, and she had started to look at her watch impatiently.

She pulled her collar up against the chill as a cool breeze whistled down her neck and made her shiver. She brushed her long, dark curls from inside the collar, the legacy of her French mother. She would have turned in her grave to see her daughter tonight. The thought caught in Dominique's throat briefly, before she put it in the mental box that was never opened ahead of a good bottle of wine.

She noticed Marlon, the bouncer at the Illuminati nightclub, watching her, taking a little too much interest in her movements. She made sure her lithe, tanned limbs moved her hair seductively as she clocked him noticing. She imagined him getting hard as he carried on staring, which made her smile.

That was part of her skill. She gave him a coy wave before his attention was diverted to stopping another surge of drunks from trying to get into the club ahead of those who had already queued for half an hour.

She was on the cusp of heading home, convinced there was no point in waiting any longer when she saw Porsche lights in the distance. It was a gift she had if you could call it that. She could tell you the make of any car by the shape of the headlights. Ever since she was a child, she could do it She was only eighteen now.

She moved towards the edge of the kerb to meet the sleek motor as it purred up to her, sidling towards her like a friend about to reveal a guilty secret. As the electric window hummed open, she leaned in.

'Want a date?' she asked in her usual matter-of-fact way. The driver didn't say a word, simply leaned over and opened the door to let her in for what she didn't yet know was the last ride of her life.

Chapter 13

He never knew for sure whether it would be asleep or awake by the time he'd brought it back home, but he was a professional, an expert, and he'd refined his process and was always careful when he first opened the boot of his car.

But this time he'd taken a chance. Buoyed by champagne and the thrill of the risk he was taking, he had left it unconscious in the seat next to him. He had been careful not to speed or go through red lights. He didn't want some fuckwit traffic cop to get the undeserved kudos of picking him up.

He opened the door and peered into its face. There was no movement apart from the even breathing that a deep sleep brings, but he took nothing for granted. These were powerful, unpredictable beings, and while he could never respect them, caution was essential.

Gently, for fear of waking it, he cupped it into his arms to move it inside, down the stone steps, and into the room he had prepared for it the night before. Even though it wasn't as big as some of the others, his arms were aching by the time he had lifted it into the cellars. He laid it out on the slab, ready to cleanse it the best way he knew how: the way his grandfather had taught him.

He moved to the corner of the room, lifted the monk's cowl from its hook, and pulled it over his head, feeling the coarse woollen fabric rubbing against his skin. It was uncomfortable, but it should be. It was a sign of obedience and penance.

He moved across to the small kneeler to his right, taking the crucifix that was there and placing it around his neck, watching it as it fell towards his stomach. The heaviness of the cross made it dig into his neck slightly; it felt good.

He kneeled down, taking the Bible in his hands: 'I ask you, oh Father, to help me with the work that I'm doing. I work in your name, to honour you, Lord, and your son Jesus Christ. Guide my hand so I may be strong and resilient, able to resist the aggressive nature of these beings. In Jesus's name, amen.'

He stood up from the kneeler and went towards the ornate desk in the corner, picking up the cut-throat razor to begin.

He stripped the body quickly, deftly, cutting the clothes away in haste so he wasn't surprised by anything. He was prepared for trouble but hoped he wouldn't have any.

He roughly shaved its head, its underarms, followed lastly by the pubic hair. The devil most often visited the genitals, and that was where he must be most cautious, in case he was hiding there still. He checked for marks on the body and found one profoundly suspicious beneath its arm. He was right.

His work complete, he tied its hands together with a cable tie, fearing that, otherwise, it could use its powers over him before he was able to move it to the shackles attached to the wall.

He tidied around it, balling up the shaved hair before putting it into a plastic bag and placing it in the chest in a corner with the others. He closed the drawer and turned the lock. There was no danger it could get at the chest, but he couldn't be sure about its helpers.

He was about to pick up its lifeless body, when it stirred, starting to wake from the drug-induced sleep.

For a moment, he stood motionless in the shadows, fearful even of breathing, in case the movement of his chest caused too many ripples in the surrounding ether. Beads of sweat broke out on his forehead, yet he felt cold. He started shaking. He should be in control. He was always in control, yet this time it had managed to surprise him.

His grandfather had taught him, trained him to adapt to unexpected situations. You never knew what might happen. He moved swiftly across the room, chiding himself for changing his approach, breaking the rules. It was the devil's work, tempting him with the cheap thrill of pride in what he was doing. Well, pride came before a fall – Book of Proverbs, 16:18 – but it wasn't going to be his failing.

He grabbed the knife. Why had he left it out this time? He couldn't remember, but it proved God was on his side.

He rounded on the creature as it was opening its eyes. Aware now of what was happening, fear was etched on its face as he strode towards it with the dagger outstretched. He smashed into its chest, its back landing hard onto the slab, the breath escaping sharply from its mouth as it hit the cold marble, his hand pressing down on its neck before he thrust retribution once again into its ribcage.

Lifelessness was something he had felt often; it kept him sane, made him feel at peace with himself, and it came quickly this time. But he had no time to follow the correct process. That unsettled him, made him feel like he was losing control. A cold sweat broke out on his upper lip. Had his Lord abandoned him, even briefly?

Desperate for a return to normality, he sat down at the desk in the corner to write, as both he and his grandfather had done many times before him. The note was brief, and once done, he folded the paper as he got up and prepared again to reveal his work. The process had not been followed properly, and that was sinful. He must atone for that.

He walked to the other side of the room, wiping the blood from the weapon as he moved. It must be cleansed. He then unlocked the small, purple velvet-lined oak box resting on the dresser and placed the ornate dagger gently inside.

As he returned to the body, he heard a low, child-like sobbing coming from it. A moan. He felt the anger that had built up at his vanity subside as he regained control of his emotions. That made him smile.

Chapter 14

Dawn had broken more than an hour before Cramer finally got back to the incident room. It was busier than usual as one shift was finishing and another starting, but few people wanted to head home before finding out what was going on.

She went into her office to change her muddy clothes and inappropriate t-shirt before seeing her team as they started their shift at six. Her new DS Jack Sargeant, the butt of many 'Sergeant Sargeant – so good they named him twice' jokes, had only recently been seconded to Cramer's team and had typically worked opposite shifts to Cramer. He had come into the outer office just as she was sorting her clothes out, and her other DC Max Rodriguez had only nodded to her as she walked in. He hadn't really noticed her appearance, thank goodness. She didn't feel like talking to either of them in this state.

She had learned long ago that a full change of clothes – knickers included – was something she should always have in the office. You never knew when you were going to be inadvertently covered in someone else's bodily fluids in this job. Immediately her thoughts returned to the night Adam had died. She felt the stickiness of his blood on her hands. It made her shiver. She made a mental note to double check when she was needed at Robert Kane's trial. Adam's killer wasn't going to get away with it on her watch.

She moved out of her fishbowl office into the main room to get coffee, a freshly pressed white Gucci shirt now gracing her lean frame along with a clean, dark blue Armani suit. She had already washed her hands and face in the ladies and used some loo roll wetted under the tap to get the worst of the mud off her boots. But it had disintegrated in her hands and on the boots themselves, leaving a telltale trail of mini white orbs stuck to the back of her left heel.

Trying to find a mug that was usable in the office before the cleaners had been in was like finding hen's teeth. There was a mountain of crockery in the sink in what laughingly qualified as the floor's kitchen. It was little more than a fridge, kettle, and a microwave on a Formica-covered bench, with a stainless-steel sink that somehow, over the years, had not lived up to its name. Using a visual exam, she checked which cup would take the least effort to make hygienic enough to use. It wasn't looking promising.

Ordinarily, she might have berated anyone still in the office about the general lack of cleanliness, but finding another body just emphasised the enormity of her team's task ahead. Now wasn't the time. She wanted to cut them some slack because, from what she already knew, their workload was going to become much heavier in the next few hours. The overtime was lucrative, but that wasn't why they worked hard – everyone felt they owed these women the extra effort and a perpetrator in custody.

The investigation had already been given reasonable focus and manpower, but now it was clear they were officially looking for a serial killer, Chief Super Davo had confirmed in a call on her way in from the reservoir that he wanted this to be dealt with exclusively by her team and it was their sole focus until its conclusion. Other divisions would temporarily take on the other serious crimes they already had on their books.

Formally leading the investigation, after being made up to acting detective chief inspector, was a challenge she was ready to take on. Cramer had passed the relevant exams for DCI months before and had thought that, when it happened, her promotion might have been a bit more notable than a short handshake in Davo's office and a rushed round-robin email a week later. But a promotion was a promotion. She'd take it however it came. She guessed he wanted to see how she performed before he made it official. It was easier and cheaper to get rid of her this way if she messed up. Not quite the moment yet for party hats and streamers then.

As she was pouring her first coffee, Cramer knew Rob, Leila, and various uniforms would still be knocking on doors, but Jill Traverne must have snuck past her while she was washing her mug because she was sitting in her office when she went back in.

Jill turned towards her, simultaneously taking a drag on a cigarette they both knew she shouldn't be smoking inside the building. Cramer stared at her in disbelief, but Jill glanced at the white stick in her hand before holding her wrists out to be cuffed. 'OK, go on, arrest me. I couldn't face going all the way downstairs for a smoke, and it helps me concentrate.'

Cramer smiled. She put her coffee down on the desk and walked around to take a seat in front of her computer screen. 'I couldn't give a toss about the ciggie, Jill, apart from the fact that you're smoking in my office. It was only this time last year I managed to give up. Seeing you sitting there makes me want one.'

It took all of Cramer's willpower to decline the cigarette Jill obligingly offered.

'Well, you're probably right, Cal,' Jill said – if anyone else called Cramer Cal rather than Callie, it made her bristle, but Jill had earned the right from their long friendship – and hunted around for a suitable receptacle for her fag end, finding a polystyrene cup that had been left with the dregs of coffee probably from days before. She mashed it into the bottom like she was stubbing out a memory. 'I ought to give up too. But it's like Samson, you know?' said Jill. 'Take away the cigarettes – what have you got left?'

'Health and vitality.' Cramer smiled at her. 'And you're a bit on the skinny side for Samson.'

Jill smirked out of the side of her mouth, a surprisingly unbecoming habit. Jill was in her late fifties, with black-grey hair that wouldn't have looked out of place in a Brillo factory. The grey looked as if it had sneaked up on her over the years, strand by individual strand, and gave an overall appearance of a salt-and-pepper rinse.

Jill got up from the edge of the table she had been sitting on and started searching for a waste bin to get rid of her cup. Cramer picked the bin up from beside her desk and proffered it over the desk.

'Thanks.' Jill slam-dunked. 'Now, tell me what we know so far.'

'Not much. Same scenario as before. Simms is still doing his magic, but there was another note, this time Leviticus: chapter twenty, verse twenty-seven.'

Jill started quoting: '"A man also or woman that hath a familiar spirit, or that is a wizard, shall surely be put to death."'

Cramer was astonished. 'How the hell did you know that?'

'Come on, Cal, didn't your Catholic education teach you anything?'

'Nothing the nuns wanted me to learn.'

Jill smiled. 'What else were we left this time?'

'Ankle chain.'

'Colour?'

'Silver. Why?'

Jill shrugged slightly and turned back around and looked again at the board that Cramer had in her office, a double of the much larger one in the main area of the department, that allowed her to see the progress on the case they were working on at all times. It had been put together by Jack on the night shift while her the investigators were dealing with the latest body.

The crime scene photos were juxtaposed unfeelingly with vibrant pictures of the first two victims when they were alive. Jill appeared to be focusing on the close-up shots of Angela's charred, blackened finger, and the inside of Linda's mouth. Cramer always marvelled at how Jill never seemed to be detached from her work, but always exuded calm no matter what she was saying or doing. Unless it was necessary to explode, to get a confession, a reaction. But even then, even at her loudest, she never seemed to lose that quiet control she had over herself. Everything had a purpose.

Cramer watched as Jill moved from one image to the next. 'Angela, silver ring. Linda, fifty pence... Come on, you bastard, what are you telling us with these?' said Jill, before turning towards Cramer. 'You got any ideas?'

'Nada,' said Cramer. 'I thought ideas were your area of expertise?'

Jill rolled her eyes. 'Well, it's not exclusive, any help would be gratefully received.'

A sharp rap on the door made them both jump. A young DC, Max Rodriguez, with short, close-cropped Afro-textured hair filled the doorway with his SAS physique.

'Ma'am, sorry to bother you, but we've just had a call. Another body has been found.'

Chapter 15

The latest crime scene was just ten minutes from the city's main police station on foot, and two minutes by car. Max weaved Cramer and Jill through the medieval streets of Canterbury in a marked car, blue lights bouncing off the buildings lining the narrow cobbled medieval streets.

As they turned into the high street, heading towards the bridge that spanned the River Stour, a solitary constable marked the spot where they needed to be.

'Stop here, Max,' Cramer said, prompting him to abandon rather than park the car, as they all saw the crime scene from their vantage point on the bridge. Another body, again devoid of hair, had this time been placed on the ducking stool where the city's river tours started from.

An exclusion zone stretched for three storefronts, past the Old Weaver's House Restaurant right next to the river and all the way down to a patisserie. Cramer fleetingly thought about getting the pastry shop opened to get a croissant; she hadn't realised how hungry she was until now.

The few people trying to get to work were already being diverted down side streets, taking them past the famous Canterbury Cathedral – the seat of the Church of England – or down towards the former Canterbury Tales tourist attraction – the seat of the slightly more bawdy Geoffrey Chaucer.

A few more people had gathered at the edge of the exclusion zone. Better to be there than at work. Cramer could already see six mobiles in the early-morning light filming the sorry sight. Some were the general public, but she recognised at least two journalists who had already arrived having got wind of what was happening, one of them being Jason Baird. He was like a bad penny for Cramer, always turning up when she least wanted to see him, although there wasn't a time she could think of when she would want to see him in all honesty. The fact he was dating Leila made it even harder to have him hanging around like a bad smell. She never knew how much information he was getting from Leila, and it made Cramer suspicious about Baird's interest in her DC.

Cramer stood silently for a short time, looking above her, left to right, and downriver as Jill watched motionlessly. Cramer pulled a face; there were no CCTV cameras directly overlooking this area. Of course there weren't – who expected something to happen on the river? She walked towards the patisserie where she saw one ball camera on the top of a post. She stopped and looked back at the scene, then fished her mobile from her pocket to call Rob.

'Rob, can you get hold of the footage from the ball camera in the high street for last night? I want you to go over it.'

CCTV review was one of the least glamorous but most useful aspects of police work and she knew Rob would be grateful for the break from the door-to-door that had occupied him and Leila for the last few hours.

'Sure, boss, am I looking for something specific or just suspicious?'

'Both. Either.' She realised she wasn't making much sense. 'I don't know yet, but our suspect has staged a real spectacle on the river this time.'

Rob hesitated. Cramer felt something wasn't right.

'What?' she asked.

'I know. I've seen what you're seeing.'

'How the hell—?'

'It's on Facebook,' Rob interrupted. 'In fact, it's spreading on Facebook. The image is grainy, but you can see there's a body. On the ducking stool next to the Old Weaver's House.'

'Shit. Hang on.' Cramer put their call on hold and opened her own Facebook. The algorithm threw up a slew of fitness and diet gurus as an opening gambit on her timeline. She'd been looking at how to lose a few pounds, and apparently, this was the result of a speculative previous cast around. But after a quick search, she immediately saw two images of the latest victim. Thankfully, you couldn't see as much detail in the footage as in real life, but it was unmistakable from where she stood: the victim hovering precariously over the River Stour in the town centre. She closed the app and went back to her call.

'What can we do to put a stop to this, Rob? Get in touch with the media team and see how they can help to slow this down at least.'

'Maybe say it is a hoax or something?' Rob offered.

'Ooh, great idea, because then I would have a lot more explaining to do when it came out that it wasn't!' Cramer countered.

Rob sounded chastened. 'OK, bad idea, sorry, guv. Let me see what I can do.'

She wasn't convinced they could do anything, but they could stop even more people from gawking right now. She strode over to the constable who was guarding the cordon.

'Can you get something, a sheet, anything, to hang across the bridge to stop people looking at her?' She pointed to the body, just as several other uniforms turned up to help. He nodded and headed off to one of the various squad cars now stationed nearby and started marshalling troops to prevent workers from heading into offices with windows overlooking the tragic sight.

Cramer asked Max to oversee the uniforms who were taking control of the scene at the bridge as the crowds started to build while she and Jill pulled their forensic suits from the back of their car, put them on, and headed down the side street next to the river. You couldn't access the side of the Old Weaver's House from the street directly, a situation made obvious as they made their way down the slippery cobbles, which had been soaked by the fine, clinging drizzle that had started a few minutes before. The only way to access the ducking stool was through a fire escape for the restaurant that was shared with the Canterbury River History company and was being guarded by another officer. Cramer showed her warrant card, and the officer, who was also wearing gloves, pushed open the door to let her and Jill in.

Cramer and Jill walked through the white peeling door, onto more of Canterbury's dark, uneven cobbles. A door ajar on the left revealed a bin store with spiral stairs to the restaurant kitchen on the right. There was a faint smell of bleach in the air.

As they passed around to the left and wound their way onto the deck towards the ducking stool, Cramer heard Jill gasp, startled by the sight of waders hanging from a peg.

'For fuck's sake!'

Cramer smiled behind her mask. To be fair, it did look like a man's legs without an accompanying torso.

To the right, perched on top of the ducking stool, was their latest victim, the deep, scarlet hole beneath her left ribs visible despite the strange angle she was sitting at. Her legs had been shoved up underneath her and her head lolled backwards over the edge of the stool, with her arms dropped on either side. She looked young, very young.

'Who called this in?' Cramer shouted back to the officer standing guard at the door.

'Dog walker, ma'am.'

'Isn't it always?' Cramer mused to Jill. 'If it wasn't for dog walkers, the countryside would be littered with undiscovered corpses.'

'I think this one would have been spotted soon enough,' Jill quipped.

'Ma'am, DS Gulliver and DC Johnson are on their way,' the officer at the door interjected. Cramer nodded. It was going to be a full complement of staff, most of them working overtime now, which Cramer would have to get signed off by Davo. Paperwork was a bitch.

The SOCOs arrived in numbers, filing through the open door, and the victim's modesty was swiftly protected by a tent – no easy feat given she was hanging partway over the river. Arc lights were set up inside, making the scene look far too bright and unreal in the morning sun, which was rising and burning off the drizzling clouds.

They began scurrying around like big white ants, across all areas that had been cordoned off, making sure no part of the scene was missed, doing fingertip searches as they went. There was little space to work in and until they knew how the body had been transported, the street which offered the only land access, as well as the river, had to be considered part of the scene.

Cramer looked from where they were standing towards the bridge and the high street as workers and shop owners moaned to the officers there about their need to get to work.

Inside the forensic tent, sporadic camera flashes momentarily competed with the sun and arc lights as the scene photographs were taken. It was strange. The darkness and clouds that had initially greeted them somehow seemed more appropriate to the crime scene than sunlight. But everything about this case was at odds with something.

'Ladies.' Dr John Simms nodded, as if he was about to offer cocktails. 'I thought we'd left this party just a few hours ago?'

Cramer grimaced. 'You and me both.'

The three of them moved inside the tent that was now covering the body, and stood in a semicircle, staring again at the sad centrepiece. The victim was a young girl, with dark tanned skin, almost Latin-looking, her eyes stuck wide open from the terror she had faced. Victorian investigators believed the image of the killer was etched on the retina of the dead, and looking at her now, it was easy to understand why. Cramer wished to herself it was that easy. The girl was small, probably no more than around five foot three, and very slight, which would have made it easier to lift her onto the ducking stool. Even so, she was at a precipitous angle over the Stour, so it would have required real strength. Her scalp had what looked like fresh cuts, clearly visible with no stubble of regrowth. With all her pubescent body hair removed, she looked little more than a child.

'How long has she been here?' Cramer asked Simms.

'Not too long, given the level of rigor mortis. I'd say she's only been dead a few hours, but I'll know more with the temperature readings...'

'... which you'll take when you're ready to move her, I know,' Cramer interrupted, repeating his mantra from earlier that day.

He smiled. 'Very good. You know more about all of this than you let on.'

Cramer rolled her eyes at his patronising tone.

Given the prominence of the staging this time, there was little chance the body could have been left long before someone spotted her, thought Cramer.

'What about the note?' Jill asked Simms.

'They haven't always been in obvious places,' he said. 'For the second victim, we came across it only after half an hour or so at the crime scene.'

Simms moved towards their latest victim and began to examine her visually under the arc lights as he talked into a Dictaphone.

'No other injuries apparent. No bruising or visible residue on the wrists.' He clicked off the recorder and turned to Cramer. 'Suggests she hasn't been tortured like the others.'

So far, none of them had mentioned the most obvious feature of this sad scene: the silver spoon lodged in the girl's mouth. Jill was the first to point it out.

'Well, that symbolism is pretty unmistakable. But she doesn't look rich. Beautiful girl, but her skin isn't in good condition, like she hasn't had a proper meal in months.'

'The sores around her mouth suggest a drug habit,' Simms added. 'The great and the good have enough money to hide it better.'

Cramer smiled sadly. Simms wasn't wrong; she knew it from a close, bitter experience.

Outside, Charlie, one of the forensic techs, was coming in from the high street with the familiar evidence bag. He'd found the note. He panted up the road, his belly rolling pendulously from side to side with the effort, and pointed a stubby finger back towards where he'd come from.

'The note was over there, stuck between the base of the railings on the bridge. Not sure whether it was placed there or blew there in the wind.' He drew in a long breath at the end of his short speech and leaned forward to put both his hands on his knees, sucking in air as if he might be about to add to the body count right there, before looking up again at them. 'Probably the former.'

'You all right, Charlie? You look a bit... hypertensive,' Simms said.

Charlie's face had turned the deep red that only those with high blood pressure can achieve. 'Yeah, I'm fine,' he gasped in reply, 'Just forgot my medication this morning.'

Cramer moved towards him to relieve him of the latest bit of evidence. 'You should take care of yourself, Charlie.'

Simms pointed towards the evidence bag down by Cramer's side as Charlie left them. 'What does it say?'

"Then Pharaoh also called the wise men and the sorcerers: now the magicians of Egypt, they also did in like manner with their enchantments," Exodus seven, verse eleven.'

She looked over at Jill to see her reaction. 'Know that one?'

Jill looked offended.

'Sorry,' said Cramer. 'It's just you did before.'

'I'm not some religious freak, you know,' countered Jill.

'Unlike whoever is doing this,' said Cramer.

Jill wagged her finger in admonishment. 'Don't jump to conclusions about someone's mind. Psychology is as much an art as a science.'

Cramer moved back into the tent towards the body, kneading her temples. For the first time, she was beginning to feel the hours she'd worked piling up behind her in a bastardised Doppler effect. She knew she was hurtling towards a sonic boom in her life; it was a question of when, not if. Simms and Jill followed her in.

'How long do you think it will be before you can deal with the post-mortem?' Cramer asked Simms.

'I'll do it this morning. Two bodies within twelve hours – doesn't make sense to hang around. He's speeding up, so should we.'

Cramer nodded wearily, wishing she had enough energy right now to speed anything up. She turned to leave the tent again just as Rob entered. His face contorted in a pained expression. 'Oh shit, I don't believe it, he said.'

'What?'

'I know her.'

Chapter 16

Rob closed his eyes and shook his head. 'Her name's Dominique Monroe. I knew her a few years ago on Vice – she was only fifteen then. I'd hoped she'd cleaned herself up by now.'

Jill suddenly became more alert. 'She's a prostitute?'

'Yeah, a particular favourite for a lot of punters, thanks to her age and "exotic" appearance.' He looked at her shaven head. 'She had fantastic ebony-black hair. Could have had such a different life. Now look at her. Fuck.' He shook his head.

They remained completely still, staring at the girl, at the spoon in her mouth, at the scene in general. Then Jill suddenly turned to move out of the tent towards the only entrance door to the scene. She shouted back towards them.

'Rob, I need to get back to the station now.'

He looked at Cramer for confirmation.

'Fine, yeah, take her. And Rob, get hold of the Historic River Tours people – we need to know how it would be possible to access this point from the river. There must be a launch somewhere that can be accessed by a vehicle.'

'Will do, guv.'

He followed Jill out of the tent, but turned around and took a deep breath.

'Guv, the media want information. Keep asking for an interview with you, especially now two bodies have been found so close together. Can you talk to them?'

She sighed. The last thing she wanted to do was get involved in a press conference. She had a love-hate relationship with the press, mostly erring on the side of hate. She looked at her watch. Less than an hour had passed since they got to the scene.

'I thought Davidson was dealing with that?' The Super rarely missed an opportunity to put on his uniform, having shined his epaulette insignia, and stand in front of the cameras to take some glory for everyone else's hard work. But he was being uncharacteristically shy about this case.

'Well, he's changed his mind,' Rob said, almost spitting the words out in frustration.

'For God's sake!' Cramer mused for a second. 'I know why he cancelled – he doesn't want to be the one to share that we have no leads yet.'

Rob looked straight back at her. 'Well, we don't, guv.'

He was right. No solid leads, no firm suspects, and, so far, no palpable connection between their first two victims other than the notes. Now the body count had doubled in two days, doing the same social media, online and offline checks to find connections between them, if they even existed, was going to take more time and much more manpower. Cramer needed to regroup her team, get back to basics, see what they were missing.

'OK. Get everyone together in the briefing room. I want to go over everything we know so far, look at any patterns. Get everyone there in the next hour. Including Leila, once she's finished talking to her press buddies.' Cramer stabbed a finger in the direction of the assembled media on the other side of the bridge where Leila was chatting.

'DC Johnson!' Cramer bellowed in her direction, causing her to turn around. 'Put your boyfriend down, we have work to do.'

Leila had recently begun dating Jason Baird. But the press – and Baird in particular – made Cramer's skin crawl. The DC started to make her way back towards her boss with a face like thunder.

Rob carried on. 'What about the interview?'

Cramer barely considered her reply. 'Fuck 'em – Davo can worry about that.'

Chapter 17

Jill was sitting at the desk in Cramer's office when she got back from the scene more than an hour later, a King James Bible in front of her, beavering away like a Sunday school child. Jill looked up when Cramer knocked on her own door. 'You didn't waste much time,' Cramer said.

Jill motioned her over with a conspiratorial wave of her hand. 'I have a theory about why he's leaving us the things he is, bearing in mind the religious or occult aspect to all of these killings.'

Cramer looked over her shoulder into the incident room to see the swollen numbers of the team, now all present. 'Explain it to me at the same time as everyone else. Incident room. Five minutes. Have you got copies of the first two post-mortem reports?'

'Not yet.'

'I've got a set for each of us.'

'Thanks, most of it is in here anyway,' Jill said, pointing to her bird's-nest hair. *It would be easy to hide a lot of things in there*, thought Cramer.

Cramer walked out of her office to the end of the incident room and clapped her hands to attract everyone's attention. She always felt an idiot doing that but shouting rarely worked above the hubbub.

‘OK, as most of you are already aware, there have been some developments.’ Classic understatement. ‘Jack, what are you still doing here? Shouldn’t you be in bed?’

Jack should have finished his previous shift five hours earlier and was not due back in until later that evening, yet he was sitting in the front row.

‘Saw on the news two bodies were found, so guessed it would only be a matter of time before we got the call. Decided I’d beat you to it, guv.’

Cramer smiled. ‘Well, if we didn’t have to deprive you of your beauty sleep, Jack, we wouldn’t have.’

Jack was used to the ribbing from his colleagues. Years of rugby scrums had given him cauliflower ears, but Cramer knew his bulk would have been beneficial in any ruckus. No doubt plenty of drunks had thought twice before taking him on, making him a popular partner on the beat. But his real strength was in surveillance. Despite his size, he was the perfect grey man thanks to his military training.

Jack’s belly laugh triggered a ripple of laughter that moved around the room like a Mexican wave before Cramer raised and lowered her hands to get complete silence again. In the meantime, Jill had moved out of Cramer’s office towards the incident board in the department.

‘You all know Jill Traverne, so I won’t waste time on intros. Hand these round,’ Cramer said as she picked up a pile of folders that were on the desk in front of her, and each of the twenty officers present took one from the top and passed them on. Inside lay the disturbing pictures leering down at them from the board behind her. It was one thing seeing them slightly blurred at a distance, but up close and personal in the folders, it instilled silence in the room.

Cramer’s voice sliced through the deafening quiet as she carried on with the briefing. ‘As most of you know, another two potential victims have been found in the last few hours. Rob has already run the prints on the first girl, but we have no hits, so it looks like she doesn't have a record. We believe from her previous photographs and description that it's Amanda Morrison, the journalist. We haven't got a formal ID yet, so treat that one with caution. We are currently trying to get in touch with her partner. But, with what looks like a third connected murder, we are now officially investigating a serial killer.' A low rumble of chatter went around the room and Cramer waited for it to calm before carrying on.

'The other girl' – she pulled two police headshots out of a file – 'we know, from an ID at the scene and her prints, is Dominique Monroe. Eighteen years old, has been working as a prostitute in and around Canterbury for about three years now.'

'What was left with the bodies this time, guv?' Jack asked.

'Amanda Morrison, if that is confirmed, was wearing an ankle chain. Dominique had a silver spoon in her mouth. Details of which, may I remind you, must not leave this room. If I hear anything about any of this from anyone not in here right now, your life won't be worth living.'

She shot Leila Johnson in particular a warning glance before continuing thanks to her closeness to her boyfriend Baird.

'And while, yes, I know the images of Dominique were on social media, none of the ones circulated were clear enough to show this.

'But perhaps more important is where she was found. Dominique's body was found sitting on the ducking stool in the middle of town, where the Historic River Tours base is, next to the Old Weaver's House Restaurant. So far, we aren't sure how she came to be there because access to that area is very limited. It could be she was taken down the river, but that would be a very labour-intensive way to dump a body. It's more likely that our suspect accessed the side entrance to the pontoon from the fire escape between the two businesses.'

Rob interjected. 'It should be locked after hours, but one of the restaurant staff we spoke to claims it could have been left unlocked. It wouldn't be the first time. I also checked the CCTV from the ball camera like you asked, and there were a few cars coming and going in that area, but nothing that looked out of the ordinary.'

Cramer nodded, along with others in the team.

'Are we thinking he may have an accomplice then, guv?' Rob asked.

'We can't rule it out – we can't rule anything out yet. We know these crime scenes are being staged, and the staging is getting more elaborate, and more public.'

Another murmur went around the room.

'OK, quieten down, please. Jill has a theory about why each item is being left with each body, so I'll let her explain more.'

Cramer nodded to Jill to move forwards, and the officers shifted uneasily in their seats.

Jill laid out her papers on the desk in front of her before starting. She looked unusually nervous.

'Well, as we have discussed before, this looks like the work of a man, either attractive or certainly not threatening, as these women must have spent time with him willingly before being kidnapped. They'll feel comfortable with him. He won't appear to be a threat.

'He will be strong – it takes a lot of power to move a body of any size any distance, and with Dominique' – Jill flicked through to the latest crime scene photos – 'he will have had to have lifted her above shoulder height to perch her on that stool. Even for someone as small as she is, that would still be some feat given the dead weight.'

Nods from all confirmed they agreed so far.

'He has a need for control, to control these women. It may mean he has a significant area elsewhere in his life where he lacks control and these acts make up for that, help to balance everything. That controlling tendency also fits in with the ligature marks on each girl's wrist.' She pointed to close-ups of this on the board, the brown rust residue clearly visible. 'They are being held bound, so they have no ability to resist physically. So, while he wants to control, he's not sure of himself, is insecure in his own ability.'

Another series of murmurs and paper rustling interrupted Jill's flow briefly before she continued.

'How's he getting them to go with him, though, even if they had spent time with him? It could be they know him and feel comfortable, but we haven't found anyone yet that both Angela and Linda knew. So, I would suggest he must be drugging them somehow. I can't see how else it would work.'

'There hasn't been any evidence of drugs so far,' Cramer followed, addressing the room. 'All toxicology screens have been negative. He could be using something like Rohypnol or GHB, because we believe he's holding them before killing them, and that would disappear from the bloodstream completely in a few days. We'll have to wait for tox results on the latest two victims to see if we can take that further.'

Jill nodded in agreement before she continued. 'He's leaving us Bible quotes with each victim, so he is either very religious or motivated by religion. He could be lashing out at something in his youth. He may well have been abused himself in some way. The Bible quotes are an obvious link between all four victims—'

Cramer interrupted. 'You'll find details of the last two notes on the sheet at the back of the file.' There was an extended shuffling of papers before Jill carried on.

'But I think there is a greater link here. The first three victims, we believe, were taken from in or around the Cognoscenti nightclub. The first two definitely were, based on the last known phone mast pings from their smartphones. We already know from interviews over the last few days that Amanda, before she went missing, was last seen there. We have to treat that as a key link.'

Cramer cut in, 'But their phones were turned off before they left the venue, having previously been left on for more than two weeks solid. It suggests he's doing that, so he has a reasonably good knowledge of law-enforcement procedures.'

'Or regularly watches *CSI*...' said Jack, eliciting knowing laughs from those around him.

Jill carried on regardless. 'Either way. He must know we can find out from someone's phone signal the vicinity where they, or at least their phone, currently is. It could be someone who knows police procedure. So, it could even be one of our own, or someone close to someone in law enforcement, or someone who has spent a considerable time in our company, and/or prison. No one can be discounted at this point.'

Cramer watched Jack's fist tighten involuntarily. The idea that it could be one of their own never went down well, but Jill was really getting going now.

'The number three has enormous significance in the Bible, and in literature, for that matter. The three wise men; Peter betrayed Jesus three times before the cock crowed; the Holy Trinity. Even when it doesn't feature directly, it features indirectly in multiples. The mark of the devil is 666. Judas was paid thirty pieces of silver to betray Jesus. There were twelve disciples. Do you follow?'

Cramer looked at the blank faces staring at Jill before she continued.

'I think he is finding these girls in threes, and with Dominique, he may have started another three. We just need to find out for sure where she was last seen to determine if, and potentially where, he has shifted his focus to. Rob has suggested Dominique had turned tricks near the Illuminati nightclub. Quite why the clubs locally have Italian names, I'm not sure anyone knows...'

Rob interjected. 'Yeah, there is plenty of traffic around Illuminati – she often picked up tricks when the club emptied out. There was a bouncer there, Marvin, or Martin, something like that, who had a soft spot for her and always looked out for her in case she got in trouble. That's probably as good a place as any to start looking.'

Cramer nodded her agreement, but Jack had started scratching his head partway through Jill's assessment of events. 'Sorry, Jill, but you know, this sounds like bullshit to me. If this guy is as mad as a box of frogs, who's to say he's working in any kind of pattern?'

Jill countered in her most understanding-psychologist tone. 'What makes you think he's mad? Angry, perhaps. I could agree with that. Mentally unstable, again, there are likely to be some elements of psychological "break" involved here. But these are not the actions of a madman in layman's terms, Jack. These murders are handled meticulously. There's preparation, method, a ritual, if you like, to be completed to satisfy his reason for killing. We don't know what that is yet, but it's there. And he is intelligent. *Very* intelligent. We just need to hope that collectively we're more intelligent, or that he slips up. Or both.'

Cramer took a deep breath. They were all hoping for that.

Jill continued. 'Besides, even if you were right, Jack, and this' – she turned to look at the board behind her before looking back at the sergeant – 'was the work of a madman, which I don't believe for a second, this is what we have got to work with. God knows you have bugger all else at the moment.'

Jack's face had got redder as Jill had carried on talking. He had well and truly had a strip torn, the kind of response Cramer had seen only a few times before. A few faces fell towards the floor. Despite this woman not actually being a copper, they all knew she was right, and had come up with what sounded like the most decent leads to follow so far.

Jill carried on, now addressing the room and not just Jack: 'If we wait until we're certain about his reasons or his ritual needs, we'll be too late. We'll have lost someone else.' The weight of her words hung heavy in the room.

'That isn't the only thing that becomes apparent either, when you look at what's being left with the bodies,' she continued. 'Yes, the mode of killing is different – the similarity is the stab wound under their left ribcage, but that doesn't finish the job. Instead, we have fire, hanging – we will have to wait and see what comes of the PMs before we know the latest two. But there is a theme. Angela, the first victim, was not married, yet was found wearing a silver wedding ring. The second victim, Linda, was a married mother of four, whose wedding ring had been taken off, and instead, he left a fifty-pence piece inside her mouth. The third victim, assuming it was Amanda and therefore a journalist, was left with an ankle chain. Now, it could be hers, but it's unlikely. Now we have Dominique, a prostitute with a silver spoon in her mouth. Do you see?'

The room was still. Everyone seemed afraid to hazard a guess at what this crazy-haired lady was getting at for fear of looking more stupid than they already felt. Even Cramer remained bemused.

'He's telling us who's next, folks. Linda was married, hence the wedding ring left with Angela. The third victim, assuming we're right and it is Amanda Morrison, was a journalist, so she is paid to pass on information, hence the money in the mouth of Linda. The ankle chain used to be a sign of prostitution, hence Dominique.' Cramer was pleased to know she wasn't the only person whose mother had told her that. 'And the silver spoon. That is telling us that the next victim is...'

Chapter 18

'Someone rich,' Cramer and Jack chimed in together as if they'd rehearsed. If this case could get any worse, it could only be by having a high-profile family involved, and there were more than enough in the county for that.

'Or well connected. Exactly,' Jill said. 'That's where we need to be looking, and I think if you can find where Dominique was last seen, you may be able to determine where the next snatch is going to be. And stop it.'

The room erupted into chatter as the gravity of what Jill was saying sank in. If she was right, it could blow this whole case wide open.

Cramer moved to stand next to Jill to take control of the room again.

'OK, OK, we've got a lot of work to do. Jack, you get in touch with Vice and follow up on Rob's recollections, see who Dominique's known associates were and track them down to find out when she was last seen alive.

'Rob, you need to be ready to head to wherever Dominique was last seen. We don't have time to lose. I want you to check on the last known phone mast ping from the last two victims' mobile phones, find out when they were last used – and where they are now, if they're still active. If we can place these victims in the vicinity of either club as Jill has identified, that will give us a better idea if her theory is right.'

Rob nodded.

Cramer continued. 'Leila, get in touch with the relatives of each of the victims. Get hold of any iPads, computers, work or personal mobiles, or anything else they might have used that we haven't got yet and go through them to see if there's anything to tie these women to each other. Get the backup files from their mobiles and recreate them since we're not likely to find them. The usual – email, WhatsApp, Facebook, Messenger, Snapchat, TikTok, Instagram – if they are linked in any way, I want you to find it. Check their work computers too, I want these all nailed down.'

Leila looked perplexed. 'But, guv, we have already gone through Angela and Linda's social media and there was nothing.'

Cramer was unimpressed. 'We've got two new victims that I know we haven't done any data analysis on, so do it again and cross-reference everything. Contact lists might shed some light. Double-check, triple-check it if you have to. We have two new names to research and something there could give us a vital lead.'

Cramer pointedly turned her attention away from Leila and back to the whole room.

'We need to get ahead of this bastard. Someone somewhere knows who's doing this, even if they don't know it. Maybe his behaviour has changed. Speak to the local vicars again, rabbis, any religious sect that might be harbouring someone like this without realising. Or actually realising, which is worse. Leila, Rob, get Max to help you. We must be sure we're covering everything Jill has come up with. Hopefully Simms will come up with something forensic in his post-mortem too. And Max, get me a list of the most wealthy and influential families in the county. We need an idea of who might be targeted next.'

Nobody moved. They were all in stunned silence.

'What are you waiting for?' Cramer shouted. 'Come on, let's stop this before we have another body!'

Chapter 19

As the office started to hum with activity, Jill and Cramer retreated into her office. Jill went to light a cigarette before stopping short in the scrutiny of Cramer's steely gaze.

'I know, I know.' She hastily re-holstered the cigarette in its box before she sitting down on the other side of the desk.

Cramer looked at her quizzically. 'Good work, Jill. But how did you come up with all of that so suddenly?'

'Well, it wasn't that quick, I just haven't felt comfortable outlining it until now. But with Dominique being found today, everything seemed less of a coincidence, and more of a plan.'

Cramer ran her hand through her fringe to get it off her face. It was such fine hair that its touch felt like an angel's breath on her forehead. Irritating.

'Well, it's the best information we have to work on so far. Apart from the Cognoscenti and now Illuminati connection, there's nothing else that strings these women together. At least, not that we've found, and the Cognoscenti guys came up with nada on CCTV that would be useful. And so far, no witnesses.'

Jill pursed her painfully thin lips. Physically she looked as fragile as a sparrow, but she had the constitution of an ox.

'People don't want to get involved. They abhor what's going on around them, but won't do anything about it.'

Cramer nodded. She knew this all too well. 'I know. I'm in court in a week for the, umm... trial.' Cramer didn't need to say which. 'But try as we might, we can't get a witness who will talk.'

Jill gave her an encouraging smile and Cramer looked away. Sessions with Jill had made her stronger when thinking about Adam's death, but she still found it hard to articulate. Although she wouldn't have a choice in court.

When Cramer glanced back up, Jill seemed to have her mind somewhere else. 'What's up?' she asked.

Jill took a deep breath. 'I was just thinking about the possibilities. Who might be his next target, assuming I'm right about the wealthy family.'

Cramer stared at her intently. 'Well, we should plan for the worst and hope for the best. We need to warn relevant people, but without telling them how we have identified them as possible targets.'

Jill sighed. 'Don't some of your family still live in the county, Cal?'

'Well, yes, but why are they relevant to...?'

Jill pursed her lips and tilted her head to one side in a silent pose, which said everything loud and clear. 'Are you kidding me?'

Cramer slumped back in her chair and let out a sigh. Jill was one of the few people who knew about her family and background. She hated to think that her personal life might start to get mixed up with work. But there was a real risk these two worlds – which she had successfully kept apart for nearly ten years now – could now collide.

She faced Jill with a resigned look and drew her hands down both cheeks. 'Yeah, OK. I'll make the call.'

Chapter 20

He'd been watching it for some time now. Watching. Waiting. It couldn't be rushed. He had two or three under surveillance at any time – it was important to keep tabs on those that had the power to commit ultimate sins against him. Against all others.

His grandfather had taught him well, to be patient, to understand there was too much at risk if you acted too early. You needed to study, to see how it interacted with its surroundings, with other people. Hunting took time. It took patience. It took skill. He had all three.

He remembered how he'd honed his skills. He started fishing with his grandfather. The peace and tranquillity of the process. Waiting, waiting, waiting for that moment. That second when the float dropped below the waterline as the fish took the bait. Then the excitement, the thrill of the fight, of reeling in the flailing fish as it struggled, fighting for life. He could take its life or not. It was his decision. His alone. With the guidance of God, of course. But it was His will that gave him the fish in the first place.

He hadn't wanted to gut the fish the first time. But his grandfather made sure he did. He winced at the sound of the knife squelching through its flesh as he ripped it open, exposing the insides that must be removed. He recoiled at the smell and the feel of them. It made his grandfather angry, so angry. So angry that he pushed his head down into the fish innards and rubbed his face in them. Then he laughed. 'That's how to learn, boy,' he'd told him. He'd hated his grandfather in that moment. But he had a lot to thank him for now. And that was where it had begun. His training for the work he was doing now.

His grandfather gave him the skills. The tracking, the hunting, the patience. But you had to have a natural aptitude for this work. That couldn't be taught.

He'd taken on the calling his grandfather had started decades before, taken it on when the old man had become too infirm to continue it himself. Too physically weak to defend himself against the power of them. Anything and everything had to be expected, but the danger could be minimised if you handled it right. If it didn't know what you were, it had no way of defending against you. That was his biggest weapon, and he used it well.

His grandfather had told him that, sometimes, this gift skipped a generation. His own father hadn't had the gift, or the stomach, to deal with the important work that needed doing. Couldn't bring himself to challenge the non-believers, the heretics, the pagans who must be held accountable. Couldn't even bring himself to challenge his wife, to tell her how it was going to be. It was embarrassing, his grandfather had said. His father should have been ashamed.

Still. He hadn't meant to kill him that day. Especially so soon after his grandfather had passed. But time marched on, and there was no time to lose. His work needed scaling up, so he needed the family home to himself. His father clearly had the physical genetics of his grandfather and was going to live to a ripe old age, even if he didn't have the stomach to take on the work. He had been strong and vibrant. And in the way.

He let those thoughts go, refocusing on his task. Focus. Concentration. Patience. He had all of them in abundance. He watched as it left the building, headed for the station. Phone cameras made his work so much easier than it had been in his grandfather's day.

This was the one he needed to get.

He started his car as it moved past him. Not yet, but soon.

Chapter 21

Despite the long hours already clocked at their desks – they had been working for more than 18 hours in a row – there was a renewed vigour in the team as they pushed to get additional leads on the back of Jill's analysis. Cramer was working in her office when there was a knock on her door, and she looked up from her keyboard to see one of the junior officers standing in the doorway.

'Ma'am, Alex Newcastle is here to see you.'

Alex Newcastle was the lead prosecutor for their considerably large case against Robert Kane. With the case already being heard in court and her testimony due next week, he'd come to see her to go over the finer details before they met across the benches.

Cramer got up from her desk, picked up her notepad, nodded a thank you to the junior officer, and made her way down to the front desk to meet Alex.

He was sitting in the moulded-plastic reception chairs – easier to clean – in reception, going through paperwork as she waved through the glass separating the desk staff from the rest of the world to try to attract his attention. But he was too engrossed. She used her pass to buzz the door open, and the noise made him look up immediately. Cramer waited for him in the doorway as he gathered his files and leather bag together and stood up to come towards her. The man next to him, a slightly dishevelled-looking and overweight apparent counterpart, stood at the same time and followed him.

'Alex, good to see you.' Cramer held out her hand as a greeting. Alex shook it.

'Yes, well, I wish it was under different circumstances, for sure.'

She opened the door wide to allow him through, pushing it back with an extended right arm, then, almost as an afterthought as he was partway through it, Alex stopped and did the introduction that Cramer felt better manners would have made him make much sooner.

'Sorry, Caroline, I should have said, this is David Riley. He's here to get up to speed on the case as well. He's recently joined us from Edinburgh where he was working with the procurator fiscal. David, this is DI Caroline Cramer...'

'Acting DCI now, Alex,' Cramer corrected.

'Nice, congratulations! Seems just yesterday we worked on our first case together, when was that?'

'Nine years ago now,' she added.

'Long time...' Alex said.

Cramer held her hand out to Riley, but had to stop herself from wiping hers on her trousers after the clammy, limp-fish handshake she was subjected to. She decided she should try to be friendly, so put her hand in her pocket instead to achieve the desired result.

Leila was heading in the opposite direction and they all stood to one side to let her pass.

'This is my DC Leila Johnson,' Cramer said. 'This is Alex Newcastle, who I think you know, and David Riley.'

Leila nodded to both as she went through the door. 'Nice to meet you. Sorry guv, just have to nip out quickly, I won't be long.'

Cramer went through the doors with the two lawyers and continued the conversation as they went along the corridor.

'Will you be sitting in on the day, David?' Cramer asked out of politeness.

'Well—' Riley started to answer, but Newcastle cut in before he had a chance.

'He might be cross-examining. We're short-staffed and I've another case I may have to stick with because of shitty court scheduling. But I hope to be with you. Bloody clerks really know how to fuck things up.'

Cramer's insides ran cold. Kane was being represented by Marcus Hall, a man renowned for getting the guiltiest people off the most heinous charges. This wasn't the time for the B-team to get an outing. Maybe she was being uncharitable. She bit her tongue, smiled and nodded and waited to see what Riley was about before making a decision.

She ushered them both into an interview room and three coffees were duly supplied by the custody staff.

The two prosecuting barristers sat down opposite her. Alex had a file an inch thick that he was thumbing through until he got to the relevant page. She always winced when she saw the images of that night, how Adam had looked when he was dying was seared on her memory, and she didn't need any picture to remind her of the horror and sadness she felt later when she knew he was gone.

'OK, shall we get going?' Alex looked at his watch as if he had somewhere to go. Cramer knew she'd rather be almost anywhere else at this moment, but was determined not to let Adam down again.

'So, the case so far has been pretty awkward. Hall has been rebutting all points put to his client, as you'd expect, but we really don't know how much the jury is believing him or believing us. I know who I'd believe...'

Cramer snorted a laugh and rolled her eyes – yes, she knew who she'd believe too.

'It means your testimony will be much more significant than expected. You're looking like our star witness.'

She blew out her cheeks. 'No pressure then.'

A pang of guilt struck her at the flippant comment. This was about caging the man who had killed Adam, and no matter how hard it was going to be, she'd be able to leave the courtroom and go home. He could never do that again. She moved slightly in her seat and mentally reset her approach. 'Then let's make sure we nail this. Kane needs to go down for a long time.'

As they were speaking, Cramer noticed out of the corner of his eye that Riley was tapping his leg under the table, like he was nervous. He hadn't even looked up from his notepad, despite not writing anything down, or even looking at any case notes. Was he listening? It was as if he wasn't even there. Alex continued regardless.

'So, we know Hall is going to be playing on Kane's injury.' Cramer smiled at the thought. How his arm had cracked under the smack of her baton. He deserved the pain. And more.

Alex continued. 'He's still in a cast. Operations and time haven't managed to give him full use back yet. Apparently, they're still working on it.'

'Ah, my heart bleeds.' Cramer had nothing but hate for Kane.

'Yeah, well, all our hearts bleed.' Alex looked at Riley, who had momentarily looked up from his notebook. He smiled and nodded in agreement.

'But, listen, that's only part of the issue,' Alex continued. 'We know they're going to work the jury to try to find errors in the lead up to the raid. Errors in the intelligence. Make it look like Adam hadn't done his job properly.'

Cramer tensed involuntarily. 'He did his job properly. We all did. The fact that we have Hall trying to soap Kane through a loophole isn't going to change that. This is solid. Believe me.'

'I hear you, Caroline, but solid or not, you know as well as I do this has to play well to the jury. If they even suspect we haven't done the right thing, there's a chance Kane will walk.'

That sentence made Cramer wish she'd broken his leg as well.

'Well, as long as we work together on this to take him down, we should be fine.' She looked at Riley for confirmation. 'Right?' He was at least paying attention to the conversation now. He nodded and smiled, but still hadn't said anything.

'OK, well, let's go through the nuts and bolts,' Alex said. 'We want to know we're all on the same page.'

He looked at Riley. 'You want to do this bit?'

Riley nodded again, shifted in his seat before leaning forward and taking the case file and started going through the evidence with her.

It was only the second time Cramer had heard him speak.

Chapter 22

Cramer didn't talk to her parents that often, not because she didn't care about them, but more because their lives were so different. Different enough that at times, it was hard for her to find anything to talk to them about.

They weren't keen on her choice of career. They never said as much, always being verbally supportive of her no matter what. But there was an undercurrent of unspoken disapproval. They couldn't understand why she chose to do what she did when she didn't need to. They missed the point that helping people made her feel good. Police work was far more palpable and satisfying than just throwing money in the direction of any problem like they did, hoping some would end up in the pockets of those who needed it rather than feathering the nests of the already well-off. Foundations, charity galas, the Rotary Club – they had been involved in all of them at one time or another. Of course, much of this charitable giving provided a tax break to her investment-banker father. There's nothing better than finding a tax-efficient way to salve a conscience.

Cramer had her own money, left to her by her late grandfather who had started the family banking business just after the Second World War and benefited handsomely from the post-war economic boom. He'd left both her and her brother Finn a trust fund, which meant they wouldn't need to work for the rest of their lives. Finn chose this route, spending most of his time travelling around the world on an endless gap year, so long now it was in danger of becoming a gap life. Cramer had at least one niece she knew of, but given how handsome and charming her brother was, there were likely to be more children that even he didn't know about.

But that kind of life wasn't for her. She wanted a reason to get up in the morning, to have a routine, to be able to help people when they needed it most. She could make a difference, a real difference that was about much more than putting pen to chequebook. But she was conscious that if her colleagues knew her financial position, she would lose the respect she had. So, she kept it to herself, and she was happy for the few who did know about her lifestyle to think it was all down to her investment-banker husband Patrick. The truth was, her wealth dwarfed his, but since the prenup he'd insisted on before they got married had been about protecting him in the event they split, she didn't feel the need to mention her financial position in any detail. Although he knew she was wealthy in her own right, he'd always believed that he would be wealthier in the long run anyway, he was 'the man of the house', after all.

Although she didn't like to flaunt her wealth like some other members of her family, Cramer did enjoy the finer things in life. She wasn't ostentatious, but not having to worry about money was something she would be forever grateful for.

Jill's point had hit home though: Cramer's family – at least the younger generation if Jill's analysis was right – could be at risk. She didn't seriously think it would be relevant for any of her own family, after all, Kent was packed to the gunnels with the wealthy and well connected, even more so than her family. But she'd never forgive herself if she hadn't at least tried to ensure they were safe. Most of them lived in an emotional cage – a gilded cage, but a cage all the same. Common sense didn't often intrude, and their true feelings were rarely allowed out.

As the family matriarch and Olympic-standard gossip, her mother was the perfect communications hub to start with, and she hoped speaking to her would be sufficient to prevent any further calls being necessary; her mother's inability to keep anything to herself might finally work to Cramer's advantage. She'd been working for nearly thirty-six hours non-stop, and her bed was calling, so phoning her judgemental mother was really the last thing she felt like doing.

But at least she was home. Unfortunately, so was Patrick. She could see his Audi parked in front of their imposing house as she swept up the drive and pressed the button on the dash, shuddering the up-and-over garage door into life, which lifted reluctantly allowing Cramer to park her Mercedes inside. Her work car – a slightly old and slightly battered VW Golf – had clearly been returned from the garage good as new, and was sitting to the right of the Audi, so thankfully, she could at least return to normal for the office tomorrow.

She opened the side door into the kitchen as the garage door hummed closed behind her, the hazard lights flashing twice as she locked her car. She didn't feel like rowing with her husband, but sadly that's how most of their conversations ended up these days.

Not having to spend time with Patrick had been a blessing given the pressure she was under at work in recent weeks. He was like her own personal strobe light – he'd created excitement in her life when they first met and offered her a different perspective on many things. Now he was mostly just annoying.

He was sitting in the kitchen eating a sandwich, accompanied by an expensive bottle of red – poor culinary companions for sure. She walked straight past him to the cupboard to get the biggest glass she could find and poured herself enough wine to drown the day she'd had. Patrick picked up on it.

'Rough day?'

Her shoulders tensed as she gulped a mouthful of wine. 'You have no idea. When did you get back?'

'About twenty minutes ago. The conference went on longer than expected.'

Yeah, sure it did. He really thought he could con a detective inspector, she mentally checked herself – an acting detective *chief* inspector, don't forget that promotion – who wasn't born yesterday?

'Well, whatever. You do what you need to do,' she said flippantly, belying the emotional turmoil welling up inside her. She could feel herself shaking with rage and hurt but was trying to hold it together.

'What's that supposed to mean?'

She went to walk past him to head out to the hallway and through to the lounge, but he grabbed her hand to stop her before she left the room. She turned to face him, slightly shocked since it had been some time since they had been even physically close enough for that. She was about to launch into a tirade until she saw his face wasn't full of the anger it had been the last time they spoke. He looked broken.

'How did we get to this point, Cal? Is this what we have now?'

She wanted to give him the sympathy he craved but couldn't bring herself to. Why he should be feeling sorry for himself, God only knew.

'Oh, for fuck's sake, Patrick, don't. Not tonight. I just can't deal with this now as well.'

'This? *This* happens to be our marriage, which is basically in the crapper.'

'You don't think I'd noticed? Maybe you should have thought about that before you stuck your dick in a co-worker.'

That hurt. Both of them.

Cramer felt broken inside too, as far as her and Patrick were concerned, but she couldn't afford to be. Not right now.

'Patrick, just stop. Not tonight. I agree we need to talk, but really, I can't do it now,' she said, more soothingly.

'Then when?'

She bristled again as his confrontational tone resurfaced. 'When I'm ready. You don't call the shots on this one.'

He looked crestfallen but she couldn't – wouldn't – offer him any compassion after what he'd done. Her compassion for him was spent.

'I loved you, Patrick, maybe I still do. But I don't like you, not one bit. So, don't push me, because you really might not like what you see.' Her words were spitting out of her mouth now. 'Your affair ended what we had, and I am just not sure we'll ever get it back. Or that I want to get it back. I deserve better.'

As she said it, she believed it. But that wasn't always the case. There were many times when she questioned what she had done, or hadn't done, to make him look elsewhere for affection. He said it was just sex, but that wasn't something she could associate with. She required more than just physical attraction to get turned on, so the idea of just shagging someone because they were there was anathema to her.

As she walked away from him towards the lounge, she wondered whether it was the animosity she felt that made her think the very worst about him. Cramer was grateful their Georgian house was big enough that they didn't fall over each other and could live quite comfortably apart – the main benefit of having seven bedrooms with only two people living there. But it still didn't seem big enough for them both and their relationship problems. That kind of emotional baggage took up an awful lot of space.

She needed to take her mind off everything, listen to some music or watch TV, something to quieten her thoughts. But nothing was working. Her brain was on overtime and just wouldn't relax.

She had been putting it off for the last hour, but she knew she really needed to call her mother. This case was forcing them to work against the clock, but they had no idea how fast it was ticking.

She settled herself into the living room, allowed the deep, soft seat to cocoon her before she took another sip of wine – she rarely drank so chose well when she did – and finally dialled her parents' number. Unsurprisingly for someone who rarely took a breath between sentences, her mother answered.

'Hello?'

'Hi Mum, it's—'

'Caroline, darling, I was wondering when we were going to hear from you. How are you? I was beginning to wonder if you were still alive, but then I saw you on the news the other night, well, in the background, anyway.'

Yep, she always knew how to make Cal feel top notch.

'I'm OK, thanks, I'm just working on a big case at the moment—'

Her mother was way ahead of her.

'Oh yes, I know. Well, I mean, I saw... dreadful business, Caroline, I really don't know how you manage it.'

Ha! Yes, there it was, the veneer of support with an undercoat of profession-loathing.

'Well, it's very difficult, yes, and the news crews aren't making life any easier for us.'

It was true. The coverage had certainly been tough to watch and read. There was an increasing number of questions, and more pressure being applied each day by journalists following the case, especially Baird. Usually, the police tried to align themselves as much as they could with the press, but there was often friction in the relationship. Cramer had been debating with herself earlier if there was any way they could use the press to their advantage on this case, but so far had drawn a blank. Releasing the information they had kept confidential to be sure no random or mentally ill person confessed to the crimes was more important. It was frustrating for everyone. However, that wasn't the point of this call.

'Listen, Mum, I just need to check something with you, and I haven't got long.' That was a lie. She could have talked all night if she'd wanted, but she needed sleep more than chat. 'Is Charlotte back from university yet?'

Charlotte, her younger cousin, was a highly intelligent but highly strung party animal who was most likely to be in the wrong club at the wrong time. It was guesswork, of course, and Cramer had no real belief any of her family was really at risk, but she couldn't shake off Jill's concern, which had burrowed into her psyche and made itself her concern too.

'She came home yesterday, darling. Said she would try to pop round and see us tomorrow. You should come along as well – we're just having a little get-together in the evening.' That, as Cramer knew from old, meant a large number of people turning up at her parents' rambling pile, most probably drinking and eating to the sound of a string quartet. Nothing her mother ever organised could be misconstrued as low-key. 'It would be nice to see you, darling, and I am sure Charlotte would love to catch up,' her mother finished.

It would be nice to see Charlotte, for sure, but with this case and her marriage problems, she wasn't sure she had the emotional bandwidth to deal with familial socialising on top.

'Let me see what I can do. This case is taking so much of all our time. Do you have Charlotte's number, Mum? I just wanted to try to have a quick word with her.'

'Yes, I think so... Is there anything wrong, darling?'

'No, just wanted to catch up with her while I was thinking about it.'

After some rustling, small talk and general faffing, Charlotte's number was duly passed on and Cramer decided to get back to her wine. She promised to try to make the shindig, although how hard was another matter. She let her chair absorb her again but called her cousin before she could be enveloped by sleep. Answerphone. She left a message, just hoping in the back of her mind she wasn't too late.

Chapter 23

By the time she'd woken up, Cramer had missed two calls and one WhatsApp voice message from Charlotte, the latest of which had come through at 3.23 that morning. Clearly, she still liked to party as hard as ever. That was a worry, but it showed she was still OK. No one else had seen fit to call her overnight, and no news was usually good news in her job.

She opened the voicemail her cousin had left, barely able to hear her above the background noise of music and chatter. She was clearly in a nightclub.

'Callie, how are you doing? Aunty Fen' – Cramer's mother was called Fenella – 'rang Mummy and said you were trying to get hold of me for something... Let's chat tomorrow. I'm not sure what time...' She'd broken off to find out from someone nearby in the hubbub what time it was, and that part of the message had become unintelligibly garbled. '...Well, anyway, I imagine you're sleeping, so give me a call tomorrow.'

It was still early when Cramer left home, a successful ploy to avoid Patrick again, so when she reached to the station, it wasn't surprising that none of her team had arrived yet. The morning briefing was due in three hours at ten, no sense in making it any earlier unless there were developments overnight. She was grateful there were no negative ones at least. It gave everyone time to pause, take a breath, and think about their next move. Four women were dead, two found in hideously quick succession. Forensics were still to be completed on the last two victims, and they had little or nothing to go on from the first two.

The problem with forensics in the real world, as opposed to in TV dramas, is that labs take time. They are generally private enterprises, rather than government-run, and while they prioritise the work in order of importance, they cannot – and will not – drop everything to expedite results without a good reason. A potential serial killer had to be the best reason of all, but the overtime created by pushing through additional testing sooner had to be paid for somehow and getting sign off from Davo for any additional spending was never easy.

The ubiquitous office secretary had already put the morning papers on Cramer's desk. 'Does that woman ever go home?' Cramer said to herself as she glided through her office door and put her overpriced morning coffee on the table. She was greeted with grainy pictures of the scene at the ducking stool in the centre of Canterbury, their latest victim dangling precariously over the river just as they had found her. Clearly taken with a long lens and then magnified as high as possible without quite getting to individual pixel detail. Thankfully, it was almost impossible to see exactly what you were looking at. But the headline screamed the answer to that, in case there was any doubt.

Two More Bodies Found in Hunt for Serial Murderer

By Jason Baird, crime reporter

Kent Police are understood to be hunting a serial killer who could have slain as many as four people in two months after two bodies were found on successive days in the Canterbury area.

The two latest victims – who are yet to be identified – were found within twelve hours of each other at different locations in the county. The first was near Westbere lake in the early hours of yesterday morning and was believed to have been naked and stabbed according to one witness who wished to remain anonymous. The second victim was found perched on the ducking stool over the River Stour by the Old Weaver's Restaurant early yesterday morning by a dog walker.

Newly promoted Acting DCI Caroline Cramer, who is now leading the investigation following the sudden and unexpected early retirement of DCI Jeff Bruce, refused to comment on the case.

However, one witness told the Kentish News: 'The officer that was first on the scene let slip to me that this was number three. From what I know about these things, that would confirm the police are looking for a serial killer.

'It's very scary. This just isn't the kind of thing you expect to happen in this area. In any area really. It's just evil.'

'Shit,' Cramer said out loud as she slammed the paper onto her desk in disgust, even though the only people to hear it were the victims on the board in her office. She turned to her keyboard and fired off an email to the boss before he got in; this needed heading off at the pass. They needed to find out who was the first on scene and what exactly had been said, or whether Baird was hedging his bets and applying the pressure. It wouldn't be the first time.

She hit send hard on the email, then picked up the paper from her desk again. Nice way to worry the general population over their cornflakes.

Bastards. She threw the paper across the room in anger, inadvertently knocking a commendation she'd received for bravery off its shelf, shattering the glass on the floor. The injury she got at the time – she was stabbed in the right buttock by a crackhead knifeman she'd disarmed who was holding his wife and daughter hostage – reminded her it was there. The scar throbbing slightly, as if complaining about the damage to the commendation it had earned.

She was ribbed mercilessly for weeks after that injury, with everything from rubber rings to whoopee cushions left on her chair. She'd also been forced to walk with a stick when she received her award a month later, so it looked far more impressive than it really was. Sergeant Caroline Cramer, as she had been then, getting a top award for being knifed in the bum. It usually made her smile thinking about it. But not today.

She moved across the room to pick up the broken glass and put the paper back on her desk. As she caught sight of the headline again, a fire lit across her face that she hadn't felt for some time. Ever since a difficult case early in her career, Cramer found it hard to deal with the press professionally. She'd given background information in good faith to a journalist, only to find it plastered all over the front page the next day and attributed directly to her. The fallout from that nearly derailed her progress in Kent Police, but strong arrests, good exam results and heroic butt stabbings brought her back on track.

Still, she couldn't really argue with what the papers were saying. There was something odd about this case, it wasn't making sense. Four women taken, four women dead, and yet they hadn't caught a break anywhere. No forensic evidence that could help them, no fibres, no prints, no hairs, no semen, no blood – at least not from their suspect. Nothing showing up on social media to link them. No CCTV footage. Nothing.

No one seemed to know anything, see anything, hear anything. It was like they were chasing a ghost. The cause of death in each case had been different, but the signature was the same – and already confirmed in the first two victims – the gaping hole below their left ribcage which resulted in a punctured lung in Angela Downs, and in Linda Burrows, the weapon had also pierced the heart. That would have killed her. But she had still been found hanged. Why? The killer surely would have known she was dead.

She looked at the post-mortem photos of Linda's body, with close-ups of the bruising and ligature marks and rust residue on both wrists and ankles, suggesting she'd been shackled by what Simms had described as 'rusting manacles'. All they knew for sure was they were metal, and they were old.

The next photo showed the inside of her mouth, where there was a very clear puncture mark at the back of her tongue, with more rust according to forensics. Apart from it being made by something metal, most likely iron, no one had any idea what had created it. Or why.

It was impossible to find any similar more subtle injuries for Angela Downs; her body had been burned beyond recognition, leaving little chance of useful evidence. She had the same stab wound, but they knew she'd been alive when set alight from the carbon deep in her lungs; the smoke would only have reached that far down if she was fighting for breath.

Cramer picked the coffee up from her desk to take a sip and nursed it in her hands as she walked over to the board to look more closely at their photographs. The first victim, virtually unrecognisable as a woman, and then the second. How and why was he choosing them?

The faces stared back at her – happy, smiling pictures of each woman when she was alive juxtaposed by the unfeeling death mask of each after that life was snuffed out. The difference between the two strengthened the argument for a soul or spirit. There was no comparison between the living and the dead, and although Cramer had never been particularly religious, a certain 'something' had definitely left the body. A soul, a spark, whatever. One minute there, the next, gone.

'Talk to me. What are we missing here?' she said to the inanimate faces. If Jill was right, they could expect another two snatches from the same nightclub, but they needed to know what the night shift had found before deciding what to do next.

Cramer finished the last of her coffee, bending her head back as far as it would go to reach the last drops in the bottom of the cup. Her long, blonde hair was tied back in a French plait to keep it out of the way which tugged at her temples. But her dull headache wasn't being caused by that.

They needed a break in this case. Door-to-doors were fruitless. They were waiting on more data from the social media accounts, but it felt like clutching at straws. She'd been giving Leila a hard time about revisiting the data yet again, but her reluctance was understandable. Any link should have appeared by now. She slammed the used cup into the bin in frustration, before looking again at the faces in front of her.

'We're gonna get him,' she promised them.

She opened her computer screen. Front and centre was a notification that her court testimony had been brought forward. She'd be in court the day after tomorrow. She swore under her breath. Her heart started to thump harder, and her stomach pitched and rolled simultaneously.

'Fuck's sake. Thank God Alex came to the station yesterday,' she told herself, as if that would make her feel better. It didn't.

The knock on her door made her jump. Leila was standing there nervously. Cramer looked from her computer to Leila and then at her watch; more time than she'd realised had passed.

'Morning, guv, fancy a brew?'

'Yes, thanks. How did you and Rob get on yesterday?'

Leila shrugged. 'I don't know what it is with this case, it's like we are dealing with a ghost.'

Cramer nodded; they'd come to the same conclusion.

Leila turned to leave the office just as Cramer caught the newspaper headline again out of the corner of her eye. She picked up the paper from her desk brandishing it towards her DC.

'Seen this?' Leila turned just as her boss launched the paper across the desk in her direction. Leila picked it up as it was coming to rest. Cramer instantly recovered her composure. 'I see Jason is determined to give us a hard time.'

A high-profile case like this for a local crime hack was a huge deal and could lead to a job on the nationals if he played his cards right. Local knowledge and a hotline to one of the investigating officers would give him a big leg-up in his career. You couldn't blame him for wanting to grab the opportunity, but Cramer did all the same.

Leila read the headline and let out an exasperated sigh and shook her head, before wagging the paper at her boss like it was an extension of her hand.

'Guv, you do realise he is just doing his job, right? I know there is tension between the police and the press, but honestly, he's a good guy if you would give him a chance to prove it.'

Cramer bristled. 'With a headline like that? And where did he get the "serial killer" conclusion from? Leila, come on...'

Leila stiffened in the doorway and Cramer waited for her to try to defend her boyfriend, to see how she would navigate such unstable ground.

'You do know journalists don't write the headlines, guv? Subs write the headlines, and they're designed to make people read the copy. So, they sometimes feel sensationalised. But it's not down to the journos, they don't do that part of the job. And I've not said anything to him about the investigation. Honestly. I just wouldn't do that.'

Cramer had lost interest partway through Leila's spiel and was already looking back at her email. She chose not to respond to Leila's tirade, and simply glanced up at the DC, watching the anger seep slowly up Leila's neck and her face turn a hot red, before giving her a look that said, 'You can go now.'

Leila moved away from the doorway and back towards her desk in the main office, just as Cramer got up and went out into the main room herself. The team were here in force now, so it was time for the morning briefing.

Cramer's presence held the room more than normal as she took her usual position perched on the empty desk in the corner. 'Thanks for all coming in early, without asking, it's appreciated and doesn't go unnoticed.'

Team building wasn't something Cramer enjoyed or was any good at, but she genuinely did feel grateful for the team's enthusiasm to solve this one.

'Let's get going. Leila, Rob, any update from yesterday?'

Rob, who had been leaning back in his chair, tipped his weight forwards, reached across his desk for his notebook, and flipped through the pages until he found the one he wanted and stabbed it with a pen.

'So, guv, I did as you asked and went to Illuminati to talk to Marlon Brown – that's the bouncer's name I was trying to remember. He wasn't there, having worked the night shift, so I kicked him out of bed at three p.m. to speak to him. But he confirmed he'd seen Dominique the night before last turning tricks outside the club.

'He couldn't say exactly what time, but thought he last saw her about' – he checked his notebook to make sure he was accurate –'one a.m. She didn't seem to be doing much business. He says he didn't see her get into a car at all. She was just there one minute, gone the next.'

'Was she within range of the club's external CCTV cameras, Rob? Did you check?' Cramer asked.

Rob flushed red. 'I don't know, but I'll find out for you, guv.'

Cramer let it go without comment.

'OK, Leila...'

Leila almost identically imitated Rob's notebook flick-through-and-pen-stab routine. 'We have the names of people each victim has interacted with in one way or another on Facebook and Twitter recently, we're still waiting on some Instagram data. We've cross-referenced the new names through our database, but still nothing relevant has flagged. Some drink drives, a few GBHs – not unusual given the steroids floating around in some of the people we have spoken to by the look of them...'

Cramer was chewing her cheek again, thinking.

'Precious little else from that trawl,' Leila added to complete the picture.

'Yes, OK. What about the boat club canvassing? The local area around the lake? Anything to report?' Cramer raised her eyebrows in hope, but they dropped as soon as Leila shook her head.

'Nothing of note, guv. No one noticed anything that seemed out of place.'

Cramer dropped her head down towards the floor briefly before realising how negative that looked. She looked up at her team, then round at the board behind her to galvanise a response.

'Right. So, let's work what we have. Rob, Leila, get back to the club and get what you can from CCTV on Dominique. Check the tapes – we might see who she was with, what kind of car she got into. Something.'

Cramer looked back around the room. Max was sitting at his temporary desk.

'Max, you covered the wealthy and high-profile families in the area, yes?'

'Yes, guv. But given where we are, that's like finding a needle in a stack of fucking needles. There are so many notables – celebrities, old money, new money, aristocracy, even royals – it's almost impossible to make a distinction on who might be next. I haven't actioned anything because I know we need to keep as much of this as much on the down-low as possible, and I wanted to check how you wanted this played first.'

Cramer knew he was right. She needed to see Charlotte.

'OK. Well, Jill...' Cramer looked around the room to find her; she was stood at the back of by the coffee machine, scratching her head with a pencil. Cramer waved to get her attention. 'Jill, I'm thinking that given the age profile of the victims, eighteen to thirty-five, we should ignore any family locally without people in that age range.'

Jill thought for a second as she stirred her cup. 'Sounds reasonable.'

Cramer nodded and re-addressed the room. 'Then we decide how to warn them without giving too many details. We need to be a step ahead of our target, not a step behind. We need that advantage.'

Chapter 24

Cramer was thinking about how fruitless the day had turned out to be as far as the case was concerned as she turned her car into the end of the driveway of her parents' home and noticed they had replenished the gravel since she had been here last. It was crunching under the wheels of her VW – she almost never used this car when she came to see them; it wasn't worth the disdain she received from her mother. Appearances mattered so much to her mother that she simply didn't understand why other people felt substance was more important.

There were lights adorning each side of the drive, classy white fairy lights in strings between fence posts that helped to show guests the way to where the 'small' gathering was. Typical Mum. Cramer smiled and shook her head from side to side. A small gathering. Right.

At that moment her mobile buzzed in her pocket and she saw Rob's name come up on the dashboard, so she immediately answered.

'Rob, what's going on?'

'Guv, you won't believe this, but the CCTV files from Illuminati for the night Dominique Monroe went missing are corrupted. I've just heard back from our tech team.'

'Shit,' she hissed, and slammed her hand into the steering wheel. 'Is there nothing they can do to access them?'

She heard Rob sigh on the phone. 'I've got them looking into it now. I bloody hope so.'

Cramer shut the call down and slammed her hand into the steering wheel again. Were they ever going to get a break?

As she continued up towards the house, the driveway opened out in front of the impressively large front door. The property was vast, with five windows either side of the entranceway on three levels and it went back almost as far as it was wide. The grey stone it was built with was lit up too, with warm lights that presented its best angles. She looked up to the roof as she drove past, a space she'd loved to spend time on when she was growing up. This was her family home, and she had great memories of living here. Well, some anyway.

There were already more than thirty cars parked outside the front of the house, crammed into every available space, so Cramer decided to drive past and round to the side to the kitchen, where she knew she could park more easily. It also gave her the option of getting away early when she didn't want to spend any more time at the 'do' than she wanted to.

As she walked to the much smaller side door, she pushed the button on her key fob to lock her car. It was darker around the side, so she pulled her phone out of her pocket, using its torch to make sure she didn't trip up the step she knew was here.

Her first stop was the kitchen where she sought out Pierre, her parents' chef for more than 40 years. She hadn't seen him in a few months, as last time she was here he'd been away. He had always been kind to her when she was a child, giving her treats when she spent time with him in the kitchens, teaching her tricks of the trade that she never forgot. It was thanks to him that she had a love of good food and had become a good cook herself.

The delicious smell of haute cuisine wafted out as she opened the door to the clattering of metal and the shouts of the chefs: the sounds of a busy kitchen. Pierre had his back to her as he was preparing hors d'oeuvres for the party. She tapped him on the shoulder, causing him to turn around. He looked stern until he realised who it was.

'*Mon Dieu*, Callie!' She'd always loved his French accent. He'd taught her French too when she spent time with him in the kitchen. She'd also spent some time in Paris and become fluent in her late teens but hadn't needed to use it in a while. Pierre gave her a big hug. 'I haven't seen you in so long, how are you?' He gave her another hug. He smelt of cooking oil and aftershave.

'Good, Pierre thanks. Well, you know, working hard, but good.'

He laughed and threw his head back. 'You always were the one who wanted to work hard, so I'm not surprised.' Cramer just smiled. She looked at the trays of food he'd prepared with the two other members of staff brought in for the evening.

She touched his arm with real affection. 'I'd better go and find them, but I'll see you again soon, OK?'

He leaned forwards and kissed her on both cheeks. 'Yes, see you. Not so long again, OK?'

Cramer blew him a kiss as she began to make her way through the main part of the house, through the family's kitchen with its marble counters and vast island in the middle – which was immaculate, mainly because it was so rarely used. From there, she went into the main hallway, more marble with gold leaf on the reliefs on the walls and ceilings. Cramer had always felt it was gaudy when she lived here, but her mother liked it. Whatever her mother liked, her father tolerated. That's mostly how their marriage worked.

Then she moved into the drawing room, which was more comfortable but still very ornate and cold to Cramer. The doors here, which looked out to the terrace and over the extensive grounds beyond, were open and she could hear chatter, laughter, clinking glasses, and a string quartet getting louder as she moved closer.

Her mother was in an animated conversation with her old friend Elizabeth Fitzsimmons, the Home Secretary, on the far side of the terrace. The latter had her security detail with her, keeping a respectful distance, but a close eye on everyone and everything at the party.

Cramer went through the doors and stepped out onto the terrace, taking a glass of champagne from one of the waiters near the doors, who she made a point of thanking. So few people here tonight would do that, she thought to herself. She took a sip as she moved towards her mother to say hello, but Elizabeth saw her first.

'Callie, my goodness you look well. How lovely to see you,' she said to Cramer as she approached.

Her mother broke too and moved towards Cramer to do air kisses which she always hated. So pretentious. 'Darling, I'm so glad you could make it,' her mother said. She meant it, Cramer knew that, but for some reason every word that came out of her mouth sounded utterly insincere.

Cramer looked at both women. They were both older than they looked, a feature of having money was the ability to stay looking younger. Probably because there was less money stress creating lines on their faces. Or maybe it was the regular Botox injections and the ability to afford the best plastic surgeons that had more to do with it. She checked herself; no need to be unkind.

Cramer addressed them both at the same time. 'Yes, I'm fine, thanks.' She lied. She was still thinking about the case; it was getting under her skin.

‘How is Helena, Elizabeth?’ Cramer asked. ‘I haven’t seen her in a long time.’

‘Ah, I think she’s here somewhere,’ she said, looking around her to find her daughter. ‘Yes, there she is,’ Elizabeth said, pointing to the terrace below, where Cramer could also see her cousin Charlotte. ‘I’m sure she would love to say hello…’ Elizabeth’s voice trailed off.

‘Me too. I’ll see you both later,’ Cramer said, kissing her mother on the cheek before pushing her way through the other guests and down the steps to the lower terrace.

Her father was walking up at the same time. She was glad to see him and gave him a big hug, which he returned with similar enthusiasm. ‘How’s my little girl?’

‘Dad, I’m thirty-three, you can’t call me that anymore,’ Cramer said.

‘I don’t care how old you are, you’ll always be my little girl,’ he said in his soft Irish accent. He had a deep voice, a resonance that exuded power and status, of which he had both.

Cramer shook her head gently, she couldn’t really argue with that.

‘How are you feeling?’ he asked her.

‘I’m doing OK, Dad. You know…’

He did know. She’d confided in him about her problems with Patrick and Adam’s death, how hard she’d found it. He’d never shared a confidence of hers with her mother, something she was always grateful for.

‘When is the inquest?’ He was nodding to someone behind her head as he asked her. He clearly wanted to give her more attention but was being called elsewhere.

‘A few weeks, Dad. It’ll be OK.’ She wasn’t sure if she was trying to convince him or herself. ‘But I’m testifying at Robert Kane’s trial in two days.’ She tipped her head slightly lower, a movement her father picked up on and offered some reassurance.

'Well, you need me, you let me know, OK?' He kissed her on the forehead like he'd always done when she needed comfort as a child. He shrugged his shoulders in an apology that he had to leave her to greet other guests, and she hugged him again, hard, and they continued in their opposite directions on the grand stone staircase.

Cramer didn't try to catch Charlotte or Helena's attention initially, but they both spotted her anyway as she walked towards them and beamed smiles her way.

'Cal!' Charlotte called her name above the chatter, causing other guests to look her way briefly. She moved forwards as Charlotte moved towards her too and embraced her. It felt good to see her.

'Hey you,' Cramer said. 'How are you doing? How's uni?'

'Ah, you know, busy.'

'Busy? Right... busy as in getting up late, the odd lecture and then partying into the night?' Cramer smiled to show her cousin she was teasing her.

'Fuck off,' Charlotte said smiling back. Cramer laughed and turned her attention to Helena who was standing next to her, champagne glass swinging between her fingers.

'And how are you, Helena? What are you up to these days?'

Helena pushed her long, blonde hair behind her ear and took a long draw on her champagne before she answered.

'I'm good thanks, Callie. I'm working in the City now, for a PR firm.'

'You like it?' Cramer asked.

'I do! Been there for a year, and I'm really enjoying it. Getting more responsibility too, which I like.'

'Sounds like the perfect job for you, Helena, lots of parties that count as work, right?' Cramer teased her.

Helena rolled her eyes but smiled at her comment. 'Well, yeah, OK, I know people used to think that's all I was good for, but I've been working hard to show there's more to me than that. I'm very different now to how I used to be, Callie.'

'I'd heard, that's good.' Cramer smiled at her. And to be fair to her, Cramer hadn't seen any coverage of Helena recently like she'd used to. Previously she would have gone to the opening of an envelope if there was champagne and celebrities present and had been papped in various states of disarray over the years. It seemed she was growing up at last.

'And what's going on with you, Cal?' Charlotte had turned the attention back to Cramer. 'Are you working on those murders that have been on the news?'

Cramer didn't usually talk to her family about work, but given the profile Jill had come up with, this gave her the perfect opportunity to discuss it. But she couldn't reveal any details of the case either. A tightrope to walk.

She took a deep breath before answering. 'Yeah, actually, I am. I'm leading the investigation now.'

'Ahh, that's so coooool,' Charlotte cooed at her.

'Congrats,' Helena added, raising her nearly empty champagne glass towards her in a toast.

'Thanks. But it's not really cooool, Charlie,' she imitated Charlotte's drawn-out pronunciation. 'Finding dead people and trying to find the person that's killed them can't really be described as "cool".'

Both girls nodded their understanding, but without really getting it, thought Cramer.

'They're saying it's a serial killer in the news, Cal, is that right?' Charlotte asked.

Cramer nodded sagely. 'We think so, yes. We can't be sure. But we have to keep an open mind.'

'Shit,' Charlotte said. 'You sound like a copper.' She laughed.

‘Why do you think that, Cal? The serial killer, I mean.’ Helena was taking it more seriously. Maybe she had changed, Cramer thought.

‘Well, there are certain lines of inquiry,’ said Cramer. ‘But I can’t tell you anything else. Sorry, girls.’ She made a motion of buttoning her lip that made both women smile.

‘Should we be worried?’ Helena asked the obvious question, and Cramer noticed Charlotte’s eyes open wide, waiting for her answer.

‘Not worried, no,’ said Cramer, trying to not make it a big thing, even though she knew it could be. ‘But be careful. Make sure you don’t get isolated from friends, for example. Keep your wits about you.’

She could see both women nodding and noticed a fear rising in their eyes.

Cramer didn’t want them to be scared. Just cautioned.

‘But you know, I mean, that’s good advice anytime, right?’ She added the caveat that any good police officer would do with a smile.

‘Yeah... but especially now...’ Helena said.

Chapter 25

The entrance to Canterbury Crown Court is impressive. Two red-and-white-striped brick pillars stand either side of a stone architrave, holding up a wooden portico with a modern glass frontage that drops to meet the doorway of the building beneath it. The doors, reached by walking up a flight of ten steps from street level, seem slightly at odds with the building that was built back in 1995, as Canterbury needed more criminal court space. The imposing royal seal above the entrance leaves you in no doubt as to what is done inside these doors, which are made of a lighter wood than you might expect for the building.

Inside, the courts are markedly less grand; mostly light-coloured wooden benches for the lawyers, the public and the jury, with an elevated platform for the judge and the witness box. Given the aspects of life, death, and human nature playing out in this building, you would imagine there might be more imposing furniture. It was like having your future presided over in Ikea.

Cramer walked into court having been called to the witness stand. She had called her father last night, despite having only seen him in person the night before. He always had a calming influence on her, and that was exactly what she needed heading into this today.

She glanced to her left to see Adam William's wife Natasha sitting passively, dressed elegantly as always, stoically holding her stare towards the proceedings. They'd had dinner often while Adam was still alive; she'd worked with Adam for five years before he was killed.

Natasha turned her head briefly as she sensed Cramer walking past her, trying to smile, but the emotion of the day clearly overtook her. Cramer watched as she bowed her head to look at her lap, before composing herself once again, eyes forwards.

Cramer's hands felt clammy, her mouth dry. She had to be careful not to show any nerves to Marcus Hall, the lawyer defending Kane who'd been charged with Adam's murder, among other things – possession of a firearm, drug trafficking, arms dealing, and human trafficking. Hall was a shark – if the man smelled blood in the water, he wouldn't hesitate to go in for the kill.

She thrust her shoulders back, so she was standing to her full five foot eight, and walked purposefully towards the dock, nodding to Judge Robinson on her way through. He was known for being fair and even-handed, which was a relief, but even with that bit of good news, this testimony was never going to be easy.

Cramer entered the witness box, and the clerk of the court approached her and asked her to affirm she would tell the truth. She answered: 'I will.'

She settled herself in her seat and moved the microphone towards her so she could be heard more clearly. She looked at the jury: a mix of races, ages, and sexes should make for a fair trial. Most would have no idea what a low-life Kane was – the UK court system prevented his previous convictions being revealed to the jury for fear of prejudice, despite him being a key player in local organised crime – so they needed to present the toughest case they could to get this scrote off the street.

This was the difficulty – or the beauty depending on your point of view – of a jury trial. Someone as dodgy as Kane with a list of convictions as long as your arm, could potentially get off on a slam-dunk case, because he doesn't 'look' like he could do the kinds of things he actually does.

The slightly dishevelled Crown prosecutor David Riley stood to question Cramer. His substantial pot belly hung over his trousers, held back only by his tucked-in shirt, the buttons at the base straining with the effort. Conversely, his lack of pecs and narrow shoulders left a lot more room at the top of his shirt, creating a surplus of material. His grey suit was crumpled, having clearly been worn too many days in a row, and Cramer swore she saw an egg stain on his red tie. Good to see the Crown had delivered its A team, she thought to herself. Alex Newcastle was nowhere to be seen.

Riley smoothed the small amount of his remaining hair over his bald pate and shuffled from behind his bench towards the witness box where Cramer could see the sweat glistening on his top lip. Moments later, she caught his stale coffee breath full in the face as he asked his first question. The contrast with the sharp-suited Hall on the defence bench couldn't be greater.

'Acting Detective Chief Inspector Cramer, please tell us in your own words what happened on the night in question.' Riley had a strange tick Cramer hadn't noticed before, a jutting out of his chin as he got to the end of a question, as if somehow this motion encouraged his words to hit the target more effectively. How this was playing to the jury, God only knew, but she thought he looked bloody odd.

'We'd been working on a long-term surveillance of the defendant over a period of months and had received intelligence that on the night in question, a drugs drop was taking place,' she began.

The glint of light from Hall's cufflinks caught Cramer's eye, and she saw Hall smirking as he wrote on a piece of paper in front of him. He would do anything to make her feel undermined, and knowing the point at which he smirked first, she assumed he was taking exception to her use of the word 'intelligence'. She could have happily gone over and smashed his face in right there. But she had to keep calm, so breathed deeply before continuing.

'We'd convened in the squad room for a briefing before setting off for the target's home – that target being the defendant Robert Kane – and we had a total of fifty officers and five forensic analysts ready to undertake the operation.'

'What intelligence had you received about the drugs delivery, and how had you come by that information?'

Cramer shifted in her seat.

'It was a combination of sources. We had some recognised informants who'd provided details, and one of my officers, Detective Sergeant Adam Williams, the victim, had been working undercover on this case for some time, ingratiating himself with Kane and some of his associates.'

From the corner of her eye, she could see Kane taking a deeper than normal breath and opening and closing his fist. Perhaps he wanted to smash her face in too. Good. She was getting under his skin. Career criminals hated someone taking them for a ride, making out they were loyal only to shaft them somewhere further down the line. She found it ironic, since that behaviour was exactly what you got from a career criminal towards their victims. They were happy to dish it out but lashed out when it was dished back.

Cramer continued. 'Adam – Detective Sergeant Williams – had managed to get very close to one of what can only be described as Kane's lieutenants—'

'Objection.' Hall was standing now. 'Describing a close friend of my client in that way is unduly leading the jury to see him in a negative light. I refute the suggestion that there was in any way an "operation" in progress that my client was leading, and would like that comment struck from the record, and any such future comments to be avoided.'

Judge Robinson sat thought for a moment; clearly, he really wanted to overrule, but was forced to concede. 'Sustained. Acting Detective Chief Inspector, if you could confine your comments to the specific details without embellishment, the court would be grateful.' He smiled at her, apologetically. Then turned his gaze on Hall and the smile disappeared. 'However, Mr Hall, I would also ask that you make your objections, where they arise, more succinct. I don't intend to miss my bridge evening so you can grandstand.'

Hall put on his most humble face, despite clearly being irritated, stood up and bowed.

'I apologise to the court, Your Honour.'

'Drama queen,' Cramer muttered under her breath, and immediately regretted it when she realised how close the microphone was. She looked around her – it didn't look like anyone had heard. Thank goodness.

Judge Robinson signalled to Cramer to carry on. She nodded and continued.

'Detective Sergeant Williams had managed to ingratiate himself into Kane's inner circle.' She aimed that phrase directly at Hall, and he smiled and nodded. *Slimy git.* 'And as such, DS Williams was party to information that showed us, without equivocation, that Mr Kane was definitely involved in organised crime.'

‘What sort of crime are you alleging the defendant was involved in, Acting DCI Cramer?’ asked Riley.

‘We have evidence to show there was involvement in the drugs trade, in racketeering, arms dealing, human trafficking and prostitution.’

‘I direct the jury to the evidence presented two days ago in relation to what had been found inside the house,’ Judge Robinson added.

That evidence had already been presented to the court including the twenty kilos of cocaine sitting on the kitchen table when the raid happened, along with examples of the fifteen semi-automatic rifles found in the cellar, and video footage of two Romanian women held down in the basement who were, they testified, forced into prostitution by Kane.

Kane’s fist was positively pumping open and closed now, as if he was trying to rid himself of pins and needles. The only needle Cramer was concerned about was her pushing further into his skin.

She continued. ‘We’d already decided to take advanced action, and once we had the intelligence to suggest the correct date of the drugs delivery, we sought authorisation for a raid on Kane’s home, which we understood from the information gathered was also the HQ for his activities. We believed we’d get the ringleader, who we believe to be Robert Kane, and potentially catch co-conspirators in the act, but also prevent more cocaine from reaching our streets.’

‘And how many officers were involved in this raid?’ Riley looked like he was starting to get into a stride. But she’d given this information already. He was clearly more Inspector Clouseau than *Rumpole of the Bailey*.

‘We had around fifty officers from various departments involved in total, including Vice, Serious Fraud, and a tactical firearms unit.’

'And what events led to Sergeant Williams being injured Acting Detective Chief Inspector?' Riley was walking around now with his hands behind his back, as if that was going to make him more impressive to the jury. He was trying to puff out his inadequate chest, but only succeeded in causing more distress to the buttons straining at his stomach.

'The entry team was in place with an enforcer—'

Judge Robinson interrupted again. 'For the benefit of the jury, that is what you might commonly know as a battering ram.' He nodded to Cramer to continue.

'The entry team was in place with an enforcer and managed to gain entry on the first attempt. As he had first-hand knowledge of the layout of the house, Detective Sergeant Williams was one of the first to enter, along with myself, but we were flanked by a number of other officers.'

'Were these officers armed?' Riley asked.

'Yes, some were, as we believed there could be firearms on site, so took every precaution to ensure the safety of our personnel.'

Out of the corner of her eye, Cramer saw Hall smirk again.

'And what did you find in the property? How did you know that the expected drugs delivery had been made?' Riley had tunnel vision and clearly wasn't listening to her testimony at all.

'We undertook surveillance initially from a distance, and once we had confirmation the delivery had been made, we waited a few minutes to give us the element of surprise. Any sooner and there was a chance those going in or out of the house would have seen our approach. We also wanted to make sure that whatever transaction was happening inside the house was in full progress, so we would have the best evidence to present.

'At that point, I gave the "Go" order, and the team gained entry as already described. On entering the property, a substantial amount of what we subsequently confirmed to be cocaine was found in the kitchen, and my officers then completed a further search of the premises.'

'How many people were occupying the house at that time?'

'There were seven in total: Kane, his wife and daughter, two associates, and we also found the two young Romanian women previously mentioned in the basement, along with substantial amounts of cash, and a number of firearms.'

'So, you would say it was a successful operation?'

Cramer shifted uneasily again. Why the hell had he asked her that?

'In terms of the recovery of contraband, Mr Riley, yes. But I would hardly consider any raid that resulted in even a minor injury to a colleague, much less their death, a resounding success.'

Riley stiffened slightly. Her well-aimed rebuke had clearly hit the mark. Hall simply smirked again. This was just playing into his hands.

Riley continued. 'Of course, I didn't mean to offend you or in any way belittle the loss your team has suffered. Can you explain to me what happened in relation to Sergeant Williams? What were the circumstances that lead to his injuries, which he unfortunately succumbed to?'

Cramer swallowed hard and took a deep breath before she started to speak.

'The entry into the property was textbook. There was nothing out of the ordinary. Control of the building was quickly established by the leading officers, one of which was *Detective*' – she emphasised that word since Riley had omitted it – 'Sergeant Adam Williams.'

'Because he was aware of the layout...'

'Yes, exactly. The initial search of the premises was uneventful as raids go. The control of the rooms was methodical, and we were clearing room by room. Robert Kane had been detained in the kitchen soon after entry.'

'Detective Chief Inspector, you were there during the raid I take it?'

Cramer felt exasperated. He didn't appear to be listening to anything she was saying. She carried on with greater emphasis.

'Yes, I was. I was the lead officer, and once we had established entry, I was with the first officers who secured the property and two associates and Robert Kane. But unfortunately, Kane subsequently escaped from the house, and so Detective Sergeant Williams and I pursued him into the grounds.'

She didn't want to elaborate on how he escaped.

Riley continued. 'And we're not talking about a small house here, are we?'

'No, Robert Kane's property is significant. I understand that his grounds extend to around seventy acres, so it was essential he was apprehended quickly, which is why Detective Sergeant Williams and I made this our priority.'

Riley turned his back to Cramer and proceeded to lift his trousers at the waist. It seemed a strange move – there was no way they could possibly be falling down.

'Can you please go through what happened, DCI Cramer?'

'Acting DCI, Mr Riley.'

He nodded an apology. Was he doing this on purpose? She carried on regardless.

'As we entered the property, Kane was sitting in the kitchen with two associates' – she resisted saying henchmen – 'who'd made the drugs delivery. They bolted for the back door but were detained immediately. This is the main reason we managed to secure such a big haul of drugs – they'd been put on the kitchen table as the money was exchanged, when we entered the house.'

She shifted again in her seat. 'After a thorough search, we found the two women in the basement, held in a cage. A cage

– I want to emphasise that. This was alongside a large amount of money, found to be just over five hundred thousand pounds in used notes and a cache of arms in the cellar.

'It was as I was returning to further arrest Kane on suspicion of the other offences that I heard a commotion, and then saw he'd shot out of the back of the property and run across a large courtyard into the stable block. I moved to apprehend him, and Adam followed.' She knew he'd seen the potential danger and didn't want his boss to face it on her own.

'I ran into the stable block, but there was no sign of Kane. I didn't know if he was armed, so stayed close to the wall as I entered.' The sensation of the wood grain against her hand stuck in her memory as she inched her way along that stable wall.

'I was holding my baton in my right hand – I'd opened it as I was running across the courtyard – but if Kane had a gun, I would have no defence. I was wearing a stab vest, as all but the firearms officers were, but it wouldn't stop a bullet.

'Detective Sergeant Williams' – she desperately wanted to say 'Adam'; calling him by his more formal title seemed so impersonal – 'and I made our way through the outer barn area of the stables.' She visualised the stacks of hay bales on either side as they moved through, the fresh scent of straw in her nostrils right there in the courtroom.

'There were a further three empty stables to our right as we went in, with what appeared to be a tack room and office at the far end. We felt that was the most likely place for Kane to be, so we headed there.

'Adam – Detective Sergeant Williams – moved across the barn, using the hay bales for cover as we made our way closer to the office. He had a better vantage point than I had at the time and was signalling to me via a visual countdown that he wanted to enter the room.'

Cramer stopped and took a deep breath before she carried on, her hands clammy, a wave of nausea washing over her. She could feel her salivary glands working overtime and had to swallow hard.

'At that moment, the radio silence was broken, and Adam' – it felt right to use his first name this time – 'had forgotten to turn his radio down in the heat of the chase, and the hiss of his radio as one of my other officers was trying to raise me on comms made us both jump. It also told Kane, the defendant, exactly where we were.

'He was, in fact, behind the next set of bales and close enough to lunge at Adam with a knife, stabbing him in the thigh first, then in the neck before I could get to him. There is no doubt in my mind, Kane was intending to kill.'

Hall stood once again at this point. 'Objection. My client's intentions cannot possibly be known by Acting DCI Cramer, and we refute her testimony on that point.'

Judge Robinson let out an exasperated sigh. 'Sustained.'

Cramer carried on without paying any attention to Hall or the judge; she was vividly reliving that day.

'Kane made his way to the door, trying to escape. I tried to stop him and lashed out with my baton. I could just reach Kane as he ran past me to the doorway we had come through. I brought my baton down with as much force as possible.' She recalled feeling both the ulnar and radius bones in his arm crack beneath the steel rod but didn't want to share that in this forum.

She continued. 'He cried out in pain, but he still managed to push me into the wall, slamming my back and head into the wooden walls as he carried on his escape attempt. As Kane raced towards the door, it was filled with the bodies of four TFU officers, all with their weapons trained on him. He knew he had no chance and fell to his knees, dropping the knife into the straw and raising the one hand he could still move behind his head.

He shouted in pain again as the officers grabbed him and pulled him out of the doorway.'

She took a deep breath before recounting what had happened next. 'I rushed to Adam, who was now lying prone on the floor. Blood covering his hand and chest from his neck wound, and escaping in pulses from his leg, suggesting the femoral artery had been severed.' His face had told her he knew how serious it was.

She felt herself return to that moment. 'I checked his neck wound – it was bad but not pulsing, unlike his leg injury. I'd been working out where pressure needed applying and shouted for one of the armed officers to help me.

'Adam knew how serious it was and asked me to tell Natasha he loved her.' Cramer took a moment to look at Natasha and nodded towards her; she had passed on that message before, but it was good for her to hear it again. Natasha simply smiled and dropped her head to look at her lap as her face creased in pain at her loss.

'I was working hard to make sure he could tell her himself. I removed his body armour to get better pressure on his wounds, but his eyes were starting to glaze over. There was an armed officer putting pressure on his neck wound while I was dealing with his leg wound. I was already covered in so much of his blood. I tried to grasp the cut end of his femoral artery, but it was retreating into his groin.

'I shouted to the other officer to find something for a tourniquet, find anything, but it was taking too long. The blood had started escaping from his neck again and Adam was getting cold. He had to put pressure back on that neck wound instead. I still couldn't grab the end of the artery – it kept slipping away from me. There was so much blood. So much.'

She knew if she could have held it, she would have been able to stem the blood flow, but she could feel the panic rising again at that moment, as if it was slipping out of her fingers all over again. Fuck, why did Kane have to hit the two areas not protected by his body armour? Cramer was right there again, doing her best to keep her friend and colleague alive. She'd been covered in his blood, could still feel the heavy stickiness of it and smell the sweet, metallic odour.

'We all had to work fast to have a chance of saving him. I focused on stopping the blood from his leg wound until the paramedics arrived. Adam had passed out before that, but he was still alive.

'It was after he got to hospital that hope faded. They said there was nothing they could do. The blood loss was too great.'

She paused to look at Natasha again. She could see her cheeks glistening as she detailed what had happened. Cramer realised that was probably the first time she'd heard about the last conscious minutes of her husband's life. There was no question Cramer's testimony had been powerful and had a visible effect on the jury. She could tell by the way some were nodding, or looked appalled at what had happened as she had told it.

She hadn't been able to leave the scene with Adam, needing instead to deal with the aftermath of the raid, and ensure the forensics were properly dealt with. Simms had arrived within ten minutes of Adam's stabbing, and Cramer had asked him to prioritise making sure everything they could get forensically would stick.

She looked back over to Kane in the dock. His arm was in a cast, the result of her lashing out to stop him. That bastard deserved so much more than that, but knowing the pain he was still in, even after two operations, with a broken radius and ulna, thanks to her actions that day made her smile inside.

Riley cut in, as if he was reading her mind. 'And Robert Kane's injuries were as a result of your actions – his left arm is clearly currently in a cast.' He motioned towards Kane in the dock.

Cramer was incensed. Whose side was this fucking idiot on?

'It's fair to say they are the result of my trying to apprehend him, yes, but I was using reasonable force, no more. You must remember, Mr Riley, Mr Kane had just stabbed my colleague, fatally as it turned out. I was fearing for my life, and I wanted him to pay for his actions. It was a spur-of-the-moment reaction in a bid to stop him escaping.'

Hall smirked again. He was up to something, she knew it. Riley merely thanked Cramer for her evidence and returned to his seat, smoothing back the sparse strands of hair that had moved from his head again as he had leaned forward to sit down.

Hall was still rifling through the papers in front of him, and the judge was getting visibly irritated.

He eventually prompted Hall to start. 'Mr Hall, when you're ready...'

Hall turned towards the judge and reached into his jacket sleeve to pull his cuff down with his left hand, his cufflink glinting again in the stark court lighting. 'Apologies, Your Honour.'

He stood up from his chair and walked purposefully round to the witness box where Cramer was still sitting.

'Detective Inspector Cramer, good to see you again.'

Cramer tried to prevent her face from telling a different story to the words coming out of her mouth, but she'd never been good at that. He knew she had been promoted, he was just playing mind games as usual. She decided to ignore it. So, she just nodded. And tried to smile. She failed.

Hall continued. 'So, thank you for giving such a vivid account from your point of view of the day in question. I do have a few questions for you, however, as I am not sure I can see everything as clearly as you do. It is a little more – how can I put it? – murky.'

Cramer was impassive; there was nothing “murky” about any of it, but Hall was an expert in dredging up dirt to obscure the view of the jury. He was a magician when it came to making serious charges disappear. Cramer had to make sure that didn’t happen.

‘I will help in any way I can, Mr Hall,’ said Cramer, flashing an utterly insincere smile.

Hall smiled back, but he was much better at hiding his disdain than Cramer.

‘Thank you, Inspector. So, on the night in question, you had briefed your team fully before leaving the station to undertake the raid on my client’s premises.’

Cramer couldn’t see where this was going. ‘Yes, that’s correct.’

‘Thank you. And you testified earlier that you were one of the first officers on the scene once the enforcer had been used, is that correct?’

‘As I said, yes.’

‘Would you say that, as commanding officer of this operation, that was the best place for you to be? Would it not have made more sense, for example, for you to hold back and allow your other officers to do the work while you oversaw proceedings from a more operational level?’

Cramer bristled. This was one question she had asked herself in the hundreds of times she had gone through the events that day to see what she could have done differently. Trust Hall to ask her the very thing she had questioned herself. But she remained composed. That would have been down to DCI Bruce after all, but he simply wasn’t up to the task.

‘No, for this operation it made sense for me to be where I was at the time. I prefer to lead from the front, to lead by example.’

'Ah yes, I understand that, Inspector, but doesn't that leave you open to being unduly influenced by your heart over your head? You have something of a reputation for that.'

That was a lie and Hall knew it. Cramer was waiting for Riley to step up and object, but he just sat there.

She was forced to answer.

'I don't think that's the case at all, Mr Hall. I am passionate about my job, about ensuring the safety of others, apprehending criminals and keeping—'

Hall cut in again. 'I see, you think you work with the safety of others as your priority. I would say this case alone suggests otherwise, wouldn't you agree? Your colleague *died*, Inspector, and you were in charge. Perhaps a different approach could have prevented this.'

'I am well aware my colleague and *friend* died, Mr Hall.' Cramer spat the remaining words out. 'I was there, covered in his blood, trying to give him the hope that we feared – and it turned out – he didn't have. At the hands of your client.'

Hall turned away from her as if he was thinking of his next question, before turning back and fixing his eyes on her. She knew it was a ruse; he knew his next question all along – it was a play for the jury.

'That's to be determined, Inspector. At present, I'm interested in your capability and, whether or not, your running of that operation is what led to Detective Sergeant Williams's death. I mean, for instance, you have just said you wanted Mr Kane to – as you put it – "pay for his actions". You intended to hurt him in retaliation for the accidental injuries to your colleague? Is that what we are to think, Detective Inspector?'

Shit. Yes, she had said that. A Freudian slip that wasn't going to help her cause. It was true, she did want him to pay. But admitting it, especially here, was a mistake.

Cramer said nothing, just tried to hide her rising anger. Riley still was doing nothing, not even making notes. It was almost as if Kane was paying his salary too.

'I didn't hear your answer, Detective Inspector Cramer.'

Still nothing from Riley. She was going to have to respond.

'No, that's not what I meant – and it's Acting Detective Chief Inspector now, Mr Hall, as you well know.' She wanted to regain some ground, but Hall just nodded without losing his train of thought.

'But that is what you said, Acting Detective Chief Inspector.'

'No, I was fearing for my life and hit out at his arm in a bid to apprehend him and prevent further injuries to me or my other officers.'

'But Acting Detective Chief Inspector' – she knew his sarcasm was purposeful – 'I remind you, you did say you wanted him to "pay for his actions". You appointed yourself judge and jury, *Acting* Detective Chief Inspector, that's the only way it can be seen.'

'No, Mr Hall, that's not what happened, and it's not what I meant. If it's what I said, then I apologise to the court as I misspoke.' She was seething inside.

She was grateful when Judge Robinson finally came to her rescue.

'Mr Hall, if you're not going to do anything other than barrack this witness, I will ask you to desist. Do you have any further questions?'

Hall demurred. 'Nothing further at this time, your honour, but I would like to reserve the right to recall Acting Detective Chief Inspector Cramer at a future time.' His greasy smile made her squirm.

'In that case, we will end proceedings there and return at nine tomorrow morning.'

The judge rose from his chair, prompting the court to do the same as the clerk announced, 'All rise.'

Chapter 26

This was the one part of the process he hated, relying on someone else. He preferred working alone. Easier to avoid detection that way. But he needed the drug to begin his journey. Their journey. So, he had to get it. He'd already called his usual supplier, but they'd run out and recommended someone new. Someone he didn't know. But that could be an advantage, as the new dealer didn't know his buyer either.

He waited exactly where he'd been told to. He looked at his watch for the seventh time since he arrived. The dealer was supposed to be here ten minutes ago. Timing was important. He had other things to do, places to be, things to watch.

They had too much power. Too much influence. Teachers, mothers, journalists, press officers, they all had such immense power over others. But he was more powerful. He would stop them in their tracks.

His own mother had tried to influence him. To make him weak, told him to be 'kind', to be 'nice to others'. What did she know? She had no real power. Not like these. He needed to deal with them. All of them.

At that moment, a car appeared in the distance, headlights on despite it not being dark enough yet. The sound of a heavy bass beat heralded its arrival. *Boom, boom, baba-boom.*

Classless. As the car rolled up towards him, he stood back from the edge of the pavement. A young woman hummed the electric window open and leaned out, simultaneously turning her music down just slightly so they could talk.

'You after some G?'

He nodded, not willing to engage with it more than he had to. Her baseball cap on the wrong way round, a heavy gold rope hanging around her neck. He saw her for exactly what she was. A showboater. Souped-up car with low-profile wheels and spoiler on the back spoke volumes. It couldn't be trusted.

It leaned down into the side of the door and pulled out two vials of clear liquid.

'Don't get asked for it in this form that often. Took me a bit of time to get it. So, it's gonna cost ya a bit more.'

He didn't move or respond. Cost him more? Because it was something it wasn't usually asked for? Don't think so.

'You deaf or summin'?' it asked, turning and laughing at no one in particular since it was alone in the car.

He held his hand out for the vials.

'Ah nah, money first, mate,' it said, losing its smile.

Again, he didn't react. He just put his hand in his pocket and pulled out a roll of fifty-pound notes and peeled off two to give it, and its eyes lit up at the size of the roll.

He thrust the notes into its hand and snatched the vials before it had a chance to do anything but let them go.

'Yeah, all right, keep yer hair on,' it said. 'If you need more G though, you let me know, right?' It winked, confident, cocky, ready to drive its smile away to its next customer.

Funny, really. Its smile never left its lips even as he leaned in and cut its throat. He retrieved the fifty-pound notes and left, the car idling.

It would never be late again.

Chapter 27

Cramer was rerunning the court appearance over in her mind as she slowly made her way back to the office. She wanted to be impenetrable, unflappable, solid in the face of what was always going to be an emotional appearance. And she blew it.

She may have badly broken Kane's arm in the stables that day, but the bruising encounter she'd left no more than thirty minutes ago made it feel like things were evened up. She walked back into her office, threw her bag down beside the desk, and slumped into her chair. She looked out of her glass wall at the assembled team. Jill had watched her walk of shame, and Cramer motioned to her to come into her office. It was well past 6 p.m., but most of the team were working late to try to get ahead. Cramer felt punch drunk, and she needed someone to talk to.

As soon as Jill had come through the door, Cramer, unusually, asked her to shut it behind her.

Jill pulled a face. 'What's up?'

Cramer always had what she called an 'open door' policy, which she liked to implement both figuratively and literally. So, when that door was closed, the team knew not to disturb her. They could usually hear the bollocking she was giving someone in 'private' anyway – one of the many downsides of an open-plan office.

Cramer sat behind her desk and stared directly at Jill, her elbows on the desk, her fingers interlocked into a double fist.

'Fucking Marcus Hall.'

Jill leaned back in her seat. 'Ah, OK. Now I get it. What happened?'

Cramer was close to tears. 'It was a total fuck-up. I was being attacked by bloody Hall from every angle, and the sodding prosecutor let it happen. Let it all happen. Like he wasn't even listening.'

Jill reached out and put her hand on Cramer's arm. 'I'm sorry.'

Cramer had had run-ins with Hall before. He was a slippery little fucker on a good day. She wondered how most defence lawyers slept at night when you considered the scum they managed to get off on technicalities, and Hall was a master.

'I went in there to tell the truth about what happened, the raid, everything. But I was too honest at one point, that was the start of the problems...'

'What did you say?'

'I said I wanted to punish Kane for his actions when I broke his arm, which I did, that is the truth.'

'But not exactly professional...' Jill countered.

'Yeah, OK, thanks for that assessment.' Cramer spat the words out – she didn't need reminding it wasn't the right thing to say. 'I'm only human for fuck's sake.'

'OK, calm down.' Jill was getting testy in return. 'I'm not working against you, Cal, but you know as well as I do that was a bloody stupid thing to say. Especially in court. You're usually much more circumspect than that, what happened?'

'I got rattled. Properly rattled. Fucking David Riley.' She was standing up now and starting to pace around the room. 'He failed to step in at any time to stop the onslaught from Hall – just let him keep going! It was awful!'

Cramer sat back in her seat deflated and put her head down.

A moment later, Cramer felt the heat from Jill's hand on her arm. Her friend didn't need to say anything.

She smiled and put her hand on top of Jill's, just as the desk phone burst into their conversation. It was the Chief Super.

'Sir...'

'Cramer, get up here now. Right now,' he growled before slamming the phone down.

Chapter 28

Cramer wasted no time making it up to Chief Superintendent Davidson's office. He was normally more managerial than brusque, like he'd swallowed one of those 'How to encourage your team to greater things' manuals. But something had made him bark down the phone. It could be her court appearance earlier. She may as well take the hit on the chin while she was still beating herself up about it anyway.

She knocked before going in but didn't wait for an answer. As she entered, she was confronted by Davidson standing in full uniform, epaulettes glistening in the low evening sunlight that was streaming in through his third-floor office window.

Davidson's jaw was clenching and unclenching, the telltale muscle pulsing just below his ear. He was unnerved, a rare thing for him.

'Cramer, sit down. We have a situation.' He took a deep breath in, his mammoth ribcage expanding until his shirt tightened around his chest. 'The Home Secretary's daughter, Helena Fitzsimmons, didn't return home last night. Or this morning for that matter. There's real concern for her safety.'

Cramer's heart fell through her stomach and her brain stalled. She would fit Jill's victim profile if she was right, but Cramer hoped against hope she was wrong. Or that Davo was. She could only nod that she'd heard him.

Davidson continued: 'We're hoping your case has nothing to do with her disappearance, but we have to cover all possibilities.'

Cramer swallowed hard. 'Where was she last seen, sir?'

'Her security detail aren't sure'. Cramer looked incredulous as Davidson held up his hand to stop her interrupting. 'Hard to believe, I know.' Actually, it wasn't. Cramer knew a few people who had bodyguards or security and things got through that cordon more often than you would expect given the money they were paid.

He continued. 'She was out with friends in London and planned to be back home early last night. She was giving a big presentation at the PR firm she works for today – a contract they've been working on for months, apparently. We were told she left the restaurant in town before ten thirty last night to get the train back to Canterbury. But she hasn't resurfaced.'

Cramer's mind was already working on what would need to be done, and in what order. The first call would be to get the CCTV surveillance for the Canterbury West station, which she already knew was nearest Helena's home, and work backwards from there.

'I read your report, and Jill's theory...' Davidson continued.

'Helena would fit the profile, sir,' Cramer said.

'Yes, I know. I just bloody well hope we're wrong.' Possibly, but not as much as Cramer did.

'We are having a media blackout on this for now, Cramer – no one, and I mean no one, is to know about this who doesn't need to. The Home Secretary's obviously concerned for her daughter's welfare, but the political damage this could do to her would be irreparable.'

'Ah, glad to see she has her priorities right,' Cramer snapped.

Davidson's face turned to thunder. 'You don't have the luxury of being cocky, Cramer. We have four bodies, and nothing remotely resembling a solid lead. Not to mention your court appearance today, which I understand went totally tits up,' he roared.

Cramer could feel the heat rising from her neck to her cheeks. She was furious, as much with herself as Davo.

He ploughed on regardless: 'If this turns out to be related and it gets out, there will be hell to pay.'

Chapter 29

There was no easy way to break the bad news to her team. If there was a bright side, there was no guarantee Helena had become involved in their case. Maybe she got lucky and was sleeping off great sex and an awful hangover at someone's flat. But Cramer hadn't been that lucky so far. At the very least she could warn Charlotte off clubbing for the next week or two. She tried her cousin.

She dialled the number and waited. The call connected, but it was only indistinct noise.

'Charlie? It's Callie.'

Cramer heard once that dogs with names ending in the letters 'ie' or 'ey' were generally better behaved because they responded better to the sing-song nature of their name. You could be forgiven for thinking her mother and aunt had tried the same trick with their children given they were 'Charlie' and 'Callie'. Perhaps that was why her brother Finn had spent so much of his life not coming to heel.

'Ah, yeah, hi...'

'Did I wake you?'

'Umm, yeah, I mean, a little.'

Cramer laughed before getting serious. 'OK. Listen, were you with Helena last night?' It was a long shot, but worth a try.

'Actually, yeah, I bumped into her. She was just back from London, and I was waiting to go into the club near the station. I convinced her to come in for a quick drink, but she didn't stay long. Why?'

Cramer's heart started racing again.

'What club was that?'

'Illuminati, you know, the one...'

Cramer didn't hear the rest of the sentence as the blood rushing in her ears drowned it out.

'When did she leave you?'

'I'm not sure. We lost track of each other – it was heaving in there.'

Cramer's body stiffened.

'Did you see her leave?'

'Actually, head out of the door? No.' Alarm started creeping into Charlie's voice. She was no fool. 'Why do you want to know, Cal?'

Cramer had to think on her feet. 'No reason, I wanted to see if her presentation had gone OK. I'm just seeing her mum later and didn't want to appear out of touch, you know?' She seemed to be lying a lot on the phone these days, but to be fair she would be seeing Helena's mother later. Unfortunately.

'If she calls you, can you get her to call me please?' Cramer said.

She quickly ended the call and immediately dialled Rob. 'Rob, has that CCTV footage from the night Dominique went missing been sorted by tech yet?'

'I'm chasing guv, but they haven't cracked it yet. They are making progress though apparently and reckon we should be able to view them at some point.'

'Good. Take Leila and go back to Illuminati, we need to get all the CCTV files from last night as well, as soon as you can.'

Chapter 30

Helena woke up with a hangover made up of all the worst hangovers she'd ever had arriving all at once. She was cold. Stone cold. Bone cold.

Darkness surrounded her. She had no idea where she was. Had she gone blind? The blackness was so velvety thick, so complete, it was possible. Her head hurt so much she wasn't thinking straight. She tried to gather herself. *No, think. If you'd gone blind, you'd probably still be able to see some light.* She closed her eyes, opened them again. No difference.

As she sat up, each vertebrae ground against whatever she was lying on, making each feel like it was exploding as she lifted herself up. It was hard, cold – stone, marble? Where the fuck was she?

It was then she realised she was naked. Where were her clothes? And who had undressed her? Was this some kind of game? If so, it wasn't funny.

The throbbing in her head was unbearable, so she laid back again. Her mind tried its best to whirr into action. What time was it? How long had she been here? Wherever she was, she shouldn't be here. She should be at work. The team had spent weeks on this presentation – she couldn't let them down.

She tried to get up again, but her head was swimming. She didn't remember drinking that much, so why was she feeling like this? If she wasn't there, her colleagues would think she had bailed, taken a sickie. Couldn't stand the pressure. All the work she had put in to shed her party-hard reputation would be shot to hell. That wave of guilt built as quickly as her panic.

She sat up again, faster this time, ignoring the firecrackers going off in her spine. But her arms suddenly stopped, jolting her backwards. There was a heavy, metallic drag. What the actual fuck? Her wrists burst with pain, and she felt the flow of blood down onto her hand where the restraints had dug in. It was warm momentarily against her marble-cold flesh.

She stopped moving, unsure of what to do next. Isolated. Then a surge of adrenaline spiked through her body, a cold sweat breaking out on her skin as her heart fell deep into the pit of her stomach. Frantically, she yanked harder on the chains, the metal cuffs digging further into her wrists, more blood trickling down her hand. The searing pain across her body and in her head stopped her in her tracks. She was exhausted.

'Where am I? What is happening to me? What the fuck is this?' She was shouting out loud now.

Her body shook involuntarily as she wailed.

'LET. ME. GO!'

Chapter 31

As she went into the incident room, Cramer saw Jill sitting in her office on the wrong side of her desk *again*, flicking through the file they had all been given the day before.

She slowed her pace to enter her office quietly, closing the door behind her before sitting down opposite Jill, who moved the clutter on the desk to one side and went to vacate Cramer's seat. 'Sorry, Cal, I thought you would be out for longer. It's hard to find desk space in this place sometimes, let alone headspace. Hope you don't mind?'

Cramer waved her to sit back down where she was.

'Not a problem. But. We have a *big* problem.'

Jill sat herself back down as Cramer took a deep breath. 'Helena Fitzsimmons has gone missing.'

'Helena... You mean... the Home Secretary's daughter?'

Cramer nodded solemnly.

'Shit! I mean, sorry... No, I do mean shit! Is this to do with...?' Jill swept her arm towards the board full of female faces staring down at them.

Cramer moved her head to one side, lifting her eyebrows. The truth was, they just didn't know for sure.

'It's looking likely. My cousin Charlie saw her last night after she left Canterbury West station. She was in a nightclub...'

Jill went pale. 'Illuminati?'

Cramer nodded solemnly again.

'Helena said she couldn't stay because she had a big day at work today. So, Charlie wasn't that surprised when she disappeared soon after she arrived.'

'Did she see her leave?'

Cramer, silently, shook her head.

'Shit!'

Cramer, looking pained, nodded. 'If your profile is right, then she would be perfect.'

Jill leaned back in Cramer's chair and let out a long, slow breath through pursed lips while she was absorbing this information. Cramer knew she usually liked to be right. But not this time.

Jill covered her eyes and then drew her hands down her face. Cramer wanted to rewind this conversation, too, and make it different.

'Aren't they friends of...?'

Cramer cut her off. 'Yes, they are friends of my family. My mum went to university with the Home Secretary. She was at a party at my parents just two nights ago.'

Jill nodded, stunned into silence.

Cramer carried on. 'Listen, there's a complete blackout on this, Jill. Davo's orders. Only those people who need to know about this can, even inside the station.'

'You don't have to worry about me, I don't have anyone to tell but you, and you already know,' said Jill with a brief, wry smile. 'Does the team know yet?'

'No, as soon as Leila and Rob are back from the club with the footage from last night, I'll brief them.'

Jill nodded. 'Did the cameras outside the club see anything relating to Dominique?'

'We're still waiting for the techs to access the files. Bloody corrupted.'

Their attention was drawn to a commotion in the outer office as Leila and Rob came back into the room. Jack had come in early again to start his late shift. There was no doubting his enthusiasm, but he'd never been this diligent before, despite the various cases they'd worked on. But this one was really getting under his skin. He was a bruiser and definitely lacked the finesse of Adam. Something about his behaviour seemed strange to Cramer, but she parked the thought for now.

The usual banter was flying around, the team letting off steam, and Cramer walked out of the office with Jill behind her right into the thick of it.

Before saying anything to the detectives, she asked the small number of admin and secretarial staff quietly if they could leave the room. Once only the core team was left, she closed the outer office door and locked it.

The room had fallen silent. She didn't have to get their attention this time; it was given readily. The last time the room had been cleared like this was when they were dealing with a child abduction in a paedophile case which only the key staff could be briefed on. That had been one of the worst cases they'd dealt with. They knew something bad was coming.

She took up her usual position perched at the corner desk before she began.

'What I am about to tell you can't' – she looked directly at Leila – 'leave this room. On the direct orders of Chief Superintendent Davidson.

'We won't be adding any of these details to the victim boards, nor will we be leaving any information about this lying on desktops, recording messages even giving a hint of what I'm about to say on voicemails, or discussing this openly while any staff other than the assembled team are here. Is that clear?'

There was a murmur around the room of 'yes, ma'am' accompanied by the nodding of heads.

'Chief Superintendent Davidson – the only person in this building outside of this room to know about this – has informed me that Helena Fitzsimmons, the daughter of the Home Secretary, has not returned home after a night out in London.'

The team didn't respond. Cramer realised they thought this might be another case they had to take on.

'I've been reliably informed the last time Helena Fitzsimmons was seen' – Cramer took a deep breath – 'was in the Illuminati nightclub near the station in Canterbury.' Now the penny dropped. Heads bowed down briefly, and people were swearing under their breath at this development.

Cramer raised and lowered her hands to get quiet throughout the room again.

'We can't be sure her disappearance is related to our current investigation. But we can't rule it out either as it would fit with Jill's profile. Rob, Leila, did you get the footage from the club last night?'

'Yes, guv,' Rob said. 'Not without a fight, but we got it.'

'Covering all areas? All cameras? The street and the car park too?'

'Yes, everything. That was the problem. They were complaining about having to hand so much over because it seems they had a bit of trouble with some dealers last night and were sending some footage to Vice. I said our need was greater and we'd clear it with Vice and pass it on when we were done. So, they gave in.'

Cramer nodded her approval. The fight with Vice might continue later, but that was an argument for another time.

'Well, I don't need to tell you how this ramps up the focus on this case. We need to bring this girl home safe, whether she is part of this case or not. Any questions so far?'

A shake of heads was the only response.

‘OK, so, Rob, I want you to chase the techs again for the footage of Dominique.’

‘Already done, guv. They’ve finally managed to access the files from the night Dominique went missing and are working on augmenting that footage as we speak. We had no idea why you wanted the other film until now, so I kept a hold of it.’

‘Good. I want you and Leila to go through that footage alone and find any trace of Helena. You know what she looks like?’

‘I’ll find images on Google, boss, she wasn’t a shrinking violet from what I heard,’ Leila said.

Cramer nodded. ‘Doubling up resources should halve the time it will take. But be discrete.’

Both nodded their agreement.

‘Max, piece together Helena’s last movements. Get the CCTV footage from her train and the station for the relevant time. We need to follow her from London right through to leaving the nightclub. See who she might have been with or anyone acting suspiciously around her.’

Max nodded as he made notes.

‘Jill, we’ll go and see the Home Secretary.’

‘Great. We get all the best jobs,’ Jill quipped.

Cramer was stony-faced. ‘You won’t be saying that shortly.’

She turned her attention to Jack. ‘Can you work with the techs on that footage to hurry them along and make sure they prioritise that for us, Jack? I know your sparkling conversation and witty repartee will win them over.’ Cramer smiled.

‘If that doesn’t do it, I’ll try my size tens on ’em.’ Jack countered.

Cramer addressed the room again. ‘Remember, none of this leaves this room. If it does, then whoever’s responsible will wish they’d never been born.’ Again, nods of agreement and a general murmur of approval.

‘Let’s find her. Alive.’

Chapter 32

The tree-lined gravel driveway to the Home Secretary's house was around a mile in length and wound first left, then right after leaving the main road, before opening up into a large courtyard in front of the imposing Georgian property. It wasn't too dissimilar to Cramer's own house, and she'd been here enough times socially for it to feel familiar.

Cramer and Jill hadn't spoken much on their way to see Elizabeth Fitzsimmons. There wasn't much to say. They'd taken a marked car rather than run the gauntlet of the Met's Parliamentary and Diplomatic Protection detail in an unmarked one, even though Davidson had already called ahead to say Cramer would be heading there to interview the Home Secretary.

The door was answered by a small, young, stick-like woman dressed in a grey cardigan and black shift dress, with coal-black woollen tights that seemed excessive for late summer. Her skin was pale as china, a complexion accentuated by her coal-black hair. It reminded Cramer of the little girl in the red dress *in Schindler's List* when all around her is black and white. Only this girl was the negative. Her features were spiky, and Cramer felt sure her manner would match.

'Yes?' Spiky Woman said. Cramer was right.

She pulled out her warrant card and held it up, feeling that being more formal would work better in this situation.

'I'm Acting Detective Chief Inspector Caroline Cramer, and this is my colleague, Jill Traverne. We've come to see Mrs Fitzsimmons.'

The woman peered at her warrant card, almost squinting to read the name in an apparently excessive effort to assert her power. It was clear she really didn't have any, but Cramer played along for now.

'She's expecting us... And you are...?' Cramer couldn't resist asking.

'I'm the Right Honourable Elizabeth Fitzsimmons's PA Emily,' she said haughtily, as if to impress them with her importance. 'Would you like to come in? I'll let Mrs Fitzsimmons know you're here. Please follow me.'

As they walked into the foyer, Jill seemed struck by the height of the ceilings and the imposing marble fireplace in the cavernous hallway. Marble everything, in fact. Floor, inlaid sections in walls, pillars. It was like a museum, the cool marble giving a sense of impersonal luxury. It could not be called homely. A lot like Cramer's childhood home.

Large pictures of ancestors graced the walls way above head height, and the grand piano in the hall gave a clue as to the acoustics in that impressive room alone. Their footsteps echoed off the hard, cold surfaces as they walked through to the drawing room behind Emily.

Cramer went into the room ahead of Jill, and Elizabeth Fitzsimmons was sitting on an elegant sofa surrounded by antique grandeur. More gilt frames on the walls with scenes of England in various seasons adorned the walls, one of them could easily have been a Constable but Cramer wasn't sure.

The usually perfectly coiffured Home Secretary was notably less formidable than normal. Her power suit was still in place, with a skirt just short enough to show the elegant legs she had been featured for in one of the low-end, not-afraid-to-be-sexist newspapers that was read avidly by her electorate. But Cramer felt there was an air of nervousness around her that seemed out of place, a crushing unease that only someone who has lost a child, even for a short period, can really understand. She'd seen it before through her job, and years before close at hand.

Emily did the customary introductions, even though for Cramer it was unnecessary. The Home Secretary stood to greet them both. Her impeccable manners hadn't been dulled by events.

'Callie, good to see you.' Cramer could see her hesitate as she held out her hand, unsure whether to hug the daughter of one of her oldest friends or not. She opted for formality, under the circumstances. 'Well, it is, and it isn't, you know what I mean...' She suddenly looked very flustered, but quickly regained her composure.

'And good to meet you, Jill.' Elizabeth moved to the side of Cramer and offered her hand to Jill.

Handshakes done, they sat on the sofa opposite the Home Secretary, a low but elaborately ornate gilded glass-topped coffee table between them.

'Emily, could you get us all some coffee, please?' Elizabeth seemed as keen to get rid of her PA as Cramer was. Emily, clearly put out at being lowered to waitress status, stalked out of the room, closing the door behind her.

Home Secretary's postured immediately slackened, and Cramer realised this private moment was perhaps the first time all morning that Elizabeth had been allowed the breathing space she needed to start lowering the barriers. Being strong was a necessary part of the job, but at times like this, it was a façade that was hard to keep up.

Cramer could see the fear in her face. So, she started gently. 'Ma'am, I know this is hard for you, but please know we are doing everything in our power to find Helena.'

'Callie, call me Elizabeth, please. I hate excessive formality, especially from you.'

Even so, Elizabeth stiffened slightly, sitting a little straighter than she had previously. Jill was just watching and listening.

Cramer continued. 'OK, thank you Elizabeth. When did you last see her?'

'She left home yesterday morning to head into work. I spoke to her briefly on the phone during the day, and she said she was going out for dinner but would be home early as she had a big day tomorrow. Well, today. It was a big client presentation she'd been working on for weeks. That was the last time I spoke to her.'

Cramer thought about her next question, but given the account from her cousin Charlie, she felt a little awkward about what she was about to say.

'We know she left the station in Canterbury and went to Illuminati for a quick drink with friends, but they lost touch with her and didn't see her leave. Is there anyone she might know who could have given her a lift somewhere? Or would she normally get a cab home from the station?'

Elizabeth hesitated before she finally shook her head.

'No, I can't think of anyone who would have driven her home from there. How do you know she was there? Have you checked the CCTV?'

'We're looking at that now, but we know from an eyewitness who saw her go into the club but didn't see her leave.' Cramer didn't feel like volunteering exactly who that was.

Elizabeth was visibly forlorn at this new information. 'How could so many people be there, and no one see her leave the club?'

They hadn't started canvassing for information because there was no certainty about how she left unless the CCTV confirmed it. But it was a fair question.

'We're currently piecing together her last known movements,' Cramer offered. 'We have all the CCTV from in and around the club, so we'll work out when she left and whether she was alone, I can assure you. Has she ever gone missing before? Even just overnight without calling you?'

'No, never.' Elizabeth was emphatic about this, and Cramer watched as she tried to hold back her emotion. 'This isn't like her at all. She might have liked to party hard in the past, but she'd always let me know where she was and what time she was likely to be back. I purposely never gave her a hard time about it because I always wanted her to feel comfortable telling me where she was, no matter what time of the day or night. We had a deal, and we both kept our side of it.'

Elizabeth's face started to crease as the tears breached her eyelashes.

'Until now. I'm sorry, I just... I don't know what to...'

'Don't be sorry,' Cramer said. She leaned forwards and put her hand on Elizabeth's arm as she dropped her head and dabbed her eyes with a tissue that had been offered by Jill. 'We understand how difficult this is. We're doing our very best to bring her back for you.' Cramer meant every word but wasn't prepared to make a promise she might not be able to keep.

The door opened, breaking the tension, and Emily came in with a tray full of cups, milk, cream, sugar and a sterling silver coffee jug. Elizabeth quickly regained her composure.

'Thank you, Emily. Would you be a dear and finish the letter I dictated earlier? It really must go ASAP.' Yep, Cramer thought again, Elizabeth just wanted her out of the room as quickly as possible.

After Emily had closed the door behind her, Jill asked: 'Does Emily know about Helena being missing Mrs Fitzsimmons?'

Elizabeth's steely gaze returned. 'No, she doesn't. And that's the way it is going to stay. She hasn't been with me for long, and despite going through the customary background check for this job, I'm not sure I trust her. Certainly not with this. I wouldn't put it past her to try to make money from the papers if she had any inkling something wasn't right at Fitzsimmons Towers.'

Cramer and Jill nodded their agreement. The fewer people that knew, the better.

Jill continued. 'So what will you tell her we were here for if she asks?'

Elizabeth had handed around the coffees she had been making while they were talking and took the first swallow of her own. She put the china cup back down with a delicate clink into the saucer as she spoke. Its tinkling rattle exposed how badly her hands were shaking.

'She won't ask. She knows better than that. Besides. We are in the same business, after all.'

Cramer picked up her coffee and took a sip. Spikey Emily might not be good at ingratiating herself with her employer or her guests, but the coffee was delicious. She put her cup down on the table and started to leave her seat, prompting Jill to do the same. It was time to go.

'When do you have to go back to the House?' Cramer asked.

'Tomorrow. There's a bill I need to speak on and a major vote that I can't miss. For today, I can work here.'

Cramer nodded.

'If you hear anything from Helena or any of her friends about where she might be, who she might be with, please let me know as soon as possible.' Cramer passed over her card with her contact details. 'Come directly to me, and don't leave a message with any details. If I can't answer straight away, I'll call you back.'

The three ladies made their way to the door of the room and Elizabeth held her hand out to Jill to say goodbye, but ignored all formalities and hugged Cramer.

'Please bring her home, Callie.'

Cramer swallowed hard and nodded. She couldn't bring herself to say anything that might become a lie.

Chapter 33

He wouldn't be deceived by the devils that resided with it again. The last one had been too much. But this time, he was ready. It would not exert its power. He would not be vain, or proud – both sins he fell victim to last time. No, he was stronger now, more prepared.

He broke the bread and heated soup for it. After all, it needed enough energy to answer for its crimes, to allow him to be sure it needed cleansing. There were the tests to go through, and it would need some strength for those. Yes, it needed some earthly sustenance, no matter what it was getting from its attendants.

He put the food and some water on a tray and placed it down on the sideboard as he swiped the keys, heading towards the door concealing the stone stairway. He fumbled with the lock initially as he tried to open the large iron-studded oak door, the keys clattering as they hit the floor. He picked them up, put the key in the lock and turned it, the bolt opening with a deep clunk. The door groaned open, and he retrieved the tray to carry it down the stone steps. His footsteps created fresh echoes as he went down to where it was held.

As always, he waited outside the door, listening for any sounds – talking, scuffling, scuttling, animal noises, anything that would give him cause to not enter at that moment. But he heard nothing.

He put the key into the lock. It was stiff and wouldn't turn easily, but eventually the bolt slammed heavily into the lock mechanism with another deep metallic clunk, and the door opened. The glow from the stairwell created a shaft of light that cut into the darkness of the room, and then he could see it. Still chained on the marble slab, trying to turn its shaved head away and shield its eyes from the piercing light.

He said nothing, moving slowly towards it. It started to strain at the shackles. The fear in its eyes was clear. The realisation that, now it had seen him, the stakes were much higher.

'Please, I don't know what you want from me. Why am I here? There must be a mistake. Do you know who I am?'

Its words were wasted on him. He was impervious to its pleading, whimpering, its aggression, its desperation. He'd heard it all before. And, of course, he knew who it was. He'd been following for weeks, just waiting for that right moment.

For the first time, it saw itself in the light, and as it looked down, it could see it had been relieved of all its body hair. A cry broke from its lips. He smiled.

'Oh my God, what have you done?'

It cried, sobbing now, shouting, shaking, screaming.

'What have you done? You fucking nutter.'

It was breaking, good news for him. But he still had to be careful. It was capable of incredible deception and its devils could act in ways no one could imagine.

He grabbed its left arm, usually the weakest, and loosened the chain on the marble slab enough for it to reach its mouth. It needed to eat. It must eat. He put the tray in front of it to show it what he wanted it to do. If it chose not to eat, that wasn't his problem.

He lit a short candle at the end of the slab, which he got from a shelf inside the stone room. It would need to see for a little time at least.

It had now grown accustomed to the light and was watching him, the aggression in its face alternating with sobs, scared to take its eyes off him. It moved its left hand towards its head, now it had a little more freedom. It leaned its head forwards and felt the smooth scalp, all its hair gone.

It screamed out at him again 'My hair! You bastard!' More sobbing. More screaming. He just smiled at it again, before uttering the only word it would hear from another person that day.

'Eat.'

Chapter 34

By the time Cramer and Jill had got back to the incident room, Rob and Leila had been working through the CCTV footage, which Jack had managed to encourage the techs to sort. They both looked grim as first Cramer then Jill buzzed themselves in through the outer door.

'Guv, you need to see this,' Rob said as soon as Cramer entered the room. She didn't even take off her jacket before sitting on a desk behind Rob's chair to see what Illuminati's CCTV showed.

Rob took the mouse and started moving deftly around the screen, opening the footage and scrolling it forwards to the relevant time slots, which were written on a piece of paper in front of him.

'First off, Jack managed to get the footage from Dominique from the techs – no-one dared to ask how he managed it though.'

'Thank god for that!' Cramer exclaimed.

Rob nodded his agreement. 'Seems she was picked up by what looks like a Porsche 911 Carrera,' Rob smiled. 'I've wanted one ever since I was a kid.' Rob offered a wry smile. 'Nice car, so this guy has some money behind him.'

Cramer knew he was right. Her husband Patrick had one of these as a plaything. He had a thing about cars and had a veritable fleet at their home. That one alone was close to £85,000.

'Have you checked ANPRs for that particular car?'

'Yes, guv,' said Leila, 'but there was nothing relevant, no sight of that car, so no plate or anything else we can use to identify it. We were thinking if he can afford one of those, the chances are he has access to more than one car. Could be one is a four-by-four, used for the lake; the Porsche for cruising around town.'

'It makes sense, but that'll mean we're looking for more than one owned or accessible by the same individual. Get onto DVLA and find out who in Kent owns both those types of cars. There aren't going to be many people who own or have access to both,' said Cramer.

'And can we make the number plate any clearer?' she asked in hope. Rob just shook his head.

'No, the techs have done everything they can to make it clearer, but that's it.' Cramer dropped her head briefly before looking up again.

'OK, what about last night?'

Rob clicked on the next tab on his computer screen to open the relevant film and checked the notes in front of him for the timeline.

'We have Helena going into the club at just gone ten – you can see her moving ahead of the line here.' He pointed with his finger to the grainy image of a young girl with beautiful long blonde hair moving past frustrated clubbers who'd been waiting around an hour to get into the club she was being whisked into by a friend that Cramer recognised immediately as Charlie.

'Then we have her on another camera going through to the bar and getting a drink.' Rob stopped the exterior footage, before opening up the next section of CCTV, which this time was infrared as it was inside the darkened nightclub.

Helena was at the bar and ordered a drink while talking to Charlie and a few other friends, but seemed a bit disengaged. She constantly looked at her watch while waiting for the barman to pour her wine, it looked like she was in a hurry to get going.

Rob continued: 'Then, there was a bit of a commotion.' The screen was suddenly filled with various men moving past where Helena and Charlie were standing, as one of the men tried to launch a punch at another. The bouncers moved in quickly, removing the men who were continuing to lash out at each other but failing to land a single drunken punch. But by the time the melee had ended, within twenty seconds, Helena could no longer be seen at the bar.

'Where did she go?' Cramer asked. 'Have we got more footage?'

'Yep guv, just a sec...'

Rob closed that screen and opened another, where Helena could be seen deeper in the club, talking to someone off camera. She was quite animated, laughing and joking.

'It doesn't look like she was at all intimidated or nervous about who she was talking to here, so I would say she must have known them,' Rob said.

Jill had taken her place next to Cramer, so she could also see the screen.

'Not necessarily,' Jill added. 'If they'd all been barged out of the way by the fight and the bouncer activity, they could just be discussing that with someone nearby. If something shocking happens, there is a sense of camaraderie, and many people will talk to total strangers as if they know them. The shared experience gives you some element of trust that wouldn't be there before. So, we should consider that.'

'Agreed,' said Cramer. 'Can we find out who she's talking to there. Are there any shots where that person is on camera Rob?'

'No, guv, not one. Which makes me suspicious. If he or she knew where the cameras were, they would know how to avoid appearing on them.'

Cramer nodded.

'But just watch what happens next.' Rob zoomed in on the footage, so Helena was more visible on screen. She went from gesticulating to whoever she was talking to, to standing stock still and put her hand to her temple. It was a sure sign she felt queasy, but according to Charlie and the footage, she only had one drink in the club and seemed sober when she went in. Whoever she was talking to offered a hand to steady her, she nodded as if to say she was all right, and then looked around to find the exit. Clearly needing some fresh air.

The mystery person took control and put an arm around her to move her towards an exit. Still, he wasn't on screen – they could all see now it was a man's arm – but it was still just a disembodied arm helping to steady her. Helena disappeared under the camera and out of shot.

'Is that all we have, Rob?' Cramer was getting exasperated.

'No, one more outside. Hang on...'

Again, Rob closed that footage and opened the next. This camera was looking into the car park behind the club. Helena could be seen outside, holding on to a railing and leaning over, as if she might be sick. The same hand that helped her before was now rubbing her back as she leaned over the railing, but there was nothing else to see. Damn. Whoever this was knew exactly how to avoid every camera. Still nothing they could use to identify him. But Helena slumped in the footage, as if she had lost consciousness. Her body folded almost double over the railing, and the 'hand' roughly pulled her upright. Then the team saw another arm as her prostrate body was picked up and carried out of the camera shot. There was no doubting what they had just seen. Helena had been drugged and taken while she couldn't fight back.

'Fuck!' Cramer said as she slammed her hand down on the desk, making the others in the room jump at her outburst. She stayed silent momentarily, the anger boiling inside her.

'There is definitely nothing else, no footage of this guy? You've gone through everything to match his shirt, a watch, a tattoo as he is going into the club?' She knew they would have, and from the footage they had shown her, there were no identifying features. Not even a watch.

Leila spoke this time. 'Yes, guv. There's nothing to work with. It was a plain white shirt, and we couldn't pin down who was there talking to her based on that at all. There were about twenty to thirty men wearing similar shirts that night. We went through all the footage available, and the camera footage isn't good enough quality to get any finer details, so we can't identify them. We've cross-referenced as many as we can, and this one guy has avoided all video footage.'

'Dammit, we must have something!' Cramer was shouting now. 'What about footage from the station? Footage from elsewhere in the club? Something! CCTV from the street? The roads on the way in? Is there any footage of a Porsche arriving? There has to be something more!'

They looked crestfallen.

'Guv, honestly we have looked and looked. There's nothing,' Leila said. 'This is one clever bastard.'

Cramer stared at Jill briefly, who was impassive, before moving her gaze to the floor. Now was not the time to lose her cool.

'OK, well, good work. At least we know what has happened to Helena.' Not that it made Cramer feel any better. Knowing what she already knew about the fate of other victims, it made her feel worse.

'Any tox results back from the lab yet on Dominique?' Cramer asked.

Rob shook his head. 'Said it could take as much as a couple of weeks. I've chased them a few times already, and I think I am starting to piss the lab techs off, to be honest.'

Cramer fixed her gaze on him. 'Well, keep pissing them off. We don't have a couple of weeks. They'll see how pissed off I can get if we don't get something soon.

'Have we checked on the last position of Helena's mobile phone?' she added, hopefully.

'Yes, and all we can tell is it was near Illuminati. Was turned off just after the time code on the footage showed her being carried away,' Rob replied. 'The same as the other victims. He's not missing a trick.'

Cramer nodded. 'So, he knows exactly how we might track someone based on mobile phone mast pings, understands something about forensics...' Cramer was thinking aloud.

'Jill could be right, we could be dealing with one of our own here...'

Rob and Leila looked shocked, prompting Cramer to continue.

'Look, I don't like it any more than you do, but we could be. I'm not saying it is, or even that they are from this force. Might be worth having a look at all the people who might have been laid off in the last few years, Leila. Not just from Kent Police but elsewhere, anyone who might have moved into the area from a force elsewhere, work out if any of them have a grudge, or enough money to be in the position to own a couple of motors like that. Maybe an ill-health retirement pay-off from the force. But keep it between us. I don't want people getting twitchy thinking we're watching them or treating them as suspects, OK?'

Rob and Leila just nodded.

'He has to make a mistake soon, everyone does. And it could be his mistake was with Dominique, Rob. The pattern wasn't followed there – taken, killed and dumped within one night. Not normal for our target at all. There's so much with the other victims that appears ritualistic, so something went wrong with her, it must have. We need to work out what, and I think she will be able to tell us more about her killer than she ever thought possible. We just need to get those bloody tox results!'

'I have tried, ma'am, believe me I have tried.'

'Well, let me try. They'll wish they'd been more helpful to you the mood I'm in right now.'

Rob handed over the details of the contact he had been speaking to at the lab, and Cramer took it and went into her office, as Jill stayed with Rob and Leila outside.

After a lot of shouting, Cramer emerged ten minutes later.

'Right, we'll have the tox results tomorrow. And Simms has confirmed. They didn't like it, but they're sorting it.'

Cramer could see in his face that Rob felt put out that they'd pulled out the stops for her but not him, but that was the benefit of seniority.

'Me and Leila were thinking, guv, that maybe Dominique was just a chance meeting. Not planned, not set up, but something he did on a whim. That could be why he was in that car, and why it was on CCTV when we hadn't had any other footage.

'A Porsche 911 Carrera is not really a car I would choose if I was trying to avoid attention. They don't exactly blend into the background, and they're definitely not spacious inside. This might have been opportune, and that's why he dumped her so quickly. He has a plan for these women, and he went off-piste.'

Rob looked at Jill and then Cramer and back to Jill. It seemed he was after confirmation for his and Leila's theory.

‘Could make sense,’ said Jill, ‘but why change approach? If he veered off plan, he would probably panic, be angry, or upset at the change in ritual.’ She thought about it for a minute. ‘But it would explain why she was taken and killed so quickly, while the other victims had been held for longer. We also have to consider the tokens left with each victim, and if my theory’s right, then he was intending to take a prostitute. Why not have a specific one in mind? All the other victims appear to have been directly targeted, and it is becoming clearer where from. There is some significant planning going into this. He is meticulous, apart from with Dominique.’

‘He needs to be in control,’ Cramer added, ‘to be focused on the process as much as the end result. If he’s drugging them, it would give him complete control from the word go. It’s likely this would be a means to an end, a way of getting someone to comply without fuss, or any risk of a scene that would highlight what’s really going on.’

‘Doing that in a nightclub is, really, genius if you think about it,’ Jill said.

Cramer gave Jill an unmistakable look that told her never to use that word in relation to this man again.

Jill held up her hands in a defensive gesture. ‘I’m only saying!’ She changed tack quickly. ‘It is just in the first three victims, we’ve seen no sign of any drugs in their system,’ Jill added.

‘But if he was using GHB or Rohypnol, then it would metabolise out of their system within hours, so we wouldn’t find it in the forensic examinations,’ said Cramer. ‘It’s the perfect drug for this – tasteless, odourless, easy to slip into a drink. We really need to know if Dominique had it in her system.’

Cramer turned her attention to Leila. ‘What else have we got? Did you get anything more from rerunning the social media searches?’

'Guv, I genuinely think we have exhausted that line of inquiry. I have checked, cross-checked, double-checked and triple-checked the info we have had. There's nothing I can come up with at all. Nothing.'

Cramer thought about that for a moment. 'What about their emails? How far back did you go?'

Cramer could see the heat rising up Leila's neck; the last thing she wanted was another reason to give her new DC a hard time, but she knew the answer was probably not far enough. Leila sighed before talking. 'We went back three months before the first victim was found. You want me to go back further, right?'

Cramer's look hardened. 'Right. Go back at least six months. This guy is methodical, takes his time, and he must study his victims. It could be at least six months before that he was in contact with them.'

Leila turned away defeated and started looking through her list of contacts. Her silence spoke loud and clear.

Cramer and Jill retreated to Cramer's office, looking once again into the faces of the women they were working for, a gaping hole where Helena's photo couldn't be. The board simply read *Victim 5?* They could remove the question mark now, there was no doubt. The impersonal nature of that label hit Cramer doubly hard, but she had to be professional.

She walked round her desk and took her seat to face Jill, shaking her head as she sat down. 'This case is driving me crazy. Four bodies, footage of a fifth victim being taken from a nightclub, and nothing to go on. What are we missing here?'

Jill turned away from Cramer, twisting her body to the right to stare at the board. 'OK, let's get back to basics. Each time he has left us a Bible quote, so we're thinking there's a religious influence pushing him towards what he's doing. But what if we're wrong? What if it's about something else? Maybe the complete opposite?'

'Jill, I don't mean to make a statement of the bleedin' obvious, but it doesn't get more religious than Bible quotes, does it?'

'But look at what they each say.'

Jill moved over to the board and pointed to them individually as she read them out, like she was giving a lecture to a student. It irked Cramer.

'"For all that do these things are an abomination unto the Lord: and because of these abominations the Lord thy God doth drive them out from before thee", and "Regard not them that have familiar spirits, neither seek after wizards to be defiled by them: I am the Lord your God".

'"A man also or woman that hath a familiar spirit, or that is a wizard, shall surely be put to death" – Leviticus: twenty, verse twenty-seven. "Then Pharaoh also called the wise men and the sorcerers: now the magicians of Egypt, they also did in like manner with their enchantments" – Exodus: seven, verse eleven.'

Cramer stiffened. 'I can read, Jill, what's your point?'

'My point is that while there is no doubt these are Bible quotes, they all relate to the occult.'

Cramer was getting more irritated. 'Yes, Jill, I realise that. We've talked about that before and I've looked into that before. We've got nothing so far from the religious routes we've gone down, so I'm not sure where you're going with this.'

'I think we need to find someone academic who knows about and has studied the occult but doesn't practice it. That way we will get a generic view that isn't tempered by any kind of reluctance to speak to the police.'

'Right, well, let's assume for the moment that's a good idea...where do you propose we find someone like that?'

'At the university.'

Cramer thought for a moment, then smiled for the first time that day.

'Jill, you're a genius. I could kiss you.'

Her friend curled up her nose. 'Please don't, Cal, you're not my type.'

Chapter 35

Canterbury Christ Church University is spread across various campuses in Kent, and after a few phone calls, Cramer and Jill had arranged to meet Professor Simon Collinson at the faculty's history department, near Canterbury Cathedral. The whole city is steeped in history and is the seat of the Church of England's head, the Archbishop of Canterbury. But given what happens in the city on a Friday and Saturday night, you could be forgiven for thinking many of the locals have little regard for their religious roots.

The entrance to the campus was inauspicious, through a nondescript gate off a road in the city near to the Crown Court buildings, and just a walk from the station where Cramer and Jill had been in the incident room. The reception area was nothing special either; a modern mixture of grey fittings and glass, punctuated by the odd piece of wood panelling. It was a very large area though, with a café at one end and double doors that led through to a stairwell to the offices above, and a constant stream of students as they went one way and or the other, to and from lectures and the café.

The receptionist had already invited Cramer and Jill to take a seat on the mix of fuchsia pink, purple and grey furniture in the foyer area, and they didn't have to wait long before they saw a young man making a beeline for them. He was smartly dressed in chinos and polo neck, and his brown hair was close-cropped around his ears, but longer and swept over to one side on top.

'Detective Chief Inspector Cramer?' He held his hand out to Jill who simply pointed at her younger friend instead. He adjusted without a hint of embarrassment and shook Cramer's hand. She didn't bother to correct him with the 'Acting' modifier.

'And this is Jill Traverne, one of our consultants,' said Cramer, not offering more explanation. This assistant didn't need it.

'Please follow me.' He headed back through the double doors and turned left to go up two flights of stairs before reaching an office door with Professor Collinson's name on it. Cramer expected him to knock on the door, but just opened it and invited them in, offering the two seats nearest the door. The room was only slightly bigger than a broom cupboard, with a bookcase that reached from floor to ceiling on the left wall. His computer was at an angle to the bookcase, allowing the backdrop to his work to be the more interesting book spines than the plain, magnolia wall that was on the other side. There was a purple pin board behind their chairs, a nod to the colour scheme that filtered throughout the university, including the graduation robes. It added an element of 'excitement' to an otherwise drab office space. If you could really call a purple pinboard exciting with a straight face.

'Can I get you some coffee? Tea?' he asked.

Cramer answered first. 'Yes, coffee would be great, thank you.'

Jill nodded in agreement. 'Yes, coffee for me too, please, thank you.'

'I'll bring it through to you and ask the professor to come in.'

When they were left alone in the professor's office, Cramer started to have a better look around. The bookcase was crammed full of books, papers, ring-bound volumes and stapled sheets. There wasn't a lot of order on there, and Cramer thought about how many times she had looked at her own desk covered in papers, yet she still knew where everything was. Her theory was that you had to have an ordered mind to cope with chaos, that was both a metaphor for her life and her desk right now.

There were some pictures of a young woman on the professor's desk, with a little girl, presumably the professor's daughter and granddaughter. Alongside these were more papers, overflowing in and out trays, and his computer, which was somewhat ancient-looking, and felt at odds with the rest of this sparkling new university campus. On the wall to their right were a range of qualifications: a BA in history, and Masters, a PhD – all the accoutrements you would expect of a highly qualified individual.

They both jumped when the door swung open and the assistant returned with their coffee, moving some papers on the desk to make space for it.

'Sorry, it's a bit of a mess in here,' he said, as he moved round to the other side of the desk and sat down. It was as much as Cramer could do to stop her mouth falling open. He's the professor?

'So, how can I help you both?'

'You *are* Professor Collinson?' Cramer was shocked, and frankly unimpressed.

'Well, sorry, Professor, um – how embarrassing – we didn't realise it was you we'd met downstairs.' Cramer felt her face burning. 'You didn't introduce yourself as such.'

Professor Collinson just laughed. His brown hair fell forward, and he pushed it back to where it had been with his right hand, smoothing it over to the side of his head again. The style showed his young age, – he had a very youthful appearance.

'Yes, I'm sorry about that. I often get mistaken for my "assistant"' – he did air quotes – 'but I don't actually have an assistant at the moment, so I play the part sometimes. I look younger than I am – I was being asked for ID in bars long after I was eighteen. So sometimes, it's nice to use it to my advantage. I'm sure you can imagine how many times it works to my disadvantage.' He continued to smile, but both women were stony-faced. It was a childish prank for someone with such authority within the university to play, the kind of humour Cramer just found pathetic. It made her wonder if he really was the right person to be talking to. For now, she had to give him the benefit of the doubt – she needed his help with this case.

'Professor—' Cramer began.

'Please, call me Simon. The title makes me think I should be wearing corduroys and a tweed jacket over a velvet waistcoat, none of which will match.'

That did make Cramer laugh.

'OK, Simon. Thank you. We wanted to ask you about some elements of a case we're working on, but I must stress that the information I'm about to share with you is not in the public domain, and we would like it to stay that way. I need an assurance from you that this will remain confidential.'

Cramer pulled out an NDA from her bag that was used for situations where they needed specialist information from outside their own ranks.

Given his apparent propensity for juvenile pranks, Cramer wondered whether this was a risk too far, but they were here, and he was apparently the person most qualified to speak to them about the occult nature of this case. He must have realised her reservation because he addressed it immediately.

'Well, listen, I know you might be thinking I'm a little untrustworthy, but please let me reassure you. I am party to many secrets, and I understand the importance of keeping this information between us. I assure you nothing we discuss will leave this room.'

He took the NDA, didn't even bother to read it, signed, and dated it before handing it back.

Cramer looked at Jill for her view, and she made an 'OK, I believe him' face and nodded her agreement.

'Thank you, that's a relief. You're clearly very perceptive.'

He smiled and nodded. 'Right, so how can I help?'

Cramer opened her bag again, and this time, handed over a piece of paper with the four Bible quotes that had been left at each crime scene for him to look at.

'You've probably seen this case on the news. Four women have been found dead so far, and while the method by which they were ultimately killed is different, there are enough similarities that we can assume the same person is responsible.'

Simon nodded. 'Yes, I've heard about this. I'm sorry, the press seems to have been having a field day at your expense from what I've read.'

Cramer stiffened slightly in her seat. Again he picked up on the motion.

'Sorry, I didn't mean to offend you.'

'It's fine, they have, you're right.' She wasn't offended by him, just the coverage.

He looked at the paper he now held in his hand, and then fixed his eyes on Cramer as he put the quotes down on his desk and folded his arms as he leaned forwards.

'You said "so far".'

'Sorry… what do you mean?' Cramer could feel her face flushing.

'Just now, you said four women "so far". Does that mean you're expecting more? Has someone else been taken?'

Shit. He didn't miss a trick. Jill and Cramer looked at each other and knew they had to be careful how they answered this question. Jill took up the thread.

'Just a figure of speech. We're doing everything we can to make sure there aren't more. That's why we're here.'

Simon nodded his understanding and looked back down at the paper on the desk before picking it up again and examining it once it was back in his hand.

Cramer nodded her thanks to Jill. She knew she would have to be more careful about how she spoke about this in the future. Speaking out of turn unintentionally seemed to be becoming a habit.

Simon looked back towards them, having read the Bible quotes. 'So, what are these? How are they relevant?'

Cramer leaned forwards to make her point. He'd placed the paper back down on the desk, and she pointed to the quotes in turn. 'These have been left with each body, one per victim. We had thought initially it was just a religious association we were looking at, but now, we are thinking there might be more to it than that.

'I wanted to speak to some members of occult groups locally after the first two victims were found, because these quotes suggest there may be an occult connection, but as you can imagine, they were reluctant to talk to me.'

Simon snorted a laugh. 'These "occult groups" are more likely to be people locally who like to... how can I put this... "play" at the occult, and really don't understand a lot about it. They like the pagan aspects of it, playing with pentagrams, fiddling around with incantations. They like to scare others, scare themselves, feel special or "different". It's an adrenaline rush. But they don't really understand it or know what they're dealing with. There's no real knowledge on their part, so they wouldn't be able to help you. They can't tell you what they don't know.'

Cramer and Jill both nodded.

'I take it you don't practice?' Cramer was interested to find out if his interest was purely academic.

'Ah, no, I don't, Chief Inspector. I'm fascinated by the historical associations between religion and what would now more accurately be called alternative religions but have no interest whatsoever in becoming involved. That isn't to say I don't know people who do, though, and those who really know about it usually have no intentions to do harm, they're generally in it to do good. But there are some who are...how can I put it...are into darker practices. But they are very much in the minority.' Cramer was keeping an open mind. Much of this was similar to what she had learned from Isabella, so it made sense. And he was the expert after all.

He continued. 'The way alternative religion has been dealt with in the past speaks volumes when it comes to human nature, and that's what I find interesting. History, anthropology, the way that we can learn to improve our future by studying our past, and how often we are destined to repeat the same stupid mistakes because man cannot bring himself to remember the solutions to problems past. It's one of the reasons it's vital our current generation should be taught about the First and Second World War – so few of the people who experienced that are left now.'

Cramer and Jill nodded slowly, a little shell-shocked at his rant.

He realised what he had done. 'But sorry, I digress. Ask away.'

'What do those quotes mean to you?' Jill asked. 'We know they refer to wizards, magicians... but why those in relation to our victims? We haven't found any link between the victims yet, but there must be something we're missing here...'

The point was left hanging in the air.

Simon rubbed his chin and leaned forward in his chair, his elbows on his desk and the paper in both hands once again. He put it back down on the desk and looked at them both and rubbed his chin as he was thinking. 'You don't have any link between the women found so far?'

Jill continued. 'Well, there may be one, but it's tenuous. We think they were each picked up in or around a nightclub in Canterbury. But the first three were in a different place to the fourth, so even that we're concerned may not be the case.'

Simon nodded and sat in thought for a few seconds before talking.

'The first three? Three is a very powerful number in religion and literature, so it might be there is a plan to start another three from the second venue.'

'Yes, Jill said that as well,' said Cramer. 'That's the assumption we're working on at the moment. But we haven't been able to find any other links, and forensics haven't helped – no prints on the quotations, nothing on the bodies, no slip-ups anywhere that we have found. So far.' She smiled, as she used that phrase advisedly this time.

Simon nodded again and smiled back. 'What about the women you've found? Is there anything significant about them you can share with me?'

Cramer stared straight at him. 'They've all had their body hair shaved. Head, underarms, pubic hair, everything. We just don't know why.'

Simon suddenly became animated. He started nodding and rolled his office chair back to allow him to get up from his desk. He went to the bookshelf and started to thumb through the books until he found the one he was looking for. It was dog-eared, and the spine had more lines than print left from where it had been opened so often that it was no longer possible to read the title.

He started to thumb through the pages until he found what he wanted, folded the book open, and presented it to Cramer and Jill. They peered at the pages, not sure what they were expected to see.

Simon pointed to a paragraph on the page for them, so they didn't have to read for too long. It read:

The third precaution to be observed in this tenth action is that the hair should be shaved from every part of her body. The reason for this is the same as that for stripping her of her clothes, which we have already mentioned; for in order to preserve their power of silence they are in the habit of hiding some superstitious object in their clothes or in their hair, or even in the most secret parts of their bodies, which must not be named.

Cramer's blood ran cold in her veins, and as she looked at Jill, she could see this was having the same effect on her.

Cramer looked back at Simon.

'What is this book?'

He closed it so they could see the title, but they were still none the wiser.

'It's the *Malleus Maleficarum*,' Simon said triumphantly.

Cramer and Jill still looked blank.

'It's the book that provided the template for witch-hunters and the Inquisition, basically between 1450 and 1750, give or take a few years. The last execution was in the 1800s. It wasn't just about witches, it was used for heretics in general. But this did focus on the ways in which witches worked and how they should be "tried" to find out if they were witches or not.'

Cramer felt stunned. 'So, you're saying he thinks they are witches? Is treating them as witches on trial?'

Simon nodded. 'Of course, in many cases, the trials alone killed these women, so they were essentially done for, anyway.'

Both Cramer and Jill were silenced momentarily. It certainly did fit with what they knew so far, almost too perfectly.

'So, you think this could be what he is working from? His motivation?' Jill said.

Cramer jumped in again to ensure they were clear. 'You think he thinks they're witches?'

'Well, I can't say for sure, any more than you can right now. But definitely the shaving of all the body hair and the use of these Bible quotes... There's a strong argument for it. Wouldn't you agree?'

Cramer and Jill both nodded immediately, but it was Cramer who spoke first. 'Definitely. But the trials they were put through to determine whether they were witches or not. What exactly would they be? Wouldn't we see some evidence of them on the women we've found?'

Simon picked up the *Malleus Maleficarum* and flicked through the pages again, finding the relevant bit to answer Cramer's question.

'There, you can see here what they would do.' He pointed to a paragraph in the book. 'They might be asked to undergo a trial by red-hot iron to prove their innocence. The idea is that if they are a witch, they will agree because they know that the devil will not allow them to be hurt.'

'But apart from our first victim, who was burned to death so we wouldn't be able to tell, there have definitely not been any burn marks on the other victims, or any major signs of other injuries apart from the cause of death and some additional bruising, which we would expect to have come from their initial kidnap or their captivity,' Cramer volunteered.

'Ah, no, you misunderstand me,' Simon said. 'If they agreed to the trial by hot iron, there was no need for the inquisitors to force it. They had their admission right there.'

'That means they won't actually go through the trial?' Jill was warming to the theme.

'Exactly. Just agreeing to it would be enough to prove to the accusers they were dealing with a witch, because why would anyone who wouldn't be protected run the risk of such heinous injuries? They had to walk a stipulated three paces with the red-hot iron. That would be enough to do some serious damage.'

'What if they refused?' Cramer asked.

'Then they would find some other test they had no choice in,' said Collinson. 'That was just one element of their methods. Aside from this, they would torture the women to get them to confess to dabbling in witchcraft.'

Cramer almost didn't want to ask the next question, but she couldn't help herself. 'What sort of torture?'

Simon leaned back in his chair, throwing his arms open as if the magnitude of the answer was far too big to get into in a single conversation.

'There were so many ways. It could be something as seemingly simple as having to recite the Lord's Prayer without making any mistakes to prove their innocence. Or being held in extreme positions to break their will, or ducking – we have an example of that in the city already, as I am sure you know. The ducking stool behind the Old Weaver's House.'

Cramer and Jill looked at each other.

'Yes, we know – that's where our fourth victim was discovered.'

Simon nodded sagely. 'Yes, I heard about that.'

Cramer nodded. 'Go on, you were telling us about the kinds of torture.'

'Yes... There was the rack. And an extreme and rather disgusting device called the Judas Chair. Pricking was another –

literally sticking pins into the accused. Scratching, using brown rats…' His eyes sparkled as his list increased.

Jill held her hand up. 'OK, we get the picture.' Cramer felt he was enjoying this conversation a little too much, especially given they were talking about real women being hurt here. This wasn't an academic subject to her and Jill. Her heart ached at the thought of what Helena could be going through right now.

'Yes, sorry,' Simon volunteered. 'I'm just very passionate about this subject and sometimes I get a bit carried away. It speaks to the fundamental ill-treatment of women through the ages. There are examples through all periods of history where men, supposedly the stronger sex, have been so fearful of women that they have gone to great lengths to silence or hurt them. It's something I feel very strongly about – I'm a feminist.' He smiled, trying to lighten the mood.

Cramer took the cue and smiled back, but her smile didn't reach her eyes. 'Well, thank you for your help. Is there any chance I could borrow that copy from you please?' She pointed to the *Malleus Maleficarum* still lying on the desk.

Simon made a pained face. 'I don't mean to be rude, but I have a rule that I don't lend my own books out to people. I've done it in the past and almost always they haven't been returned. So, no. Sorry.'

Cramer was clearly put out, and Collinson added quickly: 'But you can find a copy of this online, which is probably easier for you and your team to deal with, as you can search on keywords and such if you want to find something specific.'

Cramer stood up, and Jill followed her lead.

'We'll do that. Thank you – really, you've been very helpful.' Cramer held her hand out for him to shake. 'But I must remind you that everything we have discussed here is confidential.'

Simon took her hand. 'No need to worry, I'll keep this all to myself, I can assure you.'

Chapter 36

It couldn't have been long since she'd last eaten the food she had been given, but Helena's stomach felt empty, like it was gnawing itself inside of her. She had no control over her body, her life, anything anymore, and that was the hardest thing to bear.

She'd been moved by her captor off the slab, but instead, her hands were now hoisted high above her head. The pain in her shoulders was excruciating. There was nowhere she could go, no way she could escape, so why was she being held like this? The lit candle had again been left at her feet when she ate. It was so close to her it felt like it was burning. Hot wax had fallen on her toes as she tried to move it further away, which made her scream in pain.

Using the light of the candle, she had been able to look around to at least some bits of the room, where the weak flame reached. There were no windows, no natural light, and the walls she could see to each side were stone. Not smooth, more like a cave, chiselled into rock. Like her father's wine cellar in their chateaux in Bordeaux. That was what it reminded her of.

But her current reality shattered that illusion as quickly as smashing a wine bottle. Their wine cellar was cool and chalky white. These walls were grey, slate grey.

The shadows formed by the candle in the room had made her fearful of what was hiding in the dark corners. Was there someone there? She was sure she could hear breathing. It put her senses on high alert. No, she was wrong. Wait, was she? Confusion overtook her.

She could make out what looked like a dresser at one end of the room, and something to the left that looked like a kind of chair. But it wasn't clear. It resembled a throne, but that didn't make sense.

The light had offered both solace and concern in equal measure for the time it was there, and once the flame had burned out and the darkness enveloped her again, the oppressive fear returned. She had begged to be allowed to use the bathroom but had been given a bucket. She used it once but couldn't get to it again after being strung up as she was now. Her bladder had refilled, but she was determined to hold it in. Her dignity had been shaved away, but she wanted to retain what last vestige of it she had left. She wouldn't sink that low.

She shivered involuntarily against the cold as the candle sputtered out. Her thoughts were racing inside her head, louder than ever. But then a noise. Outside. An animal? She held her breath. Please God, don't let it be a rat.

She wanted to be able to hear everything, but her heartbeat was the loudest thing in the room as her adrenaline spiked.

The key was turning in the lock again. Her fear overtook her, and she couldn't hold her bladder any longer. Her body shook involuntarily as she felt the warm liquid trickle down her legs, forming a stinking puddle at her feet, the combination of fear and shame overcoming her. At that moment, her bowels opened too, terror loosening them. She had lost all control.

She broke down. All dignity had been taken from her; she had nothing left to give. Why wouldn't he just kill her if that was the plan? Why was he feeding her, holding her here?

She wasn't sure anything even mattered anymore. She was going to die, she may as well accept it. She closed her eyes, and the tears flowed freely, splashing into the other body fluids below as she let her head fall onto her chest.

Chapter 37

The room stank. Faeces and urine mingled with sweat and God knew what else to create that disgusting miasma. He pulled the buff up over his mouth and nose before he fully opened the door. He wasn't afraid of it seeing him. No, that wouldn't matter at all – he was still in his robes. But he didn't want its stench to affect him in any way, to infect him. He knew historic cases, medieval cases, where that had happened before to the people doing the work he had taken on. That would be very bad.

It was exactly where he had left it – it couldn't move now it was in this stress position. No mere mortal could stay in that same pose for long, but it was managing it. Its eyes were shut, head lolling to one side. It could be tricking him, making him think it was unconscious. Or it could be sleeping? If that was the case, its incubi would be nearby. The devils that had sexual intercourse with witches would take advantage of such a position.

He stopped dead. That sound. The scratching. Where was it coming from? He held a staff in his right hand, ready to thrash any unwelcome visitor in the room.

He spun around. There it was again. Scratching. Incessant. He turned back towards it. Yes, the noise was near it. It was there.

He edged towards it, staff raised, ready to strike. As he approached it, the smell of excrement became unbearable. Was it that? Or was it the odour of sin? A fleeting movement near it caught his eye.

He tried to follow the animal with his eyes, not daring to move for fear of being bewitched by this devil's powers. It was on it, crawling over its thigh, moving up over its hip. It jumped. Was it heading towards him? He couldn't take a chance and swiped the air ahead of him, but he didn't feel any contact made.

It landed back on its thigh, then its arm again, before jumping back to the thigh, and he brought the staff down hard on the devil to kill it. He felt its flesh compress and heard a crack, followed by a blood-curdling scream.

'It shouldn't let its devils do its work. Let that be a lesson. Tomorrow, there will be another.'

Chapter 38

When Cramer and Jill got back to the incident room, Leila and Rob were both on the phone, and Cramer indicated to them they needed to finish up their conversations as quickly as possible. She wanted to discuss this development right away.

She went straight into her office and looked up the *Malleus Maleficarum* on Google. Thank goodness it offered the correct spelling as an option, because she wasn't even close with her effort.

She found a PDF version online, copied the link and sent it in an email to Jill, Rob and Leila with the subject 'Update'.

Cramer looked up out of her office and watched as Jill, who was sitting at a desk in the outer office, opened the email Cramer had just sent and looked back at her and nodded. Leila walked behind Jill towards Cramer's office, looking over Jill's shoulder as she passed before standing in Cramer's doorway.

'Guv, what did you need? We're both off the phone now.'

'Great, give me a second and I'll be with you,' said Cramer.

Leila nodded and went to leave, but popped her head back into Cramer's office. 'Brew?'

Cramer nodded. 'Thanks.'

She watched Leila head to the kitchen, then picked up her own phone and punched in the extension for Davidson. It only rang twice.

'Cramer. What do you have?'

'Sir, I have an update. Can I see you in half an hour?'

She imagined him looking at his watch as he took a bit of time to answer. When he did, he sounded reluctant. 'Well… yes, OK. But I'll only have ten minutes. Enough time?'

'Should be, sir. I'm just briefing the team, then I'll come up.'

'Don't be late.'

He put the phone down. He sounded grumpier than usual, but that was becoming par for the course lately.

Cramer picked up the case file from her desk and went through to the incident room where Rob and Jill were sitting talking. Leila moved towards them all with four cups balanced in her hands and she proceeded to place one in front of each of them in turn before sitting down. Max and Jack were just heading back into the office, and Cramer motioned for them to join the briefing.

'Guv, I've asked for that extra info from the tech guys, but it's going to take a little while for them to collate it apparently,' Leila said.

Cramer just smiled and nodded, deciding to give her some encouragement. Cramer knew she'd been harsh on her recently. 'Good stuff, Leila. Rob, anything to add?'

'Actually, we got lucky on one of the tox reports. Dominique did have GHB in her system. So, that's how he is subduing the women he's taking.'

Finally, something to work with. 'Nice work, Rob,' Cramer said.

Leila offered him a high-five. He took it readily.

Cramer carried on with the briefing. 'OK, well we've made some big inroads today. Jill and I have just come back from speaking to a Professor Simon Collinson at the university, and he was able to give us some very interesting information. I've sent you all a link to a document, well, a book actually, that you need to look at. I don't expect you to read it all, but there are some areas that are of specific interest to us in this case.'

Rob turned back to his computer to open the link, but Cramer intervened.

'Don't worry about opening it now – Jill will explain what you need to know following our conversation at the university.'

Jill looked surprised, before composing herself and moving to where Cramer had perched herself on the edge of the table, ready to take over the briefing.

Cramer looked at her as she began. 'We've all been focusing on the Bible quotes as being something relating to religious symbolism – a religious reason being behind what our perpetrator is doing. And you know Cal has already spent some time looking into the occult elements of these quotes after the first two victims were found, with little development in that area.'

Heads nodded all round.

'Well, we decided to go back to basics, addressing the content of the quotes being left, and what that might mean for our suspect. It seems obvious in one way, but we wanted to try to approach this at a tangent, and it looks like we may have got somewhere.

'Simon Collinson is a professor of history with a specialist knowledge of witchcraft, the Inquisition and how the occult has been viewed through the ages. We've just spent half an hour with him to, confidentially, discuss if there was any light he could shed on what these quotes might relate to exactly, and whether there was anything that would suggest a reason for the patterns of behaviour we've seen with our victims. We seem to have found one.'

Rob and Leila both raised their eyebrows and looked at each other, before turning back to Jill to listen further.

Cramer interjected – the explanation seemed to make such sense in the professor's office, yet it felt much more outlandish back here at the station. 'Each of the victims had all their hair shaved, but we had no apparent reason for that. But the professor told us that when the self-titled "witch finders" and inquisitors tried women suspected of being witches, they shaved all their body hair because it was thought their "familiars" or devils would be hidden in the hair and could hurt the inquisitors when questioning them.'

'When you say "questioning them", you really mean torturing them, right?' Rob said.

Jill nodded. 'Well, yes. But that's what the link Cal has sent to you relates to. It's a book written in the mid-1400s called the *Malleus Maleficarum*...'

'The what?' said Leila.

'The *Malleus Maleficarum*,' Cramer said. 'We hadn't heard of it either, but I've sent it to you with the relevant page numbers highlighted in the email, so you can read the sections we had highlighted to us, and you will see why it makes sense. It's essentially a blueprint written by Catholic clergymen to endorse the trial and extermination of witches. The theory and "legal"' – she did air quotes this time – 'principles provided a roadmap that resulted in so many innocent women, and more rarely but also some men, who didn't fit into the social norms of the time, being killed. It was only second in numbers of sales to the Bible for around two hundred years.'

Jill looked at her aghast. 'How do you know all that?'

'Google's a wonderful thing.' She winked at her.

Jill just shook her head and smiled before continuing. 'The quotes being left are also all in this book. That makes this a very powerful argument as to what he's doing and why.'

'Hang on a second,' said Leila. 'What you're saying then, is that this guy thinks these women are... witches?'

Cramer and Jill spoke in unison.

'Exactly.'

Chapter 39

Leila blew air out through her teeth as she leaned back in her seat, putting her hands behind her head. 'How could anyone think like that in this day and age?'

Cramer shrugged her shoulders. 'We may never know. What we need to do is find where they're being held and get to Helena before it's too late.'

'He'll need somewhere pretty substantial to hold these women,' Rob said. 'We know he's holding them for a few days to a week ordinarily, except for Dominique, but she seems to have been the anomaly.'

'That may have unsettled him. He may be more cautious in the coming days,' said Jill.

'But does that really help us? I mean, won't that make him more likely to hunker down and not break cover?' said Leila.

Cramer watched as Jill thought for a moment before answering.

'Not necessarily. He follows a process, and given the ritualistic nature of what he's doing, he'll find it hard to not carry on. He needs to complete the mission.'

'So, he'll be looking for another victim?' Rob looked concerned.

Jill looked at Cramer, and she stood up from the desk as she took over the briefing again.

'If the theory of three victims from each place holds water – and Professor Collinson also agreed with the symbolism outlined by Jill in that regard – then yes, we're looking at another woman being taken from the same club.'

There was a feeling of unease in the room, and both Rob and Leila looked at each other. Rob was about to speak, and Cramer watched as his Adam's apple bobbed up and down frantically, betraying his nervousness.

'Guv, Leila and I were talking earlier, and we wanted to suggest something to you. But please give it some thought before you answer.'

Cramer didn't move, waiting to see what he said next. She folded her arms, a defensive gesture as she was well aware.

Rob seemed to swallow hard again before continuing. 'We think it makes sense for Leila and I to go into the club undercover, so you have someone on the ground, eyes inside.'

Cramer's body visibly stiffened at the suggestion, and she was about to answer before Rob interrupted.

'I know what you're going to say—'

'No, you don't!' Cramer snapped back, unfolding her arms and leaning forwards on the table as she made her point.

Rob was visibly startled at her response.

'Um, sorry, guv. I didn't mean to...'

'You didn't mean to what?'

'I didn't mean to assume... to know what your response would be. Sorry. I just know what happened when...'

'Rob, cut the buttering-me-up bullshit and just tell me why you think this is a good idea.'

He swallowed hard again before he opened his mouth. It took a couple of attempts to get the words out. 'We... uh... we're pretty sure a third woman is likely to be targeted at the Illuminati, right?'

She nodded.

‘We also know the first three victims were taken from at or near the Cognoscenti nightclub, and with Dominique starting – or potentially starting – another three snatches, and we have proof now of a second there. So, we were thinking we should cover that possibility. We haven’t got any time to lose.’

Cramer had a poker face. The pressure of the case was taking its toll, and it seemed much longer than only this afternoon since they had confirmed Helena had been taken. The weight of the case was pressing more heavily on Cramer at this moment than possibly at any other time so far.

‘I’m not saying no – I’m not saying anything yet. We have two priorities: find Helena, and stop any further women being hurt. We need to focus on both, and our resources are limited.’ She looked at her watch. ‘I have to speak to Davo, but I will think about it.’ She thought about smiling to soften her demeanour. But she didn’t have it in her.

She picked up her file, which was next to her on the table, and buzzed herself out of the incident room with her ID card on a lanyard, before heading upstairs, leaving Jill, Rob, and Leila in silence.

Chapter 40

Davidson's door was already open by the time Cramer reached it, and he was busy with paperwork as she approached. He looked up as he heard her footsteps and waved her in before she even had time to knock.

'Close the door, Cramer,' he said. 'What do you have?'

She was unimpressed with the singular 'you' rather than the collective 'we'.

'Some major developments, sir.'

'Good, it's about time. Go on.'

Cramer tried to hide her annoyance at his casual put-down, but her face generally told the story that was playing in her head anyway.

'As you know from my report, we're working on Jill Traverne's theory that the women are being snatched in threes – three from the Cognoscenti, and now two from the Illuminati – we have confirmed from CCTV that Helena was taken from there last night.'

Davidson looked her square in the eye. 'Can we identify who she was with?'

Cramer sighed. 'No. He – and it was a man – seemed to know exactly where every CCTV camera was and how to avoid it. He wasn't wearing anything distinctive – a white shirt. No tattoos we could see. Nothing. We have his arms, but in an infrared camera film, and there's very little we can do with that.'

Davidson grunted. He had never been a man of many words, but his face said more than he ever did.

Cramer carried on. 'We have identified some other things from footage though. The car Dominique Monroe was abducted in was a Porsche 911 Carrera...'

'You get a plate?'

Cramer shook her head. 'Footage is too grainy, and nothing on the ANPR either – it looks like the plates have been doctored so they won't be picked up. We've enhanced the images as much as we can, but they still don't give us enough.

'We've had it confirmed though that Dominique Monroe had GHB in her system – he killed her so soon after she was taken, there wasn't enough time for it to metabolise out. That's how he's subduing his victims. I'm getting a full report from the lab tomorrow – I'll send it through.'

Davidson just nodded. He was offering nothing.

'What Leila Johnson is also working on, among other things, is trying to cross-reference information with DVLA to find anyone locally who may own a Porsche 911 Carrera and a four-by-four of some kind. Drivers who have both could narrow it down and give us a reasonable list of suspects. These aren't cheap cars, so there aren't likely to be many people who have both.'

Davidson again just nodded. He was still giving her nothing. She took a deep breath before she told him the next development.

'We also have a possible motive for the killer. We think he believes these women are witches.'

Davidson's face changed at that. 'Witches? Why the hell do you think that?'

'I know. I know this sounds far-fetched, but hear me out, sir. Jill and I consulted with a professor specialising in the history of the occult at the university, who explained that shaving all the body hair was common practice during the witch trials, so the women couldn't hide—'

Davidson held his hand up, clearly irritated. 'You'd better have some bloody good information to back this up, Cramer. And I mean more than just the word of a history professor who gets his rocks off by studying women being tortured.'

Cramer opened the file she was holding and began to go through the details about the *Malleus Maleficarum*, how the Bible quotes being used appeared in there as well as the King James Bible, including the passages about the need to shave body hair. It was all there, and it was the most plausible explanation they had.

Davidson listened without interrupting. When she'd finished talking, his face suggested he could go either way. The moments before he spoke were agony.

'It sounds implausible,' he finally said, 'but run with it. We have too much at stake to ignore any potential lead. I've given you almost as much leeway on this as I can, Callie, but I'm getting pressure from above for results, and shit runs downhill. So, unless we get some concrete answers and soon, we're both going to feel the full force of the press and the top brass

'Tenuous as this sounds, I agree it's progress – of sorts. Go with it. But keep me informed... I mean properly informed.'

Cramer hadn't realised she had been holding her breath, but she suddenly felt herself take a deep breath in.

'Thank you, sir. Just one more thing...' She really wasn't sure how far she should push it. 'I want to ask you for clearance to run an undercover operation with DC Leila Johnson and DS Rob Gulliver at the Illuminati club. It would involve more overtime. But I think it's important and could lead to information that will help us find Helena and ensure no one else is taken.'

Davidson stood up from his chair, walked around behind it, and stood looking at his various awards, his back to Cramer. He dropped his head forwards, before looking back at the wall with his commendation and the group photograph of the day he left the police training college.

'Sir?'

He didn't respond.

'Will you clear that?'

He put his head down and slowly turned around towards Cramer, leaning his hands on the desk, his pot belly, the legacy of long lunches and too many hours driving a desk, lurched over his belt. He fixed his stare at Cramer.

'After what happened last time? I'm surprised you're even asking me this.' He took a deep breath in.

Cramer looked him square in the eye, refusing to be intimidated. 'If I thought there was an alternative, I wouldn't ask you, sir. But there isn't.'

Davo stood to his full height. 'I will clear two days of overtime. If you have nothing after that, then you stop. I'm not writing you a blank cheque on this, Cramer.'

'Thank you, sir. I understand.'

'Make it count. I don't want another fucking disaster on my hands any more than you do. And the last thing I want to see is the body of the Home Secretary's daughter in a report on the evening news. You find her and get her home. Do you understand?'

Chapter 41

Cramer pulled Rob and Leila into her office when she came back from her meeting with Davidson. She needed to refocus to explain the plan to both detectives.

Leila and Rob followed her in and Cramer indicated to them both to take a seat opposite her desk. There was only one there, so Rob, always the gentleman, left that one for Leila and moved one from the other side of the room for himself.

Cramer sat uneasily behind her desk, her elbows on top of the case file, which was now open by the side of her computer, her fingers intertwined and facing her detectives.

'Davo has signed off two days' worth of overtime for you to go undercover. That's all we have, and believe me, we need results.'

The pair of them smiled and high-fived yet again. Cramer wasn't impressed.

'Look. We need to be smarter. So far, we've been one step behind, which makes me uncomfortable. Now we've a chance to move forward in a definite direction. So, I'm relying on you both to not screw this up. Are we clear?'

'Yes, ma'am,' said Rob quickly, clearly picking up on the seriousness of her tone.

'I want Max and Jack brought in on this and we need to move tomorrow. I'll make sure the uniforms sweep that area more than normal tonight. Leila, we need comms, can you set that up?'

'Yes, guv.' She got up to leave.

She headed out of her boss's office and through the glass walls, Cramer saw her go straight for the phone.

Cramer turned to her screen, ready to start processing the paperwork for the overtime, but Rob was still in his chair.

'Guv, one thing I wanted to ask. Should we be thinking of this professor as a possible suspect? I mean, he came up with that theory pretty quickly, right? I just wonder whether there's more to it than that.'

Cramer leaned back in her chair and started chewing the inside of her cheek. When he'd picked her up on the 'so far' comment, she thought there was something odd about him, like he was thinking someone else was already being held. Now Rob had raised his concerns, it solidified more in her mind. Collinson was passionate about the topic, and relatively dispassionate about the women being hurt. That unnerved her.

'I'll get Max and Jack to look into him on the night shift. We can make a firm decision tomorrow when we've got more background.'

Rob just tapped twice on her desk with his fingers as he got up from his chair and went to leave, but stopped at the door and turned around. 'I'm sorry, guv. About earlier I mean.'

Cramer raised her head in recognition of the apology. She'd nothing else to say. She struggled to talk about her colleague being killed at all. Talking about it at length, and in public just a day ago, didn't go well. She wasn't ready to bring it up again. Besides, they all needed to focus.

Helena's time was ticking.

Chapter 42

Cramer had decided to go to Simms to pick up the full toxicology and blood reports rather than have it take any longer to get what they needed. Plus, a change of scenery was as good as a rest. She felt a bit stir crazy.

Simms's offices were also at the University of Kent, where he taught part-time as a professor of forensic science, when he wasn't out in the field. By now, almost everyone would have left for the day. But she knew he always worked late, so had called ahead to let him know she was on the way. He hadn't answered, so she left a voicemail and went over on the off-chance he would still be around.

She opened the heavy door which led through to the forensic-science department, and was surprised when she saw Simms's secretary Joanna still sitting at the desk outside his office. Cramer could see Simms in one of the meeting rooms, talking intently with a woman who had her back to the glass.

Joanna looked up from her keyboard as she approached. 'Hi Callie, surprised to see you here. Can I help?' Joanna had never really been one for small talk.

'I've just popped in to see John about a report he's got for me.'

'The toxicology one? And bloods?' She went through a pile of papers on her desk and handed a thin file to Cramer.

'Amazing, thanks,' Cramer said, marvelling at her incredible efficiency. Just as Cramer turned to leave, she noticed Simms had caught sight of her and put her hand up to wave. He suddenly got up from his seat opposite the woman in the meeting room and made his way around to the door and yanked it open.

'Callie, perfect timing. You got a minute?'

Cramer nodded. Simms held the door for her, and Cramer entered, taking a seat at the long meeting table in the centre. As she passed the woman sitting down, she noticed how petite she looked. She had olive skin and long dark brown, almost chestnut hair that fell in long curls down her back and over her shoulders.

Simms closed the door and took his place again. 'Callie, let me introduce you to Dr Santi Sandalo. Santi, this is DCI Caroline Cramer.'

'Acting...' Cramer corrected.

'Yeah, but not for long, eh?' Simms said, with a wink, which made Cramer smile.

'Nice to meet you, DCI Cramer,' Dr Sandalo said, extending her hand in greeting. Cramer shook it and then got herself comfortable in her seat.

Simms looked excited, as if he was about to burst. 'You OK, John?' Cramer asked.

'Yes, yes very OK, thanks. I'm so glad you turned up because Dr Sandalo has been working on something I think could help us.'

Cramer raised her eyebrows as Simms carried on.

'Santi was a student of mine here around ten years ago and has gone on to do great things since. I'm hoping I can tempt her back here to work with me...'

'How's that going?' Cramer looked at them both.

'So far, so good I think...' Simms responded with a grin aimed towards Dr Sandalo.

She laughed at him. 'We'll see. You haven't given me all the terms yet,' she joked.

'Anyway, that's not why I asked you in, Callie,' said Simms. 'Santi has been working on something that may be useful for us. Santi, can you explain?'

'I've been working on something called the "Unique Anatomy Project" which was started in Scotland.' As she spoke, Santi began to look more animated. 'We're creating a database of hand images to teach computers to read and identify unique parts of people's hands and arms to use in criminal cases, including those against child abusers. We want to enable computers to locate and extract anatomical features from the hand. The algorithms we develop can then be used by the police to search their own databases of images to match perpetrator and suspect in cases such as child sexual abuse.

'What was originally discovered more than a decade ago was that the vein patterns we have in our hands are unique to each of us, like a fingerprint. They are formed in the fetus within the first few weeks after fertilisation, and when the heart beats for the first time, the vein and arterial patterns are established.'

Cramer was transfixed. She'd never heard of vein patterns before, let alone them being used to identify someone. How had she never heard of this? She suddenly felt very out of touch and immediately looked down at the back of her own hands, turning her palms upwards and then down again, before she returned her gaze to the woman speaking.

Dr Sandalo continued. 'We're using specific parts of the hand and arm to identify these individuals. Knuckle creases, scars, moles, and the vein patterns, which show up black under infrared light. Here, let me show you.' She pulled out her phone and flicked her finger across the screen. Once she'd found what she was looking for, she passed the phone to Cramer. The image Sandalo had pulled up showed a hand and forearm under infrared light, the veins jumped out of the images as black rivers cutting through brighter grey regions of skin in what looked like regular black and white images.

'In the very first case it was used, the jury failed to convict,' Sandalo added. 'Not because they weren't convinced about the technology, which at that stage was in its infancy, but instead, because the young girl in the case simply hadn't looked upset enough. She hadn't cried.'

This made Cramer's blood boil. Anyone with any experience of childhood trauma or working with traumatised children knows that most kids shut down their emotions, become numb. That's exactly what she had done and, as a result, she couldn't remember much of the years she spent in her teens. It's the only way of dealing with it. To Cramer, it was hard to fathom the level of icy heart you'd need to have to think that's a reason for not convicting an abuser. But she worked within the justice system and knew too well how it threw up anomalies that you couldn't make sense of. She just hoped that with the jury in Kane's case, he would get what he deserved.

'I wasn't working with the team at that stage, which I'm glad about because that would have been really hard to take,' Sandalo said. She may not have been involved with that case, but Cramer could see that Sandalo's eyes burned with rage at the thought. 'But, since then we have managed to convict a lot of paedophiles with this technology, and we are working to advance it all the time.'

'This sounds amazing, but...' Cramer looked at Simms, 'what's the connection, John?'

His eyes started to sparkle. 'We have infrared images, Callie. Of his arm, his forearm, and his hand. We might be able to use these to identify him, if he's on the database. Right?' He looked at Sandalo for confirmation.

She looked at him a little perplexed. 'Well, actually no. The database itself can't be used to just do a random search – that isn't ethically or legally allowed. Even if we did find someone to match your suspect, it would be inadmissible. But that's irrelevant, I wouldn't cross that line. Sorry.'

Both Simms and Cramer looked crestfallen. This was a potential lead that could help to save both Helena and Leila, and yet it was one they couldn't exploit.

Cramer thought long and hard before asking her next question after Sandalo's response.

'Could I send the images to you anyway? Even if you could give us some insight based on what they show, that might be useful. There is a lot a stake for so many people. I just want to explore every avenue.'

Sandalo smiled and nodded. 'Of course, I understand. As long as you appreciate that I can't breach the ethical code on this and I won't do anything illegal. But I'm happy to have a look at the images for you, it's the least I can do.' Sandalo added. 'Can you send me the images in high res?'

'How high res, I'm not sure. But yes, I'll get them over in the best way I can.'

Sandalo started patting pockets in her jacket and then put her hand into the last one and pulled out her business card. 'Send them to me at that email address.'

Chapter 43

By the time she'd caught Jack and Max up on everything that had happened in the day, and what she wanted them to do on the night shift, it was time for Cramer to head home. She'd been thinking about the undercover operation and wanted all five of them on duty. More people looking out for each other meant less chance of something going wrong. She wasn't taking any chances after Adam. The guys had been eager, which was something, but she had one more thing to do before leaving.

Even though Sandalo had been clear she couldn't trawl the Unique Anatomy Project database for Cramer, she had agreed to take a look at the CCTV images they had of their suspect's arm and hand. Cramer opened her email attached the images and sent them.

She left it a few minutes before calling Sandalo to make sure they had arrived safely.

'Ah, DCI Cramer, hang on...' Cramer could hear mouse activity on the other end of the line as Sandalo opened the files she'd sent.

'Yes, got them. Thanks. As I said, I don't think there is much I can do to help, but I will review the images you've sent.'

'I'm sorry they're not better quality,' Cramer offered, 'but if there's anything you can do with them to boost the detail, I'd be grateful.'

'They look fine to me,' said Sandalo. Her tone was clipped and she sounded a little distracted, so Cramer left her to it, ending the call feeling a little deflated.

Her phone rang again as she got into her car and she was momentarily enthused thinking it was Sandalo back already. But it was Charlie. Cramer had forgotten all about calling her, things had moved on so quickly. She answered it on Bluetooth so she could drive and talk at the same time.

'Charlie, have you seriously only just got out of bed?'

'Haha, very funny, cuz! I was waiting for you to call back, but you never did, so thought I'd call you back. What's going on?'

'Nothing, just driving home actually.'

'I didn't mean with you. I meant what you were asking me about earlier. About Helena.'

She had to be careful how she answered this.

'Oh, it was nothing. I saw her mum and asked her about how she was doing in the end, that's why I didn't call you. Thought I'd leave you to your beauty sleep. You out again tonight?'

She really hoped the answer was no.

'Nah, I'm meeting friends for dinner and having a quiet one. It was pretty heavy last night – I only shifted my hangover two hours ago.'

'Oh, for goodness' sake...'

'Don't, Callie, you sound like Mummy.'

Cramer snorted a laugh. That was the last thing she wanted – she already felt older than her years.

'OK, I'll stop. Listen, gotta go – I've just reached home. Catch up before you go back to uni though, yeah?'

The call ended just as she turned into her driveway. It took about a minute more to drive up to the house. The lights were on, so Patrick was already home. She hadn't seen him for a couple of days – he'd been away again. Apparently. But she had expected him back sooner than this. His own Porsche 911 Carrera was sitting abandoned – you couldn't call that parking – on the drive, next to her Range Rover.

She hadn't used that car in a few weeks, and last time she had it was immaculate, so the fact it was now covered in mud meant Patrick had clearly used it without asking. He knew how much that pissed her off.

Cramer parked up, grabbed her torch from the glove box and opened her door to get out and move towards it, shining the light on the mud flaps, the door sills – mud had even reached as high as the wing mirror. Whatever he'd done with it, he'd made a bloody mess.

As she went into the house, she expected Patrick to be in the kitchen – he usually was. But he was nowhere to be seen. She knew he was home – not only had she seen lights in the house from the driveway, she'd already seen his car outside, but there was also an empty wine glass on the kitchen counter. He'd been drinking again. But at least he was out of the way.

It was just as well. All she could think about was Helena. Where was she? What might be happening right now? She reached for the open wine bottle and pour herself a glass.

The front door slamming behind her caused her to flick her head up, but she only heard rushing footsteps and then the crunch of gravel as Patrick did a wheel spin on the drive, the Porsche's throaty engine growling as he hurtled away from the house. He must be over the limit. Should she get him picked up? She couldn't be sure, the wine bottle had only been one glass down by the time she poured hers.

She picked up her phone ready to dial Jack's number. She would see if he could follow him on the ANPR cameras and see where he went to. But how the hell could she explain this without him thinking it was just a domestic? And an abuse of police resources? She paused.

'Shit.'

She threw her phone down and tried to stop her mind playing tricks on her. The pressure must be getting to her.

Chapter 44

Jack had tasked Max with doing the desk research on Professor Collinson and the resulting report proved to be interesting reading.

Collinson had been something of a child prodigy; gone to Cambridge University at sixteen, having completed his A levels in the time most students were still struggling through their GCSEs. Precocious little shit.

His family had been highly talented. His mother was a theologian with a PhD. She had travelled the world as a lecturer before she settled down with his father, a biochemist, who also had a PhD – talk about being blessed with genetics. They were wealthy too, and had money to buy their precious son the best education, which allowed Simon the freedom to take exams early, something that would have been so difficult to achieve in the state system.

Jack, who always compared himself to others despite it being a thief of joy, had consoled himself with the fact that he was likely to be a better athlete than this brain box. But then Max discovered Collinson had also been captain of the university hockey team.

'Utter bollocks,' Jack spat. 'He must have flaws somewhere.'

Jack was jealous of this man although he would never admit it. But he tried to remain open-minded as he headed out to check on Collinson's address.

Leila had identified that his car was a Land Rover Discovery, but they couldn't find any reference to a Porsche 911 Carrera in his name yet, or any that he might have access to. His home address was in a village about ten miles outside Canterbury – a 'country pile' as Max so eloquently put it. Life, thought Jack, was just not fair.

He parked his car in the street closest to the back of Collinson's house. The guy had a one-hundred-metre driveway, so there was no way of seeing the property from the front that wouldn't give away the surveillance Jack was doing. But where he was would still give him a good view of any vehicle coming in or out. Jack had been trained by the best in the military, and then trained the best before he left to pursue police work.

He sat quietly in the car for a while with the lights off. Luckily, the weather was warm enough for him to spend time comfortably waiting overnight. He had coffee and a paper, which he could still read by the sodium-orange of the street lights – clearly this road hadn't been converted to LED lights as yet – and settled in for a few hours of surveillance.

There was something about the solitude this part of his job offered that appealed to him. It allowed him to make sense of some of the complications in his life, which working nights also gave him time to get away from. But just as he was settling down, Collinson's car came shooting out of the drive, headed towards Canterbury.

'Shit!' Jack threw the paper down on the passenger seat and waited until the car was just out of sight before starting his engine and putting his lights on. Doing this too soon would be a dead giveaway of a follow. But too late could mean losing the target.

He moved off and kept eyes on Collinson's car, sure not to get too close or be too obvious. He called Max to let him know that he was now mobile and checked the reg plate with him. Yep. That was his car.

He followed Collinson all the way through the backstreets into Canterbury, where he drove towards the station. Collinson stopped outside and looked like he was waiting to pick someone up. Jack stopped further back and waited.

'What are you up to?' Jack muttered under his breath.

Collinson didn't move, his car was idling with the lights on. Jack couldn't see what direction he was looking in, so decided to park up and leave his car briefly. He walked down the street towards Collinson's car to get a better view, without raising suspicion.

Play it cool, Jack thought as he ambled past.

Collinson's car was still idling at the kerb as Jack stopped to look at a noticeboard outside the station. He saw Collinson move off from his position and turn into the station car park. He might have made a mistake in leaving his car if Collinson decided to turn around and head off; it would take Jack time to get back to it and he might have lost Collinson by then. But he breathed a sigh of relief when he saw Collinson park up and get out of the car.

Jack heard the double beep as the Discovery locked, accompanied by the flash of the indicators. Collinson was then walking towards him, past the station. Towards the Illuminati nightclub.

He continued to look at the station noticeboard while also keeping an eye on what Collinson was doing and where he was going. Jack watched as Collinson got to the edge of the road opposite the club and then stopped. He looked uneasy.

Jack stayed put, following a notice about football practice with his finger to make it look more authentic. Collinson still hadn't moved. He was still opposite the club, watching. Then without warning, he turned on his heel and went straight back to his car in the station car park.

'Shit,' Jack hissed to himself, realising he was going to need to make a run for it.

He pulled his phone out of his pocket, as if he had an urgent call, and raced back to his car, where he waited to see where Collinson went next.

By the time Collinson left the car park, Jack had started the engine, hadn't yet turned on the lights, but was ready to go. He would need to do a U-turn to follow, and that had to be done out of sight.

Collinson flashed past him, back down the road they had driven up no more than ten minutes before.

Jack again waited until the right moment, then pulled the U-turn in front of another car coming from the opposite direction, resulting in the other driver sounding his horn. Not ideal – he was trying not to attract attention – but it didn't matter, as he caught sight of Collinson at the next junction and watched him turn left. Was he heading back home? Really? Jack followed.

Collinson weaved through the backstreets out of the city and back into the country. Jack kept far enough away to avoid suspicion but was close enough again not to lose sight. As Collinson drove into his driveway, Jack drove past the house and took up his space exactly where he had been before.

Jack opened his car window so he could hear when the vehicle had been locked again and saw the double glow of the indicators as they confirmed the car was secure. He waited to be sure Collinson had gone into the house before he relaxed.

The lights in the house remained on for the next three quarters of an hour, and Jack had resigned himself to not move off until he knew Collinson was asleep. After the lights had been out for about twenty minutes, he decided he would take a closer look at the property. Patience was a virtue in this game.

He moved round the perimeter of the house, which had a six-foot-high wall around two feet thick, sleek grey stone with leylandii trees growing another six feet above the top of the wall, offering the property a great deal of privacy. Jack didn't plan to trespass but would see what he could from the public highway, in case there was anything useful or relevant.

As he came around to the opening on the driveway, he noticed a CCTV camera, which would prevent him from doing anything other than passing by. Bollocks. It would look really suspicious now if he went back too quickly if Collinson checked the footage. He would have to go around the block to get back to the car.

After thirty minutes and three right turns, Jack reached his car and decided to head back to the station. He wasn't sure what he'd learned following Collinson, but often the smallest things had the biggest impact on a case.

When he keyed himself into the incident room, Max already had coffee on the go. Jack got one for himself and then sat down at his desk.

'So, anything?' Max asked.

'Yeah, maybe. I followed him from the house to Illuminati. He just stood opposite it – I thought he was going to go over, but he just stood there. Bit weird, right? But then, it was like he felt really uncomfortable, turned tail, went back to his car, and straight home.

'His place has a six-foot wall with huge trees behind, so it's almost completely shielded from the road, and there's a CCTV system that monitors the gate. I didn't have a chance to get a good look. Can we find anything online that would help?'

Max smiled knowingly and passed Jack four sheets of paper. 'Yes, really helpful. He bought his house less than eighteen months ago, and there are more than twenty pictures of the best elements of the inside and the outside still online. Take a look.'

He snatched the paperwork from Max's hand. He wasn't impressed that this desk jockey sitting comfortably inside got more out of the evening and his target than he had managed to do with boots on the ground. Old school was becoming obsolete thanks to Google. He looked through the pages, but the printing wasn't clear.

'These look in a shit state, mate. Does the printer need sorting or something? Or can I look at this online?'

'Sure, I thought you might want it printed off, though – you know, old school.' Max grinned.

Jack snorted. Cheeky little shit.

He jumped into his chair and started looking through the images online, scrolling through the pictures one by one, and then clicking to enlarge any he was most interested in.

'Interesting, right?' Max said.

'Yeah. Very interesting indeed.'

Chapter 45

Jack and Max still had two hours of their shift left when Cramer got in the next morning. She'd woken up a few hours before her alarm was due to go off. In that brief time before the reality of the day creeps in, she'd battled with her thoughts, and when sleep evaded her, she decided to just have a shower and head into the station. Wisely, Patrick had slept in one of the spare rooms again. Or, at least, she assumed he had. Thinking about it, she hadn't heard him come home last night.

Cramer saw Jack first as she entered the office. He was typing with his two index fingers as always, which was painful to watch. He was grumbling to himself as he hit the delete button hard around ten times, typed again, and repeated the pattern.

'For fuck's sake!' Jack slammed his hand on the table, furious at his slow progress. She didn't think he had any idea she was there until she spoke to him.

'Jack, what's the problem?' She asked.

Adam had been able to touch-type. It was amazing the small things that made her thoughts head back to him.

'All right, guv, couldn't sleep?'

'Don't try and change the subject, Jack. What was that about?' Cramer wasn't going to let it drop.

'Ah, just frustrated, boss, nothing major.'

'It didn't look like nothing to me. You need to get a grip on that anger, Jack, it's not helpful. For any of us.'

He looked furious, but she knew he wouldn't say anything against his boss. She wasn't surprised when he tried to change the subject.

'I think the real reason you're in early is because you just wanted to see me and Max before the rest of the crew came in – you know we're the best-looking detectives you have.'

She laughed as she walked to her office to take off her jacket and dump her bag. She would keep an eye on his behaviour, but for now, it was best to defuse the situation.

'Steady, Jack, I can't take that much humour this early in the morning,' Cramer countered already heading over to the coffee machine for the first hit of caffeine in what she knew was going to be another very long day.

When her mug was full, she perched herself on the edge of the desk to talk to the two detectives in front of her.

'So, what happened on your night shift?'

'Actually, guv, all joking aside, it was a pretty interesting night,' Jack said. 'Your professor was... well... a bit odd.'

'Really? How?' She took a gulp of coffee. It tasted bitter. Must have been stewing for a while.

'I've written a full report.' Jack picked a paper folder up off his desk and held it towards her. 'The short version is he left home in the middle of the night, went to the station and parked, stood opposite the nightclub like he was going to go across and go in, and then turned straight back around and drove home. Odd.'

Cramer had to admit it didn't make much sense. Her and Rob's instinct was spot on, and it looked like they had been right to get Jack on Collinson's back for an evening. She took the file from his hand and started leafing through it.

'Did he see you, Jack? Was he spooked?'

'Yeah, I think he was spooked, but not by me. He just... changed his mind. Something must have made him think twice. But I really don't know what. His house is bloody impressive though, guv – thick stone walls, ancient-looking, you know? He has a real thing about security too – high-end system. Not sure if he wants to keep people out, or in.'

'OK, I'll read the report. Thanks, Jack.'

She headed into her office, sat behind her desk and unlocked her computer. She had to finish her own report for Davo before he got in and wanted to clear it out of the way before the rest of the team arrived so they could focus on preparing for the Illuminati op.

A few hours later, and unusually, Jill was next to arrive. Cramer had just sent her update to Davidson and had read through Jack's report. Collinson's behaviour made it clear they should take a closer look at him; he should be pushed up to suspect status. After his activity last night, she would get Jack to do more surveillance on him.

She was deep in thought when Jill tapped on her door.

'Penny for them?' Jill said as she walked into Cramer's office, taking her coat off and putting her things on the desk in the corner near the incident board.

Cramer laughed. 'If you gave me a penny for my thoughts right now, Jill, you'd have been robbed. Besides, getting inside my head isn't a good thing – you might never get out again.'

Jill put a coffee cup on Cramer's desk and then sipped her own as she pulled up the chair. Cramer knew from her own interview training it was simply so they could be at the same level.

'What's going on? Apart from the obvious.' Jill swept her hand round towards the white board in the office.

Cramer sighed. 'I wouldn't know where to start.'

'I don't blame you for being nervous about the operation tonight.'

Cramer pushed herself back from her desk in frustration. 'Oh, for Christ's sake, Jill. Don't you start! I had that from Rob yesterday.'

'I know, but he doesn't know you like I do, so don't try to kid me when I know more about how you feel than you do half the time.'

Cramer pursed her lips. Jill wasn't wrong.

'Well, it's your job.' Cramer half smiled, then her demeanour softened. 'You're right, I am nervous. The last time I was involved with undercover work, Adam was killed. Now, in the same week I had to go over that with a fine-toothed comb in court, and we are planning more of the same in a case that couldn't be more crucial to solve quickly.'

'I know, and I understand. But that's why Rob and Leila suggested it. Having someone in the club could give us a lead we've been missing. It's worth a shot.'

Cramer rolled her eyes. 'Of course it is, otherwise I wouldn't have got Davo to sign off the overtime. But I want backup outside too, and full comms on this. Leila was sorting that out, so it had better be done.'

'You do give her a hard time, Cal, you know. I'm not sure she always deserves it.'

Cramer was impassive.

'Well, it makes it harder for us when her bloody boyfriend is writing inaccurate stories about us in the papers.'

'Are they inaccurate? Or do you just not like them?' Cramer stared as Jill waited patiently for an answer. She changed the subject.

'Jack had an interesting evening with Professor Collinson. Went from his house after dark, to the train station, parked, then stood opposite Illuminati, just looking at it. For about two to three minutes.'

'Why the hell would he do that?'

'Maybe he knows more about this than we thought. It might not be just an academic interest,' said Cramer.

'I wouldn't have said so from the conversation we had yesterday. His body language was relaxed, calm, he was a bit cocky, of course, but...'

'I agree, but the fact is he left his home to go to Illuminati. We know two people were taken from there, and with potentially still one more to be taken. It might be he planned that last night but knew Jack was on to him and decided against it. Jack's convinced Collinson had no idea he was following him, and he should know. So, as it currently stands, it was just odd behaviour we can't ignore it. Just in case.'

'He did make time in his schedule pretty quickly for us yesterday,' said Jill. 'I know having police want to come and speak to you can do that to some people, and maybe that's why he was so keen to help. Are you going to put Jack on him again tonight?'

Cramer thought about it. 'I need to. We'll need Max and me in the comms van, and I'll get Jack to track Collinson's movements for the evening. He may not move, in which case we'll pull Jack back to the club, but we need him covered. So far, he hasn't done anything wrong. It isn't illegal to stand on the street looking at a club, but the timing's off. And we don't have the luxury of taking a chance.'

Chapter 46

Canterbury was the end of a pilgrimage for him. A holy pilgrimage. He'd been working across the country during his life, but now he was back. He was home.

The famous cathedral had extraordinary vaulted ceilings, and he liked nothing more than to spend time sitting beneath them, looking up. The building's magnificence was wasted on so many of the tourists sharing this space with him. Americans. Italians. Spanish. Loathsome British. They had no idea what they were looking at or how important it was.

The history. The sacrifice. The pilgrims. The wars fought in the name of Christianity by the Knights Templar. But it was Henry II's knights who killed the then Archbishop of Canterbury, Thomas Becket, in 1170, in his own cathedral that specifically interested him.

The site of his death, where four knights hacked him apart with their swords, is marked today by the Altar of the Sword's Point. The culture associated with this seat of religion couldn't be underestimated. Yet one look at those snivelling, overweight, dim people trudging around inside it showed him how little regard it was held in now.

This was one of his favourite places. He spent time here as often as he could. The Martyrdom. He could relate to that. He made sacrifices for his work. Every day.

He overheard an American crowing over how 'pretty' the cathedral was. How degrading. It was so much more than that. But that was being forgotten in a flurry of money and tourism. Something he would change if he could.

He got up from the pew he had been sitting on in the Martyrdom, where he'd been watching the crowds as they milled around the tombs, the exhibitions. It was a tourist attraction now. A travesty. A religious Disneyland. It disgusted him.

People needed reminding of the miracles that happened there. Of the sacrifices others had made. That he had made. For them.

Chapter 47

Helena couldn't understand why he continued to hurt her. She'd answered his question, and she was sure she was right. But he'd hit her again, so it can't have been. Her reality was skewed. This was surely a nightmare.

Yet here she was, and each time the answer wasn't the one he wanted. The blows were going into her stomach. If she had wanted to sleep, the pain of those alone would have kept her awake.

She could tell that her femur had been at least fractured the previous day, the swelling and pain was unbearable as the blood surged towards it.

She was angry, confused, trying to do what was being asked of her, but each time, she failed. So, she tried again. He was getting angrier. There was no end in sight. In that moment, she got angry too. *'Fuck it,'* she told herself. *'He's gonna do what he wants anyway. I'm not playing this game anymore.'*

Her body and mind were beginning to work independently of each other, an effective bid to deal with and manage the pain she was in both physically and mentally.

In the last few minutes, her mind felt stronger. For the first time since she had been in this position, she felt some sense of calm. Detached, like she was now capable of dealing with anything that was thrown at her. There didn't seem to be a reason for it, maybe she'd just reached her limit.

He suddenly stopped talking to her. He stared at her as he walked backwards away from her, before turning slowly and heading out of the door he had come in through. Perhaps he'd seen the change in her too.

She breathed a sigh of relief. It was over for now. She could feel the fresh bruises throbbing already.

Her attention was caught by something else. What was that smell? It was like an electrical fault, a burning. Helena had resigned herself to whatever came next. If there was a fire, she had no hope of escape.

Then, he returned. This time he wasn't facing her as he entered the room; she could only see his back. He was moving slowly, deliberately.

It was only as he turned that she could see the burning white tip of the metal rod, superheated so it glowed in the darkness around her. Her eyes flashed wide.

'What are you doing?'

He stood, staring at her without any emotion in his face, moving the sulphurous white iron towards her eyes.

'This is to encourage it to get it right. If not, it's going to get very painful.'

She snatched for breath as she struggled to suck air in. She tried to back away as the near-molten metal came closer to her. He pushed his face close to hers and whispered into her ear.

'Now, tell me the Lord's Prayer correctly. Or face the trial by hot iron.'

Her face creased. 'I have told you it. I have. I know I have. Why do you keep saying I haven't?'

'Because it doesn't know the right version.'

He held the iron up towards her face again, the heat getting more intense at it came closer.

'If it prefers, it can carry this iron in its hand for three paces. If it succeeds, it will be freed.'

Helena felt a pang of hope. Did he mean it? No, he couldn't. But then, why say it if not? She argued internally about whether to take the offer. It would sear her skin, yes, but she could manage three paces she was sure. Then she could go home to the people she loved.

'I'll do it. Let me do it. Please.'

He smiled as she continued to beg. Then turned abruptly away from her, moving towards the shadowy corner of the room where she couldn't see what he was doing.

What was going on? Why was she trying to bargain with a psycho? *Fuck it.* She had nothing to lose anymore. 'Let me go, you fucking freak. You're the one in the wrong! You, no one else. You're pathetic, fucking pathetic!' She spat in his direction.

He had been bending down but stood straight up at that and turned towards her. He had something in his hands, she couldn't see what it was until he moved towards her again. His eyes cold.

'It's going to regret that. It needs to understand who's in control. And keep a civil tongue in its head.'

He moved towards her with what looked like a rusting iron contraption. Her eyes grew wide as he moved it closer to her, wrenched open her mouth and pushed the spike of some metal head piece deep into her mouth. She tried to cry out as the pain seared through the back of her tongue, but even small movements were excruciating. She was gagging, the spike pressing so close to her soft palate she vomited and continued to gag, vomiting again immediately afterwards. The tears streamed down her face, from the force of the retching and her absolute terror.

He moved behind her and she both heard and felt the contraption lock at the back of her head. He couldn't leave this on her.

Then his face was less than a centimetre away from hers. She was struggling to breathe in or out, her body convulsing again.

'I don't want to hear it make another noise,' he hissed.

She couldn't talk, or move her head properly, but blinked once to say yes. She understood.

He left her just as she vomited again.

Chapter 48

The briefing before any big operation is always full of adrenaline. Everyone knows the risks involved in doing undercover work, but the rewards are usually far greater. So, the risks have to be accepted, and mitigated.

The high tension is usually accompanied by high jinks that allow people to let off a little steam. So, it was no surprise when Leila, who normally wore a trouser suit to work, got a few wolf whistles as she entered the room in a short, tight black dress that hugged her well-toned body. Her blonde hair was left down, falling seductively onto her shoulders, very different from the tight ponytail she usually wore in the office, and perfect for a night out. Rob had come in previously in a smart but casual suit with gelled hair, which received similar responses from the group to be fair. But Leila took it all in her stride.

'All right, fellas, calm yourselves down,' Leila said as she walked through the office towards her desk. 'No point in having your mouths water for food you're never going to get your fork into.'

'I don't think it is a fork anyone is thinking about getting into you,' said Jack. The banter was becoming seriously close to sexual harassment, thought Cramer, as general laughter rang round, a noise very alien to this particular incident room. Cramer stood at the front of the room watching the scene as

Leila clipped him around his cauliflower ear. He deserved it. She waited for things to settle enough to be heard.

'All right everyone. This op has been given the moniker Operation Themis. Rob and Leila, you will be call signs "Charlie One" and "Charlie Two" respectively, Jack you will be "Bravo One" and Collinson is "Echo One". Any other suspects you see inside the club will be "Target One" and so on. Everyone clear?'

They all nodded.

'Rob, Leila, I want you to head into the club. Keep your eyes open and your wits about you. We don't know who we're dealing with but get a feel for what's going on. See if there's anything untoward and report back. Have you both checked your comms are working?'

Both Rob and Leila nodded. 'But we'll check again onsite, guv,' Rob said.

'Don't know where the fuck you're hiding your radio, Leila,' said Jack, much to everyone else's amusement.

'Don't you worry about where my radio is, Jack. It's somewhere you'll never find it, that's for sure.' A chorus of laughter rang around again. Everyone was pumped.

Cramer worked to get the room back. 'OK, let's keep our minds on the job, Jack...' The room erupted again with what she had said, and couldn't help but laugh at her own accidental word play. She left it for a few seconds to allow the laughter to recede then carried on with the briefing.

'OK, listen up. Max and I will be in the comms van outside the club, call sign "Eagle One". Any problems and we'll be in straight away. We don't have a specific target, so keep your eyes peeled. But after Jack followed Professor Simon Collinson last night, he has certainly become a person of interest. You all have a photo of him in your folders, and Max and Jack have done some good work building up background on him. So, if you see him there, be sure to have eyes on him as much as possible, but don't be distracted by thinking he's the sole focus. He isn't.'

Everyone started flicking through the pages in the folder in front of them, and Rob pulled out Collinson's picture and held it up to get a better look.

'He's definitely a suspect then, guv?' Rob asked.

'After last night's little visit to the club, yes he is,' said Cramer. 'But leave him to Jack in the first instance.'

She turned towards DS Sargeant. 'Jack, you stay with Collinson and see what his movements are, if any.' Jack nodded. 'Keep in touch, and if you've no action after a significant amount of time, we'll take a view on what to do next.'

Cramer looked around the room.

'Anything suspicious, anyone you think needs a collar felt, report it. Don't go it alone. Got it? Any questions?'

A shake of heads. Everyone was ready.

Chapter 49

He opened the glove box in his car and pulled out the rolling tool bag that he took with him everywhere he went. He ripped open the Velcro and folded out his work kit, taking the vial out of the pocket and examining it in the fading sunlight. There was still enough left for one more.

He took the syringe, removed the cover from the needle and pushed it gently through the rubber membrane, making it squeak very slightly as it entered. He tipped it up until it was level with his eyes, the clear liquid filling the space below the tip of the needle. He slid it back out slightly, so the tip was in the liquid, and began to draw it down. There was a bubble in the syringe, he couldn't risk that. It could mess up the plan.

He pushed the end of the syringe to expel the liquid back into the bottle, shooting it right to the end and letting it roll down the sides of the bottle into a pool at the base, which was again above the tip of the needle. He pulled the syringe back again and drew the liquid down. No bubbles this time. He estimated its weight, around 60kg. He stopped drawing the liquid and pushed a tiny clear pearl of fluid out again. He knew he had the right amount.

He pushed the cover gently back over the needle. All he had to do now was wait.

Chapter 50

Leila and Rob made their way into the club and got themselves drinks at the bar before finding themselves a vantage point at a table. Looking for unusual behaviour in a club like Illuminati wasn't easy. It was a pickup joint, plain and simple, and Leila was already attracting attention from some of the men in the club, which could either prove to be a help or a hindrance. Only time would tell.

'You really do look great, Leila,' Rob said. 'You have a few admirers already.'

She looked around and then took a sip of her drink. Ordinarily she wouldn't have minded the attention, but tonight was different.

'Yeah, well we have work to do, and I can't imagine your wife would be too happy if she heard you say that to me, can you?'

'No, she'd probably cut my balls off,' said Rob, involuntarily crossing his legs to protect them from the thought.

'Quite right too.' Leila laughed.

Just then both their earpieces burst into life.

'Charlie One, Charlie Two. Comms check.' The dulcet tones of Max seared into their lugholes.

'Yes, clear,' said Leila.

'Loud and clear,' said Rob.

‘OK. Remember, kids, this isn’t a night out.’ Max was laughing as he said it.

‘Funny, I thought that’s exactly what this was,’ Rob said. ‘Keep the channel clear, you weasel. We’ll let you know if anything happens.’

‘We should split up, Rob. We’re more likely to chat to people that way. You never know, you might even get lucky,’ said Leila.

Rob laughed. ‘After what I just told you? Yeah, OK. But stay in my line of sight at all times. I don’t want us to split up completely.’

‘Don’t be scared, Rob – I’m here to protect you,’ Leila laughed as she said it, but Rob looked slightly annoyed. ‘So, you stay in my line of sight, Mr Gulliver, I’m just as capable as you are of taking care of myself.’

Chapter 51

Jack had settled himself in the same spot as he had been the night before. He hadn't expected the space to be available a second night in a row, but it meant he had the same clear view of Collinson's driveway. Consistency could be useful in this line of work.

The lights were on in the house, and Jack settled in for a few hours of surveillance. That was the thing about being on plot: one day was very much like the next, until you had something change unexpectedly. You had to be ready for anything.

Just minutes later, he heard the engine of the Discovery start and saw the lights as they swept down the driveway. Jack jumped into action, again careful to stay far enough away to avoid spooking Collinson as he drove towards Canterbury.

Jack pressed the redial on his car's Bluetooth and called his boss who was in the comms van outside the club for Operation Themis.

'Guv, he's on the move, heading towards Canterbury.'

'Thanks, Jack. Keep me updated,' said Cramer. 'Let us know if he is heading towards the club when you are near enough to know.'

Collinson followed exactly the same route as he had the night before, again parking at the station. Jack parked up himself, waiting to see Collinson leave his vehicle, and used his radio to update Cramer this time.

'Eagle One, Echo One has parked in the station again and is heading out of the car park now. He's stopped again opposite. He's waiting. You should be able to get eyes on him... now.'

Cramer looked out of the window in the back door that had a limo tint dark enough that you couldn't see in but allowed the occupants to see out.

'Got him Bravo One,' said Cramer. 'Standby.' There was some shuffling while Rob and Leila were patched in too. 'Charlie One, Charlie Two – Echo One is outside now. Standby.'

Jack watched as Collinson stood on the pavement opposite the club for around thirty seconds, before he stepped off and crossed the road, heading straight for the door. He bypassed the queue of people and went straight up to Marlon, who was managing the door. He seemed to know him, and after a bit of chat, Collinson shook his hand, presumably deposited some money in the bouncer's hefty mitt and he let him straight in.

'OK, Echo One is entering now, Bravo One to follow,' Cramer updated over the radio. 'Charlie One, Charlie Two, be aware. Keep your eyes peeled for anything else that looks out of place. He's coming in.'

Chapter 52

'Got it,' Rob replied.

'We'll stay close,' Leila responded. As she released her comms button, a jolt of static electricity made the muscles spasm in her leg. She jumped as the shock belted a second time into the inside of her thigh where her battery pack was hidden. It was clearly playing up.

She had placed herself at the bar, nursing a drink as she sat on a bar stool where she could see Collinson over to her left further down the bar. Her outfit was attracting attention, and she had batted away a few guys who had been interested in her and offered some cheesy one-liners and also one girl who had started chatting her up, which she felt particularly proud of.

But the shocks from her battery pack continued, making her jump each time the shock hit her body. It looked odd, and she was starting to see some people staring at her. The last thing she wanted was to attract unnecessary attention.

She tried to hide the involuntary movements from the people she was talking to, but she was beginning to feel a bit of a freak, and the shocks were getting more intense. The club was stiflingly hot, and the beads of sweat on her skin were causing some kind of short circuit.

She hadn't told anyone else in the team, but she had no choice now. They were getting unbearable, and she had to do something.

'Eagle One, my radio is shorting out and giving me electric shocks. I have to come off comms.'

'Wait, that isn't a good idea,' Rob said. 'Can't you dry it off or something? See what you can do rather than ditching it, I'd feel a lot happier with you talking to me.'

'Agreed,' Cramer responded. 'See what you can do and let us know. I really don't want you off comms.'

'OK, give me five minutes,' Leila said. 'And for what it's worth, I have just seen Echo One at the bar. Charlie One you might want to change places with me.'

Chapter 53

As she left the bar stool, Leila caught Rob going to replace her. It was a good spot to get eyes on more of the club than anywhere else. For now, if he had to be alone on comms, then it would be the most sensible place to be.

Leila sashayed through the throng and headed to the loos. With the customary queue for the ladies now already out of the door, she would have to wait. The shocks were still coming, more regularly now, and she was covering the involuntary movements they were causing by dancing.

Finally, she got into a cubicle, hitched up her skirt and peeled the tape holding the device to the inside of her thigh. She looked at the battery unit and used some toilet roll to wipe the sweat away. But just as she did this, it shocked her hand, and it was as much as she could do to keep hold of it. There was no choice: it was duff, and frankly it was a relief to get rid of it, but it did mean she couldn't communicate with the wider team.

She balled up the cables for the unit, which looked like it should have been decommissioned in the eighties, and she shook her head in disbelief that it had malfunctioned so badly. She lifted the lid of the toilet cistern, and used the tape she had used on her body to stick it to the underside of the lid before replacing it. She hoped it would hold, otherwise Kent Police would be fining her the cost of the rig.

On the way back out, she went to the bar next to Rob to get another drink and shook her head at him to let the team know she was now off comms. He wasn't happy but relayed the same back to Cramer. Leila could already imagine her boss swearing under her breath. Another cock up by DC Leila Johnson. *Yay, go me*, she thought to herself.

Once Leila had got her drink, she moved away from the bar and planted herself at the table Rob had been at previously, which had just become available as a group of girls at a hen party decided to move on. It was close enough that she and Rob were in line of sight. Collinson was still at the bar, surveying the room. He looked sharp, Leila thought, and was getting some attention already, but he seemed distracted, like he was looking for something, or someone else.

Leila watched as Collinson got up from his bar stool and moved slowly through the crowds on the dance floor and made a beeline for her table. Leila caught Rob's attention, and his lips began to move, as he no doubt relayed this update to the team.

He sat himself next to her and started up a conversation. He was animated, clearly trying hard to impress her, and she decided to play it friendly but cool.

'Do you come here often?' he asked her.

Not very original, she thought.

'Is that the best line you've got?' She teased him, smiling to let him know it was a good-natured response.

'Yeah, well, I don't get out much...' Collinson said, smiling back at her. 'What do you do?'

'I drink and dance,' Leila said, not wanting to divulge anything to him. 'You?'

'Professor of history at Canterbury,' he responded.

'Sounds riveting.' Leila wasn't giving him anything to work with in the hope that it would cause a reaction. If he was their man, she needed to see it first-hand.

The drink she had been nursing was almost finished, and he offered to get her another.

'No, I'm good, thanks,' she said.

'C'mon, what about the "drinking and dancing"? Let me get you another, on me...' He was not taking no for an answer. He stopped one of the bar staff as they walked past and ordered a round for them both.

Leila looked over quickly to see Rob, who had stayed put. He must be able to see them both from where he was, and with a good enough view of the rest of the club from that vantage point, he could keep watch over developments.

Chapter 54

'Fuck me, he's only gone and sat down with Charlie Two,' Rob whispered into his radio.

'Keep a close eye on them both, we need to know what we are dealing with here,' Cramer ordered through the radio. 'Look out for any opportunity for him, or someone else, to slip something into a drink too,' said Cramer.

At that point, a tall girl who could only have been in her early twenties came up beside Rob and started talking to him. 'Do you want to buy me a drink?' she drawled as she rubbed his leg. It seemed to Rob like she had already had enough but was still feeling a little flattered at the attention.

'I'd love to, but I am waiting for a friend,' he lied.

'I don't mind, a male friend or a female friend?' She wasn't giving up.

Rob smiled, on an ordinary night he would have had some fun with a wind-up here, but he had a job to do.

He stood up and leaned towards the woman, who was teetering on heels that made her reach his full height of six feet. He moved towards her ear to whisper.

'It's a... secret,' he said, putting his finger to his lips as he backed away from her. She took the closeness of this move as a green light to drape herself over his shoulders – not exactly the response he had planned. She threw her head back in a drunken laugh, and nearly fell backwards, she was so unsteady on her feet.

At that point, two girls appeared who were clearly her friends, and pulled her off Rob.

'Come on, Stacey, leave the nice man alone...' Stacey pulled a face as she was dragged away, and one of her friends mouthed a silent 'Sorry' to Rob as they left. He just laughed to himself.

But that little diversion meant he'd taken his eyes off Leila, and by the time he refocused his attention on her, a new round of drinks had come, and Collinson was sitting far too close for comfort. Rob could tell by the thunderous look Leila was hiding behind her smiles. In any other situation, Collinson would have been hurt in some way by now – Leila wasn't one to hold back.

Suddenly, there was a surge of people coming onto the dance floor as an argument erupted between two very drunk men. A group of friends were trying to calm them down before things got physical, but it was a real struggle. Momentarily, he lost sight of Leila again as the group stormed through the venue, with bouncers descending on them from more than one direction. He didn't want Marlon to recognise him, so turned quickly to the bar and nursed his drink until they were out of the way.

The melee had attracted a lot of attention, and the dance floor had emptied in that one area to allow the potential fight to be contained. The bouncers took both men towards the door, with their friends in tow, and finally the club settled back into its groove.

Rob turned back around and was glad to see Leila still sitting at the same table. Collinson had started to look around himself more than at Leila, which was clearly a relief for her.

Rob had tried to keep an eye on the club clientele generally, but it wasn't easy. The darkness punctuated by flashes of coloured light and the surging crowds made this more like a bear pit than a club. But as far as he could tell, apart from the presence of Collinson, there was nothing that made him feel uneasy. He noticed Jack was now in the shadows near the wall watching Collinson, and Rob caught his eye briefly before he went back to concentrating on Collinson and Leila.

'Eagle One, Echo One looks like he is getting the message that Charlie Two isn't interested in him and is getting up from the table and heading back towards me at the bar. Nothing else so far.'

Leila stayed in her same spot as Collinson moved towards the bar, and after putting his glass down, said goodnight to the barman, and headed for the door.

'Heads up, Echo One is heading your way. He will be outside the door in the next thirty seconds,' Rob radioed in. He watched as the professor made his way back towards the door, before turning left towards the toilets.

'Correction, Echo One is headed to the gents. Stand by.'

Jack was nonchalantly making his way through the crowds before he was bundled into by another bunch of drunks. Rob thought he'd let it go for a moment, but he couldn't help but audibly groan as he watched Jack grabbed one of the lads by the lapels and lifted him off the ground, shouting into his face as he did so. His friends joined in, trying to get Jack to let go, but he clearly had a red mist and was ready to lump the guy just as the bouncers turned up again. They spent a few minutes calming him down, insisting he make peace with the guy he lifted off the floor.

'Fuck's sake,' Rob said under his breath. He didn't want to report the altercation to the boss, but Jack definitely wasn't doing his job. Jack had lost Collinson, his primary. Rob attracted his attention and motioned to him to head towards the gents, which Jack did, still in a foul temper.

Rob turned back to the room and took a long draw on his drink. He was scoping the room and turned back to where Leila was sitting. Only she wasn't.

He started off his seat and headed towards the toilets, expecting to see her in the queue, but no. She wasn't there either.

'Eagle One, I've lost sight of Charlie Two, is she with you?' he asked.

'Negative, Charlie One. Search and advise.'

The panic built in Rob as he started hurling himself around the club as fast as he could, trying to find his colleague. It was impossible to do anything quickly with the number of people packed in there now – he was sure there must be some kind of fire risk violations here. But it was no good – Leila was nowhere to be seen.

'Charlie One, situation update now,' Cramer shouted into her radio, the anxiety clear in her voice.

'Charlie Two isn't here. I've checked everywhere. She's gone.'

Chapter 55

Cramer threw the doors of the van open and headed straight into the club, her warrant card in hand to prevent any delay getting inside.

The noise and the throng inside was overpowering and there was no easy way to get through the bodies that were gyrating on the dance floor to get to Rob. He'd made it over to the table that Leila had been sitting at just too late to prevent the barman putting her glass on the tray with all the other glasses he'd already picked up. Rob followed him back to the bar and ordered him not to wash any of them, showing his warrant card as a reason.

'Max, get some backup here now,' Cramer ordered through the radio. 'We need to close this scene down. Get some of the uniforms in here pronto. And I want an update on Echo One's whereabouts too. Bravo One, report!'

'Eagle One.' The sound of heavy breathing and the slapping of boots on concrete. 'Bravo One in pursuit of Echo One, who has just left the train station. Need backup.'

'Shit, this isn't happening,' Cramer said to herself before opening her radio. 'I want any Discoverys or Porsches in the area captured on ANPR stopped. Now. Put out an all-unit call.'

Chapter 56

There must have been around two hundred people in the club that night, and each of them would have to be processed to get any information they could offer.

Cramer went to the bar, showed her warrant card and told the manager to lock the doors, turn the lights on, and kill the music. In that order.

The doors were duly closed with the bouncers guarding them from the inside. The lights went up to the audible groan of everyone in the club, and the music stopped.

The manager took to the mic: 'Everyone, sorry for the inconvenience but I'm afraid we have a police matter that has come to light this evening, and we've been ordered to hold everyone here until the police have interviewed each and every one of you.' There was a lot of noise as the reality that the revellers would neither be getting home nor getting more drunk any time soon sank in. 'I know, I'm not happy about it either, but take it up with the cops when you speak to them. Right now, I need you to just stay where you are and wait for further instructions.'

He glared at Cramer as he walked towards her. 'Have you been doing a surveillance in my club without even telling me?'

'It has been fully authorised at the highest level, and for reasons of confidentiality, we weren't able to—'

‘Ah, bullshit. You fucking come in here and do an op and you don’t have the decency to tell me about it? You’ve already taken all my sodding CCTV footage for the last few weeks, and now you fuck me over like this.’

Cramer was tempted to threaten him with harassment, but decided it was as well to leave it there for now.

‘I’d like to thank you for your co-operation—’ Cramer offered, but again was cut off.

‘Oh, fuck off, bitch.’

That was too far. She fixed her eyes on him. ‘Make sure you don’t go anywhere, we’ll be wanting to interview you too. And we’ll be doing a full drugs sweep when the forensics team gets here.’

Rob had already started to corral people into smaller groups for the uniforms to deal with as they arrived. Most of Kent’s on-duty officers must have been there by now, so anyone with any other kind of problem tonight would face a very long wait.

Cramer had not only lost Leila in an operation that better judgement may have prevented her from undertaking she also knew she was going to have to update Davidson ASAP and had already broken out in a cold sweat. Here it was. That gut-wrenching feeling of another operation going properly tits up. They needed to find her, and fast.

Chapter 57

Jack had stuck to Collinson as he wound his way back to the house. He was driving fast, but not erratically; he was totally in control. The streets were narrow but getting wider as they headed out of the city. Jack was looking for the opportunity to stop him without involving any other road users, but that wasn't likely to happen until the roads were quieter. He needed more cars to do it safely too, so Jack needed to bide his time. If Leila was in that car, he couldn't risk her getting hurt.

Collinson was heading further out of town as Jack barked into his radio.

'Where's my backup? Christ, I am pursuing a suspected kidnapper of an officer – get some bloody traffic crew out here now!'

He didn't see it coming. The elderly driver was looking the other way as he came out of the junction right across in front of Jack. He had nowhere to go.

There was a momentary screech of brakes before he hit the car just behind the driver's door. Both span round into the road and Jack's face hit the airbag, which deployed on impact.

It took him a few seconds to get to grips with what happened, then his first instinct was to check the other driver. He opened his door, and it was only then he realised his arm was hurting him, killing him. He held it close to his body as he went to the other car and tried to rouse the driver. He was unconscious, and bleeding from his nose.

Jack reached for his radio only to stop short, wincing, as he couldn't extend his arm to key the comms button. He switched to his left arm, but that was almost as awkward.

'DS Jack Sargeant requesting urgent assistance and an ambulance at the junction of Sturry Road and...' – he checked the road name –'... Reed Avenue. I've been involved in an RTA, one other casualty. I was in pursuit of a suspect and need urgent assistance to continue that pursuit.'

He looked down the road, but Collinson was long gone. It was only ten minutes to his house from here, and it was unlikely they would catch him before he got there.

Two traffic units turned up, and Jack immediately jumped into the back of the squad car.

'C'mon, let's go. We have an officer in danger.'

The two uniforms looked at each other.

'Jack, you can't leave,' one eventually said. 'We don't know how badly injured this driver is. You can't leave the scene.' They all looked over to where the ambulance and fire crews had arrived and were working out how to extract the other driver.

'Fuck, guys, don't piss me about.' He clenched his fist before opening it in a hurry thanks to the pain. 'Leila Johnson could be in danger, we need to stop Simon Collinson. You all should have been on the lookout for him anyway.'

'Yeah, we know and we were, but we've got this to deal with first.'

That sent Jack into the stratosphere, he stormed out of the back of the car, his eyes flashing with anger. The larger of the two officers got out of the car as well to try to calm Jack down, but it had the opposite effect. Instead, he pulled him up by the shoulder straps of his stab vest, ignoring the pain searing up his forearm and into his shoulder as he nearly strangled the man.

The other uniform got out of the car too and tried to remonstrate with him. 'Hey, calm down. You're in enough trouble.'

'Listen, don't fuck with me...' He could see he wasn't going to get anywhere as two more uniforms had arrived behind, ready to take him down if necessary. He changed tack.

'Get someone to Collinson's address right now and get them in there to do a search. There is a risk to life, no excuses. And arrest Collinson on suspicion of kidnap and the murder of four women.'

As Jack released the wheezing officer, his arm throbbed with a pain so unbearable he nearly passed out. Other officers who had arrived on scene minutes later were dispatched to Collinson's address and all Jack could do was wait and hope they were in time. He watched as the other driver was pulled out of his car in a neck brace, still unconscious, and intubated to help him breathe. Jack looked away and put his head in his hands. What a shit night this was turning out to be.

Chapter 58

Collinson had been home for more than twenty minutes by the time the uniforms arrived at his home. They searched his house and car to see if there was any sign of DC Leila Johnson, but they found nothing. On the way back to the station, Collinson – cuffed and cautioned – had apparently been quiet. Not much of a surprise. It wasn't every day you were picked up on suspicion of involvement in the murder of four women.

Cramer was painfully aware of the situation Leila may now be in. She wasn't at the nightclub and she wasn't found at Collinson's house, even though that didn't mean she wasn't there. He could have easily hidden her away well in that 20 minutes. So where could she be? Cramer knew in her heart Operation Themis was a risk and she should have pulled her out when she'd had to go off comms. But it was too late to deal in 'could've, should've, would've'. Now Cramer had to focus on getting Leila back safe, and fast.

The remaining detective team had recently returned from the nightclub, leaving the rest of the interviews with the uniforms. Max had already started trawling through CCTV data from local cameras in an attempt to find a relevant car. Since Leila had not been found with Collinson, it meant he may not have taken her from the club himself, but that didn't mean he wasn't involved. Up to this point, they hadn't seriously considered the possibility that more than one person was involved in these snatches, but it could be possible.

As Cramer walked out of her office, the air was heavy with concern and disappointment. But they had a job to do. They were all professionals, so none of them was going to rest until they had their colleague back.

Jack had come back to the office, his arm in a rudimentary sling having refused the ambulance crew's offer to take him for treatment. His eye had started to swell now too, and by the time Cramer approached him, he looked like he'd gone ten rounds. She was about to make it eleven.

'What the fuck happened, Jack?'

Jack nodded almost imperceptibly. 'Yeah, I just didn't have a chance, boss. I didn't see him pulling out. I hope the old guy is OK, but it didn't look good.'

'I wasn't talking about that, I meant in the club. Losing your cool. You fucking know better than that.'

Cramer looked straight at him, her face flashing anger. This was a complication she really didn't need. But she knew she needed to keep Jack working – she needed the manpower and his experience.

'Jack, you're coming with me to interview Collinson. I want Jill called in as well, so make that call before you do anything else...'

At that moment, Rob shot his chair back to join them at Jack's desk.

'I'd like to interview Collinson, if that's OK, guv?' Rob had clearly overheard their conversation. Cramer hesitated, not needing to guess the reasoning behind his eagerness – Rob felt like he was partly responsible for Leila going missing. They all did, and she knew Jack's anger could bubble up again, but Rob was too close to Leila to be objective in this interview. She didn't want to make him feel any worse though, so deflected the request.

'Rob, I understand, but I think as Jack was originally in pursuit, he should be the one sitting in on this one. You focus on the CCTV and find this bastard. He was always going to make a mistake, and whether he knows it or not, he did by taking Leila.'

Rob's face turned white, and he averted his gaze from his boss. Cramer knew exactly how he felt. She had the same reaction as she was driving back from the club herself, the weight of guilt resting on her shoulders now more than ever. Losing one officer in a drugs raid gone wrong was bad enough, losing two in less than eighteen months was unthinkable.

Cramer and Jack headed down into the bowels of the station to get Collinson released from the cells and into an interview room. She grabbed them both coffee before they went in, perhaps a mundane thing to do under the circumstances, but they were all in for a long night.

Just before they both went into the interview room, Cramer stopped Jack.

'I know you've got some anger issues, Jack, but let me tell you, if there is any repeat of that in here, I will have you suspended immediately. The chances are, with your recent behaviour, that will happen in time anyway. But right now, what I need is your help, not your fury. Is that clear?'

Jack stood impassively. 'Yes, ma'am.'

'I mean it, Jack. keep it together.'

He looked her straight in the eye and nodded. 'I will, trust me.'

Cramer nodded and opened the door to where Collinson was already seated in a chair, weak tea in a plastic cup in front of him. His floppy hair had changed from the previous day, now gelled into place, which made him look even younger. His clothes had become crumpled and dishevelled after spending an hour or more laying down in the cells.

Before they had even sat down, he started to protest.

'Surely this is some mistake? I really don't know anything about what's going on. I was only helping you with your inquiries yesterday and yet here I am today as a suspect? How on earth did we get here?'

Cramer and Jack said nothing while they were getting themselves settled, and only when they had started the video recording did they make any statement at all. After the usual formalities were dispensed with, the date, time of the interview and who was present, Cramer started her questioning.

'Professor Collinson, we have reason to believe you are involved in the murders of four women – Angela Downs, Linda Burrows, Amanda Morrison, and Dominique Monroe. I remind you that you are also still under caution. Do you understand?'

'I really don't know what I'm doing here. I didn't even know anything other than what I had read in the papers until you came to my office yesterday.'

Cramer was unmoved. The cordial conversation and first-name familiarity she had used the day before were now long gone. His highly suspicious behaviour had seen to that. It was the early hours of the morning, and Cramer's patience was wafer thin.

'Professor, can you explain to me what you were doing outside the Illuminati nightclub yesterday evening?'

'What?'

'We know you were outside the Illuminati nightclub yesterday evening. You stood on the pavement opposite the club for some time, but then didn't go in. Can you tell me why that was?'

'How, I mean, how do you even know that? Have you been following me?'

Cramer was impassive. 'That's not relevant. We know you were there, and I want to know why.'

Collinson looked from Cramer to Jack and back to Cramer again, clearly aware that he needed to offer some type of explanation. It didn't take a professorship to see how incriminating the circumstances looked.

After a beat, he held his hands up as he leaned forwards in his chair, before putting both them on the table. 'OK, I admit, I was interested in what you said after you came to see me yesterday. It sparked my imagination, and I thought I would go and see the venue for myself and perhaps why that was of particular interest to the man you're looking for.'

'Why?' Jack queried his answer.

Collinson looked a bit spooked. 'I was trying to understand what the appeal might be. Why that club? Why now? How was he looking for these women?'

'How do you know we are looking for just one man?' Cramer shot back.

Collinson backpedalled, suddenly aware that he was digging himself a hole. 'Well, you said that to me yesterday. When we spoke in my office.'

Cramer thought for a second; she couldn't remember whether she had or not but decided to bluff him anyway. She didn't want him to feel comfortable.

'I don't remember being specific about that either way, Professor, yet you've taken it as read. Seems quite interesting to me...'

Collinson suddenly took his hands off the table and put them up in a defensive pose once again. He was beginning to second guess himself.

'Oh, hang on, now look, given what you told me, it sort of stands to reason, doesn't it?'

'Does it?' said Jack.

'Well, I would say it does, yes,' Collinson said nervously. He was definitely nowhere near the cocky professor Cramer had met the day before.

'Why exactly did you go into the club tonight?' Cramer asked.

Collinson moved uneasily in his seat, his demeanour changing as the enormity of his situation became clearer. 'I told you. I was interested.'

'Really? Just interested?' Cramer leaned forwards as she tried to make him feel even less comfortable. Invading his personal space.

'Oh, come on, I am perfectly entitled to go to any club – or anywhere else, for that matter – anytime I like.'

'Yes, but why there? You didn't want to go in last night, so why tonight?' Jack asked.

Collinson sat back in his seat and folded his arms across his chest. 'I don't like where you're going with this.'

'Where are we going with this?' asked Cramer.

'I'm not naïve. I think I'd like my lawyer now, please.'

Cramer raised an eyebrow.

'Well, that's your right, of course, and if you can't afford one, we will ensure one is provided for you—'

'Oh, I can afford one, don't worry. Get me Marcus Hall.'

Cramer's guts tightened. Dealing with that man once in a week was bad enough, twice in a few days was insult to injury.

Since the interview was over for now, Cramer leaned over to turn the video off and Jack returned Collinson to the custody desk, and he was taken back to his cell. They wouldn't have to wait long before Hall turned up. There was never a good time to see him if you were a copper.

As Cramer headed back to her office, she stopped off to see what Rob had found on the CCTV so far. His hair, some standing up on end, some flattened, clearly having been messed up from running his hands through it far too frequently.

'Guv, nothing. I can't see anything. How can Leila have just disappeared with all of us there? It doesn't make sense.' He leaned forward on his desk and put his head in his hands.

Cramer couldn't make him feel better. She felt exactly the same. But she still put her hand on his shoulder to try to offer some comfort.

'Keep looking. There'll be something somewhere. People don't just disappear into thin air. They just don't.'

Rob looked up at her. 'But that's exactly what's happened.'

'That isn't true, Rob. See if Max can see anything. Fresh eyes sometimes help.'

Rob was about to protest when she added: 'Besides, I need to go and see Jason Baird, and I'd like you to come with me.'

He didn't need asking a second time. He stood up, took his jacket off the back of the chair, and was out of the door before his boss.

Chapter 59

Cramer had driven hard and fast on the roads to get to Leila and Jason Baird's house. They lived in a small mid-terrace in a village just outside Canterbury, fast work for the length of time they had been together. And while Cramer was not relishing the conversation they were about to have, she was determined Jason would hear bad news from her directly, not a nameless, faceless uniform that he didn't know. She owed him, and Leila, that much at least.

As they pulled up in the street, they could see the lights were on downstairs, the only house in the street that was awake at this time of the morning. He must not have been able to sleep with Leila not being home.

Rob knocked on the door, and it was quickly opened by Jason in his dressing gown, his dark, close-cropped hair at his temples gave way to unruly waves of curls on the top of his head which had clearly been roughed up by a pillow. His hazel-brown eyes looked dull, even though he was fully alert at 3 a.m.

Jason moved aside to let Cramer and Rob into the room, and Cramer took a deep breath before she walked in. The front door opened directly into the living room, a tidy but small space that had a mix of furniture, some modern with clean lines, some clearly passed on by relatives and presumably used as a stopgap until they could afford to replace it.

The pair moved towards the sofa on one wall and waited until Jason sat down before doing the same.

'What's this about? I woke up and saw all over social media that the police had raided Illuminati, but I can't get hold of Leila...'

The news she was about to deliver was bad, and given this was the local reporter who had been giving her team the hardest time, it was not going to be easy, either personally or professionally.

'Jason, I'm sorry to come here so late... well, or early,' Cramer said, looking at her watch but not really seeing it.

Jason looked at it, looked at her face. He was cold as stone towards her. 'What's going on? Why are you here?'

It seemed he had no idea Leila was working undercover tonight. Cramer felt a pang of guilt for how much pressure she'd put on her in the previous days and weeks having assumed she told her boyfriend most things. That stung.

She sat on the chair facing Jason, who was leaning away from her, his side towards her blocking their contact; the body language showed a lack of trust in what she had to say. Cramer didn't blame him.

'Jason, I have something to tell you, but I need to explain something else first. There's a personal and a professional aspect to this, and I need to address both of those with you.'

Jason was impassive.

'Leila was working undercover tonight on a job, and...' She didn't really know how to say it. So, she just said it. '... She has gone missing.'

Jason changed his position suddenly, the words forcing him to sit forwards.

'Missing? What do you mean?'

'We're doing everything we can to find her, and at this moment, we're working through statements and CCTV footage. We'll find her, I promise you that.'

'What do you mean? How can that happen? Don't you have backup on these operations?'

Cramer really didn't know how to respond. Yes, there should have been more backup in an ideal world, but they were already stretched on this case, thanks to police cuts, and the overtime bill was spiralling. But it was too late. All that mattered now was getting her, and Helena, back safely.

'Look, Jason, I know how you must feel. I feel the same way.'

'Hmmm, I doubt that...' He snorted.

'But believe me, we're doing everything we can to find her.' Cramer swallowed hard as Jason put his head in his hands. Despite what she thought of him, he really did care about Leila, and she hadn't appreciated just how close they were.

He looked up at her with a pained expression. 'Is this related to your ongoing case? Do you think she has been taken by the same person who has killed those other women?'

Cramer couldn't bring herself to say the words, so just nodded slowly.

'Fuck.' He stopped, pausing to take in what he was being told. 'How? I mean, how could this happen?'

'Jason, I can't tell you much about the case, as you know...'

'Oh yeah, here we go. No comment, right? This isn't about a fucking story, *Acting* DCI Cramer. This is my girlfriend we're talking about here. This is my life. I want her back. Safe.' The tears started to pool in his eyes, but she saw him fighting to stop them falling. This was the most impassioned and vulnerable Cramer had ever seen him. He looked human.

'Believe me, Jason, so do I. That's all I want right now.' Cramer was careful not to let on that Leila was not the only person they were looking for. 'I'm not going to rest until I make that happen. But, and this is not easy for either of us to talk about, we need to talk about how this is dealt with from a professional perspective by you.'

Jason looked disgusted that this was even being brought up.

'Are you kidding me? You're seriously talking to me about whether this is "covered" by me or not?'

'Look, I know it isn't easy to think about this now—' Cramer said.

'You bet your fucking life it isn't easy to think about this now,' Jason shouted. 'How could you think that's at the forefront of my mind? I can't believe it's at the front of yours. Is that all you care about, your fucking reputation, Cramer? Well, I wouldn't worry, you don't have much of one left to protect.'

Cramer bristled. 'Don't misunderstand me, Jason, don't twist this, it isn't...'

'Twist this?' He was getting more animated. 'Twist this? Despite what you think, I don't "twist" anything. I report. You may not like what I report, but that doesn't mean I'm in the wrong.'

Cramer tried to defuse the emotion. Things were in danger of getting out of hand. She lowered her voice and spoke calmly. 'I just need to discuss this with you, because I think there is a danger that if her disappearance reaches the papers, it may be harder to find her and get her back.' She stopped short of saying alive.

'Well, how long do you think it's going to be before someone else picks up on this? The operation was at...'

She couldn't help but cut in with a direct answer. 'Illuminati.'

Jason snorted in disgust as he stood up and started pacing around the room. 'Well, surely you had to interview everyone at the club as part of the investigation?' He was pointing his finger at her now, accusing again. 'So, you have a couple of hundred people who will be pissed off because you spoilt their night out, and you think *I* will be the one to blow the lid on it, right? Fuck's sake, you really do take some beating.'

Rob jumped in. 'We did interview everyone at the club, yes, but that's why we want to be clear with you about what we need to do here. It's imperative we do the right thing to get Leila back.'

'Why wouldn't that include saying publicly that she's missing? The more people looking for her, the better.'

'No, we think it could make him change his pattern of behaviour, and that would be a mistake,' Cramer said.

Jason looked interested rather than angry or upset for the first time.

'His pattern of behaviour? What do you know that you haven't told us yet?'

Ah, here we go, thought Cramer. This is more like the Jason Baird she knew.

'Look, Jason, I can't tell you anything more than you already know. But let me assure you, getting Leila back unharmed is my priority. After that, we can discuss anything you like, and I will go on the record. But for now, I need you to keep this to yourself. Please. I know we haven't got on in the past, and I know some of that has been my fault' – it stuck in her craw to say that – 'but honestly, this isn't the time for petty point-scoring. You have to trust me – I know what I'm doing.'

Jason barely contained his disdain. She understood why he would be reluctant to take her word for it. A previous operation had resulted in the death of a colleague, no breakthrough in a case that should have offered many more clues than it had, and now his girlfriend was missing in another botched operation. And she was asking him to trust her. It was a long shot, but she knew what she was doing was right. She could feel it.

'I'll work with you. But as soon as this comes out, you know I'll have to be reporting on it. Once it gets out that I knew something and kept it to myself, it could mean my job. You need to work with me on that too. Give me something no one else is getting when this is all done.'

Cramer nodded. She couldn't believe she was agreeing to it, but she really had no choice. 'Thank you. I promise I will keep you informed, but I need to make sure that everything is off the record. Until we find her.'

Jason smirked. 'Do you know what that really means?'

'It means you can't report on it.'

'Actually, no, it doesn't. That's what people think it means. What it actually means is that I can report on it, as long as I don't attribute it to you. That's why so many quotes come from an "unnamed source". But that isn't what you mean at all, is it?'

Cramer coloured a little. She felt stupid for not realising this and wondered how many other people had made the same mistake.

'OK, well, what I mean then is that I don't want you to report on anything at the moment. But when this is over, I will give you a full, exclusive interview about the entire case.'

Jason's face suddenly lost its bravado. His whole body sank.

'Just get her back. That's all I want. We'll discuss everything else afterwards.'

Chapter 60

Leila's head and body felt like she had been hit by a truck as she came to. She was instantly aware of a lack of clothes and being on a cold, hard surface. It was pressing into her shoulder blades and back; her lean torso meant her bones had no softness to ease the discomfort. She could see nothing. The surrounding blackness enveloped her completely. Panic started to rise in the pit of her stomach, but she reasoned with herself to calm down. Now wasn't the time to stop thinking clearly.

Her memory of what had happened earlier that evening was hazy. She was sure she'd been drugged. She knew she hadn't drunk anywhere near enough for this kind of hangover.

The last thing she could remember clearly was removing the malfunctioning radio in the toilets and wished she had stuck it out. Now, she was alone, and despite her knowledge of the case they were working on, unsure of what was likely to happen next.

Her head felt like it was on fire – not just because of the GHB, she presumed – but the skin of her scalp felt like it was burning. Yet she was icy cold, shivering as her body reacted to both the shock and chill of her unforgiving bed.

She tried to lift her hand to soothe the burn of her skull, but it stopped suddenly. The shackle cut into her wrist as the chain attached to the hard slab underneath her became taut. Now the ligature marks made sense.

Leila fought again to keep herself calm, her brain flipping between panic and using her training to work out the best course of action. But police training, extensive as it is, had not prepared her for anything like this.

She was suddenly aware of a noise in the darkness. A muffled cry that was unmistakably a woman in pain. *Helena*. It must be Helena. But what the hell was he doing to make her scream? The scream got louder, a blood-curdling noise that caused her to turn her head. Then she realised. The screams weren't coming from Helena. The scream was her own. Leila's body started to shake violently. She had to get out of here.

Chapter 61

The discussion with Jason Baird left Cramer feeling deflated. The idea that she cared more for herself or her reputation than her colleagues was abhorrent. It simply wasn't true.

The questioning of her integrity disturbed her more than most things, so the last person Cramer wanted to see at this particular moment was Marcus Hall, but as she pulled into the station car park, she spied his Jaguar gracing the space next to the one she had left. Clearly it paid to be a defence lawyer.

She nodded her head to Rob as he noticed his car too. 'That's all we bloody need.'

They went into the station, and as they rounded the corner, they came face-to-face with the one man neither of them could stand.

Hall was leaning across the desk in the outer part of the station near the public counter. He stood a little further along from station-regular Kevin, a homeless man who would try to get himself arrested for some minor crime, in a bid to get a warm bed and a hot meal for the night. You couldn't blame him really, and as it was now heading into autumn, there was starting to be a real nip in the air.

The contrast between the two couldn't have been more stark, as Hall, cufflinks flashing, swept his arm up from his side and forwards in an exaggerated motion to look at his Rolex Submariner – a movement lacking in any nonchalance, no matter how hard he tried. Cramer hated that kind of ostentatiousness, especially in the face of someone so clearly at the other end of the financial spectrum. His watch cost nearly £7,000 – enough to have sheltered and fed Kevin for a year. The movement had been perfected by Hall as a way of ensuring everyone was aware of his wealth. It was just crass.

Hall's dark blue suit was tailored to his toned frame. Unusually for him, he wasn't wearing a tie, so the open neck of his shirt showed the jugular notch between his collarbones. The crispness of his white shirt contrasted with his deep tan, making it look like he had just stepped off a plane. Knowing Hall, he had.

There was no doubting he was good at his job. Too good. That was one of the problems. And his integrity was inversely proportional to his earnings.

He wasn't a bad-looking man on the surface, but his seedy character shone through so vibrantly once you knew anything about him, it wasn't possible to see him as traditionally attractive. That didn't seem to stop a conveyor belt of women from being at his side; it was proof, if it was ever needed, that money is the strongest aphrodisiac.

Cramer almost visibly grimaced as Marcus's gaze fell upon them but she managed to check herself just in time.

'Ah, my dear Detective Inspector, what a pleasure it is to see you.' Hall was as slithering as usual. 'I hadn't expected the delight of your company again so soon, yet here we are.'

'Detective Chief Inspector,' Cramer corrected him.

'Ah yes, *Acting*... ' Cramer ignored his snide remark.

'Wish I could say it was a pleasure to see you, Marcus, but yes, here we are,' was the best Cramer could offer.

Hall smirked and opened his arms wide, his briefcase hanging on his fingertips.

'Oh, come, come, we always enjoy the sparring, you and me. I like to have a worthy adversary, and in you, I very nearly find that.'

This man was a total shit.

'Sorry to disappoint you, Marcus, but I've never found our "sparring" the least bit invigorating.' Cramer spat out the words. 'You simply aren't good enough at it for my liking. But hey, today could be the day we have something on your client that sticks. Even to Teflon.'

Hall laughed and shook his head as he looked towards the floor. He was so incredibly cocky that Cramer just wanted to knock his block off. But that wouldn't be the way to win this argument, and besides, he would only find a way to sue her for it. Still, it might be worth the payout.

Hall lifted his head again and fixed his gaze on hers.

'Enough foreplay, my dear, I am here to see my client Professor Simon Collinson. I cannot possibly see why you have brought him in tonight, but I'm damn sure he won't be staying.'

'We'll see,' Cramer said, as she buzzed herself and Rob through the outer door, and let it slam behind them before Hall had a chance to make it through. It was highly satisfying to hear him cursing them as he tried to get the desk sergeant's attention to let him through. A petty victory, but a victory all the same.

'Rob, tell Jack that Hall is here, will you? And get him to come down to interview room one. I'll go and get Collinson now we're ready.'

It didn't take long for Collinson to appear again in the interview room, flanked by a uniformed officer Cramer didn't recognise. She was already seated when Collinson appeared at the long window in the middle of the door, and she could see his face fall as he saw her alone, with no sign of Marcus Hall.

The officer opened the door and ushered Collinson towards the seat opposite Cramer across the table. He was showing no emotion now. The friendly smile had disappeared. He wasn't even showing disdain. He just looked at her coldly.

'Are they treating you well, Professor?' Cramer said, referring to the custody staff.

'Far better than you are, DCI Cramer,' he retorted, barely able to contain a sneer. 'I try to help you out and this is how you treat me? How dare you!'

'Oh, I dare,' Cramer responded. 'When someone makes the moves you've made on the back of confidential information, I most definitely dare.'

Their contretemps was interrupted by the arrival of Hall and Jack, and the relief was evident in Collinson's face as he saw Hall coming into the room.

'I do hope you have not been berating my client, Acting Detective Chief Inspector,' Hall said pointedly.

'Of course not, Marcus, we were just shooting the breeze.' She turned her gaze towards Collinson, willing him to disagree with her. 'Weren't we, Professor?'

Collinson said nothing, remaining stony-faced. Hall sat himself next to Collinson, and with another unnecessary flash of cufflink, opened his briefcase and took out his notepad. Cramer couldn't bear Hall and his constant classic signs of a tacky social climber. Rarely would those who had family money behave like that, but she knew enough about Hall to realise he was the exception that proved the rule. His father had been wealthy, and his father before him. In fact, she had heard from a mutual acquaintance that if you went back far enough in his family tree, Hall had an ancestor that was given a title during the time of the Tudors. He apparently resented the fact that a later forefather had become so indebted to the Crown, that to get the title back would have required a significant payment from Hall today. He had better things to spend his money on. Apparently.

After the recording of the interview had started, Hall was first to speak. 'I would like to make it clear that my client has nothing to say to you.'

'How do you know that, Marcus?' said Cramer, incredulous. 'You haven't even had a chance to speak to him, or find out what we are talking to him about.'

Hall didn't flinch. 'I was about to ask for a ten-minute break to speak to my client, something I should have been granted before we even got to this point.'

He was trying to rattle Cramer; it wasn't working. 'That's fine, Mr Hall, you speak to your client. We'll wait outside until you're ready.'

'No, you will wait further away than that – my client has a right to privacy and I need to respect client confidentiality. I don't want you listening into our conversation through the door.'

'As you well know, these rooms are soundproofed, Marcus, so don't try that one with me,' Cramer challenged. 'We will be outside, and we will be interviewing Professor Collinson in ten minutes.'

She looked at Jack and pushed her chair back to get up and leave the room, he followed suit. As she walked past the end of the table, she leaned into Collinson's shoulder so he would hear her clearly.

'Don't forget about the document you signed in your office, Professor. That is legally binding, and we will bring charges for that if you contravene any part of that agreement.'

Hall stood up. 'Are you threatening my client?'

'Not at all, Marcus. As you well know, confidentiality is important. Professor Collinson spoke to us as a consultant – I was just reminding him of his responsibilities.'

She unfolded herself from where she was leaning over towards Collinson to her full height, before striding out of the room ahead of Jack.

Just before the door closed, she held it open with her hand.

'We'll be waiting. Right here. Ten minutes.' She pointed to her watch.

Jack and Cramer stood either side of the now closed interview-room door. Jack stretched before rubbing his good hand over his face, appearing to try to remove the fatigue from their long night. The other arm was still in the sling, and his eye was now turning a deep blue from the impact of the airbag.

'You came on a bit strong there, guv, didn't you? I know you love a wind-up, but it's Marcus Hall, remember. We need to follow protocol – he'll wriggle through any wormhole otherwise.'

'I know, but he pisses me off, Jack. We have followed all processes properly and he knows it, he's just being a dick. All I wanted to do was put a bit of extra pressure on them both. Let them know we're not messing around here, even though we both know, at the moment, we don't have anything specific we can use to hold Collinson here. He has gone to a club, had a drink with a girl he met, and then left. We have suspicions, but nothing else. We need to get something from him in here' – she nodded her head back to the interview room – 'but the chances are, with Hall by his side, we're going to be shut down for now. Or shortly anyway. So, we needed to shake Collinson up a bit, make him feel uneasy about his situation.'

Jack looked at the floor as he was speaking. 'I think he already feels that, boss. It might work. But I wonder how pissed off that is going to make Hall, bearing in mind you could be facing him again over Adam in court.'

Cramer watched him searching her face for a response. The fatigue must be showing in her face too, but she held his stare.

'Yeah, well, I'll worry about that later. Let's jump the fences in order, Jack. The most important thing right now is finding out anything that will help get both Helena and Leila back safely.'

At that moment, Hall opened the door to the interview room. 'We are ready to begin, when you are.'

Cramer and Jack looked at each other before they went back into the room and reclaimed their seats at the table, before starting the recording once again.

'So, Professor Collinson, can you tell me what you were doing standing opposite Illuminati nightclub two nights ago?'

Collinson prickled. 'No comment.'

OK, so that's their game, is it? thought Cramer.

'And what about last night, Professor, what were you doing at the club that evening?'

'No comment.'

'Surely you know what you were doing there, Professor? Having an evening out? Meeting with friends? You had originally said you were "curious". What were you curious about?'

'No comment.'

Cramer leaned forwards in her seat, her elbows on the table now, moving her face closer to his. She was unsure she was going to get anywhere with this, but carried on regardless.

'You see, the thing is, we think you might be up to your eyeballs in this, Professor. And you're not giving me anything to make me think we're wrong. You could so easily put us all on the right track if we're on the wrong one, but you don't seem keen to do that.'

'No comment.'

She hadn't managed to rattle him, and the lack of interruptions from Hall made that clear to her as well. Time to up the ante.

She moved back in her seat to appear more relaxed. 'What was it like, Professor? Pushing that blade into their skin. What did they say to you? Did they beg for their lives? Is that what turns you on?'

A fire suddenly appeared in Collinson's eyes. Yes, that hit home. She pressed her advantage, leaning forwards, staring straight into his eyes.

'Is that what you need, Professor? Total and absolute power over another human being? Is that what it is? Is that what you need? To get off?'

'Fuck you,' was Collinson's response. *Nice, that was a change.* Cramer knew she was on to something. Perhaps they had found his weakness after all?

'I'm surprised, someone like you – intelligent, good-looking, wealthy, a good job, and a good title – I would have thought you could get anyone you wanted. It seems such a shame, despite all that, you still have to kidnap women to be with you. Is that what you need to do?'

Collinson couldn't contain his composure any longer.

'No, you fucking bitch, that isn't what I need, and is not what I do. I don't know what you are talking about, I don't know the women you're talking about, and I have never hurt a soul. No one. Do you understand?'

Collinson stood up to try to intimidate Cramer with his height and smashed his fist on the table in frustration, but as he did so, so did Jack, and Hall, who put his hand on his client's shoulder to calm him down. Collinson leaned forwards, his head falling into his hands as he collapsed into the chair. That was what Cramer wanted, to see him feel the pressure . To break his composure.

Hall was next to speak: 'That's quite enough, Acting DCI Cramer. If you have nothing more than suspicion and innuendo, no hard evidence, I insist on you releasing my client right now.'

Hall was right. There was nothing specific they could use to hold him for now, although the fact he had been rattled, albeit briefly, was encouraging. They had to let him go. But Cramer knew Jack would be spending more surveillance time on him. Officially or unofficially. That was for sure.

Chapter 62

By the time Cramer got back to her office, Jill was already in there, having another crafty cigarette and blowing smoke out through the open window.

'Jill, for fuck's sake, please stop smoking in my office. It's against the law. And in case you'd forgotten, you're standing in a bloody police station.'

Jill flushed a little. Cramer rarely berated her friend, especially as she was around fifteen years older, so it felt odd to tell her off. But it was a bloody cheek to have another cigarette there after their previous conversation. Jill hurriedly stubbed it out on the window itself and then threw what was left of the butt out before closing it. She wiped the ash on the window ledge away with her hand.

'Sorry, lovely,' Jill offered by way of apology. 'How are you doing?' Cramer knew Jill was genuinely concerned for her welfare. She was firefighting on so many fronts it was only a matter of time before one raged out of control; Jill would want to help damp down any areas she could to give Cramer some relief from the flames.

Cramer walked round behind her desk and sat down, her body deflated by the effort of dealing with so many things at once. She crumpled into her chair, her hands initially down by her side before she leaned forwards with her elbows on her desk and ran her fingers through her hair.

'I've been better, Jill, but you know that already. I can't get Leila out of my head. I can't lose another officer, I just can't.'

Cramer's ice-cool façade was less visible when talking to her friend, the need to stay strong and in control for her team was not as evident, and she was able to tell her how she really felt. Cramer didn't build trust easily, so she was sparing about sharing her innermost thoughts. She knew some of the team called her the 'ice queen' behind her back, but reacting to it would have made things worse.

'We will get her back. I know it. I can feel it,' Jill said. 'We'll get them both back, Cal, and we're not going to rest until we do. But one thing you have to do is prepare yourself for court later. I know you're pre-occupied with everything else that is going on, but you have to give yourself some time and space to prepare for the onslaught, because I suspect that is what you are going to face from Hall.' She spat his name out in disgust.

'What do you mean? I'm not in court today. That was earlier this week, you know that.'

Jill turned her computer screen around and moved the mouse to wake up her screen. Sure enough, there was another email she had missed in the commotion. She was being called back to testify again.

'Oh dammit! Not today. Jesus!'

'I know,' said Jill, 'I wasn't snooping, it just came up as a notification when I was in here earlier. I thought you'd seen it.'

Cramer just shook her head.

'Yes, well, I have already had the pleasure of seeing him – Hall – today. Collinson brought him in as his brief.'

Jill's mouth fell open. 'You're kidding?'

'I wish I was, but I think it was close to being round one to us. We can't hold Collinson at the moment, but I did manage to rattle him. I'm getting Jack to stay on him and keep him under surveillance, providing his arm holds up. He really should get to the hospital.'

'Do you think Collinson's our man?'

Cramer deflected.

'Not sure, but something's off. His reaction to me questioning him about the case seemed genuine, but then we also thought he was his own assistant initially too.

'I think we have enough to get a warrant to search his house properly. The initial search by the uniforms came up with nothing, but I'm not convinced and we can't waste time. I'm asking Davo to approve it. It will be a fight though – everything is circumstantial, and, of course, we went to him initially, which isn't going to play well. Not to mention another screwed undercover op behind me that I had to coerce Davo to allow in the first place.'

Jill thought for a moment. 'But with an officer at risk, he should bloody well approve it. Get someone else to speak to Davo about it. Ask Jack to do it. Or Rob. Either of them would be well placed to make the case, Cal, and you need to get your head on court this afternoon. That isn't going to be easy, and you need to give yourself the tools to cope after the last time.'

Cramer knew she was right. She hadn't slept in over twenty-four hours, and there was no doubting Marcus Hall was going to enjoy making her as uncomfortable as he possibly could all over again, especially after this morning. Her hope was that he would be tired too, having been called in to deal with Collinson's questioning.

She looked at the clock on her wall – it felt much later in all honesty than 9 a.m., but that meant she had just four hours before she would be sitting again in the witness box of Canterbury Crown Court, waiting for the inevitable grilling. Going to court was always uncomfortable – after all, the process was designed to bring those who often don't give a toss about the law to justice. Intimidation in those circumstances was a good thing. But her emotions were just about sloshing over the top of her cup of woe – something she knew Jill recognised all too well. She, at the very least, needed to head home to shower and change into some fresh clothes.

'So, what are you going to do?' Jill's words cut into the thoughts.

'OK, I'll get Rob or Jack to do it and I'll nip home quickly before I head back to court. But, and I really mean this, I want to know anything that comes up. Anything. I wouldn't appreciate any of you not telling me something.'

Jill nodded and smiled wryly at Cramer.

'What?' Cramer asked.

'You just like to take on the world when you already have enough on your shoulders, and it is at times like this the world tends to fight back,' said Jill.

'Good, I'm fucking spoiling for a fight.'

Chapter 63

Marcus Hall took a theatrical walk around the courtroom towards the jury, before turning back to try to turn the screw a bit more. He'd already made Cramer shift in her seat with his questioning and turned back to her before making his next point.

'You see, Acting DCI Cramer,' he said with a swish of his gown. 'I think your judgement has come into question in a number of ways recently, and I fear there's a pattern emerging here, a worrying pattern, that suggests perhaps you're not fit for the position you hold. That, perhaps, you should be given a leave of absence.'

Cramer's face had started to flush now with anger, but she was trying to remain cool.

'If you have a question, Mr Hall, please feel free to ask me and I will do my best to answer you.' Her voice cracked midway through the sentence.

Hall wasted no time striking upon the weakness. 'Well, let's take your current case, Acting Detective Chief Inspector. Four women dead so far, no discernible progress on finding a culprit, and yet you're still leading it. Why is that?'

'Because I am good at my job, Mr Hall. Very good. Otherwise we wouldn't be here with your client Robert Kane on charges of murder, drugs, and arms and human trafficking.' She felt like she had struck back a little, but his correct assessment of the case still bruised her.

Hall was relentless. 'Surely if you were very good at your job, you would have done more than you have to apprehend the monster hurting these women?'

Cramer was starting to feel sick to her stomach. 'Mr Hall, I don't see why any other case I am working on or have worked on has any relevance whatsoever to the night when your client Robert Kane killed my officer in cold blood.'

Hall was smiling again, he could tell he was getting under her skin.

'It is relevant, Acting DCI Cramer, because, just last night, another operation you were in charge of went wrong, didn't it?'

Cramer felt her blood run cold. Her guts turned to ice, and sweat began to bead on her top lip. Her head started to swim. He couldn't know about that.

'I am not sure what you are referring to, Mr Hall...'

Hall thundered in. 'Then let me remind you. Your colleague, a detective constable this time, Leila Johnson, was undertaking a surveillance operation, once again being overseen by you, and has not been seen since. Ring any bells now?'

Cramer was finding it hard to breathe. This was an ongoing case – he shouldn't be bringing that up in court.

'I mean, I would find it hard to believe that such a monumental moment in an operation such a short time ago would be so easy to forget so quickly,' said Hall, rubbing salt in her wounds as she fought to regain her composure. He really had blindsided her with this.

She looked briefly to the floor, took a deep breath, and leaned into the microphone so she could be heard clearly. She glanced to the press bench, and the reporters were now writing feverishly into their notebooks.

'Detective Constable Johnson was undercover with another officer, and yes something happened which meant we were not aware of her whereabouts.'

'Were not aware, or are still not aware, Acting Detective Chief Inspector?'

Cramer tried to evade answering. 'I don't see how this is relevant to the case we are in court for now.' She was hoping Riley, again the sole prosecutor on this case, would do something to stop this onslaught. Yet it was hard to see if he was even still listening.

'It is relevant' – Hall was looking at the judge now – 'because I am showing the court that your operations have a habit of running into – how shall I put this? – difficulties. Wouldn't you say, ma'am?'

Cramer looked to the public gallery where Jason Baird sat red with rage at the deception he must be feeling. She had very specifically asked him to keep this to himself, yet here it was, being aired in open court, risking his girlfriend's life and making it fair game for all the journalists because it was covered by legal privilege. But where had Hall got this from? Who'd spoken to him about what had happened at the station? That was the only way he could possibly have known about it.

'Acting DCI Cramer?' Hall was still waiting for an answer to his question.

'No, I wouldn't. There are difficulties in operations at various times, and many more have gone without a hitch than have had any kind of problem. It's unfortunate, I would agree, that two ops within the past eighteen months have not gone as I'd hoped, but I see no reason for you to try to smear me as a police officer. I am good at my job, and I know that my superior officers have every faith in my abilities.' She was embellishing here and wasn't entirely sure she was telling the truth anymore, even though she was still under oath. But it was at least the truth as she saw it.

Judge Robinson had clearly heard enough too. 'Mr Hall, I tend to agree with Acting Detective Chief Inspector Cramer about this line of questioning, and I'm calling a halt to proceedings here for today. We will reconvene at nine tomorrow morning.'

Once Judge Robinson had left the court, there was a lot of noise and activity. Journalists were racing out of the court, dialling their editors before they had even reached the doors at the back of the room, ready to impart the latest details that had been revealed in open court. Everything that had been said could be reported, and Cramer had to speak to Davo as soon as possible to set up some sort of damage control.

But first she made a beeline for Hall, who was busy putting files into his briefcase.

'Who the fuck told you that, Hall?'

He smiled at her, as if it was all a game. 'Now, Callie, you can't expect me to reveal my sources. You know that's not how this works. But it's true, isn't it?'

Cramer didn't respond to that question and asked her own instead.

'How do you sleep at night, Marcus? I mean, the shit you pull to get clients who are as guilty as sin off the hook, you really shouldn't get any sleep at all.'

'Ah, Callie, you're blaming me for the ills of the world, and I am just one man. What could I possibly do compared to the might of Kent Police? You do your job properly, and it makes my job extremely hard. But, so often, you do your job so badly, as I was trying to point out. You see, it's not down to me to help you put people away. Everybody is entitled to the best defence possible, and that's what I aim to give them.'

'For a fat fucking fee, Marcus.' Cramer wasn't about to let this go.

‘What I do is a specialist service, Callie, you know that as well as I do. And yes, it does cost. But what you must remember is that all it takes for evil to succeed is for good men to do nothing. Unfortunately for you, far too often that seems to be the case with you and your team. Apparently good men – and women – do nothing. Or certainly not enough.’

Hall had finished packing his briefcase and turned to pick his coat up from the back of his chair. He put it on as he continued. ‘So, if you don’t want evil to succeed, I suggest you do something. Anything. Make my life harder rather than easier.’ He picked his briefcase up and started to walk away, but turned back to Cramer after just two steps.

‘You see how helpful I am, I’ve even told you what you need to do to convict more criminals, Acting Detective Chief Inspector.’ He smiled his broadest grin yet and bounced out of the room.

Hall had an uncanny ability to suck all the life out of Cramer – he was an energy vampire.

Riley was standing behind her, listening to the altercation between the two of them.

She rounded on him. ‘I don’t know what you’re looking at, Riley. You were no bloody help either.’

Riley said nothing. As usual.

As she left the courtroom, Jason was waiting for her outside. It was something she was expecting, but wasn’t sure how she was going to handle another person ranting at her in such quick succession.

She walked up towards him and put her hands up to him in an admission of defeat. ‘Jason, I genuinely have no idea how he knew about that – it’s not something that should have been out in the open.’

‘Yeah, well, you told me that would potentially make it harder for you to reach her in time, as there was a danger he’d change his methods. So, I hope to God you haven't signed her death warrant now.'

Cramer exploded.

'Wait a minute, I wasn't the one who brought that up, Jason, and that fuckwit Riley—' Who, as always happens, was walking past just as she said this. He gave her a filthy look. She looked down at the floor, exasperated, but carried on in more of a whisper.

'That fuckwit Riley just left me hanging, at no time did he jump in and stop it.'

'Cramer, you know something? So much of what you say seems to be someone else's fault. Have you thought about how much of this stuff is *your* fault?'

She was dumbfounded. He carried on.

'You did run both those ops, and things did go wrong on both that have resulted in serious catastrophes. Adam Williams fucking died—'

'You don't have to remind me, Baird. I was there trying to stop him bleeding out, in case you weren't listening before.'

'Yeah, well, Leila is still missing. And let me tell you, if she doesn't come back to me in one piece, then I will absolutely slaughter you in the papers. Do you understand me?'

He stormed out of the building, leaving Cramer standing in the lobby, wondering if this day could get any worse.

Chapter 64

Cramer was incensed and barged through the doors into the custody suite, smashing the handles into the walls either side. She was determined to find the person who'd told Hall everything. It was the only explanation as to how he knew about Leila and was able to royally fuck them over.

The custody sergeant hadn't yet changed with the new shift, and the uniformed officer who had accompanied Collinson to the interview room this morning was also at the desk.

'Who spent most time with fucking Marcus Hall this morning?'

'Er, ma'am, I don't know what this is about,' the sergeant said. 'Can you explain?'

'I mean, who told him about Leila Johnson, about Leila going missing. I am sure it's now the talk of the fucking station, but it should be clear that this isn't something we need out on the street. Whoever told him has guaranteed it's going to be all over the papers tomorrow morning, and not just the local ones either, the nationals too, because he just ripped into me in court about it. And Leila's life is in even more danger now than it was.'

The officer flushed from his collar upwards. He clearly knew what she was talking about now.

'Well, I... er... he asked me what was going on. We were chatting, just chatting. He was being friendly.'

Cramer couldn't believe what she was hearing.

'Friendly? That's the last thing Marcus Hall is! There's always an agenda. So, what exactly did you say? I presume the station jungle drums have been beating hard.'

He couldn't go redder if he tried, he was already in danger of bursting a blood vessel.

'Yes, ma'am. There's a lot of concern, always is if a colleague is down. Well, you know—'

'And you think that spreading gossip, especially outside the station is the best way to help?' She was incandescent. 'You do realise what you've done? You've no idea of the problems this has caused, and I am not going to leave it there.'

She started to head back through the double doors that had not long stopped swinging from her entrance.

'I'm sorry, ma'am, I didn't think... Sorry, ma'am.'

She turned back.

'You will be sorry. Expect a disciplinary for this.'

By the time she'd got back to her office, the news of her experience in court had already reached them. Thank goodness she'd already got Rob to speak to Leila's parents in confidence, otherwise this would be the first they knew about her disappearance.

Jill was still sitting in Cramer's office, and Jack, Max, and Rob were all in the incident room. She flew in like a force of nature, putting them all on edge. It wasn't how she normally operated.

'I want everyone together now – only key staff,' she said to Rob as she blew through the outer office to reach her own. She went through her door, took off her coat, and threw it over her chair. There was no time to lose. She motioned Jill to come into the outer office too, and once all admin staff had left, she sat on the edge of the desk in the corner as usual to talk to her colleagues.

'Right, so I'm pretty sure by now you all know what a fuck-up court was today, and why Marcus Hall made me look like a fucking idiot. One of the custody officers told him all about Leila this morning. Not too much of a surprise it was all over the station, I guess, given the manpower we engaged to deal with the interviews, but Leila's disappearance is going to be all over the news.'

'Guv, it already is.' Rob handed her a printout of the local paper's take on its website.

'Shit,' Cramer hissed. 'OK, well I know you don't need me to tell you what this means. We have to find Helena and Leila, fast.'

She looked over to Max who had been working his way through a pile of papers.

'Max, what are those?'

'Tech sent over a stack of printouts of people who might be of interest to us on the emails and social media you wanted. To get the relevant info, they have gone back a year – that was what Leila asked them to do. So' – he pointed to the pile of papers – 'this is the result.'

'How long have you been working on that?' Cramer asked.

'A few hours, but it's slow, and so far, there's nothing that helps us. Some can be discounted because we've spoken to them and they either had an alibi or gave us no cause for concern. Leila had already done a lot of the data crunching on those but cross-referencing them is taking time.'

'Why the hell haven't Tech sent everything to us so it's searchable on screen? That's ridiculous, get back to them and tell them to sort it out. We don't have time for that.'

Cramer looked around at her team and caught Rob's eye.

'Rob, help Max get this sorted out. Shortcut this mess ASAP. What the bloody hell were they thinking?'

Rob swallowed hard. 'Boss, I just think that's wasting time. We need to focus our efforts in a different way, a more effective way...'

Cramer cut him off.

'And where exactly do you propose we start looking Rob? Any bright ideas? Because if you have, I could bloody well use them.'

'Sorry, guv, I know, I mean... Well, it's just frustrating. I feel helpless. And responsible.'

'Helpless is the last thing any of us is, Rob. We're her only hope and we've got to keep it together. We need to find not just her, but Helena too – it's a small mercy the press don't know about her disappearance yet. But it's just a matter of time.

'I know it seems mundane, but trust me, in all my experience, it's often the most tedious data crunching that yields the biggest results.'

Rob shook his head and looked at the floor, before looking back up at his boss and then nodding slowly. She knew he preferred action to inaction, but there was nowhere else to focus their energy.

'The sooner we get through those names, the closer we'll be to finding Leila. Just don't ask me how I know – it is a gut feeling,' Cramer said. She looked around the room. 'Where's Jack?'

Jill spoke for the first time since Cramer had got back to the office.

'Still following Collinson. Hasn't let him out of his sight since he left you this morning.'

Rob joined in. 'Yeah, that's right, guv, but apparently he hasn't moved a muscle since you brought him in. Stayed in the house, done nothing, and gone nowhere.'

Cramer nodded. She wasn't surprised after his reaction to questioning that morning, even though so much had happened since then to make it feel like it was a lot longer ago than that.

'How are we doing on the warrant to search his home, Rob? Did Jack speak to Davo?'

'No, I did as Jack went straight out. And the answer is slow, guv. Davo wouldn't entertain it, said the risk is too great. He's livid about the op going awry, and one of his officers going missing—'

'*His* officers?' Cramer cut in. 'I'd be surprised if he even knew Leila's bloody name last week, the sanctimonious bastard.'

'Yeah, well...' Rob continued, 'either way, he wasn't prepared to sign it off. Not without more evidence. Everything we have is circumstantial, he said. There's nothing solid linking Collinson with the murders, and with Hall as his lawyer, he's just not prepared to take the risk. Not yet.'

Cramer blew out a long breath.

'So, was he completely against the idea?'

'Not completely. He said he wished he could authorise the application. He genuinely wants to find Leila too, but he just won't sanction that, not without more evidence to present to a judge to get a warrant.'

Cramer couldn't really argue; solid proof was scarce for sure, but that didn't alter her growing suspicions.

But she was also aware they'd all been working non-stop for more hours than they should have been. So, she had to ask.

'Look, we're all tired, and if anyone needs a break, then feel free to head home, or get your head down for a few hours at least.'

'Leila isn't getting a break, guv, so neither am I,' Rob said.

'Nor me,' Max added.

Jill held up her hands. 'I'm with all of you for as long as it takes.'

Cramer had been working in her office for a few hours when her phone rang, waking Jill, who had fallen asleep in a chair in the corner.

It was a beat officer.

'Ma'am, you need to get here as soon as you can. We have a body.'

Chapter 65

Cramer drove with blues and twos, racing through streets of Canterbury as the blue lights ahead of them competed with the city's light pollution, pounding against the lights around them, a visual heartbeat completely at odds with a young woman whose life had been snuffed out. There was no need for them to mark the spot they were heading towards: it was the city's most famous landmark.

Cramer's heart had fallen through the floor at the beat officer's words earlier. She hoped to God he was wrong and couldn't bring herself to think about who might be their next victim. Either Helena or Leila would be equally heartbreaking, and her heart was beating so hard in her chest she could hear it in her ears. She had to remind herself to breathe.

As Cramer and Jill entered the cathedral grounds, the gravity of the situation could not be more palpable. The peacefulness of this grand building had been shattered by the number of officers now present. The crime scene cordon had been set at the perimeter, radios were hissing, and the entire cathedral grounds had been closed to anyone who absolutely didn't need to be there.

Forensics had already arrived; the arc lights that had been set up inside could be seen through the stained-glass windows, creating coloured patches on the flagstones on the way into the main entrance.

Both women had donned white forensic suits before they entered the cordon, and Cramer steeled herself for the worst: seeing Leila under those harsh lights. She almost couldn't bear to look as they rounded the corner into the main body of Canterbury Cathedral.

They walked slowly up the nave, and Cramer couldn't help but look up to the beautifully vaulted ceiling. This was a stunning building both inside and out, even tonight.

Cramer and Jill headed towards the arc lights, which were focused on a smaller section off to the left as they walked in, but they couldn't see how to get there.

'Goddamn it. How do we get down there?' Cramer swerved around to one of the uniformed officers standing nearby and repeated, 'How do we get down here?'

'To The Martyrdom, ma'am?' came the reply.

It took Cramer a little by surprise; she hadn't realised it had a specific name. 'Er, yes.'

'It's that way.' He pointed in the general direction they had already come from, which wasn't helpful.

They made their way through the pews and down the steps towards the spot where the CSIs were already working. As they rounded the corner, her heart leapt and sank simultaneously. The woman in front of her wasn't Leila. But it was Helena.

Though, it wasn't easy to tell it was Helena. Her beautiful blonde hair had been shaved from her head, like the others, and in death everyone looked less like themselves. But there was no doubting the method of her death. She was naked, shaved, and hanging above the Altar of the Sword's Point, the sculpture marking where Thomas Becket had been murdered centuries before. There was the now familiar deep red wound under her left ribcage. There were ligature marks on both her wrists and her ankles, and a pair of handcuffs hung from her left wrist. Proof, as if they needed it, that Leila had been taken by the same man.

Helena's feet were soiled and blue, and terrible bruising covered her misshapen thigh. Her head lolled to one side. The rope around her neck looked similar to the second victim, also hanged, but that was for Simms to confirm.

Cramer stood stock still, staring at the scene. Lost for words. Another loss in her life. Another life taken too soon. She hadn't saved Helena. But not only was this another victim, a fifth now, she was also the daughter of one of her mother's closest friends. Cramer wanted to avert her gaze, but she couldn't. The tears welled up in her eyes as she remembered how full of life Helena had been. Taken away. For what? The tears retreated as fire boiled up in her blood to replace the pain. Whoever was doing this was going to pay.

'Let's go Jill, we've no time to waste. We can't help Helena now, but we can help Leila. We can reach her in time.' But that time was getting shorter by the hour.

Simms moved towards the pair as they both looked at the sorry scene.

Jill was the first to speak. 'Have you found the note yet, John?'

Simms shook his head. 'Not yet. We have three guys looking outside and within the cathedral itself. But as you can imagine, there are almost infinite places for it to be hidden in a place as large as this.'

He bent down to pick up a brush from his forensic case and stood up again, his white overalls stretching as usual to cover his height. But the usual banter was missing, Cramer – along with everyone else – just didn't have the stomach for it.

'Can you let me know as soon as you have anything we can use? I mean as soon as. We need to move really fast,' Cramer urged.

'Of course. I heard about Leila's disappearance on the news – I'm so sorry.'

Cramer felt numb, her emotions buried so deep at this stage that all she could was keep moving forwards, keep the investigation going. Despite that brief moment before, she simply couldn't allow them to surface.

'Thanks, John, but don't be sorry, just give me something to work with. Yesterday.'

Cramer looked for a few more seconds at Helena before she turned to Jill and motioned that they leave the forensics team to it. She couldn't bear to look anymore.

'I'll do the post-mortem tonight, Callie.'

Cramer nodded. She couldn't manage anything else.

As they returned to their car, Cramer heard Jill muttering to herself.

'What?' said Cramer. She'd regained her composure, but all patience had evaporated.

'It's just where Helena was left this time. The cathedral. If he was religious, why would he want to leave a body there? To desecrate it? Especially given the significance of Canterbury Cathedral to the Church of England.'

Cramer offered nothing.

'But what about the placement within the cathedral? The Martyrdom. That section is called the Martyrdom. What is he telling us with that?'

Cramer couldn't bring herself to speak. They'd reached the car by the time Jill had finished talking, and they both got in without saying another word.

Chapter 66

Cramer waited for Jill to take the opportunity to analyse her while they were driving to the Fitzsimmons's property again. The pressure of this investigation, the lack of breaks, the increasingly aggressive press coverage, Leila's disappearance, Adam's court case, her situation with Patrick at home, although she hadn't gone into detail about that... In any normal situation, any one of these things would be more than most could bear. Yet she was dealing with it all. Simultaneously. Cramer had no idea how she was managing to do it, and still functioning at a high level.

She could feel her sense of humour had lessened though. It was still there, she had no doubt about that, but it was being suffocated. Cramer's job was to drive others forward in extreme and upsetting circumstances, and to do it with a smile and good humour that made working in this team more than bearable, desirable. And yet, she could feel the psychological cocktail increasing its potential to go Molotov at any moment.

As Cramer stared at the road ahead, she could feel the heat of Jill's stare boring into the side of her face. Finally, she spoke.

'How are you doing, Cal? And don't fob me off with some glib comment or other. I want to know how you really are.'

Cramer was grateful that she was driving so she couldn't look at her friend and made a concerted effort to avoid any kind of eye contact.

'Are you putting me on your couch, Jill? Are you going to bill me for this?'

'Very funny.'

But Jill wasn't giving up that easily. 'You know what I mean. I'm worried about you, Cal, and I want to make sure you're going to come out of this safely.'

Cramer snorted a laugh. 'Alive would do me, Jill. Alive would be good enough.'

They both went quiet. It was a poor choice of words given Leila's predicament. Cramer was trying too hard to cover, and she knew it.

'Sorry, Jill, I know I could have phrased that better.'

'I don't care so much about your phrasing as much as you just talking, Cal. You're not talking, you're speaking, but not talking.'

Cramer was still for a time.

'I don't know what to say, or where to start. I feel like I am surfing a wave I know is about to crash, but I just don't know whether I am going to come to the surface in the sunshine, or whether I am going to be smashed to pieces by the water. But for now, I can't worry about any of that. I've just got to keep on top of this, for as long as I can, and do everything I can to make it to the shore in one piece. Along with everyone else.'

She was talking about Leila again.

'Well, when you're ready to talk, I'm here to listen. As a friend and a professional, if you need both. Or either.'

As she said this, they turned once again into Elizabeth Fitzsimmons's drive, and parked up in front of the beautiful Georgian property.

Mrs Fitzsimmons was waiting for them her dressing gown in the drawing room, having been woken by a phone call to let her know that Cramer was on her way. Her security detail had let them in; at that time of the morning, her assistant wasn't going to be around. It was clear she was trying to hold her composure, which is no more than either of them expected, but the slight redness to her eyes provided clear evidence of tears that had dried shortly before their arrival.

This was the part of the job that Cramer hated most, and there had been many times she had thought about giving it all up so she would never have to bring such awful news to a family again. But her drive to help those who couldn't help themselves, to stop people being hurt or injured whenever possible, made this part of the job bearable enough to keep going.

Cramer steeled herself, going into the mode police officers use when they have to tell a family they've lost someone. There's a detachment necessary to deliver the news and still remain professional. Yet for this, as there was very much a personal involvement here too, it might have been a better idea to get another officer to perform the duty, but Cramer's conscience wouldn't let her. Cramer felt a responsibility to take on the task after the promises she'd made to Elizabeth. The promise that she had now broken.

'Mrs Fitzsimmons, we have some news about your daughter.'

Elizabeth seemed unable to get any words out initially, her body language spoke of both fear and excitement, which, to a great extent, was about to make this even harder for her than it might otherwise have been.

'Have you found her?' she asked, clearly hoping.

That question stabbed at Cramer's heart every time.

'Yes, ma'am.' Cramer opted for formality – she was her ultimate boss after all. 'We have.' Cramer took a deep breath before continuing. 'But I am very sorry to tell you that Helena was not found alive.'

It took what seemed like an age for the news to sink in, but once it did, Elizabeth Fitzsimmons was unable to maintain her composure. She was not known for weakness, so to see her now, her face contorted by the emotional pain of finally losing her daughter, her body shaking with emotion, was difficult for either Cramer or Jill to see as they witnessed the crumbling of hope itself.

'Is there anyone we can call for you, Mrs Fitzsimmons?' Cramer asked.

She shook her head, unable to speak for the moment. Cramer watched as she calmed herself enough to answer.

'No, thank you, but no. My husband is travelling, and... Oh, you will need to inform him too. Or would you like me to ...' Her face contorted again as the tears came.

'We can take care of that for you if you would like,' said Cramer. Mrs Fitzsimmons nodded without looking up at them. 'We'll get the details from your security officers.'

Elizabeth nodded and did her best to smile.

'Is there anything you need?' Jill asked. 'Some tea, anything?'

Again, she regained her composure enough to answer.

'No, thank you. What I need you can't give me.' Her face creased again.

Cramer moved over to her and held her hand.

'Elizabeth, I know what you're going through. Believe me, I do.' Cramer looked at Jill; she knew exactly where she was coming from. 'But I will find the man who did this to Helena, and he will wish he'd never been born.'

Chapter 67

Jack had been sitting outside Collinson's house for the last sixteen hours for what amounted to the third or fourth day in a row. He was losing count. People think surveillance is a glamorous job, but what they don't get to see is the endless hours of watching while nothing is happening, or the times you have to pee in a bottle because you can't leave your patch to head to a loo for fear of missing a target. Glamorous is the very last thing this job is.

It was colder today than it had been the rest of the week, and Jack was about to neck the last of his coffee when his phone rang. His head and arm were throbbing in unison with every heartbeat.

'Boss.'

'Jack, any movement from Collinson overnight?'

'No, none. He came back to the house after we interviewed him, and hasn't moved since. Lights out about 2330.'

'Could you have missed anything?'

Jack grunted to himself. Of course, he hadn't missed anything. He was a professional. 'No, ma'am.' His tone was clipped. 'No chance at all.'

Cramer clearly heard the testiness in his voice as her next comment was more moderate.

'OK. Shit, sorry, Jack. You may as well come off the surveillance. Collinson isn't our guy.'

'What? How the hell... I mean, how do you know?'

'Helena's body has been found tonight, so if Collinson hasn't moved, then he isn't our killer.'

Chapter 68

Leila had been trying to focus on keeping her wits about her, but she hadn't eaten in what must now be more than twenty-four hours. Or at least it felt like that long. With no light in the room, she had no real concept of time since there was no sun to offer her a point of reference, but that was her best guess.

Her arms were pinned high above her head, another thing working against her. The screams she'd heard hours ago had sent a shockwave through her. The second time they hadn't come from her. So, it must have been Helena, and then silence. Thicker and more oppressive than before. It begged the question of what would happen next. To her.

Footsteps outside. She snapped her head round to listen. Her heart started to beat faster. The lock was opened, and the shaft of light as the door opening momentarily burned her retinas. All she could make out was the shadow of a figure.

Her natural reaction was to move away, the only attempt she could make to hide her naked body from him. As he moved towards her, his face was still in shadow. He stopped short of her face by only a couple of inches.

'It will tell them to stop,' he hissed. 'It will make them stop.'

What? Stop what? Was he hallucinating? She didn't answer. His eyes were flashing with anger.

'It will make them stop, or it will get hurt. Badly hurt.' His voice was getting louder.

She hesitated, but not answering would make it worse. 'I... I don't know what you mean.'

His eyes darted away from her again, and he lunged towards the floor, swiping at something invisible to her. He ran back towards her.

'*Make them stop!*'

Leila was thinking fast, trying to find a strategy to calm him, but he was out of control. She decided to play along. 'OK, OK, I'll make them stop. Just... stand back. Move away from me.'

He looked directly at her, waiting for her to make a move. She really wasn't sure what to do next, but closed her eyes, so she looked like she was trying to control something – whatever he was talking about – with her mind.

'It didn't try hard enough, did it?' He sneered at her. 'It needs to pay for that.'

Chapter 69

Cramer felt her phone vibrating in her pocket as she stood in the outer office. She pulled it out and saw Simms's name, and she moved into her office before answering it.

'Simms, what do you have?'

'Our latest victim has some additional injuries that we didn't have with the other victims. She has a broken femur, which looks like it was done with blunt-force trauma – a stick or bar judging by the bruising. And she has been repeatedly hit in the stomach, but this didn't happen long before she died.

'There's some bruising evident, but the damage to the abdominal muscles is significantly more than the bruising on the skin would suggest. So, my thinking is her heart stopped pumping soon after the damage was inflicted, and the blood didn't get the time to break into the skin layers.'

Cramer swallowed hard before speaking. 'That suggests he's getting more violent.'

Simms was silent momentarily at the other end. 'We've also found the note, Callie, but there's a difference this time.'

'How come? What's changed?'

'It doesn't quote the Bible. It's something different.'

'But it's definitely the same paper, handwriting? Everything else the same?'

'Yes, definitely from the same person, we've confirmed it already. I wanted to be sure, and we are.'

'What does it say?'

'It's a quote. The one about evil... You know the one I mean?'

She stopped dead.

'Yes, I do. Can you send it to me, please? A picture is fine for now, I need it soon as...'

'Sure, I'll send it to your mobile now.'

She'd barely ended the call before her mobile pinged. Cramer's heart was racing. Surely it couldn't be? But she wasn't talking herself out of it without checking.

She opened her WhatsApp and waited for the image to download.

Jill popped her head around the door. 'Nothing of note in the social media data Rob and Max were crunching,' she said. 'But the bloody idiots in Tech had mixed in the DVLA data that Leila had asked for. Seems they've had it for a few days already.'

Cramer's skin broke out in a cold sweat as she stared at her colleague and friend. Had they had this data sooner, maybe they could have prevented Leila from being taken. She rushed out of her office into the main incident room, shoving her phone in her pocket after seeing the image Simms had sent.

'Who has the cars we're looking for, Max?' Cramer was waiting with bated breath.

Max leafed through the sheets to find the information. 'A few more than you might expect, there were twelve in total, not all owned by the same person. But it seems they were at the same address in all cases.'

'OK, how can we reduce the number we consider to be serious possibilities? Have you looked at the properties? How close they are to Canterbury?' Cramer was pushing hard.

'Ahead of you, boss...' Max said, pulling out the relevant files.

'Don't piss about, Max. Tell me. '

He opened the folders in order: 'Marcus Hall owns a Porsche Carrera 911 and a Range Rover. He's the only one who owns both. The other two have access to them, but don't own both. One is Patrick Cramer – any relation?' Max laughed.

Cramer stiffened. 'Um, he's my husband...'

Max's eyes widened, as did Jack's and Rob's. The silence was deafening.

Cramer felt the heat rise up her neck but remained impassive. She would deal with it later.

Max stuttered 'Er, Oh... OK. Well, he has access to a Porsche and a Land Rover Discovery registered at the same address... plus a Mercedes S-type, an Audi Quattro, a Volkswagen Golf and a Toyota Prius.'

'Yes, I know, I live there, Max. Who else?'

Rob and Max exchanged glances again. That was quite a list of cars for two people in one house.

'C'mon, who else?' Cramer was getting testy.

Max hesitated. 'Well, David Riley, the prosecutor on the Kane case. He owns a Land Rover Discovery, and his father owns a Porsche Carrera 911, and an Aston Martin DB9. All registered to the same address. So, I guess he could drive any of them.'

Cramer raised her eyebrows. 'Riley? He doesn't seem the racy type.' Again, there was silence from the rest of the team.

She recovered her composure. 'Listen, I would know if my cars were being used for anything like this, it's definitely not Patrick.' Rob, Max and Jack all looked at each other as she called them 'my car*s*', multiple. This was precisely why she hadn't shared her private life with her work colleagues before. The judgement was there within a matter of seconds, and it was likely to get worse. She ignored it for now.

'So, that leaves Hall and Riley. Max, get the information on both their properties. I want to know where they are, how big they are, what rooms they have, whether they have a basement, out-houses, how much land they have. Everything.'

Max shuffled through papers on his desk and handed her a file. 'Already done, guv.' She opened it and saw the images of her own, very substantial house at the top. She looked up to see all three of them looking at each other, not daring to catch her eye.

She cast aside Patrick's file and looked back to the rest of the images, leafing through them: the layout, the driveway, the grounds, the outbuildings. Hall and Riley had impressive homes, but both were smaller than Cramer's, a fact now not lost on her team. She took a deep breath and blew her cheeks out, focusing on the remaining two properties, pulling sheets out this time, and examining them closer to the light. Each property had underground structures, but it wasn't clear exactly what they were.

Cramer turned one paper at ninety degrees then back again before looking at her team. Not one of her officers had averted their gaze from her this time. It was like they were in shock.

'Max, get some clearer images of these structures. Is it a basement? A complex of tunnels? It could be the perfect place to hold someone.'

Rob sat back in his chair. 'Fuck me, Guv. Are you saying?'

Cramer nodded.

'Yes, either Hall or Riley could have Leila. Simms has just sent this through to me,' she passed her phone around the team for them to look at the quote left with Helena. It read:

The only thing necessary for the triumph of evil is for good men to do nothing.

Rob looked confused.

'That was the note left with Helena's body?'

Again, Cramer nodded.

'Why not the Bible quotes like before?'

'I have a theory, but we need to get this information together, fast.'

'Why do you think it's one of them?' Rob questioned.

'When I was at court today, Hall said exactly that phrase to me, and with the cars fitting, it's looking like too much of a coincidence.'

'Guv,' Max said, 'Hall's house is in more than one hundred acres of land. Nothing around him for miles. It would be the perfect place to hold someone without being disturbed. The underground area isn't so much a basement as a series of natural caves, which the property was built above in the 1700s.'

'It has to be it,' Cramer confirmed. 'And Riley? What does he have?'

Max tapped into his keyboard at what seemed like a painfully slow speed. But he soon had the details up on the screen. 'Similar, lots of land, very big house, and what appears to be a system of caves underneath.'

'Shit, so it could be either...'

Just then her office phone rang, and she headed in to pick it up. She didn't recognise the code but answered. Her adrenaline pumped even harder.

'DCI Cramer,' she answered, she couldn't be bothered with the 'Acting' bit.

'DCI Cramer, this is Dr Santi Sandalo. We met at Dr Simms's office the other day.'

'Yes, I remember, do you have any results?' Cramer didn't have time for niceties.

'Your suspect has a really unusual arrangement of vein patterns – a central island with distal and proximal radiating veins – a bit like a starburst. I've only seen that pattern once before.

'It stood out because it was anomalous compared with the many others I had seen. You're very lucky, because at that point, I was able to look back at the first research database collected in Scotland when this identification technique was being established.

'Once I had checked that, not only did I find that the vein pattern matched, but so do the finger creases, and a scar on the back of his hand near the thumb. I'm as surprised as anyone to say, but... we have a match. I wanted to call you directly to give you the details. I hope that's OK?'

'That's more than OK,' Cramer said. 'What do you have?'

'I can tell you exactly who you're looking for.'

Chapter 70

Both Leila's arms were still above her head, and the pain was excruciating, enough to make her pass out. The dried blood from her weeping wrists had rolled down in streaks and dripped onto her bare scalp.

Her body was burning with fever and she was shaking uncontrollably. Her heart was sinking through her body, a sensation she couldn't stop no matter how hard she tried. It felt like she was dying. She remembered from her police first aid training that this was a sense of impending doom, a sensation for a patient with a serious condition that shouldn't be ignored. But she was the patient, and there was nothing she could do to help herself.

As she came round, she saw a movement in the darkness out of the corner of her eye. He was there, already in the room with her, and the realisation made her gasp. There was the sound of a match striking and suddenly his face was fully illuminated in the light of a candle. Her eyes grew wide as she recognised who he was.

'You... you bastard!'

He got up slowly from the chair, he was back in shadow. Leila couldn't believe her senses were telling her the truth. She must be hallucinating.

He headed towards her, and she felt his hands undoing the shackles above her head, freeing her arms to fall to her sides. The blood rushing back into her arms should have been a relief, but she cried out as they fell back down by her sides. Once again, she nearly passed out and fell to the cold, hard floor.

'Get up,' he said in such a calm and even voice he could have been mistaken for trying to help.

She was going in and out of consciousness thanks to the lack of food. She couldn't move.

'Get. Up,' he said again, angrier than before, standing over her at his full height.

Leila tried to move, tried to get up from the floor, but had no chance of standing. Her body was too weak.

He leaned down towards her, squatting on his haunches as if he was talking to a child, and hissed at her, his face filled with anger and more malevolence than she'd experienced from anyone before. He grabbed her around the back of the neck, his hand squeezing her neck muscles hard either side of her throat as he lifted her full weight from the floor. The spasm this induced made her scream, but he didn't flinch as he moved her towards a large wooden vat filled with water.

Her knees scraped along the floor as he dragged her, before throwing her useless body against the sides and pushing her head under the water. She held her breath, pushing back against his hand with all the strength she had left, before she used her arms to grip the wooden sides to stop herself being pushed further in. But her hand slipped on the wet wood, and he lifted her head back out again causing her to gasp for air.

'No, please...' she pleaded, her body feeling weaker as his strength increased.

'It will sink or swim, without any help from its spirits.'

He wrenched her left arm round behind her back, using his chest to hold her on the edge of the vat while he pulled her right arm behind her to meet her left. The unbearable pain forced a scream from her lips, she was fighting for her life.

She tried to pull her hands free, but he held them firmly with one hand, the other pushing her head hard under the water. She held her breath for as long as she could, before spluttering as she involuntarily inhaled liquid deep into her lungs. They were burning as she desperately pushed her head backwards, trying to force herself back out of the water.

Momentarily, he allowed her head to come back into the air, and she coughed hard as water escaped from her mouth in plumes of spittle with each forceful explosion of air from her lungs. She was desperate to get air in, but with the water filling her airways, there was no room for it. She vomited as the coughing caused her stomach to convulse and the bile burned her throat as it mixed with the fluid still escaping her lungs.

This process took seconds, but felt like hours, and she was soon under the water again, her head pushed hard downwards as she struggled with everything she had to stay alive. Her body was shaking, squirming, trying to release his iron grip on both her hands and the back of her head as she fought for life. Again, she inhaled water as he forced her further in, the wooden side of the vat now cutting into her chest under the pressure. Her eyesight started to fade as she felt her consciousness slipping away.

Just at that moment, her head was yanked backwards, forcing her face towards the ceiling, the coughing continuing as her body did its best to keep her alive. He leaned close to her ear as he spoke.

'It is not going to escape me to continue to wreak havoc in the outside world. This is its destiny. Here and now. It is clear, the sorcery continues to work as it fails to still itself in the water. Its spirits should fear this test, to leave it, but no. They remain and must be forced away. It works with the devil, but I am here to stop him.'

Her neck felt as if it was ready to snap under his hold, and he pushed her head again under the water. She was low on air, energy, life. She tried one last time to escape from his grip. She pushed back again, but there was no power there. She felt weak, her heart beating hard in her chest was slowing, slowing. Her face felt cold. All she could sense was the pressure of the water. It was too much. People talk of your life flashing before your eyes when you have a near-death experience, but she saw slow-moving images, people she loved, who had loved her. It was more calming than anything, and it made her feel like it was OK to give up. But part of her still wanted to fight.

She thought of her colleagues, how they'd let her down, how she was here alone and wanted so much to see everyone again. Her parents, her brothers, her boyfriend, Jason. It wasn't fair, wasn't right.

Her body went limp in the water. The fight had left her, her body had given up. All that was left was darkness.

Chapter 71

Max blue-lighted it towards the address as Cramer spoke to Davo over the phone about the situation. There was no time for admin, and Davo would either understand or he wouldn't. Right now, she really couldn't care less. Leila was far more important.

Max raced through every red light, roundabout, and junction with more than a few near misses as they headed out of Canterbury into the surrounding countryside. Rob and Cramer were putting on their body armour as they weaved through the rural lanes. Dawn was just about to break, and the low cloud meant the golden horizon would be unlikely to progress to a sunny day; for once, the weather mirrored the mood in the car. All their energy was focused on getting to Leila in time.

'Sir, we have had a major development in the case,' Cramer said to Davidson.

'Go on.' He'd clearly been woken by her call.

'We've got a positive ID from vein pattern identification,' Cramer said.

'From what...?'

'Sir, we have corroborating evidence, one of our suspects has been conclusively ID'd using vein patterns in the back of his hand. I'm not wrong. We're heading therc now.'

Davidson grunted at the other end of the phone. 'I've never even heard of that, Cramer, so how the bloody hell can you know you have the right man? Stop right now, that's an order. Getting this wrong could mean your career. You realise that?'

She knew Davo was missing the point, as usual, and wasn't listening. 'I'm not wrong, sir,' and she really hoped she was telling the truth. 'And if we don't act, it could mean Leila's life. I'll take that chance. I won't lose another officer. I just won't.'

She put the phone down on her boss and immediately called the control room for backup, giving the location they were minutes away from.

'Is Davo putting all of this on you, guv?' Rob said from the front seat.

She took a deep breath. 'Yes. Unless I'm right, and then he'll take all the credit.'

'I know you're right, guv,' he looked at her. 'We all do. And if there's any shit, we'll take it as a team.'

'Damn right,' said Jack next to Cramer.

'A hundred per cent,' Max chimed in as he rounded a corner on two wheels.

It made Cramer smile. 'Thanks, guys. But let's focus. We're going to get there before the backup, so for now at least, we're on our own, and we don't know what we are dealing with. So be prepared.' She made a mental note to work on her motivational speeches.

Cramer and Rob were poring over a downloaded layout of the caves beneath the house from a previous owner who had opened them for tours. Their ancient existence seemed at odds with the building above them, even though they had apparently been extended at the same time as the house above had been built, according to the history of the property Max had downloaded. Thank goodness most people know nothing about how to delete old or irrelevant information from the internet, otherwise they may have had no access to the caves' layout at all.

'Max, take it easy!' Cramer said as they all pinballed to one side of the car as he went around another corner, making it difficult to focus on the papers they were reviewing. 'We need to get there in one piece.'

Max turned back to her briefly and grinned, without slowing down a bit. Cramer and Rob carried on studying the map, both now holding the handles above their respective windows in a bid to stay in their seats.

'Max, is there an entrance into the cave system directly, or do we have to go through the house?' Cramer was hoping for the former; the latter would lead them through a maze of rooms and corridors, which would waste precious time that Leila might not have.

'Yeah, there is.' He leaned back from the front seat to show Cramer on the map, looking behind briefly, then flicking his attention back to where he was going, then back again to the map.

'You need to head around that corner' – he pointed to a track that led past the side of the imposing property – 'and there should be an entrance about four hundred metres that way. It's where the previous owner started the tours from.' It made sense. Why have a bunch of strangers traipsing around your home to allow a visit to an underground cavern if you could keep them in the garden?

'Shit, Max!' Jack shouted as his colleague hit the verge and bounced the car back into the middle of the road, just missing an oncoming car before regaining full control. Max smiled and theatrically mopped his brow. He seemed to be enjoying this.

Jack shuffled the papers he was holding, then leaned back to Cramer and Rob without speaking, with a picture between his thumb and forefinger. It was of an old-style, heavy oak door with a padlock and foliage covering most of the entrance. 'We'll need a set of bolt cutters for that, Rob?' Jack said.

Rob leant forward and felt under the front seat and pulled out a set of the cutters they needed. Cramer nodded her approval.

Max switched off the sirens that had been wailing up until now. They were close, and Cramer could feel knots appearing in her stomach. She swallowed hard and worked to keep calm as she told them the entry plan.

'Rob, you're with me. We'll head to the outside entrance, and Jack as soon as you have entry, two clicks on the radio, got it? We have no idea what we're going to find in there, and for now, we're on our own. Keep any comms to an absolute minimum until we know what we're dealing with. Radio silence until I tell you all otherwise, OK?'

'Yes, guv,' the men chorused.

Max made a sharp right turn into a driveway with two large concrete pillars either side of wrought-iron gates that had been left open. That was a concern. Wouldn't he have closed these? Or had them closed? It made her start to question herself, but now wasn't the time to second guess.

As Max went further up the drive, blue lights also off now, an impressive Georgian mansion opened up in front of them, the red brick contrasting against the ashen sky. The size of the property would give them problems and getting in would be the biggest hurdle to overcome. They would have to announce they were police, but there was a danger that would give him a chance to escape before they could even find him. It was a fine line, but they had to stay on the legal side of it. This was a lawyer they were dealing with after all.

'Max, pull in just over there,' Cramer said, pointing to a patch of grass with low trees that would prevent their car from being seen from the house, although they would have already been clocked by the CCTV if it was working – the cameras were certainly visible. It was a chance they would have to take.

Max wrenched the steering wheel to plant all four wheels of the car deftly on the grass, behind the low branches. It obscured their view of the house, but that meant they could not be seen directly either. For now. They had no time to lose.

Cramer took a deep breath in and then exhaled. 'Max, you and Jack go to the front and in through the house. Rob and I will take the back.'

Rob and Cramer left the car, closing their stab vests as they went. They weren't taking a chance on any risk they could mitigate. Jack and Max made their way to the front of the house.

The three of them stood waiting for final instructions from Cramer.

'Everyone clear?'

'Clear,' Max said over the radio. Rob just nodded to Cramer.

'Go.'

Jack and Max headed towards the front of the property with the enforcer, while Cramer and Rob ran round to the side, ready to gain entry to the caves from the outside. They went around four hundred metres, just as Max had said, before they saw the doorway covered in leaves. Rob made short work of the padlock with the bolt cutters. They both extended their batons before entering, Cramer taking the lead.

There was less and less light as they went down the stone steps into the dank darkness, moving silently along the corridor. The only sound was their footsteps ricocheting off the hard walls. The grey stone through which the caves were carved was relatively sheer to the left as they were walking, and Cramer ran her hand over it absent-mindedly as she was moving further into the darkness. There were ridges beneath her fingers where the tunnel had been cut from the rock.

Cramer stopped so her eyes could become accustomed to the darkness, but even after a few seconds, there was no change. She took her torch out of her pocket and switched it on. Immediately, she could see the tunnel extended forwards and round to the left about fifty metres in front of them, and there were three strong, wooden doors to her right, each with an ornate lock.

Both Cramer and Rob's radios briefly came to life with the two-click confirmation from Jack that he and Max were in. Cramer turned to Rob, who was walking close behind her, and she motioned for him to move past her to stand on the opposite side of the first door, where she had already stopped.

They both listened carefully for any noise. Cramer leaned in towards it, straining to hear even the smallest sound. Nothing. She tried the door gingerly, and to her surprise, it opened. She motioned to Rob to follow her in. She gently pushed the door, trying to stop the old hinges squeaking.

As she walked inside, she swept the room with her torch, seeing what she now knew was a Judas Chair in the far corner of the room, the sinister torture implement that Collinson had first mentioned at their meeting in his office. Her blood ran cold at the thought any of the victims might have been threatened with, let alone suffered it.

She tracked the light to the left as she went further into the room. There were shackles hanging down from the ceiling, and as she examined them more closely, she could see dried blood. She was careful not to touch anything. There was no doubt they were in the right place.

She swung her torchlight around to her right, and in the corner was a large, old-fashioned wooden bureau. She moved forwards past Rob until she was standing right by it, sweeping the light across it. The ornate inlaid lighter wood contrasted against the dark mahogany; she could tell it was antique. The writing flap was opened, with dark blue leather padding barely visible beneath the ink well and the paper she recognised immediately from the notes left with each victim.

She pulled her sleeve down over her hand and pulled open the drawer beneath the writing flap and saw bag after bag of hair within them – twelve in total. She picked up one from the top, it had *Helena Fitzsimmons* written in the same copperplate hand on a label. She threw it back, the action prompting Rob to join her by the desk.

'Holy fuck,' he whispered. 'These all from our victims?'

Cramer nodded her head. 'And more...' Her eyes were fire. Cramer keyed her radio and whispered: 'Jack, Max. We need you here. Now.'

She flicked her head to Rob, and they both moved out of the door into the corridor again.

They moved silently to the second door, which was deeper into the tunnel system on their right. Again, they listened outside. Nothing.

They moved to the third, making the same approach. This time, Cramer heard a kind of chanting, like an incantation from inside.

Cramer looked at Rob and touched her ear. He nodded to confirm he'd heard it too. Then Cramer noticed the door was slightly ajar, a dim flickering light inside... A candle? They had the element of surprise, but he would know the cave layout like the back of his hand, so outnumbering him may not give them the advantage it ought to have done.

Cramer motioned to Rob to go to the other side of the door once again as she counted down on her fingers from three, two, then one, before kicking the door open.

'Police, don't move!'

The door smashed open with the force. A figure in a black monk's cowl, an ornate dagger in his right hand, stood over

Leila's pale and unconscious body on a white, marble slab in front of him.

The figure was aware of their presence, and, as if in slow motion, he raised his head and looked straight at them from under his cowl and pulled a hideous grin. It was David Riley.

Before Cramer could react, he lifted his arm up before bringing his left hand to meet it, and with the full force of both hands, he slammed the knife into Leila's stomach, just below her left ribcage.

'No!' Rob and Cramer yelled.

But there was no movement from Leila, no reaction to any pain. Cramer's heart sank. They were too late. *'No, we can't be.'*

Cramer raced towards him and cracked her baton over his arm to make him let go of the knife. She felt his bones give way under the force, and he screamed in pain, before turning and grabbing at Cramer with his right hand. He caught her throat and squeezed hard, his eyes alight with anger with an incredible power that Cramer wouldn't have expected.

Cramer clawed at Riley's hand, struggled for breath, but Rob loomed up behind Riley punching him in the back and forcing him to let Cramer go.

Cramer dropped to the floor and moved towards Leila to assess her condition. She knew it was bad, but how bad.

Riley, growling like an attack dog, moved to his right and picked up the iron bar that was sitting on another ornate desk in the corner and swung at Rob, forcing him to jump back out of the way. He lost his balance as he hit the side of the vat full of water behind him and just missed falling in. Riley saw his chance and pushed his way past the blood-encrusted shackles hanging in the room and fled into the corridor outside.

Rob was still getting up from the floor as Cramer shouted to him. 'Get him, Rob!'

He took off in pursuit, following Riley as he ran to the right and deeper into the caverns.

Chapter 72

'Come on, Leila, don't give in. Please. *Please.*' Cramer frantically scanned her colleague's body, looking for what to do first. Leila's naked and shaved body now also had the eerily familiar red wound below her ribcage. Her upper arm was broken, the swelling and bruising clearly visible. But Cramer couldn't get distracted, she felt for a pulse in her neck. Nothing.

She moved her closer to the edge of the slab where she could reach her more easily. Her body was wet, and the slab itself was drenched in water, helping Leila's lifeless body to slide. She looked to her right at the water-filled vat behind her, the water all over the floor next to it, and realised what Riley had done.

But no, this wasn't how it was going to end. Cramer wouldn't let it.

Now Leila was closer to Cramer, she tried to find a pulse again in her wrist. Nothing. Her neck – nothing. She was getting desperate.

'No, come on, I'm not losing you.'

Cramer thumped her chest, trying to get a response. Leila's body jumped on the slab before settling back just as it had been.

'Leila, I know you can hear me. Fight for it, for fuck's sake.'

Cramer thumped her chest again. This time, some water escaped from her prone colleague's mouth, but there was still no autonomic response.

Cramer checked her neck for a pulse again. Nothing.

'Leila, keep fighting. C'mon, please, Leila, I don't want to lose you, I can't lose anyone else. No more.'

Cramer leaned Leila's head back, pinched her nose and breathed into her mouth, watching her chest rise and fall as she did so. Then moved back to her side to start chest compressions. She wasn't losing Leila. Not today. Not to Riley.

Water was coming from Leila's mouth each time she pressed down on her chest, flooding down her cheeks and neck onto the slab beneath her. There was blood coming out of the wound with each compression too, that was a dangerous problem, but Cramer had to get Leila's heart started again.

After twenty compressions, she did another breath, before opening her radio.

'Jack, Max, get an ambulance and get down here now. Third room on the right after the tunnel entrance.'

She started the compressions again with more urgency, more water was coming out of Leila's mouth and nose. Her lungs must be full, but Cramer wasn't giving up.

She went to do another breath into Leila's mouth, wiping away the water before pressing her lips against her colleague's and breathing into her lungs again. The chest rose and fell. Cramer checked for a pulse at the side of her neck. Still nothing.

'Oh God, c'mon, Leila, please. Please. You're too young to die. It's not your time.'

Cramer continued with the compressions, her body starting to fatigue as she kept the correct pace going. It didn't matter how tired she felt, she would fall before she would let Leila go.

Cramer fumbled her radio. 'Jack, where are you? Max?'

She went to do another breath just as she heard footsteps ringing through the tunnel outside the door. There was no time to lose. She pressed her mouth against Leila's again to give her another breath, and there was a rush of water and vomit that erupted straight into Cramer's mouth.

She turned to the side and spat the vile mix out. 'Shit!' She spat a few more times to try to get rid of the taste.

Cramer checked Leila's pulse again, nothing. No, wait, there was something, very faint, but it was there. And getting stronger.

As Jack rounded the corner, Leila's chest rose and fell on its own for the first time since they'd found her.

'Jack, stay with her' – Cramer pointed to Leila – 'and put pressure on that wound. Have you called for an ambulance?'

'Done. You got her back, boss. And our backup is literally two minutes away.'

Cramer only focused on the second part of the sentence and shook her head. 'We might not have that long. Which way did Riley go?'

'I haven't seen him, guv.'

'What do you mean? Rob chased him up towards the house. Which way did you come down here?'

'I came from the house. There's a doorway through to here from the hall. There's about two hundred and fifty metres of tunnel before you reach this section, but it goes off in two or three different directions. I found you because you were shouting to Leila to keep fighting and it travelled through to where I was.'

'But they didn't come past you?'

'No, no sign of them.'

Cramer readied herself to move out of the room, picking up her baton for protection. 'Stay with her until the ambulance crew arrive, Jack. Don't let her go.'

As she raced out of the room, she hit the button on her radio. 'Rob, where are you?'

No answer.

'Rob, talk to me. Where are you?'

Her radio crackled into life.

'Guv...' Rob was breathless. They were still running. 'Outside...' Another breath. 'Towards tennis courts...' Gasping for breath. 'He's heading for a barn... Shit!' She heard a thump as the radio went silent.

She was already running to the entrance they had come in from. 'Rob? Rob...? Are you there?' No reply.

Cramer saw the light streaming in from the entrance she and Rob had used and raced up the stone steps into the fresh air. She stopped momentarily to get her bearings, her eyes burning with the brightness of the day, before racing away from the house towards the tennis courts.

As she ran, she saw Rob on the ground ahead of her. He was holding his head as blood streaked down his face and hand, a rock next to him. She shouted to him as she neared.

'Rob, can you hear me?'

He raised his hand to say he was OK, but moved nothing else. She wasn't convinced. Out of the corner of her eye, she saw Max heading towards them both.

She keyed her radio.

'Max, check on Rob before you go anywhere, and make sure you direct the backup to the barn when it gets here.'

'Guv,' was his only answer.

Cramer continued running over the uneven ground, watching carefully where she was putting her feet. She couldn't hear anything other than her breathing as she pushed the pace towards a large barn near a small copse of trees. It was isolated and for now, she was on her own.

As she reached it, she saw the left-hand barn door was open. Riley was methodical, meticulous in his moves. It could be a trap but she had no choice but to follow.

She hugged the wall as she entered the barn. Again, she felt the grain of the wood under her fingertips, triggering a flashback to the last time she was in this position. It brought thoughts of Adam flooding back, she wasn't making the same mistake twice. Inside was a brand-new tractor, and some hay bales on the right-hand side. On the walls hung old-fashioned farming equipment: long saws, ancient shears, a scythe... She looked past all of them towards the back of the barn. Everything was silent. There was no sign of Riley.

She took a single pace forward, baton in hand. Her senses were humming, adrenaline surging. She listened intently for any noise that could tell her where he was. Watching for any shadow or clue. She moved forwards again slowly.

A shadow moved to her right, slinking between the bales. It had to be Riley.

Cramer moved quickly across the floor, the straw scraping under her feet, giving her location away. She crouched behind the bales to look at where the shadow came from, but there was nothing there. She gripped her baton and felt her jaw tighten.

'Riley, you fucking piece of shit! Am I scaring you? You should be scared...'

She'd just let on exactly where she was, she needed to—

A hand was around her throat, squeezing hard from behind, her baton dropped from her grasp. She felt the coarse weave of the cowl he was still wearing as Riley lifted her off the floor and dragged her backwards as he moved.

'Scared, Cramer? I've fought with the devil and won. You're a mere inconvenience.'

Her heels dragged on the floor as he pulled her towards the other side of the barn. Her throat constricted, she was clawing at his hand, trying to release it, struggling to breathe. She fought against passing out. Riley stopped by the wall, reaching for something with his left hand.

She planted her feet on the ground, leveraging herself backwards, trying to smash the back of her head into his nose. He moved his head out of the way, then hit her hard on the side of her head. The stinging headache started immediately. His grip remained tight on her throat.

'Nice try, Cramer, not happening.'

He started reaching to his left again with his damaged arm, but he couldn't see what he was reaching for. Her vision was fading, a burst of red stars creating a mist in front of her eyes as the oxygen deprivation took hold. She had to do something.

She collapsed, her legs failing beneath her, held up only by Riley's hand on her neck, but once she was a dead weight, he was forced to lean forward as she fell to the floor, throwing him off balance. This was her only chance.

He briefly released his grip on her, and she made her move, punching at his knee as he tried to regain his feet. Her hand exploded as she connected with his kneecap, taking his leg from underneath him, and he crashed onto his side.

She moved away from him, coughing and gasping, fighting to get air back into her lungs. Riley scrambled back up and reached back towards the wall, taking the shears down and holding them in his good hand stretched out towards her.

She ran to where she'd dropped her baton and grabbed it without taking her eyes off him. Where the hell was her backup? Max should have been here by now, let alone the other officers.

'You won't win, Cramer, I am all powerful. You have no idea who you are dealing with.'

'You're delusional, Riley. I've always thought it, but now you have proved it. You sick bastard.'

He smirked, just as he had done in court the day before and started moving towards her. She stood her ground. 'No mere woman can beat me, you aren't powerful enough to win against The Witchfinder.'

Cramer wasn't cowed. 'C'mon, Riley, give it your best shot, you fucker.'

He lunged towards her with the shears. She jumped to one side, making him miss. But he reset himself and came at her again her. They were now standing facing each other close to the wall with the farm tools on.

Cramer fixed her eyes on Riley threw her baton aside and reached above her head to the scythe and pulled it off the wall, both hands now on her new weapon. The extra reach this would give her could make all the difference. The side of her head was throbbing, the swelling already starting. She could still feel the imprint of his fingers around her neck. But it all paled into insignificance to the hatred she felt for the man standing in front of her.

Riley's eyes widened as she now had the advantage, but he wasn't giving up. He lunged towards her again, this time gashing her arm with the shears. She felt no pain, even though blood spurted from the injury. She swung her right arm forwards with the scythe, but he jumped out of the way. There was no connection. Dammit.

He tried to stab her again with the shears, aiming for her leg in the same way Robert Kane had done with Adam. She jumped out of the way, smashing at his hand with the scythe to disarm him. The shears rattled to the ground out of his reach.

He ran at her using his head to body charge her, which sent them both flailing to the ground. She was winded, her mouth open wide, desperately trying to get air in. The weight of the stab vest wasn't helping. It was constricting her breathing, and she was tempted to remove it, but that would be suicide.

She'd lost her grip on the scythe at the same time, and saw Riley make a grab for it. She kicked his arm away, causing him to cry out in agony, and grabbed the scythe again.

Riley's eyes widened, his mouth falling open as he turned towards the open door. Cramer was hoping officers were already out there waiting, but she couldn't be sure. Riley wasn't getting away.

As he tried to get up from the floor, she took her chance and swiped at his leg as hard as she could, catching Riley behind the ankle, slicing the blade back to take him off balance.

His face contorted in agony long before he made any sound. He crumpled to the ground, rolling onto his back so he could grasp his leg as the blood started to seep out of his calf and through his trousers underneath the cowl. The black material started to glisten as the blood flowed. Riley was down. He tried, but couldn't stand. He wasn't getting up again.

Cramer dropped the scythe on the ground and stood over him as he curled up into a ball, his hand reaching down to his calf. She drew her foot back and planted it firmly into his ribs, causing him to cry out again.

'That's for hurting, Leila, you fucking arsehole.'

She did it again.

'That's for Helena.'

She drew her foot back further for the hardest kick, and she felt his ribs break underneath her foot as it connected and he yelped in agony. She leaned in towards him, whispering into his ear.

'And that's for not working hard enough to prosecute the man who killed Adam Williams. You piece of shit.'

She punched him hard in the head, almost knocking him out, as Max with a group of other officers reached the doors. She sat down and watched them flood in, grabbing her injured arm as she felt the pain there for the first time.

'Guv, you OK? You're bleeding.' Max shouted to her.

She looked at her arm, the sticky red now seeping through her fingers.

'Yeah, I'm OK.' She turned towards Riley who was grasping his calf with his left hand and clutching his broken arm to his fractured ribs. The sight couldn't have been more satisfying.

She pulled his head back with what little hair he had to ensure he was listening to her: 'David Riley, you are under arrest for the murders of Angela Downs, Linda Burrows, Amanda Morrison, Dominique Monroe, Helena Fitzsimmons, and the attempted murder of DC Leila Johnson. You do not have to say anything, but it may harm your defence if you do not mention when questioned something which you later rely on in court. Anything you do say may be given in evidence. Do you understand?'

He glared at her.

'I'll take that as a yes. Max, take him away. Secure the house, the cave rooms, the tunnels, and this barn. Make sure Simms gets here ASAP.'

Max nodded, cuffing and then picking up Riley, who screamed again in agony as his broken arm was pulled behind him, and his body weight put extra pressure on his injured Achilles. It was clear from the way his foot was failing to support him that she had severed his Achilles tendon.

Cramer moved close to Riley as Max lifted him up.

'You should get a tetanus for that, Riley. I'd hate you to get ill.' Cramer winked.

Max looked at the floor and stifled a laughed behind Riley as he led him away.

Just then, Jack appeared in the doorway.

'You should think about that for yourself, boss.' He'd heard her parting shot. 'That looks like a nasty cut on your arm.'

She looked down at the seeping wound. It would definitely need stitches.

'Yeah, I'll think about that. How's Leila? Have the paramedics taken her already?'

‘She’s on her way to hospital. Which is exactly where you should be going.’

‘What did they say? Is she going to be OK?’

‘She has a way to go, but she’s a fighter. You saved her life, ma’am.’

She smiled and looked towards the ground. ‘We all saved her life, Jack.’ She looked back at Jack. ‘What about Rob?’

‘Rob’s fine too. Just got blindsided by Riley. Hit him with a rock and knocked him out. The medics are with him, planning on taking him in too.’

Cramer nodded, grateful for some good news finally.

‘We found her in time,’ said Jack, wincing at his own injuries.

‘Just.’

‘Just is good enough.’ He smiled. ‘Let’s get you to the paramedics.’

‘Stop fussing, Jack. I’ll be fine.’

‘True, you will be fine, because you’re going to hospital. Right now.’

She suddenly lost all her energy as the adrenaline started to subside. She didn’t have any more strength to argue.

As he helped her out of the door, Jack suddenly stopped.

‘What?’ said Cramer, unsure what was coming next.

‘Well, I was just wondering,’ Jack said, ‘whether you wanted to go to the private hospital or the NHS one. I mean, you know, you can afford either.’ He was grinning from ear to ear. Clearly, the boys had been talking about her.

She belly-laughed for the first time in a long time. ‘You know as well as I do that private hospitals don’t have an A&E, Jack. Just get me to the paramedics, you idiot,’ she said. ‘I’ll worry about anything else after that.’

Suspect Arrested in Hunt for 'The Witchfinder' Serial Killer

By Jason Baird, crime reporter

Police searching for the serial killer known as 'The Witchfinder' have arrested a suspect following an early-morning raid in rural Kent today, bringing the terror felt by women across the region to an end.

David Riley, 42, of Knowlton near Canterbury, was arrested this morning soon after attacking Detective Constable Leila Johnson, 23, who had gone missing during a botched police sting operation two days ago at local nightclub Illuminati. DC Johnson is currently in a critical condition in hospital.

Riley, a prosecutor with Kent's Crown Prosecution Service, was most recently working to prosecute local gang leader Robert Kane for the murder of Detective Sergeant Adam Williams. DS Williams died during a drugs raid on Kane's sprawling property in Blean after working undercover and infiltrating his organisation.

Chief Superintendent Ron Davidson confirmed the arrest at a press conference this afternoon. He said: 'Early this morning, my officers attended an address in Knowlton just outside Canterbury, following information showing specific access to vehicles we suspected were used in the murders of the five women who sadly lost their lives, along with information provided by a forensic technique which uses vein pattern analysis as a means of identification.

'Unfortunately, some of my officers were injured by David Riley as they worked to apprehend him, including DCI Caroline Cramer, the senior investigating officer in the case. All apart from DC Johnson are now out of hospital and recuperating at home.'

CS Davidson stated that forensic teams found blood, hair, and other evidence at the property thought to be from the five known victims – Angela Downs, Linda Burrows, Amanda Morrison, Dominique Monroe, and Helena Fitzsimmons – but additional evidence suggests the number of victims could be much higher. Various cold cases will now be re-examined.

CS Davidson added: 'As we have reason to believe some of these cases could be more than forty years old, a specialist unit will be set up to investigate these further. There is a suspicion that some of these cases will be in other parts of the UK, so the National Crime Agency will be informed.

'We also found a partially mummified body of who we believe is David Riley's father at the property, but we are awaiting DNA tests to confirm this.'

CS Davidson refused to give more details, but sources close to the investigation suggest Riley's grandfather had been a suspect in more than one murder back in the 1970s.

The source added that Riley is expected to be charged with the murders of five women, along with the attempted murder of DC Leila Johnson and assaults on both DS Rob Gulliver and DCI Caroline Cramer later today.

Chapter 73

By the time Cramer got to the hospital to see Leila, Jill had spent more than an hour on the phone talking to her yet again about what had happened with Riley. It was now two days since they'd finally captured him, and her friend had already given her a debrief courtesy of an order from Davidson – and called her each day to ensure she was talking about her experience. Bottling everything up was corrosive, Cramer knew that, but it didn't make it any easier to talk about. So, the call was more as a friend than a professional, but at times like this, Jill was both.

Cramer's eye was still an impressive blue-black from tangling with Riley, and the white was red and bloodshot, although the swelling was receding. She'd needed ten stitches in her arm to close the wound. It was a lot deeper than she had originally thought, and they had given her a tetanus jab, which made her laugh. Thankfully, there was no nerve or severe muscle damage, and she wouldn't have any permanent loss of function in the limb. The same couldn't necessarily be said of David Riley. Shame.

But she didn't want to think about him. She was here to see Leila.

Cramer finally found Leila's room on a close-monitoring ward – thankfully she was now out of intensive care, and much sooner than anyone expected. Cramer walked up towards the door and could see Leila through the glass. Her shaved head had started to regrow, but she was still a lot closer to Sinead O'Connor than Angelina Jolie. Baird was sitting at her bedside. They both looked up as Cramer walked in.

'Hope you don't mind, I was just passing, and I wanted to drop by to see how you were doing?'

Jason stood up and held his hand out to her.

'Thank you, DCI Cramer. I mean it. I really thought I'd lost her, you kept your promise, and I won't forget that.'

Cramer shook his hand. It seemed overly formal, but he didn't seem a hugger.

'Well, it was touch-and-go, but Leila didn't give up.'

'Neither did you, guv,' Leila said, her voice fainter than normal thanks to the near drowning. 'Thank you. It seems so little to say given what happened. But I'm not sure what else I can say. So, thank you.'

Cramer smiled. 'You don't have to say anything. You're safe and you're getting better, that's all that matters. You'll be back in no time.'

Leila was smiling, but looked a little uncomfortable at that comment, something which slightly unnerved Cramer.

Leila turned her attention to her boyfriend and smiled. 'Jay, can you get me a cup of coffee from the Costa downstairs please? I just really fancy a latte...'

He looked a little surprised. 'Er, yeah sure. That's a good sign – you haven't wanted anything like that yet.' He turned to Cramer. 'Can I get you one?'

Cramer held up her hand. 'No thanks, I'm fine.'

He left the room, and Cramer moved to sit next to Leila's bed.

'That *is* a good sign, Leila,' said Cramer. 'Are you really feeling that much better?'

Leila sighed. 'Yes, I really am, but if I'm honest, I just wanted to talk to you.'

Cramer nodded, now a little concerned about where this conversation was going.

'I'm not sure I can come back to work, ma'am. I just don't think I can do the job again.' Her eyes started to blink as the tears filled them.

Cramer put her hand on her arm to try to comfort her. 'Leila, I totally understand why you're saying that, but you really shouldn't be thinking about that now. You've got to get yourself better before you can make any decisions, let alone a big decision like that. You've been through an awful experience, and we need to make sure you get the help you need to recover from it.

'The physical scars will heal much faster than the mental ones, but believe me when I tell you, Jill is the right person to help you with that. She has helped me more than you can possibly imagine.'

The tears finally breached Leila's eyes and started to fall down her cheeks. Cramer moved forwards to give her a hug, and Leila started sobbing on her boss's shoulder.

'It's OK, Leila. I know what you've been through seems so hard to deal with right now, but you will get through this, I promise you will. Trust me.'

Cramer held her for a minute in silence until she had stopped shaking as much. To see her like this was heartbreaking, but she was just so glad Leila was alive. What worried her was that her colleague might not always feel the same way as the impact of her near-death experience took hold. Cramer would make sure she did everything she could to help her deal with it.

'Guv, I do trust you. My God, much more than you know. But I don't know why you don't trust me. So many times, you were giving me a hard time before' – she waved her hand up and down to indicate the full length of her body – 'all this. And I just don't know why.'

Cramer sighed. Leila was right. She had been giving her more than her fair share of grief. Most of which she hadn't deserved. She looked down at the floor before looking back at Leila, not quite believing what she was about to do.

'Leila, right now, I am not your boss, got it? So, for today, you call me Callie, OK?'

Leila looked confused but nodded her agreement.

Cramer took a deep breath. 'I'm going to tell you something that only Jill knows about, and she only knows because of the amount of time she's known me, which shows you how much I do trust you. Right?'

Leila nodded, hesitantly.

'My sister went missing when I was ten years old. She was with me one minute – we were playing in the grounds of my parents' house – and the next she was gone. I didn't see anything, hear anything. Nothing. It has haunted me ever since.

'It's why I became a police officer. I spent so much time with officers back then, those supporting us, police liaison – although it wasn't called that back then. But I still think about my sister. Wonder what happened. We expected there to be a ransom demand, but there never was. She just disappeared.'

Leila looked shocked and saddened at the same time.

'God, I'm so sorry. That must be awful. How do you deal with it?'

'One day at a time. Even now.'

'Why a ransom demand, though?' Leila looked puzzled.

Cramer thought she may as well tell her now before the rest of the team got to tell her. 'Because of our background. My grandfather founded one of the world's biggest private banks soon after the Second World War, and the expectation was that there would be a demand for money in return for her. But there never was. There was nothing.'

Cramer wasn't sure now was the right time to be sharing. After all, did Leila really need to hear this while she was laid up in a hospital bed, half-drowned, unable to speak above a rasping whisper? But Cramer carried on anyway now she'd started.

'The press interest was intense, as you can imagine. The coverage went worldwide. It was beyond difficult for all of us. Then I'd had some other problems with the press when I was dealing with cases in my early career, being misquoted, you know. So, you being with Jason made me uneasy, created friction. I didn't know what you'd tell him and what you wouldn't—'

Leila interjected. 'You do know I would never have said anything to Jay about the case, guv. I never did say anything. I never would.'

Cramer felt guilty. 'I know, but I wasn't sure until I had to go and tell Jason you had gone missing and he had no idea you were even doing an undercover op. Leila, I'm sorry. You didn't deserve the treatment you got.'

The tears filled Leila's eyes again.

'I'm sorry. I didn't mean to upset you,' said Cramer gently.

'No, you didn't. It is just a relief to hear you say that you trust me. That's all.'

Cramer grabbed her hand. 'I do trust you. Believe me, I wouldn't be telling you this if I didn't. But please, keep this to yourself. I don't like discussing my private life at work. It makes me uncomfortable.'

'Of course I will. It's nothing to do with anyone but you and your family at the end of the day,' Leila said.

Cramer smiled her thanks and then changed the subject. She didn't want to dwell on her past.

'Listen, Leila, I know you're not sure about what you want to do, but please just do me one favour – and I am asking as your friend as much as your boss – don't make any decisions about work until you have fully recovered. And even then, don't make any rash decisions.'

Leila nodded.

'You're a bloody good copper, and we need you. But more than that, you should be looking to do this for you. If you want it, I think you can go all the way to the top. You just need to focus.'

The tears started to fill Leila's eyes again. Her cheeks, already red and puffy from earlier, glistened as saltwater fell in silver tracks down her cheeks. Cramer felt like she may have pushed too hard and softened her tone.

'Look, I want to help you get the most out of this job. I had a mentor myself when I was in your position, and I believe in passing help forwards. So, just don't be too hasty, and promise me we can talk about this again before you make any decisions.'

Chapter 74

Cramer finally got back home at around seven that evening. The paperwork involved in an arrest and the interviews surrounding it were exhausting, but she had wanted to be there to see Riley squirm as he was charged and brought to court. He was in all sorts of pain – physical, mental, emotional. It was gratifying to see, and Cramer would never say that ordinarily about anyone. But he was getting everything he deserved.

The forensics team had found so much evidence within the three rooms in the underground tunnels that he was banged to rights. Blood from each of the victims, the hair she'd found in the bags that had been shaved off each of them – the list went on. Only a properly crooked jury wouldn't convict him.

Riley couldn't keep his mouth shut once he was arrested, proud of the fact that he'd been carrying on the work of his grandfather, saving the world from witches. He learned at his knee how to deal with them, apparently. That was one screwed-up family. From what Cramer had heard from her officers so far, he had a good shot at an insanity plea. He'd even told anyone who would listen that Cramer herself was a witch and would be next. She knew he was damaged, but even so, she'd push as hard as she could to stop him getting a cushy sentence in a hospital like Broadmoor rather than doing hard time.

Cramer had called Dr Santi Sandalo back to thank her for her help. Apparently Riley had been on the original research database in Scotland from when he was in Edinburgh, having heard about the research being done during a visit to the department working on it, believing it would never link back to him. So, he volunteered images of his hands while he was in the building. His arrogance had finally caught up with him.

Robert Kane's case was ruled a mistrial, given the prosecutor was now being charged with multiple murders, and would be retried later in the year. Hopefully this time Alex Newcastle could take the reins. She would need to give evidence again. But she would cross that bridge when she came to it.

Jack, as expected, had been suspended from duty by Davo, pending investigation into the crash and his behaviour at the nightclub. He was a bruiser, there was no doubt about that, but he was an integral part of the team and she hoped he would get off with a warning. Again. But this time, she wasn't so sure.

As she went into the kitchen, she saw Patrick was already home. He had a glass of red wine in his hand and poured one for her as soon as he saw her, picking it up and passing it to her as she put her car keys on the side by the cooker.

'I saw the news. Congratulations. The press are calling him "The Witchfinder".'

She took the wine and took a sip. The warming effect helped to soothe her throat which still felt constricted days after she had forced Riley to let it go.

'Well, it's a moniker that fits. That is exactly what he thought he was doing.'

'How's your eye?' Patrick asked. 'It looks sore. Do you want some ice for that?'

Cramer suddenly felt her blood drain from her face, and just stood without speaking. She put her wine down before she dropped it. She felt weak and thought she was going to pass out.

Patrick looked concerned. 'Are you OK? What can I do?'

He stood up and put his arm on her arm. Initially, she pulled it away from his touch, before looking at him and seeing the sadness in his eyes. It was too much for her. All the emotion built up throughout the case and their last few months of arguments flooded out of her. She started sobbing, her body shaking as she tried to find support from the kitchen counter and failed.

Patrick rushed towards her this time, carrying her weight in his arms when she couldn't.

'No. I just need to lie down,' she said through her tears as she pushed him away. She didn't need him. Didn't want him.

Cramer tried to move away from him and the counter but nearly fell again through her exhaustion. Patrick grabbed her arm and refused to let go this time as he helped her upstairs.

They went into the bedroom, where he laid her down on the bed and started to undress her. She didn't stop him.

Patrick had been the source of much of the emotional turmoil she was feeling, and he looked pleadingly at her. He laid down next to her and held her close. She didn't resist this time.

'I'm so, so sorry, Cal. I never meant to hurt you, and I know how difficult this has all been. The case, what I did, your family stuff... I'm so sorry,' he whispered to her.

She was still crying, leaning on his chest, letting him hold her for the first time in months. It felt good.

The next morning, Cramer woke and found herself lying on her husband's naked chest. He was wearing pyjama bottoms, which was unusual. He'd fallen asleep on top of the covers but must have put her underneath.

She tried to think back. The last thing she could remember was parking her car on the drive. Everything else was a blur.

She moved slowly, so she didn't wake him and went downstairs to make herself some coffee. She wasn't sure how she felt about being close to him again. To be honest, she wasn't sure it was something she wanted. But a divorce would be another black mark against her in her mother's book. Still, she was past caring about that particular tally.

She put the coffee into the machine, waited for it to brew, and then poured a cup for herself. She wrapped her dressing gown closer around her as she walked into the living room. She still felt beaten up, both physically and emotionally, and dropped into the chair that always enveloped her.

She looked at her watch. The Bulgari had been bought for her by Patrick for her birthday last year, and she wondered whether the expense had been spent out of love or guilt. Davidson had given her a few days off, so she wasn't in a rush to get into work. Still, sleeping in this late was very unusual. For her and her husband.

She went to take another sip of her coffee and realised she'd drained her cup. She went back into the kitchen for a refill, just as Patrick came downstairs, his pyjama bottoms almost falling off revealing the V at the base of his torso, his bare chest still exposed, just as she had left him in bed.

She took another cup out of the cupboard and offered it to him without speaking, and he nodded as he rubbed his stomach and yawned, before pushing his hands through his blond hair. He was in great shape; she couldn't deny that.

He moved up behind her as she poured the coffee into the cup, and put his arms around her waist, kissing her just behind her ear. It usually turned her on, but today she froze, her body stiffening under his touch.

She knew what she had to do.

He moved away from her as she poured the coffee and sat at the table at the other side of the room, watching her from a distance.

Cramer sat opposite him; hands wrapped around her own cup for warmth. There was just one more problem to solve before she could properly relax.

She stared straight into Patrick's deep blue eyes.

'OK, let's talk.'

Acknowledgements

There are many people who have helped me to create this book, and as with everything of this type, I don't want to forget anyone. So, to all those who have helped me, whether by reading early drafts and giving me feedback, giving me guidance on police procedures, or simply supporting me and encouraging me in finally finishing this book – which has taken many more years than I expected – a very big thank you.

Some specific mentions go to Chief Superintendent Amanda Tillotson of Kent Police for the advice and support in reading early drafts for procedural accuracy.

Similarly, thanks go to Dr Tara Symonds, psychologist, for reading a very early draft and helping me ensure Jill Traverne's character was authentic.

Also my sincere thanks to Professor Dame Sue Black, one of the world's leading forensic anthropologists, who gave me much more of her time to ensure accuracy in this book than anyone could expect of her.

Lastly, and by no means least, thanks go to my wife, Liz King, because without her support, encouragement and cheerleading, I may never have got this finished at all.

DCI Caroline Cramer and the team return in

THE MONEY SHOT

Out early 2024

Read on for an exclusive extract.

To be first to hear news from Ali about the DCI Caroline Cramer series and more, make sure to sign up to the newsletter at www.alisteedauthor.com

THE MONEY SHOT

Chapter 1

She sat, poised, taut, like a cat waiting to pounce on its prey. She was concentrating so hard she could hear her nerves humming under her skin. The heat of the afternoon was oppressive. A single bead of sweat rolled down her back, collecting friends on the way until it dissipated into the waistband of her shorts.

The street below her was throbbing to the beat of drums and the Caribbean strains of steel bands. It was filled with people, jostling, dancing, and moving as best they could in the throng. The reds, yellows, greens, and golds merged together from that distance, like a Monet painting when viewed too closely. The carnival floats flowed past her window in an explosion of colour. Whistles punctuated the shrieks and cheers of the crowd below.

None of this interested her. She had work to do. She relaxed slightly and changed position. She could get a better view from here. The motorcade weaved through the crowd, like a shiny black snake slithering between vibrant flowers. This is what she had been waiting for. The sweat was dripping from her forehead, but she dare not move now. It was nearly time.

The first Mercedes stopped outside the hotel. As the doors opened, the car spewed out four men that looked far too big to fit into one car. The second car stopped just behind. This was it. The heat had made her hands damp, and she was losing her grip slightly. A small, perfectly attired man stepped out of the second car, his hair slicked back with oil. He had a high forehead. Good for her, bad for him. Her view was blocked momentarily by one of the other men, but she was a professional. She just had to bide her time.

The crowd surged past the group. The bodyguards, who had been looking around to check the area, were jostled by the sheer weight of numbers. That was all she needed. The cross-hairs were on his forehead. She squeezed the trigger she had been fondling for the past hour, and almost simultaneously, the Brazilian dropped to the ground, a perfect round hole in his high forehead.

She ducked down below the window ledge. She was glad it was over. Her arms had started to ache from being in the same position for so long.

The street below was in turmoil. People were screaming and running from the scene, for fear of another shot being fired. Now was the time to leave. The police at the carnival were already at the scene, but as with so many South American countries, they were slow to get organised. It wouldn't be a problem to get away, she'd done it so many times before.

She dismantled the high-powered rifle in seconds, a well-practiced routine. She picked up the suitcases she had packed earlier, went down to the foyer, and left by the side door to head straight to the airport.

Ali Steed is an award-winning journalist who is stepping into the world of novel writing. She spends much of her year in Mallorca with her wife and two dogs.

Find out more at: www.alisteedauthor.com